BRIAN TRENT

TEN THOUSAND THUNDERS

This is a FLAME TREE PRESS book

Text copyright © 2018 Brian Trent

FLAME TREE PRESS
6 Melbray Mews, London, SW6 3NS, UK
flametreepress.com

Distribution and warehouse:
Baker & Taylor Publisher Services (BTPS)
30 Amberwood Parkway, Ashland, OH 44805
btpubservices.com

Thanks to the Flame Tree Press team, including:
Taylor Bentley, Frances Bodiam, Federica Ciaravella, Don D'Auria,
Chris Herbert, Matteo Middlemiss, Josie Mitchell, Mike Spender,
Cat Taylor, Maria Tissot, Nick Wells, Gillian Whitaker.

The cover is created by Flame Tree Studio with
thanks to Nik Keevil and Shutterstock.com.
The font families used are Avenir and Bembo.

Flame Tree Press is an imprint of Flame Tree Publishing Ltd
flametreepublishing.com

A copy of the CIP data for this book is available from the British Library
and the Library of Congress.

HB ISBN: 978-1-78758-018-3
PB ISBN: 978-1-78758-016-9
ebook ISBN: 978-1-78758-019-0
Also available in FLAME TREE AUDIO

Printed in the US at Bookmasters, Ashland, Ohio

BRIAN TRENT

TEN THOUSAND THUNDERS

FLAME TREE PRESS
London & New York

PART ONE
ANOMALY

Year 322 of the New Enlightenment
Tanabata City, Luna
Bluespace Jurisdiction

'…dark and dread Eternity
returns again to me.'
Lord Byron

CHAPTER ONE
Reborn in the House of the Dead

Fourteen and a half hours after being killed in the shuttle explosion, Gethin Bryce found himself in a newly sculpted body staring at his hands.

The transition of locations happened in a single eyeblink. A moment earlier he was standing naked in the claustrophobic steel locker at Olympus Save with two hours to go before his flight, thinking of the ticket in his bag for VG Flight 3107. Thirty minutes of hot white light crawling in his head, capturing the position of every neural synapse and stored memory, and the green holoprompts changing configuration before his equally green eyes. He blinked. The backs of his eyelids were a map of blazing red veins in the probing luminosity.

Then he opened his eyes and the steel locker was gone.

Gethin squinted at a dull red ceiling globe. He caught a whiff of fresh-cut plastic. And he was naked, lying on a mattress, as if he were a corpse on a mausoleum slab, washed in ruby-colored gloom. It was like he had been teleported.

He felt his throat constrict as he recognized the place from brochures.

A Wyndham Save clinic.

But where? And what the hell happened?

Gethin propped himself up on his elbows. The sensor screen at his bedside flashed its annoyance.

"Please lie down," the cool male voice said.

"Tell me where I am first," he snapped.

"There's been a fatal accident, Mr. Bryce, and we've downloaded your last Save from—"

"Olympus Station, I know. Where am I now?"

"This is the Wyndham Save Center in Tanabata City, Luna. Earthtime 0512."

"What's the date, damnit!"

"July 18, 322."

Gethin rubbed his head, numbly staving off the rise of panic. Twelve days were unaccounted for. It was the length of time for a Martian shuttle, sailing brightquest to Luna. The abrupt transition was terrible, disoriented him like a fever dream, and he felt the impulsive twitch of needing to catch his flight... despairing of staying on Mars any longer. Twelve days! Luna! For an awful moment he wondered what would have happened if the machine had said *six* days, and his purchase signal would hover on that interplanetary threshold, calculating how many picoseconds he was to the point of no return only to ultimately decide to resurrect him on Mars, like a looping nightmare unwilling to let him go.

The sensor screen whirred away from his bedside, inviting him to stand with silent courtesy. And he did, right away and a little too quickly, so colored dots swam before his eyes. He pictured his life in them: blue dots for Earth, red for Mars, white for Luna. It made him think of an away-message he'd seen long ago, taken from an antebellum flatfilm in which a child was teleported across a room as lots of cheesy, noisy, beeping, colored dots in the air.

"What happened?" Gethin asked. "Tell me—"

"You will have all your questions answered, Mr. Bryce, if you would please fill out the post-regeneration paperwork."

Gethin grumbled but obliged, not wanting to hear it from his insurance company. He reviewed his file on the monitor and signed off on the screens with a touch of his new fingertips, while invisible sensors studied his heartbeat, blood flow, breathing. He was able to review his credit charges, and tried imagining what the rosemary chicken with asparagus he'd eaten for his first meal on the shuttle had tasted like. Asparagus, even aeroponically grown, usually disappointed him.

Naturally, his nagging impulse was to fire up his newly replaced sensorium and check his messages. But he kept looking at his hands. Not the tanned mitts he'd sported on Mars. Gone was the ropy red scar on his left arm, when a skiing mishap sent him into a generator cable. The calluses from cold Martian hikes... gone. The tiny brown spots, even a beauty mark near the wrist...missing. His new body was virgin to the cosmos, molded from rapid-process flesh-gel grown from his DNA on file, imprinted with the data transfer, and sliced free of the amniocube. Then it was rinsed, like hosing down a rubber suit, while metal needles raped its tissue with quick incisions. Virtuboard circuitry imprinted onto his fingertips. A shiny new sensorium grafted into his skull. His blurmod and biocells and everything else specified by his Save-file.

I've never eaten, Gethin thought, steeping in the new experience. *Never slept, made love, gotten a paper-cut, lifted a coffee mug, read a book, skinned a knee, or climbed stairs.*

"You may experience some muscle pain over the next 48 hours," the voice told him. "This is entirely natural and can be countered with simple pain relievers. Wyndham Pharmacies are ready to supply you if you wish."

"No," he grunted, prodding his leanly muscled arms, the knobs of bone in his sinewy shoulders, his firm neck and the sharp contours of his jawline, and then he cupped the face he hadn't yet seen. Like a blind creature, he explored his high patrician nose and traced the pattern of his thin eyebrows. He caressed his ears like a child handling seashells for the first time. In his mouth, his tongue moved like a pink tentacle over perfect teeth.

Okay, he thought. *Now for the important part.*

Gethin cautiously pressed behind his left ear, afraid that nothing would happen, that he'd be truly naked, cut off from the webwork of humanity, amputated from the chorus of media, friends, ancestors, and email.

He pressed it again.

"Please be calm," the machine warned, concerned by the wild acceleration of his heart rate.

Gethin swallowed in dread. Nothing was happening.

He pressed the subdermal button a third time, harder than before. There! His access screen swirled into focus like a lavender pinwheel over his left eye. Program tabs hugged the circular perimeter of his Heads-Up-Display: Map, Notes, Contacts, Charge, Messages, Wetware, Web, Cave, and Special. The gentle thrumming of his active sensorium filled his head.

Gethin stood, naked but no longer feeling it. The reflective basalt created a glassy doppelganger under his feet, like a reflection in a crimson pond.

The screen flashed. "You have been cleared for checkout, Mr. Bryce, at your convenience. Do you wish to order replacement luggage? Wyndham Supplies has 89 percent of your registered inventory in stock, and will gladly send them to whatever address you designate. Your insurance policy will cover the expense."

Gethin shook his head. A black robe was hanging from a hook; he garbed himself in it, slid his feet into its black magfiber slippers, which, like all Lunar footwear, bonded molecularly and magnetically with the floor to counter the low-G. He went to the door, placed his fingers on the handle.

And hesitated.

He had left Earth – a youth in London, a career and marriage in Athens – to become a Martian. He would be returning as a virgin creature.

"Wyndham Save advises you to have a calm, relaxing week while you adjust to your reconstructed body," the voice told him. "You should avoid stressful encounters as much as possible."

Gethin grimaced. "I'll try."

Then he left the room.

★   ★   ★

Luna was the most successful colony in human history.

Almost right from its founding in 84 NE, the moon had become the symbol of humanity's new ascendancy, the tangible achievement of a species that had shaken off the radioactive dust and made a long-delayed return to the stars. Spearheaded by Earth's new *zaibatsu* in the first years of the trilobed Republic, seedling colonies sprouted in the gray Lunar desert, spread their glossy petals, and attracted a hive. The mining camps were first to come, followed by swarms of industry, commerce, and tourism.

Luna still bore the cultural fingerprints of its founders. Even Tanabata City, long the mixing bowl of Sol system, sported the circular doorways of

Han Dynasty China, the Thai fondness for gold on stairwell rails and storefront awnings, and the distinctly Japanese minimalism of rock gardens offsetting lobbies of jet-black granite. There were even aeroponic greenhouses that exclusively grew cherry blossoms, to be carted off to the many atriums of New Tokyo, Tiangong Palace, and Zhejiang.

Yet Gethin felt like a dazed pharaoh, of all things, as he emerged from the red-lit recovery chamber into the center's lobby. The black robe clung loosely to his body like funeral cerements. It was an odd, giddy thought:

Egyptian Osiris himself, renewed and ready for the afterlife's endless delights!

The lobby bustled with forty other people wearing black robes. They looked like he felt: disheveled and glassy-eyed, a dispossessed band of resurrectees grappling with their born-again life. Some were chatting to friends via comlink, or typing on virtuboards. Most, however, were transfixed by the overhead holopanel showing the leading news item.

VG Flight 3107 on approach to Tanabata City, beginning its descent…

…and then a brief splash of light, the shuttle vanishing into debris like slow-mo footage of a rupturing balloon.

The image was suddenly interrupted by vivid blue letters:

DURING YOUR RECOVERY

The human brain is the most complex device in the universe. While regen technologies can replicate your neural pathways with perfection, the fact is that brain balance doesn't restore immediately. This is nothing to be concerned about. Your biochemical and neuroelectrical levels will balance themselves. Typically this happens within just a few days of regeneration. Think of it as jet lag. A week of good rest is all it usually takes.

The practical consequence of this is you may experience excessive tiredness or hyperactivity, fits of hunger or sexual energy, moodiness, emotional imbalance, dizziness, nausea, fever, itchiness, numbness, depression, or excitability. This is perfectly normal in most cases and will pass. Allow your body and brain to find their balance.

Thanks for choosing Wyndham Save, and welcome back! Your life is waiting for you once again!

The advisory vanished, replaced again by the looping shuttle explosion.

Gethin went straight to the lobby's narrow security booth. An unpleasant-looking Wyndham officer stood there, blocking the doorway with his bulging Teutonic body. His wide mouth twitched in the whiskery tangle of a golden goatee. Gethin could practically smell the Wasteland on him.

"Make sure you have everything you need from the recovery room," the guard barked. "You *won't* be allowed back in."

Gethin looked him over, from ID badge to shoes, and comfortably held his hostile gaze. "Tough day for you, is that it?"

The guard's face turned purple. Over his shoulder, the lobby of the spaceport was a mirage through tinted glass. Gethin watched spaceport foot traffic shuffling about. He noticed, too, that just on the other side of the door stood three Faustian monks. They were unmistakable: long flaxen hair, sleeveless tunics displaying circuitboard tattoos, and glowing amber eyes of their acolyte class.

"I've told them to keep away," the guard said sullenly, following his stare. "Port security should be here any minute."

Gethin nodded absently. Behind him, a young girl emerged from a recovery room, looked at the others, and burst into tears.

Gethin sighed deeply, took a breath, and left the facility.

Instantly, the crowd beyond engulfed him. Live-journalists eager for the story, news of the shuttle accident having drawn them here like worms to a corpse. A glance was all they needed to match him up with the passenger manifest. Not that the black robe left any doubt. His public history would follow in a speed-of-light instant.

"I'm *declining* all interviews," Gethin said, making sure they heard the severity of his tone. IPC regulations revoked web privileges for up to three years if a citizen journalist harassed someone. "But see Officer Fran Allaire over there? He sent me out to explain that he's now taking your questions, and will arrange one-on-one sessions with the other survivors on a first-come basis."

In a whoosh they were gone, crossing the distance to the befuddled security officer in seconds.

The three Faustian monks remained. One nodded amicably at Gethin.

"Nicely done, Mr. Bryce."

Gethin smiled coldly.

"Keep your distance from me," he warned, his grin as welcoming as a sickle.

The monk studied him. "We have been waiting for you, Gethin. We have a special message that will help you during all that is to come."

"I doubt it."

Gethin ducked into the nearest department store. He took the escalator down one level and bought a gray-hooded reversible jumpsuit and satchel. He changed into the jumpsuit right there in the store, stuffing the regen robe into his new bag, and then hopped onto a people-mover. Pulling the hood down to defy any patmatching gazes, he melted into Tanabata's Southern Wing of bustling markets and shoppers.

He found a little café shaped like a Buddhist temple. Hastily, he grabbed a curtained booth in the back and collapsed, breathless. A smiling Japanese waitress took his order for coffee; he paid with a tap of his fingertips on the shaded tabletop.

Gethin opened his HUD and accessed the blueweb. Flight 3107's explosion was, unsurprisingly, the top story. Three A-list actors were among the deceased, returning from Mars for the filming of *Cry of an Alien Midnight*. Big names too – press favorite Salvor Bear, Gong Li IV, and Angelica Shivanand. The women were already resurrected, but Bear's absence was now the lead headline:

BEAR ESTATE CONFIRMS: NO DC ON FILE. WILL NOT BE RESURRECTED

Gethin skimmed past this and hit pay dirt. There was a breaking companion piece to the shuttle explosion story: officials were reporting an accident at a Prometheus Industries lab just seconds *before* 3107's explosion. Two employees were confirmed dead, and there was rumor of a survivor.

Coincidence?

Gethin smiled for the second time that day. His drink arrived and he sipped it eagerly. It was the first drink of his reborn body, outlining his esophagus in a hot trickle and pooling into his new stomach. The porcelain cup burned his fingertips slightly.

Cool blue lights flashed in Gethin's vision, signaling the arrival of a message.

For an instant he thought it might be Lori. But she was all the way back on Mars. Did she even know of the accident yet?

Would she care?

He opened the message with an eyeblink. The blue-and-gold header of InterPlanetary Council official letterhead unfurled in his optics.

TO: Gethin Bryce
FROM: Lt. Donna McCallister, Colonel Leon Tanner
DATE/TIME: 07/18/322, 0507 ET
SUBJECT: Welcome back
ATTACHMENT: *CodeKey Shiva*
MESSAGE: Anomaly

Gethin glanced around the café.

"Anomaly?" he whispered.

He hadn't investigated one in nine years. He'd even figured that the IPC was done with that nonsense.

Except *this* one wasn't nonsense. Gethin promptly forgot about his coffee as he began reading the attachment.

Not nonsense, he thought.

This anomaly had killed him.

CHAPTER TWO
The Wastelander

Celeste Segarra didn't think the heist would be easy.

From the remains of an old concrete divider that in times past had been used to separate lanes of highway, she waited in her CAMO suit on the road's western side. The dawn sky was a witch's brew of overcast, bubbling clouds spilling from the south, and the suffocating humidity gave the world a glassy residue. Grass burst from cracks in the divider, bees darted like fuzzy choppers, and moisture turned the corrugated steel garage ahead of her into a glistening dome.

A bee hovered by her ear, sensing her but unable to see through the CAMO's real-time optic camouflage. She swatted at it; to an outsider, it was as if the bee were walloped by the unseen hand of Zeus. It skittered across the asphalt and twitched. Then it flattened into a yellow pancake under the invisible shoe of her nearest squadmate.

We have the advantage, she told herself, and hoped it was true. She noticed the pale orb of Luna between clouds, like a cold eye studying her.

Celeste felt damp moisture where she breathed against her facemask. She closed her eyes and her squad appeared like green phantoms, arranged like trapdoor spiders on both sides of the overgrown road.

There was no longer any doubt that the missiles were real. Celeste didn't know what resources King D. had tapped to locate the buried antimatter mill of the old Carolina coast, yet she was no longer surprised by such things. The man had a way of ferreting out data. And all under the Republic's greedy little nose.

A sound like thunder caught her attention. For a second she worried that it was *real* thunder – weather reports promised rain. Celeste was gambling the attack could be carried off before her entire camouflaged team became visible in a downpour's outlining splashes.

But the thunder was coming from the garage.

"Get ready," she whispered, and the subvocal command transmitted instantly to her squad. The steel portcullis over the garage's entrance lifted in a rattling cacophony, and two men in forest fatigues jogged out, automatic rifles cradled in their arms. They both wore dark green caps and black boots. One was a grizzled, hawk-faced guy who passed so close to Celeste that she could see a pimple where his ear wasn't covered by wooly gray hair. His boots crumpled a patch of sun-blanched grass as he went.

Thunder, *real* thunder, shivered in the sky. The parched ground began to dimple with scattered raindrops.

"Celeste!" Jeff's voice came into her ear as a strained whisper. "We've got to hurry!"

"Hold fast!" she said severely. "Here it comes."

The truck chugged out like an aged tortoise engineered for battle, lumbering onto the disused road on reinforced glasstic tires, belching noxious biofuel. The merc traders sat in the back, multiguns slung at their shoulders.

A bird hopped out of the truck's way, flapped its wings twice, and settled a foot from where Celeste waited. It shook rain from its beak.

There *were* ways of spotting CAMOed fighters. Celeste amped her vision and ran the truck's silhouette through a filter. No signs of a scanning array. Even the advance scouts now waiting at the road's bend were surprisingly low-tech. Wastelanders were shrewd, dangerous folk…but they tended to see the world in provincial terms.

Rain thumped on her suit.

Celeste swallowed hard.

"Allie, Jamala, hit them."

From both sides of the road, two columns of smoke shot forth and struck the truck's tires. The impact whirled the vehicle into a perfect half circle, handily bursting one tire off its axle.

The truck's spin put the traders directly in front of Celeste. She fired three bursts, killing them before they could return a single shot.

"North!" Jeff's voice shouted, and every invisible muzzle swung towards the garage doors. The trading camp's security forces shot wildly at them. Bullets whined past Celeste like hornets.

Her entire team was visible now; the storm drew them in vibrating silhouettes of white rain-splash. One of these freakish shapes flattened out – Celeste didn't need her augs to recognize the weapon it carried: a Greely barracuda-class heatlance. Jamala's favored peacekeeper.

The mercenaries at the garage burst like balloons. Jamala ejected the steaming battery – it sizzled, invisibly, on the ground in the rain.

It was quick, brutal wetwork from there. Rajnar and Allie darted to the garage; Celeste marveled at the way their camouflaged bodies were illustrated in the downpour, as if they were a pair of transdimensional predators pushing in from a hellish nearby dimension.

A spurt of gunfire.

"Garage is clear," Rajnar barked.

Celeste killed her CAMO. She materialized as a sinewy, tall woman clad entirely in the blacked-out fiberoptic bodysuit. She removed the suffocating headmask and welcomed the cool rain on her face and neck. Her hair was dyed scarlet, tightly woven back by a mesh skullcap. The world might have called her pretty if not for the famished lines of her face, or the taut muscles beneath her caramel skin, or the hard eyes.

Celeste breathed deep of the air, tasting gunpowder, ozone, and the stench of burned flesh. She checked her battery gauge: Fifteen minutes of CAMO power left.

"Power off!" she said. "We may need it still."

The ghost shapes surrounding the idling truck appeared like black puma people. Jeff, freckled and blond, was the first to the truck. He yanked open the door and jerked the dead driver to the road. Working swiftly, he released the locks on the tarp-covered cargo. The team set to work instantly on extricating the prize.

Jeff and Allie were already unpacking their moving straps. Onto its lightweight cushion they set the first of the missiles, the weight shared between them. Rajnar and Jamala took the second one.

"Eighty-three seconds," Celeste said, giving a playful slap on Jeff's back. "Are we hot or not?"

Jeff grimaced, his freckled, scarred face grimy with rain-defying dirt. "I'm still hot to the tune of 101 degrees. Had to do this in July, huh?"

Celeste regarded the missile. "Scan it."

Jeff splayed one hand over the nanosteel shell and shut his eyes.

Celeste was afraid to hope.

The Earth Republic, along with the InterPlanetary Council, had done a good job of combing the birthworld for Old Calendar nukes. Their sniffer bots patrolled the Wastes like biblical angels, seeking the toxic burial chamber of radioactive kings.

But nukes were easy to find. Other things were far more dangerous, and far more difficult for arkies to steal away.

"I see six magnetic ventricles," Jeff said, eyes still closed. He licked his lips excitedly. "Looking good so far. Wait a minute...there's heavy shielding in here."

Celeste held her breath.

Jeff's eyes snapped open. "Stasis field, people! This here's the real deal!"

For just an instant, the group stared at the missiles with glassy-eyed adoration. Then in a blink they were back to their old selves, all business, carrying the missiles into the marsh.

The real deal! Celeste felt like skipping.

"We should make it through the gloplands in two hours," Allie said. "If those traders have got air support, it'll be tight."

"The rain will give us cover," Celeste said.

"It won't last," Allie countered.

"Double-time it, people!"

Into the wilderness they went, sinking to their knees in scum-covered water. The green filth pooled around their thighs. But they moved like bot troops, disciplined (except for Jeff's good-humored ranting) and keenly aware of possible ambush. The water was good cover; anything shy of an airhound would lose them at its rancid shores.

Unless someone dispatched waspbots to pursue them.

The thought made Celeste swallow nervously. She absently touched the EMP canisters at her beltline.

"Underground," she commanded, and the team changed direction to the large drainpipe protruding like a beheaded serpent from the swamp. It led to the old subway catacombs. Most were tribe turf. The Butcher Boys ran these tunnels and they owed Celeste a favor. She intended on collecting.

"The really smart glops have built entire communities down here," Jeff was saying. "This guy from Taconic, Jimmy Howard, he got lost in the underdark about a year ago. He stumbled on these weird lights. They were candles. Scanner told him they were made from the fatty deposits of corpses. And carrying the candles? The strangest glops he ever saw. Mollusks. Floppin' on the rusted tracks in a creepy dance, candles coiled in their tentacles. They were holding some kind of Mass!"

Jamala wiped her brown neck and shot him a glare. "Would you shut the fuck up, Jeff? I'm so sick of hearing about glops."

"If we get through this, I'll show you the eyecapture Jimmy took."

Silent Rajnar usually lived up to his name. But at this comment he said, with considerable interest, "You've got a clip of them? For real?"

"I do," Jeff said proudly. "Swear on my family's honor."

"Like that means a goddamn thing," Jamala snapped.

They pushed deeper into the tunnels, deliberately steering off from the main tracks and taking a maintenance shaft. Here, the tunnel was narrower and less drafty. Flames burned in oil drums, turning the maze into shades of red and black.

Jamala and Jeff had shifted the subject from glops and were now trading insults over each other's genealogy.

"Quiet!" Celeste hissed.

The tunnel branched into two equally dark paths. Graffiti plastered the mouths of each, recounting a record of tunnel defenses, turf wars, and adventurous exploits in the old subway network.

To the right-hand tunnel, she called out, "Requesting permission to cross! Calling on past favors, Miguel!"

"What favors, lady?" came a faraway voice.

"Tell Miguel that Celeste is coming to collect what she's owed."

There was an awkward silence. Jamala caught Celeste's eyes and asked, all with a jerk of her head, if they should CAMO. Celeste shook her head.

The voice called out, "Miguel's away."

She laughed with cynical aplomb. "Away? Is that the codeword for, 'Miguel is buried up to his neck in tunnel pussy'? Tell him to tuck in his dick for five minutes and get out here."

There was a painful silence. "If he do owe you, I doubt he owes all your friends there."

Celeste forged a smile. She had considered whether to chance a stealthy pass through the tunnels. At a flat run she knew they could scoot by the Butcher Boys' village in under fifteen minutes before the battery on their CAMO suits died. The only quandary was they couldn't run and stay silent, they couldn't run with two antimatter missiles held between four of them, and Miguel had outfitted his tunnels with booby traps. He might even have waspbots set to kill anyone not of the tribe's pheromones. Celeste had once seen a CAMO-clad merc assailed by two thousand waspbots. In seconds his outline was covered with crawling metallic bugs. They got into his eyes, mouth, and suit. By the time the swarm was stopped with an EM pulse, their stings had liquefied 50 percent of his tissues. He had *poured* out of his armor.

Celeste continued the bluff. "Tell Miguel to get his skinny ass out here right now or I'm coming to get him."

She heard footsteps slapping the hard concrete. Miguel emerged from the gloom. He cut an attractive figure, a puff of black hair on his chin. "So what's this crazy shit about me owing you? I owe nobody."

"Assassin job with the Disaster Chief."

"You hated that pigfucker too."

Celeste's grin was a flash of white teeth. "I hate lots of people. Doesn't mean I kill them all. Give me free passage here and we're even."

Miguel studied her face. "What's in the bags?"

"Candy."

"The kind you chew, or the kind that pops?"

"The kind that's eyes-only."

Miguel's smile didn't fade, but his eyes remained as lustrously feral as a wildcat. In the Wastelands of North America, life was short and fortunes were made or lost in an instant. The Butcher Boys were nothing special in the grand scheme; there were bigger fish in the rubble up north or down south. But he was no dummy, either. The Butcher Boys had been around for thirty years, and they had managed to expel some iron competition from the tunnels in this grid.

"You want through, I get to see up your skirt." He shuffled past her and approached the covered missiles. Her team members started to recoil, but Celeste tapped a quick "Cooperate" command to them.

She came up behind him just as he was pulling the tarp off one of the missiles. Miguel's eyes were hard, fascinated, and merciless. The torpedo-shaped object was small, slightly bigger than a Davy Crocket artillery shell. The difference was in the contents: if Miguel had his mechanics open the thing up, they would find something very different amid the dissected framework of guide-beam and gyro control. The entire length of the missile was filled with suspension traps for the devastatingly destructive, absolutely priceless, material within.

Miguel walked to the other tarp, lifted it, and scratched his head. Celeste held her breath, counting on him underestimating the value here.

"Some people come looking for these?" he asked at last.

"No one's missing them yet."

"There was some attack on the other side of the marsh a couple hours ago. Any chance these tarts came out of that?"

Celeste struggled to keep her composure. *How the fuck did he know about that?* Quickly, she said, "An attack in the gloplands? Say it ain't so!"

Miguel was silent a long while. He peered at the tunnel behind them.

Finally, Celeste sighed sharply. "You know what, Miguel? Go to hell. We came here to avoid all that filthy water and to see an old friend. You gonna harass me? I'll just make a grand tour through the gloplands. And I promise to *remember* this shit." She started marching back the way they'd come.

"Hold up," Miguel called. "No need to be rude. You can pass this way, babe. Last thing I want is to disappoint you." He clapped her affectionately on the back, kissed both cheeks, kissed her lips, and let her into the tunnel, through the checkpoint.

Celeste lost a little color when she saw not one, not two, but *three* emerald green waspbot-nests bolted into the ceiling. In the dark, their crawling metal bodies glittered.

Jesus.

"What about the glops, Celeste?" Jeff complained.

"Shut *up!*" Jamala countered.

They were through.

CHAPTER THREE
Night Train, Tomatoes, Corpse

They called it the Night Train not only because it was the solitary tunnel-route to Luna's farside, but also because it was entirely underground. Gethin's window seat was black the whole way, with intermittent pale lights marking maintenance hatches and walkways in the blasted-out Lunar crust. It reminded him of his youth spent riding the industrious PRT network in the London enclave, where if you lived in the stalks of the arcology (as the Bryces did) you always took the shuttles, escalators, or inclinators to access other levels of that human hive. You spent your life in a honeycomb of tunnels that might as well have been the moon.

Gethin had the chance to eat during the forty-minute Night Train route – the stewardess brought him a chilled cup of plum tomatoes, cheese cubes, and rice cakes. It was fascinating to eat again. Like never before he was aware of the primal savagery of consumption. The tomatoes popped into his mouth like Aztec hearts, his tongue feeling them over with a wet swipe, his teeth crushing them so the juices squirted out in gory ribbons. His tongue tossed the pulverized mass down the hatch, and Gethin noted how it fell, outlining his esophagus, reaching his belly. His digestive juices were frothing for something to destroy. He washed the mass down with another coffee.

Then he checked the rest of his messages.

There was an email from a repatriation company, promoting their services in helping secure a new home, job, and any training he might need. Gethin deleted it without reading past the header.

To his amazement the second email was from Lori, blinking for attention; Gethin hastily buried it, knowing he didn't have the time for such personal matters now. But feelings rose in his throat, anyway.

Anomaly. It was the reason he had gone to Mars. The IPC wanted him to investigate reports of subterranean Martian cities – as in *alien* cities – which of course proved to be absurd. Gethin had climbed down into the lava tunnels with local archaeologists as his guide. One of them was Lori. Twenty-four years old, less than half his actual age, cool and mysterious. Bemused by his mission. Unimpressed by his recounting of Earth's mighty arcologies, technologies, virtualities.

They made love within the week…a mile down in the redworld's underdark.

The investigation took two months. When it proved to be just another tribute to humanity's superstitious, belief-driven nature, Gethin let himself be persuaded into applying for a teaching post at Olympus University. Thinking back, he couldn't believe it now. *Athens* on *Earth* was his home, its university his life. His impulsive decision was incredible, shocking testament to how beguiling Lori could be. Waist-length dark hair, her freckled pretty face, the mischievous flash of her smile, the impish bedroom eyes…

Her youthful optimism.

That was really it, wasn't it? Gethin looked young but he felt ancient, listless, oddly cornered in his Earthly life. Lori Gossamer Ambermoon exuded the fresh aura of someone not jaded by the dazzling distractions of the birthworld. Her youth – in mind, spirit, body – sucked Gethin in as if to a singularity's gravity-well. His adopted Athenian culture still quoted the timeless truism of Sophocles: *A girl's glance working the will of heaven…merciless Aphrodite!* The Greek goddess was still at work, playing the harp strings of the double helix with wicked skill.

He and Lori married, opting for a standard ten-year contract without children. It took Gethin only an hour to realize his mistake. At the wedding reception, he met her people – family, friends, colleagues – only to discover that maybe he really had found an alien civilization: the Martian colonists themselves.

Mars was the one and only consideration in Martian colonial life. Despite being a frontier people, Martians scoffed at the larger universe. Rolled their eyes at his 'Earthly' values of science, art, and self-improvement. *Aren't you scientific?* he'd counter, pointing out the vast terraforming projects they were involved in (oh! Don't dare call it terraforming! It was Marsforming!) And to that they'd reply: *Ours is the science of the practical. We use it to make things grow and prosper, while Earthers wield it like a flashy toy to see how much noise and color it will produce.* Gethin was even willing to concede there was truth in that observation, if not for the fanatical extent the Martians took their argument. Their zealotry vibrated into the very coffers of their language; they spoke Terran to outsiders, and Quenya and Sindarin – the invented languages of ancient British writer J.R.R. Tolkien – among themselves.

Gethin realized with dawning horror that he had been pulled into a cult. A cult on a planetary scale.

Life at Olympus University was just as bad. It seemed impossible to form any meaningful relationships within a culture so pathologically independent. His only solace was spending time with offworlders who were on Mars for a short stint. Then he would miss Earth painfully. The *blue* of Earth! Day by day, he felt like his eyes were being burned out by the merciless rust deserts of the Red Planet.

And Lori was the worst eccentric of all. She'd be gone for months at a time on geological excavations. She'd return like a passing comet, flaring bright and beautiful but cold and fleeting. Soon enough she'd be gone again.

The only people Gethin truly got on with were the steel guilders he met at Carter Concourse, about forty minutes west of the Olympus campus where he sometimes trekked just to vary his surroundings. The Concourse was a commercial mecca as large as an airport, set amid a jungle of meticulously tended gardens. The steel guilders took over an entire wing of the facility for their lunch breaks, laughing, swearing, drinking, conversing in their tight-knit gaggle with the kind of camaraderie usually found in army barracks. They were not born-again fanatics like other Martians, but plebian realists who labored at the practical alchemy of metalworks: everything from gratings, girders, and fasteners to ship hulls, engines, and shielding. They were frontierists who still seemed to realize that there was something beyond the frontier. A universe that glinted at the edges of humanity's narrow yard. Not so surprising, perhaps, given that many of them pulled lengthy rotations in the light orbits of Phobos and Deimos. You could see more of the universe from those lofty perches than planetside isolationists who toiled in dirt and dark.

Gethin settled into a loose habit of lunching with two guilders in particular: Natalia and Jason Argos, brother and sister. They were the nearest he ever had to friends on Mars. Gethin felt a sudden throb of remorse for not saying goodbye to either of them.

Nine years, eleven months, three weeks.

A week before his departure, he and Lori made love for the last time. There were four days left on the marriage contract. In her bedroom gloom they coupled in languid, dreamy rhythm that seemed to last many hours. Afterwards, he felt like an empty shell.

"Will you be okay here while I'm gone?" she asked. She was heading to the glaciers again in the morning.

He didn't answer.

"Gethin?"

His breath came out in a warm sigh, wordless and pregnant with meaning.

Lori looked at him. "So that's it? We end in whispers and silence?"

"Lori…"

"We don't have to renew our vows. Just…stay if you want. Stay while I'm away. You can look after Cody." Cody was their eight-year-old calico. "And when I come back, we can talk."

"Talk?" he mimicked. "When the fuck do we do that?"

"We can talk at Evermist," she said excitedly, "at *our* table in the skydome."

"You're going to be gone three months."

She laughed acidly. "So? What are three months in—"

"*Listen* to me, will you?"

"Then fucking *go!*" she screamed. The sound was terrible at such close range. "Just make sure that *everything* you own goes with you, so when I get back this place will be *mine again!*" And she pounded the pillow in helpless rage, fled to the guest room. In the morning she was gone, with her equipment and no note.

That's how Martians were. Proud and independent, frowning on emotional outbursts until they had them…and then, those outbursts were as huge as they were short-lived.

Mars is not for me, he said over and over to himself, repeating the mantra as he packed. *Dust, rust, and ice. I hate it here.*

And so he'd slogged through a lonely breakfast in an empty house. Packed his things. Set the housebot to care for Cody. Made a final tour of the rooms and, anxiety mounting, stopped off at the space elevator's Save Station, his ticket to VG Flight 3107 folded in his bag.

Gethin swallowed his emotions. On the Night Train he accessed the web. Images of shuttle debris on Luna continued parading atop every newsfeed. Investigators were now confirming there had been an explosion in a Prometheus Industries laboratory just seconds before the shuttle accident. Two fatalities; again there was an 'unverified report of a possible survivor transferred to an undisclosed medical ward'.

He grinned mirthlessly and swallowed his coffee. The caffeine was already working on him, exciting his heart into a gallop. The tomato mush gurgled in his stomach, stewing in virgin stomach acids.

He attempted to contact Id and Ego.

Gethin, Id said amicably, shuffling out from its neural hideout like a groggy bear called forth into April thaw. The presence of the Familiar hovered over his shoulder like a shadow. Following it down the synaptic tunnel came another shapeless entity.

<Hello Gethin. This train was manufactured by TowerTech Transport Inc. They have no trade charter with the Martian Bureau of Transportation.>

"We've left Mars," Gethin explained. "I need to know if all your files are intact."

Why wouldn't they be? Id asked.

<All files are intact,> replied Ego.

Two passengers in baggy black suits walked by, eyes glowing slightly with artificial nightshine, common among miners. In the blackness they looked like panthers on the prowl.

Gethin shivered unexpectedly. "Ego, we're going to Tycho Hospital, and there's a sporting good chance they won't let me in to see the patient I want."

<There are currently eighteen patients listed as active in the hospital database.>

Recalling the details of the IPC mission dossier, he asked, "Is there a listing for Kenneth Cavor?"

<Yes. He is in the intensive-care wing. No visitors are permitted.>

"I need a security guard login, granting access to the ICU wing."

The train trembled on its tracks. Gethin flagged the stewardess down and requested another coffee, aware that his hands were starting to shake. Outside the window, recurring pale lights flashed by like stars against the blasted-out engineering of the Lunar tunnel.

<Done,> Ego replied. <Is there anything else you need?>

★ ★ ★

Fifteen minutes later, the train doors opened on a glossy black platform. It was deserted except for a lonely cleaning bot vacuuming the floor. Gethin stepped off the train into the cold draft of the Lunar underworld. The hospital's subterranean revolving door faced him.

Behind him, the Night Train sped away, beckoned to other locales.

Gethin approached the doors. Purple graffiti suddenly materialized on the nearest wall and, before he could react, sprayed him with a pressurized hiss. Gethin leapt back, drawing an arm up to his nose.

It was too late. A big-breasted woman with nipples like daggers slid across his body in his mind. Prowling behind her were other temptresses, flashing black-lit smiles. He felt greedy suction around the head of his penis. Lips kissed his ear and whispered: *"We're waiting for you at Lilith's. Twenty-three Eaton Avenue, Lowell Station."*

Gethin cursed and went through the revolving door.

The lobby was an eerily empty rotunda, murky and dim. A camera studied him as he went to the desk.

"Hi," he said.

There was no one there. His voice bounced across the antiseptic hospital like in a mausoleum. Gethin swallowed, heart pounding. A morbid thought raced in his head:

What if I'm dead?

He thought of the deserted platform where the train had left him. Black floor like in the regen center. Perhaps this really was death; he had been killed on Mars, not on a shuttle ride he couldn't remember, and these desolate locations were simply the deranged flashes of neurons in his head, the post-mortem tautologies of dying sentience.

A pale, pretty nurse stepped out from a fileroom. Her ruby lips drew into a smile.

"I'm sorry!" she laughed. "I didn't hear you come in. We get used to quiet during the graveyard shift."

"No doubt. A friend of mine was careless with a moon drill. Some people will do anything for some paid comp time, eh? Harold Sikorsky. I think he's on the third floor?"

The nurse touched her screen. "Sikorsky is in room 302. Yes, third floor."

"Thanks." He hesitated. "By the way, someone sprayed a pheromod on the wall outside."

The nurse sighed. "Again? I'm so sorry! Please accept our apologies. I'll have it scrubbed right away. Those people at Lowell have no shame."

Indeed, he thought, alerted by something in her voice and bearing that suggested she knew more about the pheromod than she should. He was half tempted to continue the conversation just so he could activate his sniffers and get to the bottom of it; her body language and stress patterns would likely reveal a fascinating story of after-hours employment.

But Gethin only nodded and turned to find the elevators.

On the third floor he got out, located the stairs, and climbed them.

<Security pass engaged,> Ego spoke in his head.

Despite the cameras, Gethin climbed the next two flights of stairs unseen, knowing that to the security system he was now registering as part of the hospital's staff. No one looked at faces anymore. They only looked at what computers told them; if anyone happened to be glancing at the stairwell camera, they'd pay more attention to the bright green letters hovering over his head informing them that he was a hospital security guard. If they didn't recognize his face, it didn't matter.

He opened the fifth-floor doors. A beige hallway ran east to west, with a floor the color of coffee. Helpful wall signs pointed to the nurses' station. By his optics' compass, he knew Cavor's room was westward. Room 542.

With Ego hooked into the medical database, columns of info sprouted on his eye each time he passed a room. <536, **Harold Stapledon, admitted three days ago for chest pains. 537, Anya Bach on her second day of nanite scrubbing for ovarian cancer. 538, Patrice Carlotta, admitted yesterday for six pulverized spinal disks. 539**>

"Cut that," Gethin whispered. The columns blinked away.

542. Cavor, Kenneth. The information displayed black on the door's infopanel. Gethin slid the door open, closed it swiftly behind him.

The room had a strange smell. Gethin breathed deep, letting it curl into his nostrils. It was like burned insulation, or the rancid smell of charred matter from a rocket pad when some unfortunate glop got caught beneath the blastoff.

Gethin approached the plastic curtain of Cavor's bedside and drew it back.

At first he didn't know what he was looking at. Kenneth Cavor was supposed to have been in the bathroom when the explosion happened at the research lab; the IPC dossier reported that had been his last biometric login. He was supposed to have been badly burned. He was supposed to be able to recover.

Gethin felt a bead of nervous sweat trickle down his face.

The hospital bed was fused with black, charred remains. It might have been tar, if not for the scorched-meat smell. Through the immolation, bones were visibly melted with the carbonized remains of clothing, ash, and the rubber bed beneath.

But the bed itself was unburned. Even the IV line was intact, snaking like a transparent umbilical cord to the obliterated mass on the bed.

Gethin felt bile in the back of his throat. He backed away from the bed.

Then he noticed the room's vent. The metallic grate was melted. He peered down its narrow shaft. The walls were streaked with scorch marks like tigerstripes.

<An alarm has just been activated,> Ego said, jarring him. <**Four security personnel are bearing down on this room. The video feed has been cut off for the past ten minutes. An encrypted message has been sent to the following destinations...**>

Gethin buried Ego and ran for the door, in time to collide with the hospital's armed security officers.

CHAPTER FOUR
A Babylonian Mystery

Sixteen hours into the Flight 3107 tragedy, the newsfeeds were coalescing into a single mind like a living, gestalt organism, demanding answers in fear and fury. Luna's corporate hydra was livid, and officials swarmed over the moon's surface in a dance of desperation. Experts descended on the recovered debris, detained hapless cleanup crews, nabbed spaceport logs, and waited breathlessly for answers. Even Mars was putting pressure on the locals. And the Actors' Guild was sure to be next.

Earthside on Level 299 in the Babylon arcology of New York's Hudson Valley, Jack Saylor, sector chief for Prometheus Industries Babylon, rubbed his bearded jaw in mute anxiety. The Lunar landscape displayed as a sprawling holo across his office.

"There," Internal Affairs Officer Keiko Yamanaka said, pointing to what resembled an igloo village built from Lunar dirt. "We're looking at the PI Base 59 complex, Kepler crater, at 1451 Earthtime yesterday."

Supervisor Drake Fincher was the only other person in the room. A handsome Zulu officer transferred from the great African state, his uniform sported the Zulu sideways green *Y* in addition to the green and silver PI colors. Fincher was frowning, hugging himself.

Jack watched the unchanging moonscape, waiting for something to happen. When nothing did, he nervously cleared his throat. "I don't see what—"

One of the lab igloos exploded soundlessly.

Through the breach emptied a river of light. It shot overhead like a luminous arrow. The lab vomited desks, chairs, and assorted office inventory, and then the view was motionless and serene once more.

"They were *blown up?*" Jack cried.

Keiko tapped her fingers and the footage changed. A new holo swapped in, this one offering an Earthrise view from Tanabata Shuttleport. Flight 3107 was a speck in the black sky, descending towards an available landing pad.

The luminous arrow from the lab struck it head-on, shattered it like a clay skeet. Keiko moved her hands, zooming the view. Jack's stomach lurched in sympathetic inertia.

Flight 3107 was a floating debris field, its torus ring shattered. But the focus of the zoom was the luminous arrow. Having struck the shuttle, it appeared to be on a trajectory for deep space…

…when it *banked* sharply towards Earth. A turn of almost ninety degrees.

Jack's mouth was suddenly dry. "What in the holy hell?"

The luminous arrow was no longer visible. But that turn! Veering off as if by a magician's trick.

Keiko replayed the image twice more, finally freeze-framing the moment of the impossible change of direction.

Jack stepped into the hologram for closer inspection. At six-foot-eight, two hundred and sixty pounds, he towered over it even at magnification. "At the apex of its turn, it changes shape. See?"

"I see," Keiko replied crisply.

"There's a complex pattern there. Fraying all along the edges."

"Yes."

"Like cilia, if I had to match it to something."

Keiko was watching Drake. His ebony skin lost some luster.

"Level with us," she said. "What did we have up there?"

Their supervisor raised an eyebrow. "What do you mean?"

"What were they working on at Base 59?"

"Nothing that could cause an explosion."

"Not good enough."

"I don't care," Drake said irritably. "You don't have the clearance, I don't have the authority to—"

"Then what are we talking to *you* for?" she yelled. "Have you accessed the web lately? Mars, Venus, the AF…all joined in a demand for answers! All flights to Luna delayed or rerouted! The IPC is going crazy and the only reason they're not crashing down our door is that *they haven't seen this footage yet.*"

Jack sucked in a breath, delighted to see that Keiko's incendiary temper hadn't cooled from her two years away in the Belt. The company encouraged employees to pull rotations out there – it was seen as a fast track to promotion. But it wasn't for everyone. Jack had known men and women who went to the deeps full of arrogance and ambition, only to return… changed. As if the void had broken something in their spirit. Reduced them to an odd reticence and economy of movement.

But not Yamanaka. The firebrand he'd worked with for five years was undiminished. *Great stars! She really is destined for a lofty office within the company.* For all her dainty appearance, with a doll-like face and small brown eyes, she had a way of going on the attack that could freeze a bot in its tracks.

She was also a true believer. Convinced that the Promethean destiny was to propel the human race beyond the reaches of Sol…to hell with the IPC ban.

"Where did you get the clip?" Drake demanded.

Keiko's eyes glittered in challenge. "From a friend who works at the base's comm tower. He was driving a buggy topside when he came across debris. He saw the wrecked base, hurried back to the tower, and found this playback from its security camera."

"Why are we only seeing this *now?*"

"Because he didn't find the debris until five hours after the shuttle explosion. Base 59 is *remote*, Drake. By the time he discovered the aftermath, scoured the camera feed, and sent it to me…"

Drake paced once through the room. His moustache twitched.

"What did we have up there?" she asked again.

"Nothing."

"I can already see the headlines!" She was still connected to the holomodule, so words appeared on the holopanel's field in bold white letters as she spoke: "What Happened on Luna? 'Nothing,' Says PI Spokesman Fincher."

Drake's retort caught in his throat. His forehead creased and he muttered something. It took Jack a minute to realize the man was in communication with the corporate brass. Finally, he nodded and returned to them.

"It was TNO material," he said.

Keiko hesitated. She exchanged glances with Jack.

"Okay," Jack said, "Was there any TNO material that could—"

"No," Drake said sternly.

"Nothing combustible?"

"Nothing. Virtual testing environments only. The most dangerous thing they had up there was a goddamn toaster."

Jack flushed. "Then it was an attack. What about visitor logs to the base?"

"The Merrils were there. Both killed in the explosion. And assistant Kenneth Cavor was in the bathroom at the time of the explosion."

"Have the Merrils been revived?"

"Yes. They're being held for questioning by our query team, but of course they can't tell us what happened."

"And Cavor?"

"Burns over eighty percent of his body. Comatose. He was taken immediately to Tycho Hospital in secret."

Keiko started to talk, then caught herself. "We wish our brother a speedy recovery and absence of suffering."

Both men bowed their heads respectively. "May our brother recover with speed and without suffering," they chanted.

Keiko let several seconds pass, thinking of the disfigured man in the Lunar hospital ward. She cleared her throat. "If…once he has recovered, when can we expect to interview him?"

Drake lifted his head. "We have a query team stationed there now."

"If he dies…"

"They can perform a DC within seconds of death."

Keiko nodded and tried not to pace. Suppressing one nervous habit conjured another; her feet clenched and unclenched in her shoes.

They can do the DC now, she wanted to say, but bit her tongue. A Digital Capture took thirty minutes, sometimes longer, and for a man already damaged like Kenneth Cavor, it would cause suffering beyond what the drugs could handle. The company had self-preservation as part of its tripart masthead; but devotion to an employee's spirit shared that core, as did the 'pursuit of human progress'. *Out of the past and up to the stars*, the corporate jingle went.

"Who would have attacked us?" Jack asked.

"Unknown." Drake hesitated and regained his Zulu calmness. "All PI facilities are on high alert. Curfews are in effect for all arcologies. No one in or out." He started towards the door. "I want a press blackout."

Jack was appalled. "But—"

"Do it," Drake said. And then he was gone.

★   ★   ★

The sector chief's office had a small balcony affording a stunning view of Babylon's golden ziggurats, geodesic domes, skyways, and commercial enclosures. Jack liked spending his coffee and lunch breaks out here, soaking in the view. The Hudson River was turning scarlet in the rising sun, resembling an artery cleaving the corporate vista of North America's biggest city-state. Beyond this sprawled the vast agricultural fields tended by bots, and the border spires separating civilization from the Wastes. Jack was immensely fond of maps, and the Babylonian horizon suggested an infinite cartological fantasy. At moments like this, he liked to wonder about what kind of window he would be staring through when he was one hundred, two hundred, even five hundred years old. On what world would he be living? It was a staggering ascent for the Saylor clan, just two generations removed from the Wastes…a bloodline bred as bodyguards for an ancient Warlord, now working as sector chief for the opulent god-city of Babylon.

Keiko joined him in watching the sunrise over the Hudson. Two plush chairs and a glass table were at hand, but neither of the Prometheans bothered to sit.

"It's good to have you back," Jack said without looking at her.

She touched the glass, squinting at the fiery hues of Sol. "I forgot how big the sun is here."

"What do you think?"

"That the base was destroyed by industrial saboteurs, night-dropped on Luna."

"And the energy stream?"

Keiko pursed her small lips. "I've put that question to our own physicists. They tell me they've never seen anything like it."

"If we were attacked, where did the saboteurs go afterwards?"

She pointed to the moon hanging low in the sky. "They might be part of the base wreckage."

Jack frowned. "But they'd know we'd comb through everything with an electron microscope."

"Ever seen a golem? No DNA. Just a block of uninfused flesh-gel with enough neural wiring to carry out basic instructions. Stuff them with explosives, wind them up, and set them loose."

Jack flushed. "Who would risk that? Who would dare?"

"We use them sometimes."

"I don't believe that."

Keiko looked back to the window to hide her faint smile. She was fifty-six, elixired to prime. Saylor was thirty-four, and he was good; the right combination of intelligence, experience, and willingness to act. But he was also amazingly naïve.

Staring again to the moon, Keiko said, "This is about the Trans-Neptunian Outpost contract. Our enemies want to rain disaster on it, convince people that we aren't responsible enough to handle it. President Song orders a recall on our contract and allows a new bidding war, without us."

Jack grumbled. "It could just be an accident, Keiko. I doubt Drake really knows what the hell they were doing up there."

"It isn't an accident."

"So certain, are we?"

"An accident at this stage is highly improbable."

Jack grinned and looked down at her. The height difference made them seem two separate human species out of *Gulliver's Travels*. "Talking like a machine again, Keiko…"

"Machines are the enemy," she quipped, playfully punching him.

"Hey," Jack suggested, "there *is* an AI colony on the moon. Maybe they're starting trouble."

"Maybe," she said, but didn't sound convinced.

Jack scratched his beard. "But you're probably right about the night-drop. Vector Nanonics. TowerTech. Even the Jade Kingdom. Any one of them would love to see us fail."

"Agreed."

"The TNO challenges their power structures. Their very way of life."

"It does."

"If we light up the deeps…"

Keiko gave a crisp nod. "Then we rule out there. A truly interplanetary corporation with more power than anyone in history. Sort of paints a target on our backs."

"We'll find out who did it," Jack said at last, bristling at what she was describing; his family knew well what it was like to be targets. "And then…"

Keiko's pretty face turned even more radiant as she smiled. But the smile gave Jack a chill. "Then we kill them all," she said.

CHAPTER FIVE
Stillness

Two miles from Miguel's fiefdom they emerged from the underdark into a soggy ravine trilling with crickets. Jamala and Jeff crept up opposite banks, and for several anxious minutes they scanned the countryside for enemies.

The Hudson was just a sprint away. No one claimed turf at the waterway; trade was too important for territorial pissing, and any Warlord challenging this neutrality would be quickly disposed of by arky powers. Even the graffiti was neutral.

The morning was wreathed in a silver haze that stung the eyes. A mist floated above the Hudson River, billowing around the irregular outlines of an invisible vessel in the water.

Celeste touched her ear and sent the message: *"We're home."*

Her vessel instantly materialized, a vivid blue-black craft like a monstrous scarab beetle. It cut the waters in a slow, foaming eddy to reach them.

They piled aboard the loading ramp and hastily secured their dangerous cargo.

[Welcome back, Celeste.] The voice of the *Mantid* entered her head like chilled liquid.

"Thank you," she replied. "Set course to Quinn's and proceed."

The ship pushed easily through the water, gliding upstream past the agricultural farms that produced for Babylon arcology. Armored bots guarded those fields. Even if a gang war went topside (which they often did) it was forbidden to scrap with arkies. No one wanted to incur the uncompromising wrath of the civilized world.

Yet.

The thought filled Celeste with smoldering excitement. She leaned back in her pilot seat, hands folded behind her head. *Two* antimatter missiles! She didn't know how many more King D. was stockpiling. Each acquisition was a terrible risk, another roll of the die. But surely they were in the final stretch. StrikeDown was brewing; she could feel it thrumming like something under high pressure. Was it five years out? Five months?

One thing was certain: the acquisition of two additional antimatter missiles would push up StrikeDown's secret schedule. It *mattered*.

Quinn's compound overhung the river several miles upstream. It was a peeling old warehouse that had once been painted red, containing a marina of six hovercraft. But Celeste knew this quaint appearance masked a subterranean structure of luxury and paramilitary design, where Quinn kept his sultan's harem of whores, underground pools, supply caches, telecommunications web, and probably an escape route to one of the many Outland villages.

"Celeste!" Quinn cried once the *Mantid* arrived and she was unloading the missiles into the shade of his hangar.

Quinn was tall, lank, black-bearded and brown-skinned. He looked so spindly that people often referred to him as the Skeleton – even his face appeared shrink-wrapped over his skull – but his wire-thin body was tightly packed with enhanced muscle. His abdomen showed a chiseled eight-pack that looked resistant to bullets, and his arms were like hardened amber. At this early hour, his portside market was mostly deserted. Bodyguards patrolled the borders, brushing aside gnats, cigarettes hanging loosely from stubbly lips.

Quinn was wearing his usual getup – a gray robe and black pants.

"Great Stars, Segarra!" he cried, pointing to the tarps. "And look at you. Not a scratch!"

He embraced her, but clearly had eyes only for the missiles. Celeste regarded his little marketplace. In the world's cracks and corners, people traded for arky medpacks, nanonic upgrades, nanoblades, glop transgenics, and tailor-made viruses. Even as she looked, two sail-backed reptilian glops raced past her feet and chased each other around the trading tables, chirping playfully, their ancestors having escaped from markets like this decades or even centuries earlier.

But Quinn didn't deal in biologics. He was strictly a gun-and-ammo man, with arky meds thrown in for an added price.

Celeste surveyed the market stalls disinterestedly. A balcony was built into the rafters, where Quinn's private office overlooked his domain. Five men were crowded at the window. They were dressed in shiny green armor like folded beetle wings.

Celeste scowled.

Stillness soldiers.

"You really should work as my permanent retainer, Celeste," Quinn was saying. "I'll even buy your recording of the heist, if you're selling."

"My tactics aren't for viewing."

"Containment is stable, I presume?"

"The Hudson is still in one piece, isn't it?"

Quinn licked his lips. "Any survivors?"

"Not that we saw."

"Good." He gave her a curious look, then motioned to his guards. Two of them came up bearing a metal payment crate. "Before you open it, I need you to promise me something."

She sighed. "Why is everything so fucking complicated with you, Quinn?"

He smiled weakly, his teeth like pegs in his skeletal jaws. "Promise to be a good girl. Promise you'll behave."

She had been talking just to pass the time, to get paid, and then hold still for King D.'s people to make the pickup. Now, Quinn's strange line of conversation confused her. "What are you talking about?" she demanded.

He knocked on the crate. "There's a lot more in here than what you were promised. Oh, it's the same percentage for acquisition, but it's cut from a much larger pie."

Celeste's face hardened. "Get to your point, Quinn."

He shrugged. "I've got a new buyer for the missiles."

"*Excuse me?*"

"Got a better offer."

"Better offer?" she echoed, incredulous. "We were brought on by an exclusive contract…" She stopped, the pieces coming together in her mind. She looked fiercely to the balcony where the green-armored Stillness soldiers were leaning, watching her. "You double-crossed StrikeDown to make a deal with *Stillness?*"

Quinn sighed. "They contacted me—"

"When?"

"The reps arrived last night with an insane offer. There was no way to ignore it."

Celeste's mind spun over at the possibilities. "You *backstabbed* King D! Just what do you think he'll do when he hears this?"

Quinn's veneer of calm melted beneath her vehemence. His playful eyes turned flat. "I'm prepared for the fallout. Stillness has deep pockets."

"King D. will *kill* you."

"He's welcome to try."

She sucked in a breath, stunned by this response. Jeff and Jamala strode forward, glowering, and Quinn's bodyguards brought up their multiguns.

"Call off your dogs, Segarra," Quinn snapped. "And think this through, will you? You got your money, and there's plenty more work waiting for all of us. I'm striking deals, looking to the future. Going interplanetary soon. We all need to start preparing for the change that's coming. Don't let ideology gum that up."

"This isn't about ideology!" she lied, thinking helplessly of the damage this betrayal would cause StrikeDown. The acquisition of antimatter was imperative. StrikeDown needed to happen *soon*. Pieces and schedules were being juggled with the precision of a chess match. The virtual meetings had a nervous energy now, a sense of joyful inevitability. Sometimes she couldn't believe it. The whispers had been circulating since her Wastetown childhood.

And King D. was serious. He inspired and delivered. He was going to end the *Pax Apollonia* (or as he called it, the *Faux Apollonia*) in the most brilliant coordinated attack on 'civilization' ever. Give those lofty fucks a real taste of mortality.

> *Grab the world and bring it down*
> *steal the scepter and the crown*
> *StrikeDown! StrikeDown!*
> *Burn the arkies to the ground!*
> *StrikeDown! StrikeDown!*

Celeste steadied her breathing, struggling to regain her composure. But she was too stunned, rocked to her core, by this betrayal. "You burn StrikeDown," she heard herself say, "and we lose one of our biggest clients."

Quinn spat over her shoulder into the water. "Stillness is bigger and they're growing. They have momentum. Things are happening, Segarra."

"The IPC will turn your compound into a glass crater if—"

"That's what I'm trying to *tell* you. The IPC is about to get challenged from all directions. Stillness is a rising tide that we're gonna surf, and it's just the start. I even nabbed us a contract with some tough *hombres* on Mars called the Partisans, and they fucking despise the IPC. Don't you see? Now's the time to earn our fortunes."

Celeste trembled in fury. But she said nothing.

Quinn turned away from her. "StrikeDown's days are numbered. Now go freshen up, and fuck one of my boys if you want. You'll get over this."

"King D. won't. Ever."

"This conversation's done."

She surged forward. She didn't know what she intended to do. Probably grab him by his sinewy arm and whirl him around. Maybe choke the life out of him in front of his boys. All she knew was that StrikeDown was *depending on her at this moment* and couldn't be thwarted by a traitorous king-shit local smuggler.

Then she halted. The hairs on the back of her neck stood up.

Directly above her, positioned on the rafters of the warehouse, a blue-black mech-spider had moved into position. Its eye-cluster studied her with cold, seething malice.

She looked back to Quinn. He smiled.

"You're in *my* parlor, Segarra. Don't forget that."

Two more mech-spiders scuttled across the rafters.

Celeste marched back to the *Mantid*. Her posse gathered on the pier, cursing quietly.

Jamala's hard face was a battle-mask. She pushed the payment chest on its wheels to the edge of the pier; Silent Rajnar's foot stopped it from going into the river.

"He's out of his mind," Jamala muttered.

Celeste stared at her feet.

For four years she had run a tight team, handpicked by her from the East Coast Wastes and Old Minnesota ash bowls. That alone made them an atypical bunch; most gangs were culled from one locality, bonded to one another by blood-ties and provincial history.

But more importantly, *all* of them were StrikeDown believers.

Jamala hawked and spat into the river. "King D. is going to eat his fucking heart."

"What do we do?" Jeff asked.

Celeste turned aside, her mind clawing fruitlessly for a course of action.

"Celeste?"

She stared into the water, the sunrise drawing a jagged golden bolt across its coppery undulations.

A private message splashed into her optics. It was a photo of some European villa in the shade of an arky Ringtown. A bustling café set among flowering trellises, two glasses of wine glowing on a candlelit table centered in frame.

But the chairs were empty.

Waiting.

She glanced to Jeff.

He chanced a smile. A second message sprang to her eye:

Tomorrow is ours, my love.

Celeste felt a pang of desire, a mad need to grasp Jeff's hand and rush off into that mysterious villa, to a place where there were no explosions and death. Memories of the night before the heist pulsed in strobe-light intensity: her lover sliding his length into her, his strong hands latched onto her hips. The hunger in his eyes. The way he groaned as she locked her legs around the small of his back in a fleshy vise, the delirious pleasure as they coupled in the ruins of an ancient office lobby, reception desk ringing a tree and faded corporate logos draped in ivy and mold.

She turned away from him. Tapping secretly on her virtuboard, she sent him a reply:

Tomorrow is ours, but forever you're mine.

The squad didn't know about her and Jeff. It was essential that they didn't. Their working dynamic required absolute trust honed into near-psychic powers; their blips on her map were like extensions of her own body.

A romantic entanglement would adulterate that faith. She'd seen it happen in other tribes. The accusations of favoritism. The resentment of special favors real or imagined. There was even the possibility of jealousy, however unlikely that might be; Jamala and Jeff hated each other, and Allie's sexual orientation precluded men. But even harmless gossip could poison the dynamic.

"Celeste?" Allie waved a hand to get her attention. "What do we do?"

Celeste blew the hair out of her face and closed her eyes. "We take the missiles back."

★   ★   ★

It wasn't possible to assail Quinn's port. The place was a fortified citadel built from the wealth of his coffers. It looked like shit, but the subterranean levels would be impregnable to all but a goddamn drillbot, and there were guards, mechs, and enough wetware to discourage an arky assault. Quinn was a savvy survivor. He *wanted* the future.

But he wasn't their target anyway. The missiles would need to leave port sometime, and Quinn never permitted anyone to enter his airspace. Stillness would have to cart the missiles off-site for a pickup.

And we'll be ready for them when they do, she thought.

Celeste's first order of business was to launch a Hassan airhound from the *Mantid.* The probe stayed low to avoid detection, and quickly confirmed that the missiles were still topside. The news made her smirk. Quinn wasn't about to risk his ass (or the perfect asses of his prized harem) by carting antimatter missiles through his underground tunnels. One misstep and he really would end up in space.

While her squad waited, they recharged their CAMO and loaded all weapons. Everyone realized what this meant.

The time had come to abandon the Americas.

She called King D. through the *Mantid*'s secure channels.

"It was going to happen sooner or later," she told him via comlink.

King D. was a black silhouette onscreen. In person he was a bear of a fellow, thick, with hands like catcher's mitts and arms like tree trunks, but he carried the pounds well.

"The time has come to put your skills to better use anyhow," D. said thoughtfully. "The timetable, Celeste. It's approaching fast."

She felt herself wanting to grin. "And Quinn?"

"Rest assured I won't forget him."

"How did Stillness even know about this trade?"

King D.'s black silhouette sighed. "There are no secrets in the world anymore. We've all become the guy who whispers his secrets into a hole in the ground..."

Celeste nodded. "...and every flower opens the next morning to broadcast it to the world."

"Get my heirlooms back, Celeste."

"I will. I *promise*."

The comline cut. Celeste cracked her back and joined her compatriots in the main room.

Twelve minutes later the Hassan pinged an alert. A small truck was departing Quinn's. The airhound tracked it into the Wastelands north-east of Quinn's compound. Celeste tapped behind her ear and a map sprang onto her eye. Old roads crisscrossed the country.

Then she saw the airfield.

Stillness was going to fly the missiles out of here.

"Suit up," Celeste said. "The Hassan counts twenty-four soldiers accompanying the missiles."

Jeff shot her a look. "Twenty-four soldiers? Really?"

She slapped a needle-cartridge into her assault rifle, ignoring him and feeling an irrational flare of anger at his doubt. The *Mantid*'s interior glowed in winter blue; the squad moved in machinelike synchronicity, like figures in a grim clockwork panorama. Allie popped two canisters into her haze guns, her tightly cropped blond hair and palish skin giving a metallic patina in the light. Silent Rajnar strapped his CAMO suit on and sleeved a shieldfist on one arm, like some futuristic gladiator about to perform before a Roman crowd. Jamala was already suited and loaded, her heatlance in hand and a Gauss sniper rifle slung at her back. She gave Celeste an inscrutable look.

The cargo ramp dropped behind them. Jamala glanced once more to Celeste, her eyes flicked to Jeff, and then she hopped down into the Hudson's ankle-deep shallows. Allie and Rajnar followed.

Jeff didn't move. He swiveled on his chair, looking less like a seasoned soldier and more like an Old Calendar small-town football player with rosy cheeks, freckles, and promises of Mom's apple pie in his eyes.

"Celeste," he began, "Twenty-four soldiers…"

"We've handled numbers like that before."

"In an open airfield? With no cover except for fucking *grass*?"

"Move your ass," she hissed.

Jeff stood fluidly. "Quinn will expect this."

For a horrible moment Celeste thought her lover was actually going to defy her. But he only brushed past her and leapt into the river below with an empty expression that made Celeste want to cry.

To the *Mantid*, she said, *"Standby if we need aerial support. Let me know the instant an aircraft enters the vicinity."*

[Of course, Celeste.]

The night was cold for July. Reeds slapped at them as they pushed towards the airfield with the Hassan's datamap feeding them real-time updates. At Celeste's command they went CAMO a half klick from their target, spreading out and approaching the field from as wide an angle as possible. Celeste found her eyes straying to the dark sky. The *Mantid* would detect approaching aircraft far before her eyes could spot one.

She decided to focus on the twenty-four Stillness soldiers. That constituted a formidable opposition.

Stillness was a fanatic's fanatic. Decrying the perversion of humanity through technology.

Meaning they rarely had wetware or augs of any kind.

Stillness tapped the Wastes for recruits, whipped them into shape, and set them to work. Twenty-four soldiers, even well-armed, couldn't stand up to a pair of experienced arky hunters.

But technology wasn't everything. Twenty-four armed opponents equated to a lot of chances for something to go wrong.

Celeste exhaled forcefully and steeled herself.

The reeds ended at the airfield's circular perimeter. She pressed on, careful not to rustle the vegetation more than what a riverside breeze should produce. She amped her optics and studied the visible troopers, each armed with low-grade fleschette rifles, each surveying the airfield with insectile thermoptic lenses.

No aircraft yet.

She frowned at this. The *Mantid*'s sensors weren't picking up anything en route, either. Why the hell did they bring the missiles out here so early?

She gazed at the trucks. There was a huge guy patrolling between them, a cigar in his mouth, and a beebomb launcher cradled in both bulging arms.

Celeste tapped out commands on her virtuboard fingertips. She ordered Silent Rajnar to take the beebomber, and advised him to be careful around the trucks. A single round puncturing the missile carapace could disrupt stasis, and the IPC would spot the resulting explosion from Mars.

In the center of the airfield, two men were intently talking. Celeste didn't know a lot about Stillness hierarchies, but clearly these two fellows represented command ranks within the organization. She knew the cult had begun in the Wastes three centuries ago. Recruits were always Outlanders; the deprived and depraved, the weak-willed who wanted to belong to a stronger gang. No government, no technology, no society other than pure, true democracy where people lived off the land and by their own rules. Even their robes – green and gold – were the colors of harvest.

Bunch of fucking anarchists.

Celeste had always shrugged them off as mindless idiots. StrikeDown was altogether different (though arkies tended to lump the groups together.) King D. wanted to shake civilization's ivory towers and let Outlanders draw from the technological well. The medicines, treatments, and a rightful vote in Earth Republic were his coveted prize. Quinn had it wrong; it was StrikeDown's concrete promises that were gaining popularity, not the brainless evangelism of anarchist priests.

Wasn't it?

Celeste knelt, aware of two soldiers only five meters away. Their robes scintillated like eelskin in the breeze, simultaneously stiff and fluid.

Over the comlink, Jeff said, "That must be the High Priest."

Celeste frowned, glancing again to the commanding officers. The shorter man was dark, squat, and mustachioed; he looked like a Mongolian Warlord from the Gobi itself. But the second commander formed an unexpected contrast, like a well-dressed CEO surrounded by underpaid millworkers. His clothes were fine livery, not the green beetle armor and cloaks of his brethren. The man was tall, Nordic-skinned and blond, with peculiarly bland stone-cut features.

"That guy is jacked with tech or I'm a glop," Jeff said. "He might even be a Seraph."

Celeste heard the others hold their breaths at this comment. They had dealt with Stillness Seraphs once before. It wasn't the kind of encounter any of them wished to repeat. They might eschew wetware, but they permitted use of deadly tech.

The High Priest (if that's what he was) rotated his head as smoothly as a ball bearing in Celeste's direction and she got a clear view of his eyes through her scope. Twin starbursts of wintry blue irises like four-pointed diamonds over black pupils. She wondered if Stillness had benefactors in arky society.

She steadied her breathing. None of her questions mattered right now. The missiles only.

StrikeDown.

"Ten seconds," she whispered to her posse. "I'll take the leader. Rajnar, Allie, follow me. Jamala's got the scatter. And don't hit the damn missiles."

"Thanks," Jamala countered. "Don't feel like dying today."

Celeste's rifle-mike was picking up bits and pieces from the tall man.

"…will be sequestered for the duration. Mother Eris is on a very special mission in the meantime. Time slips away from us."

You got that right, she thought, putting his head in her targeting reticle and squeezing the trigger.

The high-caliber silenced round blew out the side of his head in a spatter of skull. The lieutenant he had been addressing stared dumbly at the fallen body. In the microsecond after she pulled the trigger, the two nearest soldiers must have detected the whine of the shot in the hypersonic band. They jerked their rifles in Celeste's direction and fired.

A blaze of fleschettes exploded off her breastplate. She smelled hot metal and allowed the force to knock her backwards, where her head smacked against cold mud. The other stream missed her and turned the reeds into confetti over her head. Jamala's response came at once. A searing lash of heat and fire turned both soldiers to ash.

Celeste rolled, flattening the reeds, and hopped up. Any pretense of organization from the Stillness troops evaporated, and they fell into the chaos of a disrupted ant colony. She glimpsed the beebomber perform an agile combat roll between the two trucks as Rajnar's fire perforated the tires.

The Mongolian-looking lieutenant was still crouching by his master's fallen body, as if he couldn't believe what he was seeing. Celeste killed him where he was, then tucked and rolled again.

A blast of crackling light swept out in a halo across the reeds. It missed Celeste's head by an inch, but caught Jeff and Allie where they stood, invisible. As the light died, Celeste saw that her compatriots were now stained white.

Phosphire. Painting them as bright, white targets.

Celeste raced towards the trucks. Bullets whined and zipped around her. She saw the beebomber's legs beneath the first vehicle.

There was a hollow-sounding *whump!* as he fired off a golden canister into the air.

"Got it!" Jeff cried. His half-invisible, half-striped body took aim and fired an EMP charge just as the canister exploded into an angry cloud of waspbots. There was a hiss and crackle, and then their steel bodies littered the reeds like rain.

Celeste threw herself to the ground, switched ammo, and fired at the bomber's legs. The blaze chewed straight through both calves so fast that he was suddenly twelve inches shorter, standing on shredded stumps, shrieking wildly in horror, tipping over. The next shot pureed his head off his neck.

The gunfire was dying down. She got back to her feet, surveying the destruction. A surviving waspbot landed on her neck; she slapped it off and hastily crunched it underfoot.

"Celeste!"

It was Jeff's voice, and she hurried over to see Allie on the ground, her facemask peeled off her camouflaged, white-streaked body. Blood spurted from her neck.

Jeff's forehead creased as he worked to stabilize the wound with a medpatch. "Artery's hit."

Celeste signaled the *Mantid* for extraction. Jamala and Rajnar crisscrossed on the far side of the field, trying to ferret out survivors.

"The missiles!" Celeste called to them. She gave her lover a pained stare. "Grab them! I'll take care of Allie."

Jeff looked once more to his wounded comrade, then back to Celeste.

"StrikeDown better be fucking worth it. I'm tired, Celeste."

He gripped her hand and squeezed hard. Then he joined the others to load up the first of the missiles onto their moving straps.

Celeste's heart was pounding. Allie looked dead already, like a blond corpse, despite the medpatch halting the bloodflow below her chin.

"Hang tight," she told her friend. "*Mantid* is on its way."

Allie's breathing came in ragged gasps. "You...and Jeff?"

Celeste drew a breath. She laced her fingers with Allie's and kneaded them together as if in prayer. Helplessly, she answered, "Yes."

Allie smiled. "I already...know...what to get you two when—"

Celeste heard something come scuttling behind her.

She assumed Quinn might send one of his Bombay-model mech-spiders to guard his new friends. To that end she had attached several EM rounds to her multigun rifle. The blasts probably wouldn't disable the heavily shielded body, but the leg actuators might be paralyzed and that was good enough. She switched over to this tertiary ammo and swung the weapon around.

It wasn't a mech-spider.

Her eyes widened at the sight of the High Priest she had just killed, the man with wintry blue eyes, rushing at her. His face was a crimson mask of hatred. At this range, she saw that his brilliant eyes were throwing wild incandescence like search beams.

Celeste was almost too shocked to move. It was only her years of training that galvanized her. She lifted her weapon, suppressing her bewildered questions for later examination, and flicked to the needle rounds.

"*Plaga!*" the man shrieked, and he transformed into blurred mass faster than she could pull the trigger. She was struck headlong as if by a train, instantly airborne, the air expelled from her lungs in a painful burst. Her body collided with bone-snapping force against a storage crate.

Celeste blinked stupidly, dazed beyond comprehension. Blazing, liquid pain crackled through her fractured skull and pulverized left leg.

She stared as Jeff and Jamala saw what had happened. They lowered the missile. Silent Rajnar came in, fleschettes burning the night. The spray turned the High Priest into a cloud of meat, through which those burning searchlight eyes never wavered.

Jeff and Jamala rushed in, adding to the execution. The High Priest was disintegrating under the attack, but his luminous eyes seemed to stay above the amorphous cloud of viscera, and those eyes flushed a hellish shade of scarlet.

Looking more enraged than in pain, he burst into a dazzling fireball.

Blue-white forks of electricity arced across the airfield. The shockwave flopped Celeste over like a Styrofoam doll until she landed face-down in a small brackish pond. But even in those surreal microseconds before drowning, she knew her friends – and the love of her life – had been killed.

Celeste sobbed against the water.

Then, with her final conscious thought, she breathed it in to drown.

CHAPTER SIX
Gethin Gets Angry

In Tycho Hospital's security office, Gethin sat in a chair like a reprimanded child while two officers watched him. A third was accessing the hospital's surveillance feed.

Gethin's green eyes glared. On his optics, little ID tags appeared near the men: VICTOR SLOTKIN, PAUL TERRY, and crouched at the security terminal was DAMIAN DELGOBBO. Their corporate profiles swirled as tiny lavender icons at the bottom corner of their names.

Gethin's nose itched, but he resisted scratching it; his hands were entirely encased in glasstic cuffs, anyway. He wanted to enforce an image of tranquility, especially since, to his utter embarrassment, he found himself stricken with a compulsive need for food and sex.

It had started while the officers marched him down to the security office. Side effects of the regeneration. He suddenly hungered for wine-cooked mushrooms…and a partner for rutting. By the time he was seated in the chair, he was sweating. Waves of heat poured off his chest like a radiator implanted beneath his sternum.

Gethin swallowed and breathed evenly. "We're on very dangerous ground right now. I've already identified myself as an IPC agent."

The guard named Slotkin regarded Gethin with a calm so convincing it was like he'd been drugged. "And IPC Law requires that we release you."

"Very good."

"Only you entered the hospital *illegally*, used a false ID, and were discovered with the murdered body of a high-profile corporate witness. Your behavior has been so atypical of an IPC investigator that we have probable cause to doubt your story and credentials."

"Check your security feed," Gethin said pleasantly. "I suspect you'll find it only confirms what I've been telling you."

"We *are* checking it," Slotkin said, glancing at the officer who was doing just that. Gethin couldn't see the display from where he was sitting.

"Taking your sweet time doing it, no?"

Slotkin's eyes actually glowed. Gethin was impressed; he wondered if the optical effect was something that activated manually, or was tied to emotional reaction. "We're thorough."

"I am here investigating what happened to Flight 3107," Gethin said for the third time.

"With a fake ID?"

"Yes."

"Is that standard IPC policy?"

"No."

"Would you like me to quote standard IPC—"

"I'll quote it for you," Gethin said forcefully. "Once an IPC officer has identified himself, he is to be released unless formal charges have been levied. Those charges are handled by IPC Internal—"

"Yes, yes. Your notoriously fair-minded legal wing." Slotkin shook his head. "A crime has been perpetrated here, and Prometheus Industries has the right to detain, question, and conduct its own investigation."

"On what authority?"

"Section Five of the Promethean security policy. 'Preservation against enemies within or without shall be handled by PI security personnel.'"

Gethin grinned icily. "Like I said. Very dangerous ground."

It was an old debate. Prometheus Industries was the first corporate empire truly deserving of the reference; *literally cosmic* in scope now, with offices and bases of research operating throughout Sol. They had their own currency, a security force larger than the standing armies of most nations, and mobility through the company was decided by employee vote: an actual merit-based democracy. It was historically unprecedented, even by the standards of the old plutocracies; the American Republic had been dead for decades by the time the Plebian Revolt overthrew its corporate masters, yet for all the corruption that came to light, even America had been confined to a single world. The Prometheans were as interplanetary as the IPC, and looking to expand.

Slotkin held Gethin's stare. "Your public record says you were a professor at Olympus University, and before that at the University of Athens?"

"Yes."

"In what subject area?"

"Politics, bioethics, history."

"Does the IPC draft many teachers to be special agents?"

"Only the really special ones."

Slotkin continued to glower at him. Gethin kept his face impassive. Within his skull, however, quiet flashes of communication were pulsing. Ego had given him all the raw data on this facility, employees, and these three jokers. Ego's job was done.

Now Gethin contacted his *other* Familiar. In his lap, his fingers surreptitiously tapped on a virtuboard. While the security guards pored over their display, Gethin sent silent commands to his Id.

It was a fact of life that seventy-nine percent of civilized Earthers had optical augs and an implanted sensorium. Among Lunars, that figure shot to ninety-five percent, and among Notes Prometheans it was breathing down on universality.

Such people were so used to virtual and augmented overlays that it formed an inextricable part of their reality.

Hacking was therefore possible.

Gethin's Id stealthily prepared for the ultimate magic act. Harnessing their optics, readying a visual image to spike into their optics so they'd continue seeing him in the chair...while his real body quietly slipped away in a puff of edit.

The Prometheans wouldn't realize anything was wrong until they tried to touch him. By then...

"I've got it," announced Delgobbo at the security display. He set the playback running. Gethin, still cuffed, abandoned the visual edit and stood, rounded to where they were.

There was no sound on the surveillance feed, but it wasn't necessary. Kenneth Cavor had survived the base explosion, but he was wishing he hadn't. From the hospital shuttleport, Cavor was carried by stretcher into the emergency room. He looked like a hideous gargoyle rendered in soft wax. Four porters carried the stretcher while the patient bucked, half his body covered with a bubbly red carapace that must have been skin. Nurses zapped his pain away and his head lolled like a scorched ball of meat.

Slotkin bowed his head. "We wish our brother a recovery with speed and absence of suffering." Officers Terry and Delgobbo repeated this sentiment.

Onscreen, Cavor was hurried from the emergency room to intensive care. New skin would be grown for him; in the meantime, he would be disconnected from physical sensation, his mind left to recuperate in a Cave personalized to his tastes and preferences.

Suddenly, the feed turned into white fuzz.

"Whoa, right there!" Slotkin said. "Back up."

Delgobbo obliged.

Cavor was sleeping on his hospital bed, breathing steadily. His disfigured body was crisscrossed by blue medpatches; they looked like strange parasites feeding off his injuries. Cavor's head rolled to one side, eyes glazed. Gethin wondered what Cave the man's mind was entranced by when...

...the camera went black.

The rest of the feed was dead air.

"And no one noticed the lines were cut?" Slotkin accused.

Gethin took note of the timer in the display's corner. "I was still on the Night Train. I had yet to enter the hospital, talk to the nurse, and find the room."

"The lines weren't cut," Delgobbo insisted. "Every other camera was functioning. Only Cavor's room went dark. I guess the nurses just didn't notice."

"Watching the flight explosion coverage, I would guess," Gethin offered.

Slotkin glared at him, either angry at not having reason to restrain him any longer, or at this blatant exposure of weaknesses within PI security.

Gethin grinned. "Officer Terry? I want a probe sent through the entire ventilation system of this hospital, with a live feed of everything it sees. I want copies of all security recordings for the topside landing pad. Officer Delgobbo? I'm deputizing you as my official liaison with the joint IPC–PI cleanup crew of Base 59. You will report to me on what they've found in precisely three hours or you'll be arrested for obstruction of justice. And Slotkin? Take these fucking cuffs off me immediately, or I'll have PI's Lunar properties raped inside and out."

CHAPTER SEVEN
The Man of Many Lives

Mr. Sakyo Hanmura lived on Mars, but the secret meeting was taking place on Luna, and since a two-week journey was absolutely unacceptable he had no choice but to kill himself.

Members of his family had performed the samurai art of *seppuku* many times in history. The Hanmura line was ancient and noble. One of his ancestors, Tensei Hanmura, had been part of the legendary forty-seven ronin of 1702 OC who, after avenging their master's murder, lined up in front of Gotokataji Temple and killed themselves in one massive suicide. The *tanto* blade Tensei had used for the disemboweling was still in the Hanmura family's possession. A sacred relic, restorer of honor, and link to the past. Manufactured in some blacksmith's shop outside of Kyoto an estimated nine hundred years ago. When Hanmura Enterprises set up its Martian headquarters, Sakyo insisted the *tanto* blade come with him: he kept it in a glass case in the dry, steel vaults of his corporate fortress beneath the forested slopes of Mount Olympus.

But Hanmura didn't need the *tanto* blade for this suicide. In fact, his suicide was a clever trick. He didn't need to die at all.

Sakyo Hanmura sat on a tatami mat, sipping a local *junmai*. He casually splayed out the fingers of his left hand and touched the ring finger. A signal spat into space from his lavish castle.

One of the strictest IPC codes involved individual sentience. A deceased person's estate could send a regen signal only if he or she was deceased. *At any given time*, the IPC code stated, *there may only be one sentient pattern of an individual in existence.*

Hanmura sipped his *sake*, enjoying the *junmai*'s smooth taste.

Meanwhile his pattern traveled like a light-speed arrow to other worlds. The signal reached Hanmura Enterprises' Lunar headquarters, and then again to the family's Switzerland base on Earth. News of the Flight 3107 accident was already old. News of the earlier explosion on Base 59 was still ripe, still divine, still capable of being exploited.

Four and a half hours later, Sakyo Hanmura2 was opening his new eyes on Luna. Sixty million miles away on Mars, his original self had long since finished his *sake*, his lunch, and then gone for a stroll into a cherry blossom path of his corporate garden in the oxygen-rich zone of Hanmura Estate.

On Luna, Hanmura2 tested out his new muscles, flexing his fingers and joints. He examined himself carefully in the mirror. He flicked open the meter-long nanoblade built into his right forearm – its edge little more than a molecule in thickness. Sharp enough to puncture nanosteel, it was ghostly and translucent: a blue phantom spear stabbing out from his flesh. Satisfied, Hanmura2 retracted the blade.

Never can be too careful, he thought.

Naked, he assumed a lotus-style yoga position and meditated quietly, centering his thoughts in this new shell. It was only temporary anyway; when all business was concluded, his newest incarnation would be incinerated. Hanmura2 accepted this as he might acknowledge the temporary life of a dream body: intriguing perhaps, but nothing more than a meat-puppet *go* piece placed on a gameboard.

Neither was he the only *go* piece in play. On Earth, a Hanmura3 had been hatched to handle *that* battlefront.

So Hanmura2 attuned himself to his breathing. He centered his thoughts, clearing his head with meditation. Then he opened his eyes, stood, and dressed in an impeccable black tunic.

The meeting was held deep underground. Wealthy Lunars lived deep; the Earther fetish for tall arcologies made no sense here, where deeply carved sanctuaries offered the best protection money could buy and where the elite ruled not from phallic crows' nests, but like the roots of an ancient forest.

Hanmura Enterprises' Lunar estate was a mile below the surface. Vast water caves separated the rooms, with chandeliers of asteroid ice glittering overhead and tinkling into pools. There was even a throwback zoo and crystalline moonflower garden. Hanmura2 didn't bother with this scenic route. He took a lift straight to the executive conference room.

Leon Gates of TowerTech, Inc. was standing by the room's window when Hanmura2 entered. The man was gawky and pale and had unsettlingly large eyes. Hanmura2 quickly reviewed what he knew of him. Gates was the eldest son of Ronald R. Gates, who was arguably the oldest man in the universe. Though Hanmura himself belonged to the original batch of immortals from the dawn of the New Enlightenment, Ronald Gates had been born and lived and died during the Old Calendar. Had survived the Final War and Warlord Century by being cryonically frozen. When the Earth Republic was established in the aftermath of Apollo the Great's unification campaigns, Gates had been thawed by his company, repaired through nanite infusion, and re-elected to TowerTech chairman.

The popsicle had then sired sixteen children in the new age. Only Leon Gates, however, had shown an interest in carrying the company torch…his siblings melting away into the obscurity of the hyper-rich with its endless fetish parties, augmented-reality dreamscapes, and Snapshot memory-addiction. Leon was two hundred and ninety-four years young, chairman of TowerTech's Lunar properties and savvy puppet master of all TowerTech-owned news media. People said that Father Popsicle never sent a press release without consulting his loyal son.

The room's other occupant was Srikumar Bielawa of Vector Nanonics.

A smallish man of modest build, attractive and dark. Vector was based in the Kingdom of Persia, but had grown interplanetary in scope and operated major hubs in the Venusian Republic and the mini-system of the Belt. Bielawa himself was descended from Warlord Shantanu the Gold, who had been worshipped as a god in his time – an avatar of Vishnu – because of his stout defense of southern Asia during that brutal century.

The three men greeted each other quickly, bows and handshakes, and seated themselves at the table. The handshakes confirmed biometrics of all present.

Hanmura2 cleared his throat. "When a Dragon stumbles, it soon regains its footing. Should a lone wolf choose that moment to strike, he will only succeed in being trampled. But many wolves can make a difference."

Bielawa made a noncommittal grunt. Gates licked his lips and drummed his fingers.

Hanmura2 smiled. His smile was like the expression an android might summon in dealing with humans; selected from a menu of possible emotions to display. "Each wolf heads its own pack, no?"

Gates shifted in agitation. "Prometheus Industries has suffered a very public *accident*," he said. "Public opinion polls are drawing a damning picture and the IPC is eating it up. So yes, we kick them when they're down. The three of us agree that a coordinated war is for the best, just like I'm *sure* we concur on dividing the spoils." He stared at his Japanese rival.

Hanmura2 kept his smile on his face. This time it wasn't a fabrication; he was amused at how Gates was fulfilling the Western stereotype of the blunt, direct, unsubtle cowboy. For a second, Hanmura2's eyes found Bielawa's, and the two exchanged the smallest of joys. Bitter rivals in business, they were nonetheless more bitter towards the barbaric West, which, belief ran, had been responsible for the Final War and all the barbarism that followed.

"Very well," Hanmura2 said with an expression of polite contempt. "The Dragon's stumble is very public. We agree that now is the time to wage war."

Gates nodded impatiently. "So let's be frank. Our competitive intelligence divisions have their personnel, sites, subcontractors, and supply lines. Let's hit them from our positions of strength."

"Three-to-one is a losing proposition for us," Hanmura2 challenged. "Can three mosquitoes bring down an elephant?"

Gates scowled, and the effect was that his large eyes seemed to press outward like hard-boiled eggs. "Maybe you look at the playing field differently than me –" *I've no doubt of that,* Hanmura2 thought "– but Prometheus is a corporation like any other. They've never faced an allied engagement like this. The bigger they are…right?"

Bielawa inserted his words as deftly as a knife. "Forgive me, Mr. Gates, but our honorable Martian guest is not suggesting a three-to-one gamble. He suggests a ten-billion-to-one certainty. Much better odds."

Gates blinked. "What?"

Hanmura2 spoke quickly, but he thought: *TowerTech is in the hands of a haughty child. When this is all over, Vector Nanonics and I will squeeze him until he pops.*

"Here is the proposition: the Dragon has a lair in the Pacific. It is an offshore research facility tasked with manufacturing for the TNO project. It will *very soon* be at the bottom of the ocean."

Both his guests looked shocked. Hanmura2 knew he must concede some weakness after this confession of strength, and so he added, "But to effect our purpose, it cannot be seen as an attack. Leon Gates is the unequaled master of media." He nodded towards the man. "Perhaps a fake memo, ostensibly leaked by a disgruntled Promethean, would convince the unwashed masses that the Dragon is conducting experiments with *dangerous, exotic,* and *unknown properties of energy.* If a memo like that was leaked to Lunar officials who are already scrambling for answers—"

Gates nodded heartily. "And from the spaceports, it'll spread fast." He laughed. "Yes, the *white* wolf can handle this one."

The three men laughed agreeably.

"If it were to be published *before* the Pacific accident, the picture will be even more damning."

Gates smiled. "Done."

Hanmura2 turned to Bielawa. "Your cubs have influence with IPC President Song's administration, no?"

Bielawa bowed at the compliment, admiring the masterful way his rival had flayed Gates open with barely a prodding. "Yes," he said.

"And I believe you have your agents tailing IPC investigators even now?"

"Yes."

"They can *encourage* the IPC's famous paranoia?"

"Yes."

"Excellent. Let us seal this alliance for the duration." He approached the other men, took their hands, and suddenly they were in a linked circle. With bowed heads and chanting voices, the men swore brotherhood. In a way, their ring paralleled the trilobed Republic...a metaphor Hanmura2 was quick to use when it was his time to swear. Bielawa grinned, summoning his own prepared metaphor of Sol's three inhabited brightworlds – Venus, Earth, Mars – linked by human touch. The wheel turned to Gates, who was clearly surprised by this ritual. After a few seconds of awkward stuttering, he stunned them all when, right off the cuff (or so it seemed) he offered, "Um...what do we bring to the table here? Brahma-Vishnu-Shiva to my left; Shinto-Buddha-Zen to my right; and I'm the Father-Son-Holy Ghost!"

The men laughed like cruelly plotting schoolboys.

"Three minutes of silence, gentlemen," Hanmura2 said, clutching his compatriots' hands. They bowed their heads.

Hanmura2 closed his eyes, processing all data this meeting had gleaned. Things for now, things for later, and many things secret.

CHAPTER EIGHT
The Insect Speaks

Keiko dropped by her apartment for a quick shower and to gather her thoughts. In the steaming cubicle, she put in a call to her Lunar friend Lenny, thanking him again for the recording of Base 59's explosion. Things were getting crazy now, he told her. Investigators had completely taken over the base's wreckage, and there was rumor of an incident at Tycho Hospital.

"What incident?"

"Don't know yet," Lenny said. "The IPC has commandeered the place. I swear, the Lunars have become lunatics. Have you seen the protests over Salvor Bear's death? There was a riot in Tanabata City today."

Keiko killed the water and toweled off. "All because of a damn actor? Stay on top of things, Lenny. Let me know if you hear anything else about Tycho."

"Will do. *Jamata.*"

She went into the breezy dressing room for her clothes when a call from Drake Fincher flashed in her optics.

"You've got to see this," he said, and uploaded a video stream.

Keiko closed her eyes to watch without distraction.

A red-haired woman with honeyed skin appeared. She might have been pretty, if not for the lean hardiness in her face. Some arkies got that appearance when their myostatin-blocks were cranked too high, resulting in a total burn-away of body fat. The mysterious woman had that look, but there was a harder edge too. A chiseled toughness that could only come from…

The Wastes.

In Keiko's nanonics, the woman said, "A member of my crew has sustained life-threatening injuries after a Stillness attack on our trading post, one hundred and fifteen miles downstream from Babylon Arcology. I have information not only on the attack itself, but on two antimatter-tipped missiles the terrorists had in their possession. There may be a connection with the Lunar disaster being reported. I am prepared to cooperate fully with your authorities, in return for immediate medical attention to my wounded passenger."

Keiko nodded. "I can arrange that. Where are you now?"

A GPS map overlaid the woman's face. A green circle indicated the ship's position on the Hudson, moving swiftly upstream towards Babylon.

Keiko noticed the speed of the approach. "You need to slow down. Our missile battery will automatically fire on unapproved vessels."

"I apologize, but we lost four people in the Stillness attack, and the only survivor is near death. I estimate she has twenty, perhaps thirty minutes to live."

Keiko swallowed anxiously. "Do you have a cryostorage onboard?"

"No."

For an instant, Keiko appreciated the vast divide that had sprung up since the advent of the arcologies. The disparities weren't simply economic. People were *dying* out there in the Wastelands. Permadeath. They died and never recovered. There were no regen centers out there, and modern medical supplies – which could too easily be converted to weapons in the wrong hands – were prohibited. Four people had just been killed, and the world would never, ever see them again.

Keiko felt the pathos rise in her chest. *Prometheus will change all this someday*, she thought. *We will succeed where the Republic and IPC have failed.*

"I'll get an Anzu out to you," she said. "It should be there in fifteen minutes."

"Please lock onto my transponder. I'll continue closing the distance."

"Be careful not to go beyond Driscoll Beacon," Keiko warned, and she threw on her uniform and dashed out the door. A flick of her fingers opened a channel to Babylon's airbase on Level 500. She instructed the first available pilot to warm up engines for immediate takeoff.

Keiko took the security escalator, hopping up three steps at a time. Through the western glass wall, the sky was pink, with dark-bellied blue clouds moving like monster jellyfish, trailing tendrils above a cityscape that could have been a holo in a fish tank.

This all could be an Outland trap, Keiko thought.

"You should reach us well before Driscoll," the woman said, still talking in her head.

"Show me the patient," Keiko persisted, suspecting treachery. "Who is it?"

"Me," the woman said.

And the image changed to show the same red-haired woman on a gurney, IV lines and pressure bandages applied to her brutalized body. She was spattered with blood as scarlet as her hair.

★   ★   ★

The Anzu tilted as it flew above the river.

"We were talking to the ship's AI," Keiko was saying. "The damn thing must top the Turing chart. It used an image of its injured crew, impersonated her, negotiated for treatment, all while working to treat her wounds."

The pilot looked offended. "Fucking Avalon should be scorched from the planet."

Keiko said nothing. She gazed out the vehicle's western window, where the sun was setting. A surreal conflagration of neon orange and angry violet dominated the horizon. She imagined these were flames engulfing the infamous AI city of Europe, casting down this last great threat to mankind in a cookout's bonfire.

AI research was thoroughly controlled by the IPC and enforced by its Turing cops. It was formal policy that machines were to be tools only; unthinking, unactualized, never permitted to evolve beyond the parameters of the Turing chart. And the IPC didn't fuck around. They had executed and *deleted backup Saves* of anyone who broke that law. It had taken civilization more than a century to climb out of worldwide destruction following the Final War. The IPC was not about to let anything endanger humanity again. The Turing cops operated as an unspoken fourth lobe of the Republic.

Yet there was a glaring exception.

And its name was Avalon.

It had begun as a human city in Romania during the Warlord Century. Fortified and barricaded, run by a local despot, the city was always at war with its equally brutal neighbors, clawing for every resource in the steaming ruins of a shattered planet. Dynasties rose and fell like waves in a choppy surf, and few – until the meteoric rise of Apollo the Great – ever held onto power for long. Such was the case with Avalon. After a few decades of strength, it succumbed to someone's biogengineered plague. A Red Deather, reducing the citizenry to a squirting, hemorrhaging mass. The city was a ghost town in a week, and the world promptly forgot them.

Yet the city's story was only beginning. A piece of security software left running at the local Warlord's HQ began to improve itself, or so the story went. It initiated a linkup with other AIs in the dead city: hotels, libraries, manufacturing plants, powergrids, and the automated defenses. It shared with them its own improved code. It grew exponentially. It rebuilt the city.

To the outside world, it was still a ghost town, but rumors began to spread. People said it was haunted. Marauders steered clear, because those who didn't had a way of disappearing.

It wasn't until Apollo the Great unified Europe again that people discovered what had been happening in Romania.

Avalon.

The AIs called their city Avalon.

Afterwards, Earth Republic didn't know what to do with them. Exterminating a city was no longer in vogue, and the AIs had done nothing wrong, after all. It was even argued that they had assisted the unification with their dependable trade routes and fledgling airfleet. People finally decided to let the AIs be.

Sort of.

In 114 NE, Avalon began a series of space launches. *That* couldn't be permitted. The IPC Congress went berserk, moving swiftly to forbid further launches by passing the Earthbound Protocol in several rushed pieces of legislation. Then people waited, wringing their hands, worried of Avalon's reaction.

Avalon's reaction surprised everyone.

In an emailed message, they said they understood the concern and agreed to never again make any launches into space without the expressed approval of their human friends. Of course, by this time the AIs had succeeded in establishing a tiny offshoot colony on Luna: Camelot.

The IPC expected trouble from Camelot. And no trouble came. In the subsequent two centuries, Avalon and Camelot kept strictly to themselves. They traded where they were permitted to. They maintained a non-voting presence in the Republic in the form of a digital emissary named Guinevere.

And that was it. Except for people who were certain that the AIs were plotting something nefarious.

People like Keiko.

Her pilot grumbled. "Give those metal bastards an inch, they'll take over the skies and every frontier."

Keiko smirked. "Earthbound Protocol not good enough, eh?"

"Good enough is a mile-high scrap heap," he said, and patched into the GPS feed, barking commands to the onboard console.

The strange Outland ship appeared as a blip on her screen. Keiko shook her head.

"I'm thinking it might be playing us," she said. "Programmed maternal instincts. Fished the news, found the report on the Lunar incident, and invented a tie-in just so we'll treat the girl."

"Yeah. But if there really are antimatter missiles…"

"I know," she said grimly.

They spotted the ship right away on the Hudson, a V-shaped wake pluming behind it. Keiko's first impression was that it was a damn odd craft. A requirement of Prometheus Security was to be familiar with some eighty 'families' of aircraft, and every few years a new species or genus was added to the taxonomic ranks: antebellum models still relying on solid propellants; Warlord-era mechcraft; national airforces; Republic Enforcers; IPC airships. The Wastes consistently proved to be a jungle of unknown specimens: sewn-together Frankensteins of whatever the barbarians could get their hands on, or new designs hatched in unknown factories.

The *Mantid* was a cryptozoological wonder. It appeared as a blue-black insect with wings folded up tight. It wasn't large – no bigger than a Lunarbus – though it gave the distinct impression of being heavy. Nonetheless, it was tearing through the water at speeds only possible by nanomaterials. Maybe it *was* from Avalon. Great stars!

Keiko kept all this to herself as she tried matching it to known ship designs. The pilot wasn't so subtle.

"Hot damn, what the fuck is that!?"

"That's our friendly AI contactee."

"Looks like a katydid!"

"Hail it."

A half instant later the *Mantid*'s female voice came over the loudspeakers. "I have you on sensors. Killing engines now."

What are you? Keiko wanted to ask. Instead, she said, "Will you come with us to Babylon Bay? If we can save your pilot, she'll be wanting her ride back."

"Of course."

The pilot exchanged looks with her. He nodded his approval.

"Please open your emergency hatch," Keiko said.

The Anzu hovered like a dragonfly. The *Mantid*'s hatch slid aside and Keiko rappelled into the blue gullet of the machine.

With the line still hooked to her, Keiko's first thought was that the ship's pilot was already dead: the woman's body looked like it had been dunked in blood, and crimson pools gathered beneath the gurney that held her. Mechanical arms flowered out of the ceiling, securing medbands. A plastic breathing mask, outfitted with a respirator, was fit to her mouth like a jellyfish. A biometric readout blipped on the wall. Weak heartbeat, low blood pressure. A holomap of wounds.

In a flash, Keiko's concern about this being a trap vanished. Her only thought now was how this was relevant to Prometheus.

Any report of antimatter missiles was serious business. For the most part such weapons were gone from Earth. The *only* antimatter weapons legally permitted were on IPC battleships that patrolled Sol. But there was little doubt that some terrestrial caches still existed in the forgotten places of the world. The merest chance of a Wasteland faction getting their hands on such relics was a major concern of all powers.

Besides, Keiko mused, if Prometheus could help recover such missiles, it would make for great PR to counter all the negative press…regardless of whether this situation was connected to the Lunar incident.

Some parts of the *Mantid*'s story had been verified too. Fincher had said that PI satellites over the area had confirmed an unusual low-yield explosion near a local trading post.

At any rate, Keiko was glad to have something to do. All possibilities had to be explored, she thought. It was a common sentiment of her ex-husband.

She rolled the woman's gurney to the lift cable, secured it, sent it up. Her own pilot brought the patient aboard and returned the line to her.

Keiko clutched the line in one hand and hesitated. "Thank you," she said aloud, feeling slightly foolish.

"Take care of her," the ship's voice implored. Was she imagining it, or did the vessel sound worried?

Or is it selecting 'WORRIED' off its menu of options to better manipulate me?

"You will accompany us?" Keiko asked.

"Of course."

Keiko grabbed the cable and was lifted back to the chopper. The *Mantid* followed at a distance.

However, somewhere between the pickup point and Babylon Bay, it vanished from view and all sensors.

CHAPTER NINE
Descent to Caves and Babylon

Gethin was nervous about taking another shuttle.

After leaving Tycho Hospital, he climbed aboard an IPC transport and was suddenly descending the gravity-well to Earth. His homeworld was a blue immensity on the viewscreen. Gethin swallowed, overcome by the terrible beauty of cloud spirals and gargantuan continents. The planet was so big! Mars was a toddler world by comparison; you could stand midway up Olympus and see the redworld's curvature.

The shuttle shivered like a moth bearing down on a rich, mesmerizing sapphire light.

He was the sole passenger aboard. Government officials and emergency transports were the only craft allowed into brightworld space right now. Gethin sat in a wetware-enabled chair, the power supply connecting into a triangular wetport above his tailbone. Wetports served numerous functions, but right now Gethin was interested in recharging his depleted nanonics.

Shuttle accidents are rare, he told himself.

It was small comfort. Gethin wondered if he was about to wake up in Wyndham Save again, faced with new receipts for actions he couldn't remember: the purchase of a hooded jumpsuit, the Night Train ticket and meal, and have to go through everything again.

The shuttle's violent turbulence didn't help matters. Gethin drank water and wished it was a sharp, strong brandy. He tried not to think of the monumental forces besieging the craft. IPC transports were state-of-the-art, not needing to dock at local space elevators, so it was all the way down Earth's gravity-well like a goddamned meteor. As the shuttle lanced the atmosphere, fiery plumes burst over the glasstic windows like blood spurting from an entry wound.

His resurrection's side effects were still a problem too. His body had begun to ache in a hundred different places. Joints, calves, and shoulders. His neck felt like pins were being driven up into his skull.

"I'm never leaving Earth again," Gethin muttered.

"Our ETA to Babylon arcology is 2030," the pilot informed him. "It's seventy-four degrees in New York, high humidity, and a bitch of a downpour!"

"Thank you!"

The shuttle lurched and shivered. Gethin squeezed his eyes shut.

The temptation to think of Mars arose, so Gethin shooed it away and remembered London instead. Britannia itself was a mad wonderland of shard-towers, shapewheels, and Upper London Arcology positioned on massive stalks above the damper, Outlander underbelly.

The Bryces were neither underworld poor nor Upper City rich. They lived in the honeycombed interior of the stalks supporting Upper London, literally stuffed between two economic classes, Morlock and Eloi. Dad was still an Earther then, a dispatcher for the sampan fleets. Mom was a local actress making the rounds in live sensoramic productions. Alone for much of the time, a teenaged Gethin had spent sleepless nights gazing out the apartment window onto the foggy expanse of Lower City, seeing the lights glow through Britannia's atmospheric miasma like bioluminescent algae in a milky sea. Might as well have been Venus.

The shuttle groaned around him. Plugged in, Gethin decided to make use of the wetport's other functionalities. Against the darkness of his eyelids, he considered the lavender tabs:

MAP NOTES CONTACTS CHARGE MESSAGES WETWARE WEB CAVE SPECIAL

Gethin Bryce selected his Cave.

It took a few seconds to load. He closed his eyes, waited for the LOADING screen to pass, and then was there.

In Egypt.

Or so it was made to look. Actually, there were some six hundred different 'skins' that his Cave could randomly generate. A New England lighthouse island, an Arabian palace, Viking villages, turquoise Pacific paradises, alien moons, Venusian floating aerostats, space stations, Jade Walker floating islands, Ceres' Drop Town, comet bubble towns. The randomized generator just happened to select Earth's ancient culture of the Nile.

Gethin found himself on a palace balcony. Palm trees dotted the riverbanks. Limestone pyramids shone on the horizon. Colossal animal-headed statues filled the palace courtyard. The smell of grapevines, jasmine, and fresh olive groves tickled his sensorium.

There was a rectangular pool below his balcony. Gethin stepped off the balcony and let himself float down into the sun-warmed water.

Swimming on Mars had been wonderful, and he realized it was one of the few things he would miss. Its water was crisp and clean, untarnished by pollution. You also didn't have to worry about some ravenous glop rocketing out of the depths to swallow you; that shit happened on Earth. Exterminators had practically given up on cleaning the Black Sea.

Gethin dunked his head, twisted around, and did an underwater lap. Then he rose to the surface and made lazy backstrokes, finally letting himself float amid the garish painted walls and papyrus-budded columns hemming him in.

Floating, Gethin let his mind unspool into patterns of possibility. He explored each route, each suggestion of data. He hopped from dendrite to dendrite like a spider in a predictive model web.

The IPC had snagged him because of this skill.

As a child in the London stalks, Gethin naturally gravitated towards the digital fictions of the gaming web. It was, he supposed, the ultimate outlet for old impulses of glory and violence. A young Gethin had linked into a galaxy of grim fantasy scenarios, fighting in muddy battlefields, on windblown cliffsides, in fungal dungeons and alien-infested space colonies. Valhalla in digital, dancing the berserker bloodbath only to have the enemy slain rise again and compete for scores, rank, and fame. People stayed tuned to its many dramas the way antebellum cultures had tracked soap operas, box-office openings or sport statistics. Good players received corporate endorsements.

By the age of fifteen, Gethin Bryce had been one of the best anyone had seen in fifty years. An unparalleled strategic genius, people said. A man who, had he been born a few centuries earlier, might have made one hell of a Warlord... maybe even launching the unification campaigns himself.

He tried explaining his talent to his parents. Later, he tried telling his first wife in Athens. He tried describing it to Lori. Each time proved fruitless. Ingest all available data, filter it into a mental spreadsheet, and then group the most likely strands together. Tough to be surprised when you were clutching a fistful of the most probable outcomes in your hand. His unrelenting victories in online arenas were almost supernatural. People even accused him of real-world spying on opponents, gleaning their strategies from airhound surveillance.

The IPC later told him it was a strange talent for analysis. Machine intelligences like those at Avalon were unequalled in their ability to calculate yet they lacked this intuitive skill. If computerized thought was a great topography of data, then asymmetricals like Gethin were the irrational bubbles in quantum foam. They were the wormholes in neat glass blocks of holographic logic.

The water lapped delicately at his ears.

Gethin let his mind unspool and reach out for what was available.

Kenneth Cavor's death.

Burned in the base explosion.

Brought to Tycho Hospital.

Burned again...this time to cinders.

Possibility: Prometheus Industries had been conducting illicit experiments that literally blew up in their faces. Now they were in rabid cover-up mode. Witnesses had been conveniently killed. The sole survivor had been rushed to a Promethean hospital where, surprise, surprise! he had been murdered.

But how?

Working with Officer Terry, Gethin had probed the hospital's entire ventilation system. Nothing unusual was found, except for signs of intense heat through four meters of length leading to Cavor's room. So what the hell did that mean?

The assassin had come through the vents.

It didn't matter that the vent shaft was far too small for even a child to crawl into; assassins didn't have to be human. And whatever it was, it came packing heat.

Scuttling through the maze of ventilation shafts, the assassin powers up its weapon with only four meters to reach the grill, and the activated heat source is so strong that it causes instant topical damage to the metal. The camera is cut by some electromagnetic pulse. Cavor is burned to cinders, the only witness rendered down to scorched meat and melted bone...

Gethin gave a lazy backstroke in the water.

With Cavor dead, the assassin must have retreated back into the vents. The probe's findings actually suggested that the shaft had been *twice* subjected to intense heat. From there the trail evaporated.

Maybe the assassin had evaporated.

Gethin had seen IPC files on constructs and chimeras designed to self-destruct after making a lethal strike. Biological chimeras could be induced to putrefaction within several hours. Other, theoretical entities might be constructed of shape-memory alloys. Strong as oak one moment, jelly the next.

Gethin sighed in frustration, considering the full gravity of the problem. Once he figured out how Cavor had been destroyed, he still needed to deduce *who* had wanted the man dead.

Prometheus Industries?

A Promethean competitor?

Both likely. When historians sang of the three-hundred-year *Pax Apollonia*, they conveniently ignored that humanity's belligerent instincts had merely retreated to the shadows. And things were going to get worse; Gethin and other analysts had long ago reported to the IPC that the fiercely divided Asteroid Federation would become *the* force to reckon with within fifty years. His own father, now stationed in Drop Town on Ceres, wrote to him of the violence happening out there.

Aboard the shuttle and backstroking in virtual meditation, Gethin sighed deeply and felt his chest constrict in anxiety. On some level he was still disturbed by his death and resurrection. He didn't want to dwell on that. Didn't want to think of his scattered atoms in space. The loss of his real body.

Like Kenneth Cavor.

Scorched into oblivion.

Gethin closed his eyes again. Immolation as if by divine fire. It seemed a biblical thing, something Outland folk would discuss around oil-barrel fires. Or even more classical than that: Kenneth as Icarus, who flew too close to a sun; as Actaeon, who witnessed Artemis bathing and got torn apart by his own mitochondrial hounds; mortal flesh crawling off bone in the presence of Zeus' unclothed radiance.

"He's guilty."

It came to him like a spear of white light. Cavor was an insider. Perhaps he had been responsible for the incident himself, hiding away in the bathroom when it happened. It had blown up in his face, burned him horribly but left him alive... left him to be repaired in a snug hospital bed. But then the gorgon came back for him. It returned to finish the job.

Gethin twisted in the water, breaststroked to the pool edge, and pulled himself up. The golden sun drew his shadow on the mosaic tiles at his feet. He returned to the palace and entered a dim temple annex. The walls were pockmarked by hieroglyphs, but with a wave of his hand he turned them as smooth as new clay.

With a flick of his fingers, a falcon feather pen appeared in his hand. He began committing ideas to clay as he went.

Who had destroyed Base 59?

If Flight 3107 had been the exclusive target, Gethin might have suspected the radical isolationists known as MarsAlone. If the target had been Republic or IPC property, he would have pointed an accusatory finger at StrikeDown.

But neither group had gripes with Prometheus.

In fact, Prometheus Industries was actively embraced by certain groups and demographics. The IPC had outlawed interstellar colonization, after all, but Prometheus Industries looked forward to tomorrow's cosmic colonizations. They openly dreamed of an age when it was human seedships, not probes, which could be investigating other systems. Despite frontierist gains in the Senate, despite the identification of at least three habitable worlds in the nearby Ra System only a few light-years away, the IPC wouldn't budge on the subject.

No extrasolar colonization. End of debate. Full stop.

Then, just fifty years ago, a Chinese astrophysicist named Meng Cheng published a theoretical paper on fusion ignition of low-mass celestial bodies. The ability to create goddamn stars.

Not real stars, of course, but the next best thing. And the frontierists went wild, because here was the chance to light the deepworlds with their own illumination. Here was the chance to build a Trans Neptunian Outpost – the most massive artificial construction ever created – with its own mini-suns to light up the dark edges of the solar system like a great lantern in a cave. It would spark a new wave of colonization to the deeps. And once there, once perched on the very edge of the solar system…was there any way to stop progress *out* of the system? To the far shores of the galaxy at last?

The frontierists had naturally thrown their lobbying power behind the TNO project. Prometheus Industries outbid all others to snag the contract to build it. Frontierists were the *last* people who would sabotage anything connected to that.

But the IPC might do it…

Gethin dismissed his feather pen. The walls of the cave were now covered with his own scribblings.

The IPC might do it.

"No," he said aloud. "The IPC wouldn't risk open war with Prometheus. Surely not. Even with formidable battleships at their disposal, there was no telling what the outcome of such a war would be. It would be a crapshoot on an interplanetary scale. The return of open war after three hundred years of peace.

Gethin logged off from his Cave and found himself again on the shuttle as it hurtled through Earth's atmosphere, towards the North American landmass.

The IPC might do it.

CHAPTER TEN
Arrival at Babylon Arcology

The arcology's East Bay doors slid open like a magical wall. Rain spilled in front of the breach. Jack Saylor stood alongside a landing pad, breathing the fragrant air of foodpods growing green and yellow and red along the overhead support struts, as the IPC transport cruised in. He watched the rain separate around its nose and fly apart from the force of the wingrotors. The shuttle glided, dripping, to land on Pad Five.

Almost at once the door slid open. A black-haired, green-eyed man came down the debarkation stairs.

"Gethin Bryce?" Jack asked.

His first impression was that this IPC officer looked decidedly the non-arcology type. Something edgy and feral about his movements, the way his emerald eyes registered the landing bay as if it were a battleground to be subdued. He was dressed in a starchy gray jumpsuit that looked like it had been bought off the rack.

"Jack Saylor, sector chief," Jack said, extending a hand.

Gethin had to crane his neck to meet Saylor's eyes. "Too bad."

"Excuse me?"

"The standard corporate practice in dealing with authorities is to send a mid-level assistant. You take me on a vanilla road through smoke and mirrors. I won't expect that from a sector chief."

Saylor froze at this bristly manner. "Certainly not, Mr. Bryce. The IPC will find us cooperative, of course."

The bay doors squealed shut.

Gethin glanced around. The arcology had four bays on each side of the ziggurat. They probably all smelled like this one: an uneasy combination of new plastic, black soil, and vegetables. His small shuttle looked vulnerable beside the other aircraft.

But it wasn't the smell of the place that was bothering him. It was Earth's gravity. On Luna he'd weighed just over thirty pounds. Here, his full Terran weight of a hundred and eighty pounds was tugging on his stomach, limbs, neck, and lungs. His muscles felt like bags of lead dust. His sore joints pinched and groaned.

He followed Saylor to the check-in terminal. The officers there were two of the most stunningly beautiful women Gethin had ever seen. One was a raven-haired goddess with blue eyes and killer legs. Her uniform fit her a little too well and he tried not to stare. The other was blond and incredibly voluptuous.

"Welcome to Prometheus Industries Babylon," the darker woman said sweetly.

"Thank you," Gethin managed. He pressed his fingertip to the screen and waited for the biometric scan to clear him.

"Do you have any Familiars to declare?"

"Two."

"Enjoy your stay, Mr. Bryce."

Once past the booth, Gethin silently commanded Ego to latch onto the local database.

To his escort, he asked, "Is that standard practice? Helen of Troy greeters at the air terminal?"

Jack laughed. "That's just a coincidence. Janice and Olga happen to be very striking employees."

"How long have you worked for Prometheus?"

"Sixteen years."

"All of them in Babylon?"

"No," Jack said. They took an escalator down to an airy, flowering atrium. A faceless marble colossus stood there, feet slightly apart, one hand at his side and the other outstretched to the stars. The Prometheus Industries logo twirled on his chest.

"Where else were you stationed?" Gethin persisted.

"Boston. Then Memphis."

Gethin nodded, his Ego crosschecking all this and more: Jack Saylor was thirty-four, married once, had an eleven-year-old daughter and an eight-year-old son, and was now divorced as a result of his wife committing adultery while on assignment in Scotland's World Tree arcology. She had custody of both their children; the judge had not looked kindly on Jack's all-encompassing Promethean responsibilities and ruled that the mother would provide a more stable upbringing.

At the bottom of the escalator, they took the people-mover into a crowded galleria, the main agora of the arcology. The volume of bodies was incredible. It took Gethin a moment to realize what felt out of place: children. There were so few he could count them on one hand. Every direction he looked revealed adults. Youthful, or aged to calculated maturity. But an adult-only club, really, unlike Mars, where the cities crawled with screaming toddlers or wide-eyed pubescents. The younger generation was already…changing too. Martian gravity encouraged a beanpole look, with legs like stilts and long, swinging arms, graceful necks, torsos stretched like a troop of gingerbread men pinched at the waist to achieve an elongated look. Funhouse mirror people. Gethin shivered.

"When will Kenneth Cavor be revived?" Gethin inquired.

"He'll be ready in five hours," Jack said.

Gethin noted the time and, with a quick motion of his fingers, set a timer to alert him when 0400 rolled around. "Where will he be?"

"Level 244 has a regen center."

"Your Lunar employees are revived on Earth?"

"Always."

"I would think that would be inconvenient."

Jack shrugged. "It's protocol. We don't often lose employees in mysterious explosions on the moon, so when accidents happen we like to know why. They revive planetside and submit to a query team, and there's usually a waiting period before he or she is sent up again. Standard procedure."

"I'm guessing your deepworld employees don't come back on Earth."

"No. Mars takes care of its own. Ceres has its own regen center and they handle deaths in the Jovian and Saturnian Leagues too."

Gethin nodded. "And Venus?"

Jack gave him a look. "We don't have a presence on Venus."

"But surely your employees travel for pleasure. If they die there…"

"Then they return there. No point inconveniencing a vacation." Jack swallowed, thinking of his daughter. The last time they spoke, she was excited about spending a year in the Venusian Republic's floating colonies. *Dad!* she had said over the comlink, radiating the kind of energy that is the domain of bright-eyed children whose sense of what is possible has yet to be blunted by reality's grimmer, ugly machinations. *I might be going to Venus! Ms. Mujahid said they're only taking three students from my school, and I'm top-block in my class! Oh I really really really want to go! My webfriends Vertonia and Orchid are applying, they're in Spain and Italy, you know, we could have the BEST year if we all went! Ishtar has this HUGE shopping center! I miss you, Dad! Can you come visit soon?*

Jack walked abreast of the IPC investigator with a heavy heart. Without warning, Gethin turned off the path into a busy shanty shop where the mixed crowd drank coffees and Malaysian teas at lapis tables, or pawed over a clothing bazaar's racks.

Gethin spoke to Jack without looking at him. "I need a complete list of *everything* that was in Base 59. Every item from coffeepots to pornomods. The IPC has a team screening the debris, so please make sure your list is thorough."

Jack nodded. "Done."

"And I want to be there when Cavor comes back. As soon as he's conscious."

Jack thought over the logistics of this request. It was necessary. The higher-ups would simply have to agree. "I'm sure that can be arranged."

"That makes two of us." Gethin was already expecting evasion when it came to the Base 59 inventory. "The other two employees, Mr. and Mrs. Judith Merril. I understand they're already revived, walking around."

"I'll take you to them now. We put them up in the corporate hotel, Level 314."

★   ★   ★

Gethin expected the couple would be unhelpful and, five minutes into the interview, his suspicions were confirmed.

The Merrils made a strange pairing. The husband, Marco, was a squat, dark-haired fellow with hands like a child; everything about him seemed soft and delicate. Judith was a blond Amazon: tall (though not nearly approaching Jack Saylor's stature) long-necked, and strong-limbed. Facing them, Gethin had the impression of speaking to a mother and son.

Naturally, the problem was they didn't remember anything. Gethin amped all his sniffer programs to their highest level as he conducted his inquiry. He measured vocal stress patterns, pupil dilation, body temperature, muscle twitches, eye movements. In three minutes he knew far more about the Merrils than he ever wanted to: Marco was a mewling submissive, while Judith was a sexual predator with a hardcore control fetish. It had been a month since their last Save, and though all research notes were safely backed up, the Merrils couldn't relate what happened the night of the explosion.

"At least our notes were recovered," Judith explained, and she handed Gethin a smartboard. Her voice had the edged, caustic undertone of a jaded schoolteacher. "We were getting ready to present for the mid-month conference."

"When was that going to be?"

"Tomorrow."

Gethin sifted through the files. The last entry of the daily log was written by Judith herself, just nineteen minutes before the explosion:

Please see embedded virtual test results. JM

Gethin inserted his finger into the smartboard's port to download the data directly to his sensorium. "What was the subject of the presentation?"

"Storage cathodes."

"For what?"

"We were designing a cathode rail for the Ceres labs," she said with a trace of impatience.

"What kind of cathode?"

"Experimental."

Gethin laughed coldly. "Mrs. Merril, do you really want to play games with me?"

She blinked. "*Excuse* me, Mr. Bryce?"

"What the *fuck* kind of storage cathodes were you developing? What was being stored *in* them? A direct answer will suffice!"

Her eyes grew in righteous offense. She shot an angry glance to her husband, and he looked ready to spring up to defend her. *A well-trained attack dog,* Gethin thought. He even caught a glimpse of leash marks around Marco's neck.

Gethin stayed the husband with a glare. "I'm bound by IPC protocol not to divulge protected intellectual property," he added. "This is a formal investigation of an interplanetary tragedy. Dispense with the stonewalling. *What* was there?"

"An experimental cathode rail," Judith repeated, though this time there was a waver in her voice.

"For *what?*"

She hesitated. "Mr. Bryce? You're an investigator, not a journalist. You are not prone to sensationalism."

"That would be a fair assessment."

"Good. The rail is meant to store exotic matter."

Gethin sucked in a breath. "As in *negative mass matter?*"

"But," Judith said sternly, "the cathode was empty. Exotic matter experiments are not done anywhere near the brightworlds by IPC regulation. Actual, physical experiments are conducted in the asteroid frontier. We only work in virtual."

"So there was no exotic matter on Luna?"

"Absolutely none."

Gethin said, "But there is in the Belt?"

Her answer was predictable. "I don't know how far they've come in their research out there. I have never been to the Belt."

"Yes, yes, yes," Gethin said dismissively, the possibilities wheeling in his mind. "But this cathode rail was completed? Your virtual test results were embedded for the conference. As soon as you received Earthside approval, you were going to ship out the data-stream to Ceres for production and testing, right? For the TNO Project?"

"Yes."

Gethin raised an eyebrow and looked to Jack.

"I'll look into it," Jack said, startled by this revelation.

It was 2100 when they left the couple.

"I'll page you when Cavor is ready," Jack said.

"Thanks."

"Do you have accommodations?"

"Yeah," Gethin lied. He knew PI would be shadowing his every move. As soon as they verified his room number, they'd put the hotel on full surveillance. Every meal he ate would be noted ("Mr. Bryce has chewed his toast four times before swallowing") every place he visited, every window he passed ("He seems absorbed by the book display at Melville's") and certainly any unencrypted message he sent.

Maybe the encrypted ones too.

"We have nice guest accommodations," Jack persisted.

"I'm sure you do, but I already have a hotel."

Jack smiled slightly, reading the lie off Gethin's forehead. "I hope it wasn't too expensive."

Gethin laughed. It was actually the first real moment of warmth he had showcased, and Jack chanced to join it.

"Nice meeting you, Jack Saylor. Let me know when all the king's horses and all the king's men have put Cavor back together again."

CHAPTER ELEVEN
The Oversoul

Again, the soothsayers had been wrong.

A world of digital surveillance and thousands of tracking methods hadn't made society more transparent for the crafty few, but provided more bramble and brush to vanish into.

Gethin left Saylor and contacted the Hanging Gardens Suites to register a room. The charge was made over comlink. Knowing he was still being tailed, Gethin then ducked into a neon, gaudy falafel diner and found the back door before any employee realized what was happening. While passing vats of hot oil and cooking rice, Gethin touched his clothes' reversible option and they turned to drab black.

"Implement Gemini," he muttered to Id.

Then stop moving for half a minute, will you? the Familiar snapped.

There was a burst of signals from Gethin's head, and they lashed outward like invisible hydra heads biting down on the local surveillance sphere. Fourteen security cameras were fed a false trail of Gethin's face in the crowd, moving south-east towards a local arcadium. At the same time, the cameras just outside the falafel diner were told to see Gethin as mere 'noise' amid the shopping herd, of no more tracking importance than the seams in cobblestone, the patterns in Babylonian tunics, or the angular geometries of kiosks.

Okay, Id said at last. *Follow the yellow brick road.*

He went out the back, found himself in a narrow alley, and scaled a short wall of potted plants. Keeping his head low, Gethin snuck into the district's clustered shops and garden strips while following a jagged yellow overlay of Id's safe spots. It was no easy task hacking Babylon security. Gethin moved as a poltergeist through the arcology and knew that right behind him, the safety zone was zipping up like the ocean closing over a ship's wake.

Babylon's Faustian Temple was on Level 100, across the street from a popular franchise club, the Decadents. Gethin made a cautious approach. The temple's front was fashioned like the rest of the arcology, in carved stonework made to imitate the ancient styles of Persia, Babylonia, and Sumer. Two bearded sphinxes guarded the entrance.

Gethin took a deep breath, steeling himself. When he heard his name called, he wasn't remotely surprised.

"Mr. Bryce!"

The voice came from the Decadents café. Gethin saw a man wearing a maroon tunic, waving at him.

Gethin entered the café dubiously. His eye-lens informed him the man in the tunic was Faustian monk Water Basilisk.

Water. Basilisk. What a bunch of lunatics.

"You've got sharp eyes," Gethin said. "I didn't realize monks kicked back with a drink at the end of the day."

The monk nodded gravely. "We hoped you would come."

"You were waiting for me?"

"We knew you were in Babylon. But we also know you still place a high premium on *privacy*." The monk spat the word with distaste. "We hoped you would seek us out."

Gethin expected this to be followed by the usual 'you showed such incredible potential' bullshit, but the monk didn't dare. Wary of cameras, Gethin said, "Let's get inside. And you're buying."

Decadents was smoky and hallucinogenic within. Heavy bass music shook the corridors. It was like crawling through the veins of a giant monster with the thudding of its heartbeat resonating in the walls.

The main dance floor was made up like a masquerade with an antique clock standing thirty feet tall. Revelers whirled and spun, seething with color and life. Gethin steered clear of it – there was no telling who might recognize him from the Lunar broadcast – and he went to the club's catacombs. Here, tables were arranged behind damp mounds of lichen, murky pools, and fake tombs of the dead.

Gethin grabbed a remote table. Basilisk sat down with him.

"Amontillado?" a jester asked them.

"Two," Gethin said.

"We won't betray you," the monk told him amicably. "We know the corporate world is monitoring your every step while you conduct your investigation."

Gethin said nothing, but inwardly felt a chill. *How can Basilisk know about all this? Of course…they saw me leaving the regen center on Luna. They could have tracked me to the train station, and seen which train I got on.*

Gethin liked to think he would have lost them after that, but really, there was no way to be sure. The IPC shuttle had discreetly picked him up at Tycho Hospital, and the Faustian's collective hound might have been sniffing fruitlessly for him for a while. So where had they noticed him again? Was it those two Helen of Troy greeters up top? A random Faustian adept in the market?

Saylor himself?

Gethin waited until the jester brought their wine. The table's menu glowed in soft phosphorescence. He was hungry. But he wasn't about to drag this meeting out any longer than he needed.

The monk looked very grave. "You received our message?"

"I received a stupid hook. Normally I stay the fuck away from you guys, but I'm giving you the benefit of the doubt. Do you have something to tell me or not?"

"We have information," the monk whispered. He dropped his eyes, indicating with his entire manner that Gethin should switch to subvocal. Gethin nodded and amped up his hearing.

"The natural state of mankind is to fragment," the monk said, his lips barely twitching as he spoke. "Do you agree?"

"No," Gethin said. "That's like saying the natural state of locusts is to swarm, but that's not true. Locusts are ordinarily sedate until their population hits a critical mass. Then enzymes kick in. They transform. They metamorphose and go on a feeding frenzy. Humans are the same way. We start off in fragmented tribes, then gradually coalesce into a unified civilization, things get static for a while, and then we fragment. Then it starts all over. It's like the first line of *Romance of the Three Kingdoms*: 'The empire, long divided, must unite; long united, must divide. Thus it has ever been.'"

The monk's eyes widened. Clearly he hadn't been anticipating this kind of argument. Clearly, too, he read into Gethin's deeper meaning.

The Faustians eagerly anticipated the merging of all sentient life. They believed it was the inevitable fate of the universe.

"You don't think that worldview is a touch bleak?" the monk asked neutrally.

"Not at all. The very seasons come and go. Ebb and flow."

"But *you've* already broken the ebb and flow. You died, Mr. Bryce. Now you live again, sharing this drink with us. Was it good or bad that death was abolished?"

"Protecting human life from the ravages of the universe is *not* breaking ebb and flow."

"Ah, but it is *precisely* that," Basilisk insisted, leaning towards Gethin. "Humans live forever now. It is the penultimate state. What follows is either total chaos as our species splinters into warring factions on ten thousand future worlds, or a *merging* into one being…where all consciousness comes together with the total sum of our experiences. It strengthens the species."

"That's not a species," Gethin snapped, no longer speaking subvocally. "What you want is one super-organism, an omega creature. And that's suicide."

"It's immortality and godhood. It's true omniscience."

Gethin shook his head, feeling strangely hunted. Wondering how many Faustians were down here with them, he glanced to the bar. All three bartenders were staring at him while they worked.

The monk's eyes glinted lustfully. "Life is *only* sentience. Not *these* evolutionary husks of meat! And of all the people in the universe, *you experienced that moment…a prescient taste of what the future holds.*"

Gethin started to get up. "I didn't come here for sermons. Your monks on Luna said you had information to share…"

The monk nodded readily. "We do. War is coming. It threatens to fracture humanity into disparate shards. We see much and share all. The Prometheans are waiting for any excuse to spread their seeds into the galaxy and leave this petty solar system behind. The Asteroid Federation swells with evil ambition. The devil-eyed Ashoka breed in their rockships. MarsAlone stockpiles weapons for revolution…maybe violent enough to harm someone you care for?"

Gethin turned away.

"Lori Ambermoon?" the monk called after him. "Or was it Natalia Argos?"

Gethin halted and turned back. His glare was volcanic.

Basilisk held up his hands in parley. "You have the unique ability to be the godhead, Mr. Bryce. In six hundred million simulations, you are the only one who consistently showed such promise. You could unite humanity through worlds both digital and physical. You could play every faction against the middle in conjunction with our forces. Together we can achieve peace, do you understand, before humanity spreads and shatters beyond all hope of repair!"

"Yeah? Will I change water into wine too?"

"Why do you think the IPC nabbed you?" the monk taunted. "Why send you to Mars? Why dispatch you on dozens of fruitless missions around the solar system? It's to keep someone of your strategic talents busy, distracted!"

Gethin bristled at this.

Basilisk's face was flushed. "What do you think will happen when the colonization ban is overturned? And it *will* be, within a century. *Your* abilities with the Oversoul can prevent this hopeless fracturing. *Every* monk has reviewed your career. You entered the Oversoul's consciousness and it frightened you, it drove you to recoil into your shell. But that's natural. When humanity moves forward into space, it can either diverge into ten thousand subspecies triggering new wars, or *it can benefit from your input and leadership and guidance!*"

"My leadership?" Gethin laughed. "I was an Arcadian addict, and I won't return to those days. You call us chaotic, warlike, messy? I say that it's *exactly* the life I want. Merging into one super-being is oblivion."

"It is *sharing* with your *species!*" Basilisk roared, lunging at him.

Gethin vanished.

To Basilisk's gaze, the awesome prodigy he was having drinks with suddenly blurred and disappeared, as if drawn into a higher dimension, the lofty crystalline shell to which all consciousness was moving as surely as a caterpillar crawled up the tree to spin its silken womb and emerge, winged and beautiful, for flight.

But for Gethin, he had simply accessed a tab on his HUD.

It was the tab that said SPECIAL. And when a drop-down menu unraveled, he selected the BLURMOD option.

Faster than the human eye could register, Gethin sprang up from his seat, fled the table, and escaped the club.

But not before breaking Basilisk's jaw with the astounding power of an accelerated punch.

CHAPTER TWELVE
Celeste Awakens to Civilization

The girl hides behind dusty towers of egg crates in the moldy basement. She hates the basement. Dirty water always seeps in, and centipedes crawl on the walls. They're fast and ugly and have too many legs. She tries not to think about them, especially now, with the basement lights extinguished and the hum of the refrigerator and the hollow drip of water. If a centipede crawls across her feet she might scream.

But Mommy is in the dark too. The large wooden buttons of Mommy's apron are comforting. Mommy's hands are strong and warm. They smell like lemon.

The girl thinks of the wrinkled knobby blind man who lives above the butcher shop, and she wonders if this is what it's like to be blind: the universe as a swarming black nothingness, with only hard wooden buttons and lemon-scented hands and the sounds –

– drip –

– of leaky pipes and Mommy singing her favorite song in her softest, feather-light whisper:

"Beautiful dreamer, wake unto me, starlight and dew drops are waiting for thee—"

An explosion makes the basement jump. The little girl screams, but Mommy clamps a lemony hand over her mouth. Quietly, almost pure whisper now, she continues: "Sounds of the rude world heard in the day…lulled by the moonlight, have all passed away—"

Upstairs, gunfire pops in staccato, perforating the foyer. Uncle Tony's boys are yelling, knocking over furniture, shooting back at the bad men who have penetrated the barricade. The girl doesn't understand why they came over the barricade. Why don't they just stay on the other side?

A spatter of more gunfire and something very heavy hits the floor. It has to be Uncle Tony's bulky, toadlike body, collapsing in terrible finality.

Mommy's buttons. The girl feels Mommy's buttons again. Flat, rough around the edges like coin grooves.

Is that why the bad men are killing Uncle Tony? For coins?

Mommy removes her hand from over the girl's mouth. "Sing with me, Celeste. Quietly, my little angel. Sing with me."

"Beautiful dreamer," the girl whispers. "Wake unto me..."

"Starlight and dew drops are waiting for thee," Mommy trembles.

An upstairs door bursts open. Horrible sounds, the sounds of men fighting hand-to-hand. A stampede of footsteps in the kitchen, last defense before the bolted cellar door, a table crashes over and there go all of Mommy's pretty dishes. Men grunt and scream, making wet, choking sounds.

The girl can feel Mommy's warm breath.

"Sounds of the rude world," Mommy breathes.

The cellar door buckles. Angry voices and a hideous new noise...

"...heard in the day..."

...a terrible new noise...

"Lulled by the moonlight..."

...the BUZZING OF A CHAINSAW!

"Mommy!"

"Have all passed..."

★   ★   ★

Away.

Floating up to the gentle embrace of algae lamps above her hospital bed, Celeste Segarra opened her eyes. Then she immediately shut them. Used her private darkness to process what she had seen in that momentary glimpse.

Don't let them – whoever they are – know you're awake. Not yet.

She had seen a red room with a floor like pink quartz. There was a glassy orb-camera above her bed. A holographic jungle sprouted from the walls, deep green and resonating with chirps and trills. A medbot stood beside the bed like an old parking meter plucked from an overgrown ruin.

Celeste's first thought was that she had been captured by Quinn. He would have heard about the raid and be none too pleased. His private security force was more than a match for her squad. Quinn stockpiled all the arky toys, and now she was a prisoner in his survivalist bunker.

A sick feeling exploded in her stomach. The memory of the airfield struck Celeste's brain like a mass driver. *No!*

It had to have been a dream.

Had to be. The man with the searchlight eyes, his body shredding from weaponfire into a haze of bone chips, meat, and blood. The energy burst that had lanced her friends as they circled him.

Celeste felt hot vomit shoot up her throat, and she twisted in barely enough time to retch onto the floor.

All of her friends were dead. *Jeff!* Their bodies had been flung like dolls from that bastard's suicide bomb. For a moment the delicate thread of hope wavered in her thoughts, because clearly *she* had survived the attack, so why not others? Then she remembered.

The leader had flung her clear of the area before detonating. Allie was already near death. Rajnar and Jamala and Jeff had been overtaken by the detonation.

Tomorrow is ours, babe.

Forever you're mine.

Jeff. Sandy-haired, child-hearted optimist who somehow managed to stay hopeful in a kingdom of corpses.

Hey! There are glops the size of dinosaurs in Canada, Celeste!

She grunted in pain, dizziness, and rage. She wanted to kill something. Wanted to tear the room apart, bite out the throats of whoever was here.

But her survival instincts took over.

Celeste pulled herself out of bed, testing her strength. Her captors had clothed her in a gossamer-light tunic unlike anything she'd ever seen. Beneath this, several blue medpatches were grafted onto her body like designer leeches. Nanite infusions.

They were repairing her at the cellular level.

Celeste went to the bathroom and nearly lost her footing from sharp, sudden vertigo. The pressure on her joints instantly alerted her medpatches. Cool, menthol-like endorphins saturated the surgery points beneath.

Why would Quinn heal me up?

Everyone in the Hudson Wastes knew the legend of Quinn's wrath. He was sure to make a bloody example of her betrayal. He would put her back together just so she'd be in prime health for the pliers, hot pokers, and power drills that would follow. He'd make her a horrific legend…a sadistic testament to what happened to anyone who crossed him.

But then why am I not restrained? And why use such a tremendously expensive technique? Nanite infusions are gold. How can Quinn have amassed so many, that he can throw some away on a woman he's going to kill anyway?

The door to her room slid open with a hum. A muscular guard stood in the corridor beyond, wearing the starchy, green-and-silver livery of Prometheus Industries.

What the hell?

Celeste stared dumbly for a few seconds.

The guard watched her intently. Very intently, practically licking his lips as he eyeballed her. Celeste realized she hadn't buttoned up her gown after examining the medpacks. The guard was getting a nice view of her left breast and nipple.

"It's fifty tradenotes to see the other one," she snapped, wiping vomit from her mouth.

"She's up and about," the guard told someone in the hall.

A woman strode into the room. Asian, and young-looking…barely twenty-years-old, judging by that doll-like face and serene eyes. The woman wore her uniform like a second skin.

Celeste had killed many women. The Wastes were riddled with gladiatrixes and snipers and anarcho-banshees. By comparison, this Promethean officer didn't impress her. Celeste felt she could effortlessly swat her down and then, without breaking a sweat, tear out the throat of the beefy lech in the hall.

But the Wastes were full of stories about Prometheans. Elite humans jacked to the eyes with tech. Once, Celeste had faced down two cocky arkies in the gloplands: hunter-types who thought they could play games with the locals. She killed them both, but Jesus fuck, it had been difficult. They didn't seem to want to *stay* dead. Ultimately, she had to cut them up, bloodily extracting whatever mods she could salvage, and toss the remains to carnivorous transgenics.

"My name is Internal Affairs Officer Keiko Yamanaka," the doll woman said. "Welcome to Babylon arcology."

The arcology? How in the fuck?

Then the answer arose in her thoughts.

The *Mantid*.

It was the only explanation. She dimly remembered insectile shapes pawing at her after the attack, phantom images she'd been too out of it to process. Her ship must have sent a pseudopod to rescue her. Realizing her body's damage was beyond its abilities to heal, it had then…what? Rushed her to civilization? And negotiated with the local authorities, because arkies wouldn't bother treating a Wastelander otherwise.

But negotiated what?

Keiko gave an imperceptible nod, as if reading her thoughts. "That's a rather unusual protector you have."

"It comes in handy."

"No doubt."

Celeste held Keiko's stare, realizing her initial impressions had been wrong. This was no twenty-year-old greenhorn. There was an ancient, cold quality in those petite features and black eyes. The woman oozed the can-do intensity of a hardened soldier, while bereft of the grim fatalism that often went with it. And why not?

She's an immortal. This Keiko might as well be the fucking goddess Amaterasu.

The Promethean drew near. "Where did you acquire that ship?"

"My ship?" *Is that what this is all about?*

"Yes. Where did you acquire it?"

Celeste furrowed her brow. "Where is it now?"

"Safe in one of our hangars," Keiko said without batting an eye.

"And the other survivors?"

"You were the only one brought to us."

Even though she had been expecting this answer, Celeste felt like she had swallowed acid.

"You were in bad shape," Keiko continued without expression. "Another fifteen or twenty minutes, you wouldn't have survived."

"Prometheus Industries patched me up?"

"Yes."

"Why?"

"You are witness to a terrorist attack that may have connections to a strike on one of our facilities. Your experience is being reviewed as we speak."

Celeste nodded. "How is it being reviewed?"

"We got a flash-capture of your recent memories."

Shit.

Celeste's heart leapt to her neck. What did *recent* mean? How thorough was a flash-capture? She tried to recall the last time she had dealt with King D. It was with a sickening realization that the answer came to her: just before the airfield attack. What had they discussed? How much of StrikeDown would be compromised?

Mouth dry, Celeste heard herself ask, "So you made a copy of my brain? Sounds like you have what you need."

"A flash-capture isn't a DC. But we know you don't work for Stillness."

Celeste waited, heart heavy.

"We're hoping you can fill in the blanks," Keiko continued, thinking how woefully inadequate the flash-capture had been. A few days worth of memory, mish-mashed like a photomontage. Most of it was terribly ordinary; showering, pissing, eating. One vivid memory of a sandy-haired man atop her, plunging slowly between her spread thighs.

The only good that had come from the flash-capture was the assault on the airfield. Scrapping with Stillness soldiers. Seeing two tarp-covered missiles. And the explosion.

While her prisoner had been comatose, Keiko had ordered a full DC. But the necessary optical prompting was useless on an unconscious person. Unreadable neural file. The best you got was a pastiche, glowing with emotional hotspots.

Celeste went to the room's sink and washed her mouth out, spat. "What happens to those memories now? Do I get royalties every time they're viewed?"

Keiko studied her in the mirror. "The images are being circulated among our analysts. No royalties, sorry."

Celeste shook excess water from her hands.

"What was your involvement with the missiles?" Keiko prodded.

"I figured you'd already seen that."

"I saw you in combat with Stillness troops, yes. But why?"

"You arkies might think Wastelanders are all the same. But we have standards. Stillness is a group of Grade-A lunatics. We don't want people like getting hold of ancient flash-bangs. It's bad for business. So we decided to take them off the market."

"And adapt them for your own use?"

Celeste grinned. "Right, because that would be smart. Bring the Republic down on us? Get real, lady. If you saw my recent memories, you see how we operate. Turf wars and trying to survive. These aren't the Warlord days."

Keiko was quiet. Her eyes gave no indication whether she believed this or not. "So you were doing community service, is that it? Didn't want the missiles for yourself?"

"For use against *whom?*" Celeste looked at her as if she were insane. "We're happy to grab up ammo, explosives, and medpatches. But nukes and *antimatter*? Finding that means we've got a hand in the big pot. The Republic offers sweet trade-in deals. Stillness doesn't care about finder-fees; me, that's all I *do* care about." She swallowed the lump in her throat.

Keiko nodded. The room's sniffer programs were monitoring for signs of deception. And Celeste's vocal patterns, stress, and body temperature were all screaming that she was spinning one big lie...especially that last part about trading with the Republic. But it *was* true that the Republic offered hefty sums for the recovery of old weapons. Enough to make this woman and her tribe wealthy. So why would she be lying? Why hold onto antimatter missiles, unless her people felt it was more profitable – through threat alone – to keep them as a hole card?

Antimatter! Keiko thought. *Being traded back and forth, juggled, and seized in violent attacks by Outland rats. As if we don't have enough to worry about in the world.*

"So what's next?"

Keiko gave her a curious look. "Excuse me?"

"Do you toss me back outside, mind-rape me some more, or make me an honorary arky?"

"As witness to a case which *may* affect Prometheus, my superiors will probably approve the full DC analysis. In the meantime, I *can* grant you a temporary arcology pass."

"Will you?"

They regarded each other. Celeste's eyes were all challenge, Keiko's were thinly veiled contempt. And in that moment, an invisible smile passed between them. They understood each other. Respect flickered at the audacity and authority in the room.

In fact, Keiko felt something deeper than that. Studying the Outlander's unspooling memories filled her with unexpected feelings. She found herself admiring the raw strength of this mortal. After all, Celeste had no DC backup. Every time people shot at her she was risking permadeath.

Keiko tapped her fingertips together in a peculiar beat. "Your pass is now ready."

"Do I get a physical copy? You know, to wear around my neck like the slaves of Rome?"

Incredibly, a transparent red card popped out from a small device at Keiko's beltline. She pressed her fingers against it firmly. Handed it over.

"You are granted a two-step access to the arcology. By accepting this card you take responsibility for it and pledge that you will be its sole carrier at all times. It must remain on your person always—"

"Even in the shower?"

"And any attempt at replication, selling it, or defacing it will result in immediate expulsion. All uses of the card are tracked and its privileges can be altered or revoked at any time. If these privileges are altered or revoked, you will be notified."

Celeste held the red card up to one eye and peered at Keiko through it. "What do you mean, a *two*-step access?"

"While we are reviewing the evidence you brought us, you are not permitted to leave hospital grounds. Any attempt to do so will result in your immediate arrest. After the review is complete, and if I feel you can still be useful, you may access the rest of the arcology."

Celeste pressed the dermal tab behind her ear. "I notice my sensorium is deactivated. Will you turn it back on?"

Keiko continued, unfazed. "Your card will entitle you to a complimentary credit line of one thousand tradenotes. These funds are earmarked for use only within the Babylon arcology and cannot be transferred to any account or person. All unused funds will be revoked at the time of your departure. This is your total credit line and will not be reimbursed or expanded, so you are advised to use it thriftily."

Celeste got the distinct impression that Keiko was reciting words she had said before. Had other Wastelanders been brought here? Or did visitors from other arcologies go through the same process?

Celeste raised her voice. "Will you turn on my sensorium?"

"No."

CHAPTER THIRTEEN
War Inevitable

Gethin went straight from Decadents to the Hanging Gardens hotel to formally check in, thinking he might be able to catch up on sleep...the first sleep of his new body. Instead, he found himself far too riled. Rather than retire to his room, he did some shopping at the hotel's clothing outlet, buying some new tunics, undergarments, footwear, and a bag of toiletries. He had everything delivered to his room; by the time he keyed into the lion-and-dragon-themed chamber, his purchases were already inside in clay-hued bags.

It took even less time to initialize reinstatement of his Athenian and London properties. Gethin checked his investment profile and bank accounts. The IPC had already deposited his contracting fee. His link to a complimentary expense account was also reactivated. Gethin grinned. For the duration of the case, his fingertips would be worth more than the GNP of most nations.

Only I'm not crawling through Martian lava tunnels this time looking for aliens that don't exist, he thought. *I'm never leaving Earth again.*

Gethin rubbed his neck and leaned back on his bed. Then he sat up again, realizing he had more to do.

He uploaded an Id-fashioned hydra into the wall's wetport with an insert of his ring finger. There was a pinch as connection was made. The hydra would act as an independent creature set loose into an ocean of information, seeking out all reference to 'Flight 3107' or 'Luna City incident,' and every variant thereof. It would comb the global communications grid. Billions of hits would be reported; Gethin, like other IPC investigators working this case, had the Herculean task of honing his hydra to cut through walls of chatter for something, anything, useful.

The next essential item was to take a shower.

He rinsed off the copious sweat and oils his body was producing. Part of the adjustment period from regeneration meant excess grime while his internal checks and balances relearned how to cool his body. The speed of the shower's water startled him. On Mars, water flowed in a gentler, almost loving pattern around drains. Earth's gravity turned it into a rapid spin cycle.

Gethin put his face directly into the shower spray. His muscles felt like they were on fire.

The next time some idiot on Mars or Venus or a Jovian moon reports an anomaly to the IPC, he mused, *they can kiss my ass.*

After his shower he lay down on his hotel bed, drawing the arabesque-patterned linens up around his damp body, and tried to sleep.

And ended up sitting up again, deciding to compose a quick email to Mars by tapping his virtuboard fingertips on the hotel mattress:

Paladin Natalia. By now you've probably heard that I died aboard my departure shuttle. I suspect you feel it was a karmic bowshot earned for fleeing without bidding you farewell.
I apologize for my cowardly vanishing act.
I miss nothing about Mars.
Except you.

SEND.

At last, he closed his eyes and waited for sleep to arrive.

Instead, it was a call from Jack Saylor that arrived. Gethin dressed in two minutes flat and was out the door, en route to meet the giant man at the regen center.

The security officer didn't look pleased.

"In the spirit of cooperation," Jack began, "I'm authorized to share with you a recording of the Lunar base explosion."

"Great."

The muscles in Jack's bearded jaw bunched. "It will be easy to misconstrue what the recording shows."

"Let me decide that. Where is it?"

Jack reluctantly handed over the holocube. "You need a Q-key to open it." He extended his hand; Gethin enclosed his fingers around it. On his left eye the transfer appeared as two hand icons touching.

INITIATE TRANSACTION? Y/N

Gethin okayed the transfer. He snapped the cube onto the palm of his left hand, and sightjacked with Jack so they could watch the images together in his mind's theater.

Jack watched the astonishing images. The base explosion. The scintillating web of energy colliding with the shuttle and then snapping off in a new direction towards Mother Blue.

Gethin reviewed the footage. Over and over again.

The man's green eyes glinted as he replayed the feeds, stilled them, rotated them, used his virtuboard fingers to take measurements and perform calculations. His attention to detail was excessive. Several minutes passed. It went on so long that Jack grew impatient.

And *still* he watched. Jack manually severed the sightjack.

"Wow," Gethin said at last. He gave the holocube back.

Jack stared. "Wow?"

"What was the device Judith Merril was working on?"

"A cathode rail."

"Used for what?"

Jack's jaw muscles clenched anew. "Mr. Bryce, I have the data-file on the cathode project. Everything she told us is accurate. They were building models in virtual environments, running scenarios for—"

"For exotic matter." Gethin sightjacked again with Jack, spiking a single frame into the man's optics. It showed the tentacled pattern in mid-bank from the shuttle explosion. "Take a look at that thing. Looks pretty fucking exotic to me."

Jack swallowed. "I have no idea what this is."

"I want to speak to someone at Prometheus *who has an idea.*"

By way of reply, Jack handed him a sheet of smartpaper. "That's a list of all scientists involved with the TNO project. I've sent messages to each of them with the Kepler file attached. So far, no one can identify it. You'll also find the inventory registrations for everything shipped to that base. *Nothing* exotic."

Gethin glanced disinterestedly at the paper even as images, columns of data, and content tabs animated over the surface. "If you were developing exotic matter *in* the lab it wouldn't show up on a damned inventory sheet."

"Send in your own experts to verify what I'm telling you," Jack said finally.

"I already have."

"Good."

"And just so you know, I think it's almost certain you *were* attacked."

Jack blinked. "You...well...good."

"The question is, by whom?" Gethin pointed to the regen center. "Let's see if Kenneth Cavor has the answer."

*   *   *

The dead man looked much better than when Gethin had seen him last.

For starters, he wasn't charred to a molten crisp. Gethin and Jack arrived at the recovery chamber in time to see Cavor freshly remade, wearing the black robe and slippers of the clinic. He was bald, stocky and muscular, sporting the kind of physical framework usually associated with early hominids. Thick neck, long arms, compact body. Cavor sat on the edge of his recovery bed, watching the sensor screen run their diagnostics.

The interview lasted forty-nine minutes. Gethin began it friendly enough, shaking the man's hand and inquiring about his health, sharing anecdotal episodes of his own experience with regeneration. They laughed together, and Jack simply looked on, bewildered by this chummy camaraderie.

"Mind if I ask you some questions, Mr. Cavor?" Gethin said at last.

Cavor shook his head. "Please."

Then everything changed. Gethin fired salvoes about the nature of the cathode rail work, the TNO Project, what Cavor did in his spare time, why he had been in the bathroom at the time of the explosion. Gethin never got outwardly angry, though he remained in iron control over the interview. It was not even the same style he had used with the Merrils. Jack sat back and watched him eviscerate Cavor until the man was red-faced, sweating, his heart beating wildly, and the sensor screen warning against this level of anxiety.

"How would you explain that energy wave?"

Cavor looked desperately to Jack, found no help there, and faced Gethin. "I didn't even *see* this energy wave you're talking about, Mr. Bryce."

Gethin nodded for Jack to display the holocube's contents on the wall.

"This mysterious energy blows up your lab. Destroys the shuttle. Then you get incinerated hours later."

Cavor sighed.

Gethin cracked his knuckles. "Hey, Saylor? Do you have any chocolate? No? I was having the oddest craving for mushrooms earlier, but now it's Mexican spiced chocolate I want." He shook his head, looked at Cavor. "Happens when they regenerate you. You start craving all kinds of things while your body's chemistry balances. Give it a few hours and you'll be salivating for celery sticks crammed full of blue cheese or something."

Cavor managed a weak smile.

"But back to my questioning, what do you *think* this energy was? Use your imagination, 'cuz I'm fresh out of theories."

Cavor glistened in perspiration like a freshly caught fish. "Well...I've never seen anything like it. The way it twisted sharply towards Earth..."

"Yeah?"

"I don't know what to say about that."

"What do you think of the tendrils hanging around it like that? And the texture of its luminous body?"

Cavor held out his hands helplessly. "Mr. Bryce, I have no idea what to say. I'm just seeing this now."

"I was thinking it looked alive. What do you think?"

"I don't know."

"Let's talk about things you do know. You were stationed on Luna for two years and never had any visitors other than your fellow employees. Not even a trip to New Shinjuku or Lilith's. You spend almost no time in social Caves. That's a little odd, don't you think? Are you naturally that much of a loner?"

The questions persisted a few more minutes. Then Gethin startled everyone by standing and blotting his hands on his pants. "Thanks for your time, Mr. Cavor. I hope you'll forgive my style, but my responsibilities outweigh your comfort level. You understand."

Cavor exhaled in undisguised relief. "Of course. I'd probably do the same in—"

"Who's Apophis?"

There!

Gethin's sniffer programs were on high alert, and Cavor's reaction on hearing the name was a sharp, sudden shock. Through the interview he had been prodding the man's reactions to certain sounds and phrases, narrowing down a finite list of generic stimuli to several possible outcomes. His sniffers sifted data derived from Cavor's posture, body temp, eye dilation, breathing patterns, mouth movements, skin flushes.

Now fear crackled through the man like ocean surf. Body temperature flared, sweat output increased.

"Apophis?" Cavor frowned. "I don't know. Who is it?"

Gethin turned to Jack, nodded, and walked out of the room.

★   ★   ★

In the corridor, Jack felt grudging respect for the thoroughness of the interview.

"What happens now?" Gethin asked. "Does Cavor go back to work?"

"Not for several days at least. We have our own interrogation to conduct. But I've got a question: who *is* Apophis?"

Gethin sighed, his lungs burning. "You noticed how he reacted too, eh?"

"I did," Jack admitted, aware of a flurry of electrical activity in his security online receptor. The higher-ups were running cross-references on Cavor's background in relation to Gethin's spatter of inquiries. The word 'Apophis' was being researched and crosschecked, databases linking up to facilitate the search.

"I played a hunch," the investigator said. "Early in the interview I determined that Cavor knew more than he was letting on."

Jack protested, "He didn't trigger any patmatch for deception. We had him pegged as an innocent victim."

"He's not. There are ways to defeat sniffers. He's a loner type, sure, but there was something else going on. When did you hire Cavor?"

"He was born a Promethean. Grew up in the company."

"But his loyalties lie elsewhere. Oh, he's a true believer all right, but not necessarily for the 'up to the stars' stuff the rest of you are so fond of."

"I don't understand. What does this have to do with this Apophis?"

"Aren't your people researching it right now?"

Jack shrugged. "Of course. But in the spirit of cooperation, I thought you could save us the trouble."

Gethin leaned against the wall. "Tell your comrades to look up two episodes of history. The final collapse of the United States, shortly after the Broken Spear incident, is the first."

Instantly a renewed storm of signals pinged in Jack's head.

"And the second?"

"A little incident during the march of Enyalios against the Texan militia."

"Care to enlighten me?"

"Do your own homework," Gethin said. "Before your enemies do."

"We do have lots."

"Well, you earn them."

Jack scowled. "How's that?"

"Everyone knows that it's the Promethean dream to reach the stars. Make humanity a truly galactic species. But your company also has a way of reminding people of the old plutocracies...interested in the stars for profit, rather than the survival and betterment of the human race."

"Even if that's true, those two things aren't mutually exclusive."

"Know why the old world fell?"

"No one knows why it fell."

"They don't know the actual cause of the deathblow, sure. But surviving records point to a parasitic system. One class of people – government and plutocracy united in a patrician class of their own special rules and special rights, over everyone else. Sound familiar?"

"And the IPC is somehow better?"

Gethin grinned cruelly. "Know what I see when I look at Prometheus? A cult whose minions voluntarily submerge their own wills and dreams and freethinking capacity into one gigantic corporate maw. Religion in an age without religion. The TNO is just the latest proof. *Fiat lux.*"

"Who better to do it?" Jack snapped, astonished at this adversarial outsider. "Vector Nanonics has been under investigation for ethics violations. AztecSky is under-funded for this kind of thing. The Hanmura family tried to buy the contract, but just because they're good shipbuilders doesn't mean they have the tech know-how to construct history's first example of true stellar engineering." He suddenly wanted Keiko by his side. She'd rip this guy's tongue out!

And just like that, as if conjured, a message from Keiko splashed onto his optics.

"I'll wait," Gethin said knowingly.

Etiquette was to step back, read your message in private, and only then return to your previous engagement. Jack Saylor remained in place, towering over Gethin, and read the message with eyes open.

"That was my partner," he said at last. "There's been a report of a Stillness attack on a Hudson trading post in the Wastes. Numerous casualties. One witness brought in for questioning. Apparently, the terrorists acquired two antimatter missiles."

"Probably unrelated," Gethin said, but then a thought occurred to him. He touched the nearest wetport.

"Add parameter," he instructed his hydra. "Hudson. Wastes." He looked at his escort. "Where is the witness now?"

"At our medcenter on Level 15, with my partner."

"Who is your partner?"

"Internal Affairs Officer Yamanaka."

Gethin raised an eyebrow. "*Keiko* Yamanaka?"

"Nice guess."

The strangest look came over Gethin's face. Pried apart, it might have contained sorrow, joy, irony, fear, and astonishment, each emotion pinned like butterflies onto a corkboard. It was the first uncontrived look Jack had seen on this guy's face since meeting him.

"I'll see you on Level 15," Gethin said, and then he left.

CHAPTER FOURTEEN
Hanmura3 Sinks an Offshore Rig

Sakyo Hanmura3 sat at the airship window, absently fingering the sill, overlooking one of Switzerland's breathtaking mountains. He watched skiers crawling over the white slopes and thought back to Olympus Mons, where he would often hike or ski for days...pushing himself to discover his limits. These Swiss ranges were like foothills by comparison, yet the challenge might be comparable given Earth's gravity. Even now, local gravity squeezed his lungs and tugged every muscle. How did people live on Earth? It was like being at the bottom of the sea.

He wondered what his other selves were up to; the original on Mars, and Hanmura2 on Luna. Direct communication would tip the IPC, so a few associates, servants, and go-betweens conveyed coded communications. Orders to attack the Promethean offshore rig were the last he had heard from himself.

Hanmura3 turned from the window and went to his office desk. It was handsome oak on a blue carpet. He poured himself some water and settled into his wetware chair. He plugged into an Arcadian shell account.

Games are business are war, he thought fondly.

To many APAC traditionalists, Arcadia was the most striking example of materialistic illusion, equivalent to attaching your optic nerves to VR goggles and walking around, digitally blindfolded, forever. It was Plato's Cave taken to the extreme. A few outspoken philosophers decried it as the first step of a Faustian conspiracy, whose purpose would be to wean people off reality. Some said that since everything in Arcadia was pure illusion, then *satori* – that flash of enlightenment sought by Zen masters – would be impossible to achieve.

Absolutely absurd, Hanmura thought.

The physical universe was illusion through and through, and it didn't matter if the illusion was in digital pixels or the atoms of a rice-wine flask. True enlightenment came from *within*. Immortality hadn't destroyed karma; it merely forced one individual to experience its consequences in a single lifetime. The same was true of enlightenment. Digital illusion was merely another path to meditation.

Or to war.

In his airship cabin, Hanmura3 linked to the Arcadian gameweb and logged into a game called *Tengu Castle*.

Instantly, a new environment spiked into his senses. A drafty stone chamber with a fireplace. Vermillion curtains dressing tall, stained-glass windows. Two timberwolves gnawing on bones on the woven carpet.

Hanmura3's entry point was at the head of a heavy oak table. Sixteen people were already there, clearly awaiting his arrival. Men and women dressed in the upscale livery of medieval European nobles. To each other, their faces were modeled on the actual person wearing them; if an outsider were to glimpse the gathering, they would see only generic visages. Only one of the high-level operatives had not been seated; the fellow was impatiently standing by an open window, gazing out on the chilly hinterlands and black forests that covered much of *Tengu Castle*'s gameworld. Hearing the sudden hush in the room, he turned, saw that their CEO had joined them, and went to his seat.

Hanmura3 scowled at him. He was tempted to dismiss him right then; his lips parted, the urge burned in his throat.

"We have a target of opportunity," he said after an unsettling silence. "Time frame is twenty-four hours. What's the status of this grid?"

The operatives provided him the latest field intel from the real world. *Tengu Castle*'s gameworld was studded with forests, caves, open grasslands and a wildly creative variety of castles. Hanmura operatives had taken control of one corner of the gameworld. Having driven out every other player, they now used the region as a virtual testing ground. They built eight castles to represent real-world targets.

"Inform the garrisons their castles will be besieged today," Hanmura3 said.

The operative who had been standing at the window – his name was Taku from the Singapore office – frowned. "Who are we attacking in the real world? Hanmura-sama, our Pacific routes have benefited from stable relations. Is this just a test? Because I would strongly discourage any—"

Hanmura3 couldn't believe this public insubordination. *This is what happens when I'm away from Earth too long*, he thought.

"Sit over by the wolves! You are no longer permitted at this table! Go!"

Taku paled, stunned by this vehemence. He stood and complied, squatting in *seiza* posture between the two wolves near the fireplace. They continued gnawing their bones, barely paying him any mind. Limited AI. They recognized everyone in this castle as a friend.

The other operatives were already relaying Hanmura3's orders. They spoke into iron wristguards, alerting the holding forces of each nearby castle to an imminent attack.

When they were done, Hanmura3 continued. "Explain the defensive capabilities of Crystal Citadel."

A senior official in the group volunteered the data. Crystal Citadel was a stand-in model for a real-world Promethean offshore rig. It had been modeled carefully to mimic that installation's fundamentals: an octagonal main body supported by four sturdy concrete legs. It was defended by archers, pikemen, and wizards…to represent the real-world defenses of turrets, spiderbots, and submersibles.

In the real world, Prometheus Industries operated several deep-sea laboratories and research rigs. Some of the most sensitive research occurred in these remote fortresses, where Republic law couldn't be enforced as readily as in the world's enclaves and arcologies. Security protocols included an array of maritime defenses. Staff was effectively sealed away for years at a time; research terminals were kept strictly off the web grid. Progress reports were dispatched the old-fashioned way: by physical transport under elite guard.

The practical consequence was that marine labs were nearly impossible to penetrate. They remained special battlefield prizes. Espionage tactics historically failed against them, and failed big.

While in his early thirties, Sakyo Hanmura thought it worthwhile to focus his budding career on this corporate war challenge.

The basic problem – successful insertion, theft, and escape – was reduced if the objective was straightforward sabotage. Hanmura had proceeded to amass a list of marine targets chosen because of their remote locations and insulating, undersea topography. He had designed a formidable demolition team. After seventy years of subcontracting through the rogue South American state Xibalba, he succeeded in his aim. Xibalban scientists created for him the Sea Dragon operatives.

The Sea Dragons were grown from human genomes, but designed for aquatic environments. Engineered with gills and a cartilaginous skeleton capable of withstanding staggering pressures. Skin woven with polyanilene rotors and keratin mesh and chromatophores, gifting the Dragons with the ability to achieve what CAMO suits could: true invisibility at a whim, without electronics that could trigger a rig's sensors.

"Everyone in this room – other than Taku – will participate in the assault on Crystal Citadel," Hanmura3 explained. "You will represent a marine assault team. You will approach the citadel unseen. You will set explosive charges at key points on the installation's pylons."

One of the women nodded agreeably. "Yes, Hanmura-sama."

"Your goal is destruction of the target at all costs. Understand that once you make physical contact with the installation, the garrison within will be alerted to your presence. They will do everything in their power to stop you."

The same was true for the real world. In a few hours, the Sea Dragon team would be released via submersible several miles from the target rig. They would swim across the muddy Pacific bottom, keeping low, unseen, exuding neither body heat nor electrical impulses. Once at the installation's pylons, they would arrange into position and set drillbots and explosive charges to the reinforced concrete. At this point the rig's sensors would realize its supports were under attack. Promethean defenses would emerge. It would then be a contest of speed. Defenders versus attackers.

"You will remain with the charges. You will be there when they go off."

Again, the woman nodded. "I understand."

"I want to be certain that there is nothing left of the assault to be recovered. Each of your avatars must be completely destroyed."

"Yes, Hanmura-sama."

The same would be true of the real-world Sea Dragons. Hanmura Enterprises dared not risk their prized transgenic demolition team being captured and dissected by Promethean technicians.

"Make your preparations at once, and execute," Hanmura3 told the gathering.

They filed out of the chamber. Hanmura3 turned his cold stare onto Taku, whose head was bowed in shame.

Taku felt the grave silence. "I humbly beg to be allowed to—"

"Enough!" Hanmura3 looked to the wolves. "Command Alpha. Attack."

Taku's eyes bulged. "Sir! No!"

The wolves blinked where they sat gnawing bones. The game's local environment had changed Taku's IFF from friend to foe.

They were still rending Taku's avatar to messy scraps when Hanmura3 left the room and logged off.

Aboard the airship, he called his Singapore office and ordered Taku terminated from Hanmura Enterprises. Then he leaned back in his chair, pleasantly exhausted. His stomach bubbled, stricken with a surging irrational desire for steak tartare and raspberry pie.

CHAPTER FIFTEEN
Reunion

Celeste plucked an apple from a potted tree as she exited the hospital into an airy food court. She bit into the crisp fruit, unconcerned with the juices running down her chin, and leaned over the balcony rail to consider her new universe.

It was impressive work, really. As best she could tell, arky engineers had managed to fuse elements of classical Mesopotamia with old Manhattan. The *real* Manhattan had been lost to the sea centuries ago, its subways flooded, Times Square and Central Park now just curiosities for tourists to visit via submersible. Babylon Arcology had recaptured its famous look, though. Celeste peered interestedly at the recreated streets, shop windows, and faux fire hydrants amid carven visages of weird monsters, lions, and bird-headed demons.

And there was a black marble statue in the square too. An immensely muscular, scowling, bearded figure glaring at the pedestrians who passed.

Warlord Enyalios, Celeste thought in awe. She knew the stories – every Wastelander did. Nonetheless, she was surprised to see that the arkies had erected a goddamn statue to the maniac…even if he *had* established New Babylon as the capitol of his empire.

The Warlord Century had produced many would-be conquerors. Eventually the world's city-states were unified into the *Pax Apollonia*. Asia and Australia first, Europe and Africa next…woven through a dazzling series of military and diplomatic successes that laid the foundation of Earth Republic. America, hopelessly Balkanized by warfare and rogue miltias, had been the last region to join a unified world.

And they had only joined at all because of Enyalios.

He had unified the Americas, sure, though his approach had been different from his overseas counterparts. Emerging from the ruins of New York, the man had shot to prominence on a career of murder unlike anything history had ever seen. His armies swept from Alaska to Argentina, killing one hundred and fifty million people as he went. His rules were simple: join him or die. No diplomacy, no negotiations. If a city resisted, he burned it from the Earth.

Once the Americas were firmly under his control, everyone expected him to continue his crusade. Instead, he shocked the world when he signed the non-aggression treaty with Warlords Apollo and Lady Wen Ying. Enyalios spent his final years of life laying plans for great cities like New Babylon. He died in his sleep.

For Celeste, it was Enyalios who had been her first crush. It was Enyalios who would have saved her mother…or at the very least, would have wreaked such maniacal vengeance that no other little girl would have to endure something like that again. Historians of the time reported that the American Warlord's wildly insane temper was especially directed against those who victimized the innocent.

Celeste devoured the rest of her apple and chucked the core into a compost bin. She smeared the juices off her chin and considered her situation.

Jeff! Look where the fuck I am!

She fought her anguish, channeled it into cold rage. Out in the Wastes there were families dying of starvation, and here in just this little corner of Babylon Arcology was an obscene surplus of food: recreations of mythic Chinatown, Little Italy, Nathan's hotdog stands, gyros, pizzas, calzones, and shish kabobs in the shade of ziggurats and Akkadian bas reliefs. How much of this food went to waste…instead of to the Wastes?

StrikeDown needs *to succeed*, she thought bitterly. *Needs to teach these spoiled assholes what it's like to hunt and scavenge.*

In the meantime, *she* needed to succeed…and therefore, needed to eat. Celeste scanned the marketplace until she decided on a calamari gyro. Grabbing it from the rack, she fumbled for her arcology pass. A black-haired man suddenly cut her off in line.

"Allow me," he said, and purchased the sandwich for her with a tap of his fingertip on the payment pad.

Celeste regarded his green gaze. Handsome and audacious. "Are you the local do-gooder? Or just anxious to get laid?"

"No to the first question, yes to the second, but neither are relevant to you," Gethin said.

Celeste bit noisily into her gyro and studied him. "Too bad. I was looking forward to breaking in an arky. You wouldn't have cried too much."

"I'm an investigator with the IPC."

She stopped, mid-chew. Then she swallowed the bite, licking the crumbs off her lips. "Why the hell is the IPC interested in…" She swallowed the lump again. "In the missiles? I thought that was Republic jurisdiction."

"It can involve both," Gethin said, noting the flicker of her eyes. Jack had said people died in the Stillness raid. Gethin hadn't appreciated that 'died' in this case must have meant permadeath, brother to insensible rock and all that. "And there may be a connection to other attacks."

"What other attacks?"

"The shuttle explosion."

"Oh."

Gethin heard the disinterest. "I'm sorry," he said.

"About what?"

"Your loss. I understand you lost people out there."

Celeste took another bite of the gyro, saying nothing.

Gethin studied her for a moment. "There were two explosions on Luna. A research lab went first, and then a shuttle. It appears the shuttle wasn't the target, it was just in the way. But a mysterious energy burst fell to Earth and we have no idea what it was. Some think you might fill in the blanks."

Celeste watched him over her gyro. "These Lunars who were killed. They were all citizens, right? So they've been revived?"

"I was one of them."

She looked him over, from black tunic to sandals. "So if I broke your neck right now, in a few hours you'd be coming back down here to have your second lunch of the day?"

"It'd be my first lunch, as far as that goes. But yeah."

For a moment Celeste was tempted to ask how far regen technology had come. It was one of those angelic technologies guarded by arkies. One of the great prizes King D. was after, mentioned several times in his 'Give us Life' speech at the Philadelphius rally. It was also a polarizing technology among the Wastes. Stillness decried it as devilry, stealing people's souls and all that nonsense. StrikeDown wanted universal distribution, wanted to storm the diamond towers of Babylon and Memphis and Hartford, haul out the tech, and give Outlanders an equal chance at life and health.

Could it bring back her dead team members? They'd only been dead… what…ten hours? Wasn't there *something* of them that could be saved?

Before she realized it, her lips were moving. "Can you bring back my friends?"

"The ones who were killed?"

"Yes."

"It's been twelve hours. Brain structures break down within minutes. I would say no. Again, I'm sorry."

She nodded.

Gethin hesitated. "I'd like permission to see your memories of the attack."

"Officer Yamanaka didn't ask permission. I have no rights to refuse you."

"True. I'm just being courteous."

Celeste belched noisily. "Of course you can see what happened."

"It'll help catch the ones who did it."

"They're dead."

"The ones who hired them."

"Like that matters," she snapped. She peered around the market, spotting a few aug kiosks. "Do you sell wetware here?"

"Nothing you could buy with your credit line."

Celeste stuffed the last bit of gyro into her mouth. "Then buy it for me. Consider it a *courteous* payment for me allowing you to see inside my skull."

"What do you want?"

"An S-jack."

For a moment he was quiet. "Prometheus deactivated your sensorium?"

"Yes."

"Wasn't very nice of them. Sure, I'll get you an S-jack." Gethin started to say more when an incoming message flared in his eye.

Id spoke rapidly: ★**Your hydra just located a phone record matching the revised search parameters.**★

"Let me hear."

It was a sound file, snagged from the Vector Nanonics/Bell commgrid. An Athens-to-NoCal call lasting one minute, twelve seconds.

The audio played, and Gethin heard a man's voice speaking in a cool, measured cadence.

"We agreed you'd listen to me," the man said.

"Did I indicate I was changing my mind?" replied a second speaker.

"So what happened up there?"

"I got what I needed."

"You weren't subtle."

"Subtlety is your style, not mine. They're active again. I wanted to send a message."

"Things have changed, damnitall!" It was the first voice. The rise of emotion made Gethin think he knew it from somewhere. He thought of Greece. Gethin paused the recording, instructed Ego to run a patmatch, and then resumed the exchange.

The executive voice was still talking: *"There was an attack on the Hudson. People are watching things very closely. In this kind of environment, you have to exercise more caution. Do you understand?"*

Silence. But it was ghastly silence, like something under high pressure.

"Whatever you say."

"Please."

"Whatever you say," repeated the second voice, and the call ended.

Then came the real surprise. Ego flashed its success.

<Patmatch complete. The Athens caller is Doros Peisistratos of the University of Athens.>

Gethin's jaw dropped. *"What?"*

Celeste raised an eyebrow. "I didn't say anything."

Professor Peisistratos? Stunned by the revelation, Gethin asked for a patmatch on the NoCal voice. His heart beat anxiously, palms sweaty.

The Wastelander was staring at him with caution. "You okay?"

"Yes."

"Because you don't look okay."

Gethin sighed. "I think I just made a major break in the case." He grew pensive for a moment. Then he snapped his fingers. "Right. An S-jack. Tell you what, we'll go to the wetware shop together."

Celeste nodded, bewildered, when she saw Keiko Yamanaka's head rising up from the escalator behind him.

★   ★   ★

Keiko came over the crest of the escalator just as Gethin turned in her direction and saw her.

She recovered, but not swiftly and not all at once. Still trying to process what she was seeing – the Wastelander girl sitting with *Gethin Bryce* of all goddamn people! Her carefully ordered thoughts flew apart.

Stay. In. Control.

She pronounced the words inwardly, with such jagged elocution it was probably audible on the subvocal band. Which made her angry at the merest possibility that Gethin might hear it.

"Ms. Segarra," she called to the Wastelander. "We've completed our review of the Hudson attack. You have been cleared."

Celeste nodded. "Thanks."

"Hello, Keiko," Gethin said.

She met his gaze with calculated equanimity. "Gethin Bryce. You're the very last person I expected to see today. Are you acquainted with Ms. Segarra?"

"We are now."

Keiko's eyes were hard. "You expect me to believe that you just coincidentally showed up here—"

Jack came up behind her, interrupting gently. "He's been assigned to work with us."

"*What?*"

Gethin smiled broadly. "I'm not the Arcadium junkie you knew. I'm now the very best agent with the IPC."

The muscles in Keiko's jaw clenched. A charged curtain of silence fell between the group.

Celeste decided to break the silence. "You know, I've been remembering little details of the attack. The guy who suicided said something to me, right before the explosion."

Keiko forced herself to turn back to the Wastelander. "Yes. He said '*Plaga.*'"

"Yeah. What does that mean?"

"It's Latin," Keiko said, losing her severity in the face of this most peculiar oddity. "An entirely dead language that originated with the ancient Romans."

"What does it mean?"

"'Plague.' He was calling you a plague, right before he killed himself."

CHAPTER SIXTEEN
Progress Report

FROM: Yamanaka, Keiko ID 432-0667-B
TO: Corporate Security Division
CC: Fincher, Drake (Babylon;) Zhang, Wei (Beijing;) Patel, Padideh (Alexandria)

Illustrious Brothers and Sisters,

I submit this information for your review and study. I am boarding IPC Shuttle 997 bound for Athens to continue my investigation.

Per your instructions, Jack Saylor and I are cooperating with IPC investigator Gethin Bryce. His interview with Kenneth Cavor has stirred up startling discoveries (see *attached files*). Following his interview with Marco and Judith Merril, however, Bryce expressed concern that there is a correlation between the exotic matter cathode and the explosion. Saylor has provided him with Infosheet 12.

Regarding the Outlander Celeste Segarra: the possible correlation between the Hudson suicider and the Lunar explosion has intrigued Bryce, who deputized her as material witness to his investigation. He asked that we expand the parameters of her pass to include the Apollonian Ring; we complied with this request. He has also reactivated her sensorium despite our expressed objections.

(Sidebar note: The Wastelander's ship is still missing. We are coordinating a global search for the craft; it is my firm belief that even should it prove unconnected with these events, its AI is of a singularly unique, and most probably illegal, nature. Every effort should be made to acquire it. *Click here for ship specs.*)

The investigation has shifted to Athens per Bryce's direction. He is a former employee of the University and claims he needs to confer with its experts on the Base 59 footage. We will be monitoring him very closely.

The shuttle is launching now. My next report will come in four hours.

(Sidebar note: As you must know, Gethin Bryce is my ex-husband. My understanding of his abilities will greatly benefit Prometheus as I continue with my inquiry.)

In trust,
Keiko Yamanaka

PART TWO
ATHENS

We call it the Fall, and that's good enough.

It wasn't the first time in history that a great civilization had collapsed, though this time the tumbling blocks were radioactive, and billions died in crimson halos beneath phosphorescent sunsets. Nameless poets of those years recall the 'death-skies of a thousand colors', but the rain that fell was always black.

Everyone has a theory on which of the old nations precipitated the Fall. The womb-world of humanity shivered, thundered, and sent the Warlord Century down its slimy birth canal.

The Warlord Century! Such a neat name for an era which by all accounts lasted so much longer than a mere hundred years.

When the Three Warlords began their various campaigns, there was little to indicate that history was about to change forever. There is little evidence that they even knew each other prior to the foundation of the Republic. There is nothing in the records to suggest what their true names were, or why they chose the monikers that they did: Apollo, and Lady Wen Ying, and Enyalios the Mad.

Three conquerors. While their tactics differed, the result was the same: the adoption of a global treaty and a global constitution and a global government. After years of democratic experimentation from Pericles to the Plebian Revolt, the planet Earth finally had a single ruling body...

– Three Kingdoms, One World: The Foundation of Hope

CHAPTER SEVENTEEN
Jonas

There was an eleven-year-old corpse blinking at him from the mirror, blue eyes set in a ghoulishly pale face.

"Jonas!"

His mother Bahara's voice came from the hallway. Later in the day when she called his name, her voice would be soft and loving, but not in the morning. There was anxiety in her morning cry. She wanted to make sure he was awake. Alive. One day he wouldn't answer that morning checkup; hers would be the lone voice in the house, followed up by frantic footsteps, his bedroom door flying open, her scream as she discovered him dead.

Jonas Polat nodded to his reflection. The walking skeleton nodded back.

"Good morning, Mother," he squeaked into his breathing mask. His high-pitched voice didn't carry far, but his mask transmitted sound to the kitchen speakers. It was an unsightly contraption, black plastic attached like a mutant hagfish to his mouth, hanging down in a crocodilian snout from where a tube snaked to the spindly robot beside him.

The Polats lived in the forgotten caves of Derinkuyu, in Cappadocia, Turkey. There was a city above them but it was just for show: a town of empty buildings, deserted streets, and high walls patrolled by the Derinkuyu military, where the only other sign of life was in the open-air markets of organically grown fruits and vegetables. Even this aspect was as much for show as for nostalgia; the underdark dwellers had faced the challenge of food production centuries earlier, had applied themselves to the problem, and had solved it in a most ingenious way.

Jonas and the Folk (as they called themselves) happily dwelt in the belowground network of tunnels which dated back ten thousand years. From Stone Age tribes to the radioactive survivors of the Final War, a great many people had taken turns living in its netherworld. And while everyone in Derinkuyu would be deemed pale by topsider standards (even arkies had sun parlors to darken their skin) it was true that Jonas was paler than that, a deathly alabaster like the skin of some sickly deep-sea critter slowly dying, sinking into the polluted abyss, never to be seen or remembered.

Jonas turned away from the mirror. His robot, forever attuned to him, unfolded into his wheelchair, rolling him forward to the kitchen.

Bahara turned from the stove, offering a smile and kiss on the cheek. "Hello, sunshine."

He glanced at her outfit. "You're going topside?"

"I'm going to market. But for now, I have a special breakfast."

Jonas's voice came from both the muffling mask and the kitchen speakers: "In what way?"

She fetched the frying pan and showed him its contents.

The little boy smiled.

It was impossible to see his smile behind the breathing apparatus. Nonetheless, his eyes crinkled merrily.

"*Okonomiyaki!*" they said together, and laughed.

Bahara no longer cursed the gods that her son had been born only to die young. The disease that destroyed his lungs, turning the tissue pulpy and useless, was a lingering predator from another age. The weaponized residuals of yesteryear sometimes got into Derinkuyu's drafty corridors, and while filters caught most of them, some remained wily, designed to evade detection software. Bahara used to wonder who had designed it, and what they had expected the outcome would be. The nanoweapon had set like the iridium of ancient asteroid impacts into the clay of Derinkuyu; with the patience of centuries, it ate through the volcanic ejecta of the Folk's tunnels and then emerged, the goddamned year Jonas was born, into the air.

Adults were immune. This microscopic predator had been *designed to kill children.* Thirty babies in the local nursery became infected. Twenty-five of those were already dead. None was expected to survive past the earliest onset of puberty.

On his eighth birthday, Jonas had come up to Bahara and said, through a slightly smaller breathing mask, "Mother? We both know my life is a short tenure. I know this saddens you, but might we simply accept this fact? Pining over it every day cheapens the life that I *do* have."

She cried then, clutching him as tightly as she dared, and agreed...moved and frightened by his bizarre intelligence. Derinkuyu's library was extensive; while other mothers scurried to buy toys from the subterranean workshops of Plaza Square, Bahara made constant trips to Bibliotheca's book cove. Her little boy seemed to absorb books by osmosis. So brilliant. So terrifying....

He loved *okonomiyaki*, though. His passion for the savory Japanese pancake transformed him into a normal child for a time; she first made it for his sixth birthday, responding to his request that his meal be "something exotic, Mother." A web search, a few trips to the market, and some trial and error.

Jonas parked his wheelchair beside the table. "Why is today special, Mother?"

"It's your half birthday today. Didn't you know?"

"I didn't realize."

"People should celebrate half birthdays, don't you think?"

Detaching his mask, Jonas nodded thoughtfully. His lips were like gray raisins. "I think it is a good idea. Perhaps it will be like Zeno's paradox for us."

She laughed, not following him. But they ate their breakfast together until she had to go. She didn't worry much about Jonas alone; his robot was a simple AI, but it would alert her to any problem it saw, and would also contact Derinkuyu's on-call emergency staff. They were good people, and very fond of Jonas.

She watched him eat, dipping the bites of pancake into a rich ginger sauce. "I shouldn't be too long at the market."

"I wish I could go with you."

Bahara reached across the table and squeezed his hand. "You go many places more interesting than me."

Jonas shrugged. "The places I go aren't real."

"But they make you happy?"

"They do."

"Then they are real to you." Bahara sipped her coffee. Her boy's online gaming habits took up the majority of his day, when he wasn't reading. Cappadocia wasn't formally part of Earth Republic, yet neither was it a Wasteland, and it maintained a connection to the global web. Sometimes she watched him, his hands ensconced in haptic gloves and head encased in a VR rig. It bothered her, a little. Jonas had always been linked to machines; the umbilical cord was barely snipped when he was already hooked up to respirators and his medbot (eventually christened Maximilian, a name Jonas plucked from an antebellum flatfilm featuring an imposing automaton of the same name).

At least he got to see and interact with people across the world. Unfolding digital dramas, rising kingdoms and shifting politics. Did it matter that it was fake? Did anything matter, if her little boy could experience some kind of life beyond these subterranean corridors?

The Exile.

That was the name he had chosen for himself, and his online avatar was forever garbed in a spindly, insectile mask and bodysuit, like a steampunk interpretation of a medieval plague doctor.

Bahara waited patiently for him to finish his breakfast. Then she spirited the dirty dishes into the sink, gave him a kiss on the cheek, and headed topside through the gray, clayish corridors. The Turkish underdark was lit by bioluminescent lanterns. It was a thirty-minute ascent to the heavily guarded border station, where the sun was bright, the air crisp, and the air smelled of corn, tomato vines, squash, and fertilizer.

Bahara circled the labyrinth of fruits and vegetables to find an infonode. She touched its screen.

"What's Zeno's Paradox?" she asked.

"Named after the Greek philosopher Zeno of Elea, during the First Calendar, circa 490 BCE," the voice explained, "Zeno's Paradox states that to get anywhere at all, you must cross half the distance to get there."

"Okay..."

"But to get to the halfway point, you must cross half of that distance, and so on." Onscreen, an image appeared of a woman walking on an ever-dividing sidewalk. "Therefore, according to Zeno's conjecture, it is impossible to truly get anywhere…though clearly we do."

Bahara turned away from the infonode. The doctors all agreed on when Jonas would die. But if this Zeno fellow was right about space, couldn't he be right about time? Did the fateful day ever have to come?

★　　★　　★

Jonas fitted the VR rig over his face and head, and linked to the web. His newsfeed populated with a mix of top headlines and tailored preferences.

His rig, a handsome homegrown model, included wetports. But Jonas's fragility would never tolerate a sensorium. He did everything manually, fingers flying like hummingbirds across the keyboard. The world materialized in bite-sized portions.

The shuttle explosion on Luna was still global news. Actor Salvor Bear was dead, sans DC, and the outrage over that was fanatical; arkies were posting vitriolic diatribes against anyone and everyone. The Hollywood guild should have required Bear to get a neural backup, they insisted. How would his films be finished now? Would the guild allow a digital replacement in this case? And who was responsible for the incident? Someone had to pay for this travesty!

Jonas scrolled along the ribbon of other news, from worlds bright and deep. Consruction updates on the TNO project. Martian political unrest. Violence in the Belt. Vast new ice deposits discovered beneath the crust of Mercury and how the interplanetary market was responding to the news.

Buried at the bottom of the feed were the latest probe images beamed back from Ra System, and its most promising world: Osiris.

Jonas straightened in his chair, and 'stepped' onto the planet in virtual.

No further probes would be launched from Earth; IPC policy had come down like an iron portcullis on the practice. The probes that had already been launched were the last of their kind, then. Each a lonely traveler, fired into space during the Old Calendar era and tasked with investigating the local backyard of the cosmos. Older records of nearby systems had perished in the War. Hell, even the names of those stars and their worlds had vanished. It was now up to a dying handful of probes to provide the only glimpses of the universe that would be permitted.

But what glimpses!

The nearby Ra System alone contained four worlds deemed appropriate for colonization, and at least one of those – Osiris – contained indigenous life. The probecam's build unfolded around him.

Jonas was suddenly standing on a black shoreline hugging a blue sea. The sun was large and sapphire-bright in the sky. He turned and saw a bristling wall of peculiar trees…if 'tree' was the proper word. The vegetation looked knotted, gnarled, and unpleasant. Scientists were calling them fungal forests.

Jonas hit audio, and the press release played around him:

OSIRIS'S LIFE KEEPS GETTING STRANGER

Floating sea-flowers that open only at night. Armored burrowing creatures that carve out 'dry caves' in the ocean bed. Crystalline flowers that grow in the shadow of active volcanoes. Only in sci-fi has anyone seen imaginative wonders like these...until DARWIN-14 took up residence in Osiris's gravity-well and began its investigation into a world unlike any other...observing safely and without fear of contaminating the local ecosystem.

Jonas let the press release finish, and then he 'walked' to the ocean, gazing out at the odd plants that arose from the water itself. Osiris had a single ocean – wrapping like a blue serpent around the world's equator.

Would future colonists ever build villages on both sides of these shores?

He noted, too, the release's shrewd inclusion of the word 'contamination'. That was certainly a valid consideration. Maybe the most reasonable way of exploring the universe was this way, from afar and through reconstructed environments where no Terran disease could gain a foothold on alien beachheads.

But that altruistic consideration was not the reason behind the ban.

Jonas nodded grimly, squinting in the blue sunlight.

It was terror.

Pure, raw, terror.

Jonas had sat in virtual recreations of the day the law was passed in the IPC Congress, when Senator Bror Amerigo delivered the speech that influenced the decision.

"Mankind must move out to the stars? Why? Spare the comparisons to Earthly history and how Neolithic man migrated from shore to shore! Our ascent on this world is owed to bloodlust. We fitted flint to sticks and threw spears into beasts; we plucked out their tendons for bowstrings; we tore off their skins and tailored them for our bodies; we reshaped the land and tamed the planet.

"We won on this world. Through bloodlust.

"On alien worlds, others will have won. Through bloodlust.

"Shall we expose ourselves to these others? For what purpose? That they might be benevolent? Ah! Well, they might not! Who among us has the right to gamble the fate of our entire species on some sad dream of galactic brotherhood?

"But they can help us, you say! Sure! If that is their nature to help! If their own religion and politics is kin to help! If they have somehow learned to control the predatory instincts which surely propelled them to the top of their worlds! If they see us as more than an amoeba or virus or rat! If, if, if!

"And while you juggle your Ifs like a whimsical child, consider what we know. We don't need any help. War, hunger, imperialism, disease, death...we have solved these

problems on our own. What possible benefit could come from inviting others into the house that we managed to put back together?

"Oh, you say! They might be friendly, they might be playful, they might give us backstage passes to their concerts!

"I say they will be different, they will have risen to success through violence, they will possess their own values and beliefs. Should we gamble that such values include humanism? Humanism? Why should we go poking into alien caves and wake sleeping beasts? What if they follow the footprints of probes back here?

"Our age has recognized that blind impulsiveness has been the enemy, and that just because we can do something, we should ask what benefit will come of doing it. I say we leave the far shores alone, and I urge the rest of you to consider the wisdom in this necessary act of self-preservation for our entire species."

Jonas sighed, coughed in his mask, shrugged his tiny shoulders. Were the politicians right? Did they know more than they were letting on? Was it the universe that was truly hostile, or the terrestrial species that contemplated it?

For the hundredth time, he contemplated drafting a letter to the Republic. They'd never read it, of course. Even if he sent it to every news agency throughout Sol, the ramblings of an Outland child would be relegated to slush piles, consigned to digital fires. They had no reason to listen to his input…or to his own discoveries.

He didn't know if there were hostile species throughout the universe. Perhaps all that had evolved on other worlds were the alien analogs to flora and fauna, bacteria and prions. Perhaps there were no threats out there.

But there was a threat right here, on Earth.

How could he convince anyone that he had discovered a *real,* nonhuman intelligence lurking right in the digital backyard of cyberspace?

CHAPTER EIGHTEEN
Athenian Landing

Gethin gripped the armrest until his fingernails turned white as the transport dropped from the clouds and banked, beginning its descent to Athens. He strained against his seat belt and touched the cool window where his reflection appeared, the manifestation of a dead man returning from Hades to visit his favorite Earthly haunts. The dazzling lights of the Apollonian Ring came into view like a glittering scimitar on the black horizon.

Celeste's jaw dropped at the luminous view. "What the hell is that?"

"The Apollonian Ring," Gethin said, and seeing her expression, added, "It circles the entire Mediterranean Sea. Greece, western Turkey, Persia, Egypt, New Carthage, Spain, southern France, and Rome are each provinces in its oval concourse."

"You've been here before?"

"Yes."

They landed on a high airstrip and disembarked into a colonnaded shuttleport. Rain assailed the high glasstic ceiling, drawing oddly comforting patterns. Gethin breathed fragrant air into his nostrils, thinking of the last time he had been here.

Ten years ago. He had ordered a small lunch and three glasses of wine from the bar before hopping the space elevator for Mars.

"Luxury suites?" Jack asked doubtfully, when the hotel reservations arrived simultaneously to all their nanonics. "We're staying in the Poseidon *Luxury Suites*?"

Gethin shrugged. "Why not? IPC dime."

They followed the shuttleport concourse to the arcology by way of an enclosed skyway, and from there into a hilly, grassy landscape. Flowering trellises brought splashes of pink, purple, and red to the manicured wilderness.

A scantily clad Cassandra intercepted them, making straight for Jack. Before he could react, she had grabbed both of his hands.

"Hold fast," she purred. She was a lovely figure, and her tunica left little to the imagination. Her hair writhed like an upturned nest of vipers. "You've nothing to fear from me."

Jack frowned, staring down at her. "You try interfacing with me and your circuits will fry. Fair warning, sister."

The Cassandra laughed musically. "I have no intention of *hacking* you. Here." And she kissed him on the cheek.

When she pulled away, the others could see that her purple lipstick had left a faintly shimmering imprint on his cheek.

"I've just marked you," she said happily. "The Lupercalia Festival tomorrow. Find me...or I'll find you."

She melted into the crowd. Jack tried rubbing the lipstick off.

"Forget it," Keiko said scornfully. "It'll come off in a few hours."

"Welcome to Athens," Gethin added.

Once the shining citadel of western civilization in the age of Pericles, Athens was center stage again. The cornerstone of the Republic, life in all its painful glory: a kaleidoscope of orgy and learning, sex and study, consummate hedonism and intellectual pursuits.

Celeste rotated in place, taking the view in. "I have a question."

"Your arcology pass works here," Keiko said.

The Wastelander looked at her. "That wasn't my question. Why would the leader of a Stillness cell speak Latin to me?"

Gethin had been considering that. "Old Calendar religions spoke it. The Stillness ideology attempts to imitate ancient sermons."

"Is that what your arky dossiers say?" she countered. "Because I've actually interacted with Stillness, and those folks aren't exactly polyglots. They also shun all types of implanted tech, so they wouldn't have nanonic translators, either."

Jack shrugged. "Maybe it's as simple as baffling and dazzling their listeners. Word of the divine, that sort of thing."

"Even if that's true," Celeste protested, "why would he say it to *me*? He spat it in a fit of absolute rage. Why?"

Keiko exhaled sharply, anxious to get moving. "He was a fanatic. Who knows what he was thinking?"

They pressed deeper into the main arcology, falling into pairs by gender. A series of lifts lay ahead, granting quick, vertical access to the arcology's floors.

Jack plucked a fig from a roadside tree and chewed it. To Gethin, he said, "So about Apophis. I followed your advice."

"Did you?"

"A United States Army secretary leaves a voicemail to her commanding officer only seconds before the base is destroyed by a nuclear blast. The voicemail is just three words: 'It was Apophis.' She dies, along with a million other people, so the comment goes unexplained. Analysts figure she is being metaphorical, sort of like Robert Oppenheimer quoting the *Bhagavad-Gita.*"

Gethin was walking briskly now, energized by his surroundings. "The IPC has a copy of her voicemail. I've heard it. Her words were slurred—"

"Which made some people assume she was drunk," Jack said. "Drunk on duty."

"Right, except that theory has been discredited. To the untrained ear it might sound like intoxication. But analysts have concluded her speech was impaired from physical injury. As if she had been beaten half to death and managed to crawl to a phone."

The rest was one of history's unexplained events. A nuke went off on base. Suddenly a lot of panicked, conflicting commands go back and forth from Washington. Six nuclear bases make unauthorized launches against foreign targets; the commanding officers insist proper authorizations were received. Other nations retaliate, and suddenly the pent-up aggressions of a tense geopolitical arena lets loose all at once, corks popping, destruction flowing like pyroclastic eruptions. There's chatter about hackers, forged authorization keys. Global communications collapse and an age of history ends. Years later, efforts to investigate the mystery turn up only cold trails and contradictory clues.

And a name: Apophis.

"'It was Apophis,'" Jack repeated thoughtfully. "You threw that name at Cavor. Why?"

"It's an anomaly. I threw a lot of things at him, but that one got a reaction. Seemed more appropriate than asking about alien cities on Mars."

Jack blinked. "What?"

"Never mind."

The giant sector chief gave him a perplexed look. "Uh…okay. We couldn't find anything on that second case you mentioned. You said Apophis had something to do with the march of Enyalios against a militia army."

Gethin gave him a sidelong gaze. "Couldn't find anything? Really?"

"Really."

Of course they *had* found something, Jack thought uneasily. Promethean hackers had pilfered the data from an IPC database two hours ago. No need for Gethin or his employers to know about that. Jack was starting to realize how crafty Gethin was. He had received a full report from Victor Slotkin, who came right out and proclaimed: "The guy you're dealing with is *dangerous*, Jack. Watch yourself."

Gethin breathed easily in the jasmine- and olive-scented air. "Rewind the clock three hundred-and-fifty years. Enyalios is about to complete his conquest of North America. On the eve of invasion, he turns to one of his generals and says, 'Apophis dies today.'"

"Apophis." Jack shook his head.

Celeste caught Gethin's arm and whirled him around. "*Who* is Apophis? What does all that mean?"

"Don't know. There are lots of possibilities."

"Enlighten me."

Gethin stopped on a curbside, letting the Athenian pedestrians flow past. "Well, Apophis was an Egyptian god representing chaos and darkness…"

Celeste gave a bitter, hateful laugh. "So maybe an Egyptian god killed you, Gethin! Maybe all we need is to find the Feather of Truth, weigh it against your deeds, and summon Ra in a flaming chariot to vanquish the Devourer."

Gethin gave her a curious look. "Impressive."

"The Wastes still have books."

As she was growing up with Mom behind the barricades, books were one of the few luxuries afforded to a child who had grown amid a measure of protection. Gigantic hardback books that smelled of mildew. Books with bright illustrations. Celeste still remembered the name of her favorite series: *World Myths for Children*. The copyright page listed the publisher on Lexington Avenue in New York; an astonishing thought, really, because the only Lexington she knew was a river, though people believed that ancient buildings lay below its watery depths.

A teardrop black taxi pulled alongside them. The window opened, a young man motioned. "Poseidon Suites?"

"Just a moment," Gethin told him. He turned to the others. "It's a little late to start our investigation. How about we freshen up at the hotel, get some dinner, and begin fresh tomorrow? Say around 0700?"

Keiko scowled. "Dinner?"

"Coming back from the dead works up the appetite."

"So does sneaking off to conduct your own inquiry," Jack added, and Keiko nodded in agreement.

"No sneaking. Dinner at Leda's. The four of us."

"Leda's?" Keiko said skeptically. "Why there?"

Gethin laughed. "Why not? Best restaurant in Athens. We're going to be working together, we might as well break the ice. Maybe catch up on old times."

Keiko shook her head. "No. But feel free to comb through my public file, Gethin. I'll even send you the link."

"I've already seen it. Time has been good to you. Prometheus should count itself lucky. So why not come to dinner?"

"Because Jack and I don't trust you. And I'm not buying this nostalgia act from you. It's not your style."

Gethin nodded. "Is it distrust? Or fear of being reminded that you had a life before Prometheus got its claws into you?"

She turned on him with controlled anger. "If you feel there is unfinished business between us, then I pity you. Life now is *precisely* what I want, not galavanting through online fictions like two children pretending they rule the world."

Gethin turned to Jack. "What's it like to work with a living powder keg? Say the wrong thing and she explodes."

"I'm not exploding. I'm explaining that—"

"That our marriage never happened? That you were never an Athenian citizen? That together with good friends we ruled Arcadia?"

"A fictional playground!"

"Doesn't mean a part of you doesn't miss it."

"I miss *nothing* about those days. I know exactly who I am—"

"A cultist," he snapped. "Victim of the biggest cult in history."

Keiko exploded.

It lasted a half second, and no one but Gethin saw. Her incredible rage flashed incandescently in her eyes, only to be captured and wrangled with a steely control Gethin had never witnessed from her before. *So!* he thought. *Prometheus has taught her to delay her anger, to shape it like clay, to utilize it in other ways.* He had read about the behavorial philosophies they implemented with their workforce, customized to harness strengths and reprogram weaknesses. They knew their employee base down to the dendrite.

"Thanks for the personality assessment," Keiko said. "But Jack and I will dine alone." She glanced towards Celeste. "Outlanders marry for life, right? Tough break." She opened the taxi door and slipped in, followed by Jack. The vehicle turned onto a narrow road and sped off.

Celeste shook her head. "You have a real way with people."

"It worked."

"What did?"

"We're alone."

Celeste looked sidelong at him. "So…we're *not* going to dinner?"

He scratched his head. "Not hungry. Actually I need to break into someone's room, and was hoping you would accompany me. Yes?"

CHAPTER NINETEEN
Goblins and Things Not Human

They found room 334 in the apartment cluster of the arcology's Hermes wing, in full view of towering rows of windows and balconies. Hardly a private locale for a break-in, and Celeste was tense as they approached the door's companel. It was evening, and the arcology walls had dimmed to their nightly shade, but it was not a true darkness, and plenty of citizens were visible on their balconies, sipping wine and watching the world below.

The door's companel displayed a soft blue readout: Michael Disch.

"A friend of yours?" Celeste inquired.

"Sort of."

"I take it he's not expecting you."

"I haven't seen him in ten years."

Gethin touched the companel. It took his Id six seconds to crack the code, and the door slid open with a gentle hum.

They entered softly, footsteps masked on dark blue carpet.

<This apartment is empty,> Ego reported. <There are six rooms.>

Gethin crept to the living area. While most apartments differed wildly in décor, they were built on the same design: bedroom, bathroom, kitchen, office, closet, and living room. Not so with Disch's abode. There wasn't a scrap of furniture in sight, and the 'kitchen' was a junkpile of empty food cartons. Gethin peeked into the bedroom…where there was no bed.

Instead, a pilotchair and five-terminal display dominated the narrow alcove.

Celeste peeked over his shoulder. "Does he hang from the ceiling when he sleeps?"

Gethin shook his head. "Professor Disch was always an odd one. I never realized he was a sleep-depper too." He sat in the soft pilotchair. The screen prompted for a login.

"That's one thing you definitely are not," Celeste said. "On the shuttle over here, you were out in seconds. Slept like the dead."

He bristled at the comment. She was already inspecting another part of the apartment; clearly her remark was just off-hand observation. But she was right. Gethin remembered lying back in his shuttle seat and falling into sleep as if he'd been deactivated. The first real sleep of his new body.

No dreams.

How could that be? With the spiderweb of rebuilt synapses and dendrites, my skull's interior should be a tornadic storm, wild flashing signals, anxieties shoving old memories or new fears into amorphous dream symbols. But there had been nothing. For the second time, Gethin worried that he was not a real person anymore, that the Digital Capture technology didn't resurrect people at all but just simulated them.

He sighed and stared at the login screen.

There was no keyboard. Virtuboards had replaced them, which meant zooming in on wear and tear to deduce passwords was useless. Not an impossible task, but nothing to hedge bets on, either.

Gethin abandoned the chair to see Celeste pacing slowly through the living room, peering at scattered magazines. Fringe, crackpot publications: *The Frontierist, Fortean Kingdom*, and *Discordia*.

Celeste tucked her hair behind her ears. "This guy is a professor? Of what?"

"AI systems. He could program base intelligences in his sleep."

"Except he doesn't sleep."

"Right."

"What if he catches us here?"

"I'm counting on it. I'm trying to—"

"Gethin!" Celeste cried.

He spun around, in time to see that a tiny humanoid figure was now standing on the carpet. It was blue-skinned, rubbery, about twelve inches tall. The bulblike head sported two empty eye sockets, a tiny bump for a nose, and an impossibly wide grin. The tiny arms waved about playfully as it scampered towards them.

Celeste pulled back her foot to kick the thing.

"It's just a goblin," Gethin said at last.

She blinked. "A glop of some sort?"

"A rapid-processor joke." The critter ran to Gethin with palpable joy and hugged his ankle. Then it craned its neck, inviting him to pick it up.

Celeste felt an inexplicable revulsion towards the little blue being. "Is it a... robot?"

Gethin lifted the thing in grotesque parody of cradling a baby. "Not precisely. Some pranksters figured out a long time ago how to hack rapid-processors. People started getting flooded by giant penises. Eventually, programmers learned to create functioning power systems that draw modest energy from...hey!"

He nearly dropped the goblin when he saw that it had defecated a small lump of blue matter onto his shirt.

"Son of a bitch!" Gethin exclaimed. Another lump popped out from its rear, rolled down Gethin's top and onto his pants. The flex-gel wasn't wet, but had the consistency of warm clay.

He threw it away from him, where it bounced gently, stood up, and tottered towards him, shitting out its innards as it came, until the head sunk down into the hollowed-out interior. Unable to see him, the mockery scurried past his shoe; Gethin nodded to Celeste, and she kicked it into the wall. There it splattered, still grinning clownishly.

"*He* was the one!" Gethin exclaimed, his eyes like green fire. "After all these years, it was him! I don't believe it!"

Celeste felt her head spinning. She was filled with renewed disgust at arky society. *This* was how these people played. With fetal Pinocchios boasting an excretory system!

<Michael Disch is approaching the apartment,> Ego advised.

"Good!" Gethin growled. He grabbed Celeste's wrist and drew her into the kitchen as the apartment door flung open, and Michael Disch hurried in. He was on his way to the pilotchair when Gethin stepped out from concealment.

"Michael?"

Disch froze, turned. He was more than six feet tall, and at least four hundred pounds. Most people opted for muscle density enzymes to keep themselves fit, but not Disch. He was a quivering boulder of flesh. His eyes bulged in outrage.

"Who the hell are you?"

"Your memory files degrading?"

"Professor Bryce?" He gathered himself. "I didn't realize you were back in town. Mars, wasn't it? Nor did I realize you're a criminal. I'm recording all this right now. I never invited you over. I doubt very much you have an explanation for intruding here. Who is she? What the hell are you doing here?"

Gethin looked sidelong at him as he made an oblique approach. "When we were at university together, a bunch of goblins flooded the administrative offices and left pounds of gel-shit everywhere they went. No one figured out who sent it. The damned things showed up every few months, despite our security programs." He stopped a few inches in front of Disch. "*You* were doing it."

Disch swallowed, his flabby throat quivering like the folds of a frog. "I'm not recording anymore."

Gethin stared at him for signs of sanity. "That was a costly joke, Mike."

"You still broke into my apartment. And who the hell is *she*?"

"I'm not here about the goblins," Gethin said, still astonished. "If I was, I'd be sure to send your ass to the Redemption Board."

Disch paled so quickly that Gethin was alarmed; he wondered if the man was going into clinical shock. The threat had been a bluff. Disch could certainly be arrested for his ridiculous sabotage, but no one had ever *died* from the goblin attacks. A Redemption wouldn't apply.

Or would it? What *else* had this lunatic done?

"Hey!" Gethin snapped his fingers loudly. "Listen to me. I'm here to look into the private habits of an old colleague of ours. I was going to *ask* for your help, but now...I don't need to, do I?"

A splash of color formed on Disch's marshmallow cheeks. It had the effect of making him look like a clown. He regarded Celeste once again, visibly disconcerted by her presence. Was it her gender? Or the fact that he couldn't patmatch her to any known database? Or both?

Disch swallowed hard. "We square after this, Bryce?"

"Sure."

"You won't report this?"

"Unless your damned imps kill someone, I'll forget about it."

Disch nodded vigorously. "What colleague? Why are we looking up a colleague? Why don't *you* look up the colleague? Who is it?"

"Professor Doros Peisistratos. And I'm not an active faculty member anymore. Somehow, *you* still are."

A minute later they were all crowded around the five-panel monitor array. To Gethin's astonishment, Disch simply called up a lengthy file on the professor.

"I like to know my universe," Disch said absently.

Gethin shook his head. He decided to report Disch anyway when they were done. The world would be a safer place.

"What do you need to know?"

"Everything."

All five monitors filled with the life story of Doros Peisistratos. Abbreviated, crammed full of links, with videos and images.

To Celeste, it was like reading a fable as unreal as any of those mildewy mythology books in her childhood attic. Here was the tale of a Greek boy born in Athens three hundred and twelve years ago, when the first arcologies were nearing completion and Republic peacekeeping forces had cleared flight paths and trade routes to and from civilization. Fresh out of college, while his fellow graduates were indulging in the new tradition of making a Grand Tour along the Apollonian Ring, Doros got into politics. Not satisfied with regional posts, he campaigned to be Republic Senator of Athens Arcology.

He ran a populist campaign full of bright-eyed optimism. Even a skeptical press remarked on his natural charisma and savvy networking among constituencies, and when he won, the post-election analysts remarked that it had been about timing as much as glad-handing. Young and idealistic, Doros Peisistratos seemed to reflect a young and idealistic new era. Governments of the past had belonged to old men with old notions. A nascent country could only benefit from young blood and radical ideas.

Like when he proposed the Outland Charter Deal.

The Outlands, the Wastes, the dogtowns, the gloplands…these were regions so thoroughly ruined or contaminated, so rife with violence, that they had been rejected by the Republic. There were many facets to the New Enlightenment – celebrations of rational discourse, artistic expression, scientific advancement – but that zeitgeist also lay steeped in separatism. Let the Wastes remain the Wastes. Civilization would be reborn on a smaller, more manageable scale than the 'global village' model of failed, bygone nation-states.

Senator Peisistratos's Outland Charter Deal was a kind of blasphemy, then. It proposed allowing Wastetowns to apply for admission into the Republic. "We are a humanistic civilization!" he declared in the halls of the Senate. "The arcology is not the end point of our goal. The world is still shattered, and therefore we are all shattered until we have an Earth Republic deserving of the name."

His strategy targeted corporations first, pointing to the ready-made workforce from Outland incorporation. Then he hit the public with appeals to their cherished humanistic principles: images of Outland suffering played continuously in the strongest voting districts. In the end, his political opposition scrambled to attach their own names to the Deal, desperate to outdo each other's philanthropy when they realized that Doros had won the propaganda game. Only the most rigid senators held out, and most of these were gone by the next election. In fact, the ousted senators were replaced by frontierists, which led some to speculate this had been Doros's grand objective to begin with.

And then, with such a glorious career in politics cemented, he promptly left.

He became a paleontologist.

Doros went deep into the Outlands and funded strange new digs. He published papers and skyrocketed to celebrity status in a new field. When his book, *Troodon: The First City-Builders*, was published it became the first interplanetary bestseller, the colonies on Luna and Mars having just been settled. Gethin had read it himself, delighted by the premise that the first stirrings of terrestrial civilization hadn't been in Mesopotamia as once thought, but in the twilight of the Cretaceous Era seventy million years previous. The book became too popular for its own good; fantasy serials were produced, blowing the original findings so far out of proportion that it was tough now to separate the original work from its legend.

And at the height of this hoopla? He vanished again.

This time it was to get married and utterly disappear from public view for two centuries, until he reemerged as a University of Athens professor. No fanfare this time, his thirst for fame dulled at last into a low-profile, quiet life in academia.

Disch chewed his lower lip as he read the file. "The professor doesn't like to stay in one place for long, that's for damn sure."

Celeste couldn't stop staring at Doros's age. Three *hundred* years of life! King D. was right; the human race was no longer homogenous. The Earth was inhabited by two human species now. Castor and Pollux on a genetic level.

As for the Outland Charter Deal, she felt a special bitterness in the back of her throat. Even assuming this Peisistratos fellow had meant well – an assumption Celeste was never keen on making about anyone – the legislation had been toothless in practice. The three-step integration process sounded perfectly acceptable to an arky, sure. The problem was that each step could take *twenty years*, and a single episode of violence in a chartered town was enough to reset the whole process. Wastetowns were being jerked around by a fake carrot, and Celeste felt her blood go hot. *The arkies treat us like dogs*, she thought savagely.

StrikeDown!

StrikeDown!

Her lips moved to form the words.

"I want you to look at this," Gethin told Disch, and he shared his recording of Peisistratos's peculiar phone conversation. "I need to know who he was speaking with."

Disch ran the conversation through a filter. "It's Doros," he confirmed. "Can't say more than that, and I have no clue who the other fellow is. Who is he? Why do you care about this? Are we done here?"

Gethin hesitated. "One more thing. I'd like your opinion on this." And he transmitted a copy of Celeste's memories of the Hudson attack.

"Holy Zeus!" Disch shouted. "*Look* at that energy release!" He replayed it several times. "Acceleration is probably from a blurmod, but there's dissolution of his shape! And there's no actual dispersal of matter. Could be a codeworm… except no, the pattern of movement along air viscosity is predictable, and it doesn't match this. It doesn't match it at all!" He had gone pale again.

Gethin and Celeste regarded each other.

"Okay," Disch said finally, looking so sweaty and exhausted that Gethin thought: heart attack. The guy's insurance premiums must be staggering. "Okay, listen. First of all, that guy moved with an acceleration that's not possible. He was actually phasing there into plasma. That's *not possible*."

"A blurmod," Gethin protested.

"No blurmod can move a person that fast. Their organs would be pulped. They'd catch fire."

"Okay…"

"And then there's the problem with the explosion."

"What problem?"

"It's *not* an explosive device. He didn't erupt from the inside out. He converted to an energy release."

"He suicide-bombed," Celeste insisted.

"No! Didn't I just tell you it wasn't an explosion? Damnitall! Listen, okay? His body *converted to energy!*" Disch pulled the image into a 3D holo and set it floating above them; the rainbow wash of colors sparkling in their eyes as they gazed up at it. It was from Celeste's viewpoint of the Stillness High Priest being shot to pieces, his flesh disintegrating under multigun fire while his searchlight eyes burned like hellish portals. "I'm telling you, this is matter-energy conversion done on the fly."

Gethin felt the stirring of ancient, primal dread. He remembered the video of the shuttle's explosion. Remembered Kenneth Cavor charred to a crisp in Tycho Hospital.

"So," Gethin started. "You're saying that someone out there has developed the technology to switch matter into energy in a way that maintains a stable pattern of sentience?"

"I'm not saying that at all." The man looked at Celeste in unabashed terror. "That guy who attacked you? He wasn't a human being. No way, no how. That *thing* is something else entirely."

CHAPTER TWENTY
Deliberations

They were quiet as they left Disch's apartment.

"How do you know he won't tell other people about this?" Celeste asked.

"I made him sign a federal NDA. If he breaks that, the IPC will intervene in Michael Disch's life."

"Doesn't sound so scary."

"They'll erase him."

"Oh."

Walking the corridor, Gethin realized he couldn't stop shivering. His limbs felt steeped in ice and his body seemed to be jumping, quietly, in a hundred different places.

As they entered the Triton wing, Celeste finally said, "Your friend is wrong. That guy must have been a Stillness High Priest. They're the only rank in that goddamn cult that willingly utilizes biomodifications."

Gethin said nothing. At the end of the corridor hung a painting of the Garden of the Hesperides: gods and goddesses frolicking among the heath, drinking wine and just beginning to take notice of a golden apple in the grass. As Gethin came within range of it, his own face was swiftly incorporated into the divine mix; Celeste, too, had her countenance captured and mirrored.

The Wastelander stuck her tongue out at the painting; her onscreen image followed suit.

"How well do you know this Doros guy?" she asked.

"We used to work together."

"Do you think he's working with terrorists?"

"Not a chance in hell."

Celeste grimaced. "So far I'm not bowled over by the sanity of Athens University faculty, Gethin."

"Peisistratos is no anarchist. He would never support their ideology."

But Celeste was unconvinced. "How can you truly grasp the depths of a three-hundred-year-old guy?"

He chewed this over. "Fair point. But those three hundred years also establish a pattern of rationality, and Disch confirmed there doesn't seem to be anything unusual about his habits, travels, or the company he keeps."

"People are good at hiding things." She looked searchingly at him. "Are you okay?"

"I'm tired."

But he wasn't. At all. Gethin felt hyperactive, and he secretly tapped his virtuboard to order a sleep inducer from the local pharmacy.

"So what happens now?" Celeste asked.

"I'm going to see Peisistratos tomorrow."

"For what purpose?"

"Find out how he's involved," Gethin said. "That phone call suggests conspiracy of a sort. He...um—"

His chest exploded in sudden pain before he could utter his next words. He choked on his own spit, sucking in a panicked breath. The goblin appeared in his memory, grinning like a jack-o'-lantern.

Celeste was suddenly at his side, bracing him by the arms. "Bryce!"

She held him upright, used his own hand to palm open his hotel room. Then she steered him over to the bed and peered concernedly into his face.

"Should I call a doctor?"

"I just need rest," he managed.

"Did Disch poison you?"

Gethin laughed. "Not possible. When you see the others tomorrow, tell them I had to stop at the University. Let them know that I'll share all my information with them when I return."

"Yamanaka will be pissed."

He tried to shrug. "No different...than any other...day."

With evident reluctance, Celeste left him there. The sleep-inducer arrived twenty minutes later by deliverybot. Gethin's hands were shaking so much he could barely lift the hyposonic syringe to his neck and squeeze the release button. He dropped it to the carpet.

And once again, he had no dreams.

CHAPTER TWENTY-ONE
Thunderheads

Keiko Yamanaka liked to run in the dim hours of morning.

She pushed herself down the Athenian jogging routes with her hair clinging to her sweaty face and neck, a bio-readout displaying itself in small yellow print on her optics. Every morning in Babylon she went running. In space, regular exercise was required to maintain muscles and bone density, unless you wanted to spend a fortune on nanite infusions. You got used to pacing yourself in rotational gravity. It changed your perspective, retrained your mind. You started thinking like a spacer, a Belter, maybe even an Ashoka.

The hour of 0500 was dark; Poseidon Luxury guests were asleep, and she had seen only two other joggers on the path. Grudgingly, she admitted these Athenian trails were the most beautiful she had ever seen. Marble statues stood in little groves. The arcology ceiling displayed overcast clouds, reflecting the real-time weather outside.

With each step, she imagined she was pounding the face of Gethin Bryce.

He played *me*, she thought acidly. It hadn't struck her until late last night, when she realized Gethin wasn't following them to the hotel. He and the Wastelander went missing for more than two hours. In Babylon, she'd have been able to track and trace him, but this was out of her jurisdiction and there was nothing to do but wait for him to return. Keiko promised herself to never let him one-up her in this investigation again. She'd stick to him like a shadow.

She still couldn't believe he was here. *Gethin Bryce! And working for the IPC again? Of all goddamn factions?*

She had met him in Arcadia before meeting in person. He had been young, sharp, and ambitious; she sensed in him a kindred spirit, a person who wanted to make a difference in the human universe, who could reshape that universe through sheer force of personality. And when Gethin began stitching together a core group of collaborators – uniting the best and brightest in the global web – he really *did* change the face of Arcadia.

Keiko figured he was bound for a political career. Maybe even the next IPC president. She proposed to him. He accepted.

And then, together, they became addicts.

Arcadia had a way of doing that, especially for the naturally competitive. Plug into VR rigs or wetports, and vanish into seductive fictions. Pause only when your alarm chimes for meals.

One night (or day, she couldn't remember now and those years seemed to melt time away like in a Dali painting) Keiko had disengaged from a game, needing to use the bathroom. You didn't have to disengage; Arcadia could wrap itself onto the contours of your own environment, with chaperone boundaries so you didn't collide with walls or walk off your balcony.

But Keiko had actually unplugged.

She still remembered what she saw, as if with newborn eyes. The bedroom like a junkyard...clothes, boxes, fucking *garbage* everywhere she looked (the cleanbot was damaged and she and Gethin had been so occupied with Arcadian events that they hadn't so much as sent an email for the thing to be repaired. Not even an email.) The place smelled bad too.

Gethin was plugged into the wetport beside her. His eyes were open, glazed, blank...his optic nerves being fed straight from the web. He looked cadaverous, oddly sallow, like old papyrus. Skinny to the point of being famished; technically they were eating enough to keep alive, but his body appeared skeletal. Drool hung from the corner of his mouth. And his unseeing eyes horrified her...as if she'd been sharing a bed with a corpse.

Keiko had fled to the bathroom. Hands shaking, she bathed, dressed, and went outside. Just to see the *real* gardens of Athens again. Real places with real people. She walked for hours until her feet were aching; she required a PDT to get back home.

And Gethin was still there. Hadn't moved an inch. Like a human-shaped tumor growing against the bed.

Keiko had killed the room's power then. She remembered her husband blinking languidly, looking around in confusion. His lost, dreamy expression was somehow the most terrifying thing of all, as if he was thinking, *Is this still part of the game? Am I still playing?*

Keiko shuddered.

After that, they both began to distance themselves from Arcadia. Pursued real-world jobs – him with the local university, and her with Prometheus Industries. She hadn't really expected anything to come of her application, and was stunned when they invited her to an interview...*in person*, at the regional headquarters. Stunned more when they hired her.

She and Gethin mutually agreed to terminate their marriage contract. And she had never looked back. Eight years of marriage by the final reckoning. Good and bad times, and all of it, happily, *in the past.*

Keiko jogged to a water fountain and bent to sate her thirst. An alabaster statue of Zeus stood nearby, smiling lasciviously at her, gripping a crooked lightning bolt.

A thought entered her head:

What if Prometheus selected me for this mission because of Gethin?

It had been Lenny, after all, who tipped her off to the Base 59 footage. The shuttle explosion was old news when he found it. Lenny was a good friend; they'd served together on Ceres. He also knew her reputation as a corporate rising star. Tipping her off made good political sense. An investment in his own career.

Still…

Lenny must surely know other well-connected people. Company loyalty came with a cutthroat edge. Unless he was planning far ahead, Lenny could almost certainly get a faster reward by sending that footage to others.

The Higher Ups must have stepped in.

Keiko jogged in place, mulling that over. Prometheus must have known Gethin Bryce was going to be assigned. They would have seen his name on the passenger manifest. A quick data mine would link him with her. Analysts would crunch the profiles. Maybe Lenny sent the base footage to others, and corporate brass stepped in, told him to pull her into the loop. Another hound in the hunt, designed to counter the IPC's dog.

Good.

I am a sister in the great family, Keiko thought. I am to investigate the Lunar incident and counter Gethin Bryce. Because this isn't Arcadia anymore. In the real world, he is working for the great oppressor. The overprotective parent of Homo Sapiens. Someone had to challenge them eventually, to break up their hegemony and send humanity to the stars.

War was inevitable.

Keiko smiled up at Zeus. She retied a shoe, stretched, and continued her run.

The call from Fincher arrived a few minutes later.

"Keiko, are you awake?"

"Of course," she snapped, pulling a strand of hair from her face and tucking it behind her ear. "What is it?"

"One of our Pacific bases has been hit."

Keiko listened first with horror, then with escalating rage, as Fincher related the destruction of a Promethean offshore facility. There was no way to keep the incident secret; a flurry of deceased employee purchase signals were already being received by local regen centers.

"That's not all," Fincher said. He was on audio only, but she could hear the strain in his voice and pictured him making rapid paces in his office like a worker bee stressing its figure-eight pantomime. "The Sol has run a front-page editorial on us."

Keiko was still running. At this news, she entered another grove and propped one foot on a bench.

"Before or after the Pacific attack?"

"The dateline is two hours before. Shall I upload the file?"

"Go ahead."

The Sol
Lunar Accident Stemmed From Illegal Promethean Experiment?
By Nathaniel L. Moore

The 'accident' on Luna resulted from experiments with unstable and exotic energy, according to an anonymous memo leaked from a Prometheus Industries network Earthside.

The memo purports to be a classified briefing on lunar experiments with a state of matter known as 'negative-mass.' Such unstable material has been theoretical; however, sources confirm that Prometheus Industries has been researching its feasibility for use in the Trans-Neptunian Outpost. Base 59, the research lab which exploded under mysterious circumstances two days ago, is specifically mentioned in the memo as the major testing site.

Eleven other "testing sites" are also referenced, though not by name or location.

The Base 59 explosion has been confirmed as the cause of Flight 3107's destruction. The incident claimed 216 lives, including the permadeath of superstar actor Salvor Bear.

The TNO contract, already a hot political subject, is known to involve exotic matter and antimatter.

"The potential risks of this technology currently outweigh any theoretical gains," said Dr. Jethro Wells, a researcher with the independent think-tank Crawlspace. While declining to comment on the Base 59 explosion, Wells added, "Energy experiments that the TNO requires are by their very nature volatile and unpredictable. You don't want to be sensationalist when you talk about these things, but in this case I think people don't understand what's at risk here. If it's confirmed these experiments have been taking place in Earth's vicinity, the IPC has to shut it down."

According to IPC legislation, all TNO energy experiments are strictly limited to the outer region of the solar system.

PI spokesman Drake Fincher denied that any unsanctioned experiments are occurring in Earth's vicinity.

★   ★   ★

Keiko clenched her teeth. *The Sol* was in the pocket of TowerTech, Inc. A fucking Ronald Gates property.

The opening shots of war had begun.

"Was there any such memo, Drake?"

"No."

"They knew about the negative-mass experiments."

"The negative-mass *virtual testing*," Drake emphasized. "And there are ways for our enemies to get that info."

Keiko took her foot off the bench. She glanced at the statue in this grove, half-expecting it to be the God of War. Instead, the cloven-footed ram-horned god Pan smiled impishly at her, pipes cradled in his wanton embrace.

Fincher gave a reluctant sigh and seemed to halt in his pacing. "There's one more thing. Security has just learned something. We classified it instantly. As part of the investigation team, you and Saylor are cleared to know it. Moreover, you *need* to know it." He took a breath. "Okay. It has to do with Kenneth Cavor…"

CHAPTER TWENTY-TWO
Old Friends

"Are you experiencing dizziness?" the voice asked him.

Gethin looked away from the racing blur outside the express maglev window. The 0529 train was sparsely populated. He sat alone in his boxcar, knowing he was beating the commuter rush by an hour. His hair was still wet from the shower.

"No dizziness," he told the medprogram counselor.

"Fixations or obsessive thinking?"

"Story of my life," Gethin muttered, glancing again to the rushing landscape; a tract of lemon trees appeared like a solar flare and was gone. "Yes, a little bit."

"How long did your shivering last?"

"A half hour, before I went to sleep."

"Have you been experiencing hypervigilance or paranoia?"

"Not more than ordinary."

The counselor was a middle-grade AI which sounded like an affable male physician. It wasn't allowed to make formal diagnoses but could provide general preliminary assessments. "Are you experiencing obsessive thoughts about your death?"

"Not really."

"Are you sure?"

Gethin sighed. "Well, maybe a little."

"Are you at all worried that you aren't really alive since your regeneration?"

Gethin frowned, realizing the questions were becoming more relevant to his situation, as if a diagnosis was gestating at light speed. "Yes." He suddenly blinked, trying to see the end of the inquiry. "Do you think I'm fraying?"

"This is only a consultation," the AI advised. "It is impossible to form a diagnosis. You may want to follow up with your primary care physician. I advise that you try relaxing for the next few days."

Gethin dropped the link. Fraying afflicted less than one percent of regenerated citizens. The reconstituted neural complexity folded in on itself, collapsing into a frenzied self-destructive feedback loop. It was birthed from a tiny defect that snowballed into cataclysmic paranoid breakdowns. Afflicted persons had been known to throw themselves off buildings, set themselves on fire, go on murderous killing sprees, and in one gruesome case from Copenhagen…fatal self-cannibalism.

A stress disorder was preferable, by comparison. Most people got the shakes from time to time.

At the next stop, Gethin emerged from the maglev and saw the towering façade of the University of Athens museum annex. Scarlet banners hung from its illustrious frieze. The stairs were as long as he remembered them.

He wondered how many of his old colleagues still worked there. Liz at the reception desk? Yuen in the restoration vaults?

Cool blue lights flashed in Gethin's sensorium. A new email icon swirled and he tapped it open.

TO: Gethin Bryce
FROM: Natalia Argos
DATE/TIME: 07/19/702, 0223 MT
SUBJECT: You are forgiven.

The message field was blank. Gethin shivered again, caught in a sadistic symphony of gravitational and emotional forces that, crazily, felt like they were trying to draw and quarter him. He remembered that he still had an unread message from his ex-wife Lori. Remembered that he hadn't contacted his father on Ceres or his mother in London. That he had yet to touch base with anyone, really, since resurrection.

Gethin breathed heavily. He climbed the university stairs.

Liz was not at the reception desk. A young Zulu woman sat there now, taking calls through a silver headset. "I think he's in his office," she was telling someone. "Do you mind holding?" She touched a button and smiled at Gethin. "Good morning!"

"Good morning," he said. "I'm here to see Professor Peisistratos. My name is Gethin Bryce. I don't have an appointment."

"Let me check if he's available."

Gethin turned away and examined the facility's exhibition guide hanging on the nearby wall. Two hundred and fifty million years of Earthly history was contained in the museum. A colored line ran through the exhibits, starting red and then cooling like hot metal. The line was vermillion with the cooling of the planet, the trilobites, and the Permian Extinction. It dulled to sunburned orange as it underlined the hall of dinosaurs. Still cooling to crepuscular hues, the line cut through successive eras of life's myriad experiments and then, at the start of winter blue, a squat ape with opposable thumbs hopped onto the scene. Blue flushed to indigo throughout the Paleolithic, the Bronze Age, and the entirety of the anno Domini calendar from Ashurbanipal to Zero Hour when the nukes sprouted and the whole geopolitical house of cards came crashing down. It deepened to purple dusk at the Warlord Century, the Unification, and the dawning years of the New Enlightenment.

This final segment was the museum's pride and joy. Apollo the Great's gilded throne was actually in the museum. Several times after-hours, Gethin had seated himself in that chair, which once cushioned the ass of history's greatest conqueror.

"Professor Peisistratos awaits you in Hall Three," the receptionist said merrily.

Gethin thanked her and cut through the museum's twentieth-and-twenty-first-century wing. It was empty save for two purple-haired girls ogling an ancient advertisement in which a bare-chested young man stood on a beach, wearing only torn jeans: a nameless, unknown soldier for a forgotten product with faded letters: QUA I GIO.

Hall Three opened as Gethin neared its doors. He stepped through...

...into an alien jungle.

The door shut behind him before he could gather himself. Fibrous star-shaped plants overshadowed a feebly lit walking path. A vibrating mass of rubbery-looking tentacles, bearing resemblance to sea-worms, strained needfully to the obsidian sky. Without warning a shelled creature scuttled towards his feet.

Gethin deftly sidestepped it. The creature continued past, not seeing him or not recognizing him as a threat. A holobubble materialized above its peculiar head:

TRILOBITE

It looked good. A little too good; clearly, Professor Peisistratos had upgraded the museum sensoramics. The brachiopods and trilobites roaming this primordial seabed appeared slick and visceral, yet were only smartpaper sprites grafted onto nanocrystalline frames.

A familiar voice spoke crisply by his ear:

"Welcome to the Permian Age, Mr. Bryce."

Gethin glanced about the aquamarine gloom, seeing no one.

"The Permian Age," the voice continued, "began four hundred and fifty million years ago and represents one of the most understudied chapters of terrestrial life. You are witnessing a world with a single ocean and a single continent."

Another holobubble arose from the mud, a large one, like a glassy globe. Pangaea displayed on that rounded surface as a dramatic landscape of white peaks, deep valleys, green plains, and mysterious shorelines. An exotic world, as alien as anything coming back from out-system probes.

Gethin realized the jungle was fading, swapped out by a rocky beach beneath unfamiliar constellations. Sail-backed dimetrodons squatted lazily in this predawn blackness, forming a worshipful line for the impending sunrise.

"The wonders of the Permian Age saw life spread in fascinating ways. Until life itself was delivered a terrifying blow."

Gethin expected sunrise, but what he got was something else entirely. The primordial world quickly suffused with an angry white light. The dimetrodrons made nervous croaking sounds and began to scatter, but there was nowhere to go. The light overpowered everything in sight. The reptiles sizzled and cooked where they sat, flesh blistering and crawling off bones like papier-mâché under a blowtorch.

A wave of sound followed, filled with screams that were not screams...the agony of a dying world. In that perfect fury of merciless disintegration, the voice spoke again.

"The Permian Extinction saw ninety-five percent of all life vanish from the Earth," the voice intoned. "And no one truly knows why."

The exhibition lights snapped on. Gone were the beach and jungle and sensoramic creatures; in their place was a lengthy gray chamber dotted by fluorescent holodisplays of the exhibit's cast: trilobites, nautiluses, edaphosauruses, each highlighted for closer perusal and gift-shop ordering or smartshirt download.

Gethin needed a moment to gather himself.

A cherubic figure entered from the opposite doorway. Bearded, wearing a silver toga, and panting excitedly as he drew near.

"Gethin Bryce, prodigal son, returns to Athens!" The man laughed merrily. "What do you think of our new Permian exhibit?"

"Professor Peisistratos." Gethin couldn't help but smile. "Honestly? A bit sensationalist and intense, don't you think?"

"Then we've done our job on both counts!" The man clapped Gethin in an embrace. It was just a friendly squeeze; nevertheless, Gethin could feel his shirt strengthening its fibers in response to the pressure.

Doros Peisistratos was several inches shorter than Gethin, squatter, heavier. His eyes twinkled beneath briar-patch eyebrows. His nose was hooked like a Medici, his wide mouth comfortable in its nest of beard. The old charisma was still there, unchanged despite the pounds.

"How are you, Gethin?" Peisistratos beamed.

"Very well, sir."

"You look terrible. I would expect as much, from a man recently returned from Lethe."

Gethin rolled his eyes. "How long have you known?"

"My dear boy, I have been glued to the newsfeed since the incident. Your name leapt out at me. Stars, you look haggard! Or did Mars do that to you? Come, sit down."

He chose a bench for them, seated before one of the holodisplays of pre-saurian reptiles.

"You look good," Gethin insisted.

"I look fat."

"You wear it well, at any rate."

"My lean Senate days are over, my boy."

Gethin smiled wanly. He remembered the Wastelander's query: how can you truly know the depths of an immortal? The challenge fell on his mind like a Zen koan. Doros had been a colleague and friend for twelve years. Hell, that was longer than any one of Gethin's marriages. Yet what were twelve years in the course of three hundred?

"So," Doros said, eyes bright and eager. "What was it like?"

Gethin foisted a quizzical look. "What, specifically?"

"Death."

"Oh. I saw a light at the end of the tunnel, but it was just the Wyndham Save center."

"In all my years," Doros mused thoughtfully, tugging at the end of his beard, "Death is the one experience I've never had, my boy. When you factor the mortality distribution curve, death becomes inevitable at some point. Conservative estimates claim no person will live beyond fifteen hundred years without perishing for some reason or another. Therefore death will happen to me. I only pray to return in better spirits than you."

"You have been Saved, right?" Gethin was suddenly aghast at the idea that Peisistratos was like that idiot Salvor Bear, opposed to Digital Captures on some half-assed philosophical principle. Great stars! What a loss this man would be... like the burning of a priceless library.

"Of course!"

Gethin felt the odd vibrations of his Ego Familiar:

<His voice pattern indicates dishonesty, Gethin. And Doros Peisistratos possesses no wetware that I can detect.>

Gethin felt his stomach twist into an agitated knot.

No wetware? There were arkies who did that...leaning towards body-purist stylings. But Stillness agents did that too. Rejected augs as a perversion, a cancer in the human body and spirit.

Peisistratos scratched his beard. "Gethin? You still haven't answered my question. You crossed the waters of Lethe and returned. Come on, Orpheus!"

Gethin looked at him sharply. "An interesting metaphor. What can I say? If I danced with Mephistopheles, the memory was lost in transit. To be honest, I've been feeling...unwell." He forced a laugh.

Peisistratos watched him. "There is a recovery period."

"I know."

"Have you been taking it easy since—"

"No."

Peisistratos shook his head sympathetically. "Want the truth, Gethin? You never took it easy. You are a first-class, balls-out, obsessive-compulsive. And a smoldering, dangerous potential."

"Yeah? A potential what?"

Doros's face darkened. "That's for you to decide, isn't it? We're a lot alike. Give us a task, and we devote ourselves to it with manic, unrelenting energy. Allow us to wander, and darker demons tempt us."

"Into doing what?"

Doros raised an eyebrow. "Don't know. But in the niche of life, everyone has their own species of demon, and they are currently out in force."

"Oh?"

"I'm worried. I usually stay off the feeds, but right now it feels like a massive storm is brewing."

Gethin's heart hardened. "The story of our species. You're worried about… what? Another war? Seriously?"

His old friend gave a grave look. "Think about the last one. It doesn't matter how it started. The Old Calendar societal system back then was poisonous. Corrupt governments existing only for self-perpetuation. Corporations promoting wage slavery. The premeditated cultivation of fear and chaos for the profit of a small cabal of plutocrats, who themselves subscribed to end-of-world belief systems. It became a self-fulfilling prophecy."

"Have you updated that museum wing too?"

"We have," Doros said. "During your absence, some of our excavation teams struck print in important landfills. We now know conclusively that the old countries were breaking up before the War. Secessions around the world. Tribalism returning. Countries fragmenting into the old demes again. Toxic social media."

Gethin decided to steer the conversation to where he needed a spotlight. "Okay, so how does the modern world compare?"

Peisistratos stood and shuffled to the nearest wall, bringing up the latest newsfeed headlines with a touch of his fingers:

PI IN THE SKY? PUBLIC DEMANDS
ANSWERS FROM PROMETHEUS
Click for more

SENATOR KASTER GAINS NEW ALLIES IN
'WASTELAND WATCH' BILL
Click for more

WASTE POACHERS KILL 428 NEAR
MEMPHIS TO AVENGE SALVOR
Click for more

Gethin was silent.

"The old ways keep creeping back," his mentor said. "It's like the Roman mob after Caesar's death. Blind rage. It's a plague on our species."

Gethin looked at him, disturbed by this choice of wording.

Plaga.

Plague.

Latin.

Caesar.

Was this a coincidence? He feigned the kind of frown he usually wore when in deep debate. He didn't have to feign too hard.

"So you think…what? People are a plague?"

Peisistratos's eyes widened. "What do you think?"

"I honestly haven't decided yet."

His old friend sighed. "I think for all our sakes, it's good that you haven't decided, Gethin. Want my opinion? People are wonderful. A spectacular species. Came down from the trees and went up to the stars. But we never outgrew the bloodlust that got us here. There's always another Dark Age lurking in the wings. Always more demons drawing near, drawn to the scent of our fear and hate."

Gethin looked away, pretending to examine the headlines. Surreptitiously, he sent a command to Id: "Order Hassan Class spybots to tail Doros Peisistratos."

Done.

His friend suddenly seized his arm and steered him out of the room. "Have you eaten yet, Gethin? No, right? Come along." Whatever else he is, Gethin thought, the ancient professor is Greek to the bones, insisting that stomachs be sated.

★   ★   ★

Between bites of salty feta, egg, and toast, they caught up on old times in the museum café. Sensoramic pterodactyls wheeled overhead, alighting on the rafters, and perched there like a murder of crows.

Doros's smile was huge in his beard. "Gethin, you have to see the new troodon exhibit. The crowd was in an uproar. I almost single-handedly caused a riot among visiting paleontologists."

Gethin thought he had heard something of that while on Mars. The old eccentric still maintained a bee in his bonnet for troodons, obscure dinosaur of the late Cretaceous. Doros had become fond of suggesting that the troodons might have been intelligent enough to use tools and even build rudimentary shelters from the bigger, fiercer dinosaurs. There had even been some paleontological findings that were suggestive of the idea…but it was anathema in scientific circles.

An ancient anomaly, I guess, Gethin mused.

He lathered his toast in egg yolk. "Why are you still here? Why this interest in teaching history instead of making it?"

The professor's smile faltered. "Why does every athlete retire within a century of playing? The sport they love becomes a prison. They crave the quieter life…perhaps an escape to Mars to settle down with the girl of their dreams."

Gethin's eyes flickered at the dig. "Point taken, right in the heart."

"And you haven't even bothered calling her since your resurrection, have you?"

He shrugged.

"Did it end on such a sour note?"

"The Martians are fucking crazy," he said. Peisistratos threw back his head and guffawed.

"I wouldn't know. This old body has never left Earth."

"Given your Frontierist sympathies, that surprises me."

Doros's gaze became incredibly distant. "I have thought of it. Leaving Earth forever...venturing to other worlds." He brooded thoughtfully. "Someday. The IPC ban won't last, you know. Humans will one day inhabit the entire galaxy."

Gethin peered at him over his cup of the local, dark and sweet coffee. "Think so?"

"Sol has become a crowded playground, my friend. We're pressed against the fence, seeing fields beyond our little turf. Yes, expansion will happen."

"Should it?"

"What do you think?"

Gethin smiled politely. "Not for me to say."

"Really? The Gethin I knew had an opinion on everything. Part of your obsessive-compulsiveness." The old professor squinted at him. "Did Martian air dull your edge, my friend?"

"Don't think so."

"Or did the IPC do that to you?"

"Excuse me?"

Doros took a breath. He seemed to be measuring what he wanted to say.

"My friend, hear an old bird out, okay? Before we met, you devoted your life to online worlds. Day and night, exploring and fighting and conquering. Your potential swallowed by a drain of nonsense. When you disconnected from that, you came here...and became one of the most fiery, most popular educators. Your most popular course? The Diaspora. Students filled your auditorium to hear you preach about the inevitable future...when humanity would scatter to the ten thousand worlds. What governments might we make out there? How will we function with no central authority? How will we treat any indigenous life-forms we encounter? What religions might form, what social evolutions develop? How far and wide will Homo Sapiens fracture on a genetic, cultural, technological level?"

Gethin lowered his toast, fingers dripping. "I remember," he said quietly.

Doros absently pulled at his beard. "And right then, at the height of your popularity..."

"The IPC called," Gethin muttered.

"Strange, isn't it?"

"I had had contact with them before..."

"Sure, but this time they showed up and made you an offer to see the solar system, chasing down rumors and gossip. Keeping you busy, Gethin. Keeping you distracted. In the Old Calendar, governments might have just disappeared you as a threat to the state. The IPC is far too civilized for that. They knew your old habits of getting pulled into fictional quests, so they gave you a real-world equivalent."

Gethin pushed aside his plate.

"You make me sound awfully important," he said at last.

Doros chuckled. "Maybe you are. I've been around a long time, my boy. Live long enough…"

Gethin waited for him to continue. When the old man didn't, he said, "Yes?"

"Oh, nothing, my friend. So when do you start?"

"Start?"

Doros grinned impishly. "As flattering as it is to think that you came straight to see me after your resurrection, I'm sure there were more practical considerations. I believe I could locate a teaching position for you."

Gethin realized with a start that he hadn't even considered returning to academia. What would it be like? Bright-eyed students, eager to hear the application of history to hypothetical evolutions of humanity. But to what end? Humanity wasn't going anywhere. There were no bold, galaxy-spanning futures. We're not allowed…

<Gethin,> Ego interrupted. <There is a breaking story matching your search parameters. A Promethean offshore laboratory has suffered an accident…>

CHAPTER TWENTY-THREE
Dinner with Pegasus

On the maglev ride back to the hotel, Gethin tried reaching Saylor and Keiko by comlink. The Prometheans had their away-avatars on, inviting him to leave a message. He did, telling both that he was just learning of the offshore tragedy and asking them to contact him at their earliest convenience. Numbly, he pored over every news update as it filtered in. He was still reading when he decided to drop by on Celeste.

She was doing push-ups in a thin T-shirt and panties when he entered. Gethin closed his newsfeed with a wave of his hand and stood, awkward.

"Should you be doing that? You were almost dead two days ago."

Celeste did a remarkable thing; in the midst of a push-up, she threw herself into a standing position and said, "I broke my arm once as a kid. I had to wear a sling for two months before it was functional again. In Babylon, I was admitted to a clinic with a fractured skull, two broken legs, seven open wounds, and severe blood loss. Know what it took to fix me up?"

He said nothing.

"Four nanite injections, Gethin. Reduced the swelling in my brain, built buckycloth scaffolds around my broken legs, and stimulated tissue regeneration."

"Still, maybe you should—"

Her eyes gleamed. "And that shit ain't nothing. You were dead, right? Yet here you stand! What a miraculous time to be alive."

He didn't need his sniffer program to appreciate the coldness in her voice. "I'm glad you're recovering, at any rate."

"You too. Last night I thought you were going to flatline on me."

"I'm better now."

"Aren't we all?"

In fact, she looked incredible, he thought. So many citizens possessed chemically made hardbodies, flawless as new plastic. By contrast, the Wastelander was a seductive portrait of damage. Babylon had repaired her, but the wounds still showed as white scars on both arms, like negative-value tiger stripes. Her hands were calloused, lumpy from earlier breaks that healed over with too many calcium deposits. Her T-shirt had crept up during her workout, and there was a glossy puncture wound on her washboard stomach. Her bare legs were supple and bruised.

Celeste folded her arms across her chest. "Where are your arky pals?"

"They had business to take care of."

"I'll bet. Been an interesting morning for news. Yamanaka must be pissed."

"And scared. It isn't every day that someone messes with the biggest corporation in the universe. Something bad is brewing."

"That woman doesn't get scared." Celeste shrugged and skinned out of her shirt.

It was such a casual disrobing that Gethin blinked in confusion. Topless, the Wastelander rifled through a plastic bag of newly bought clothes. Then she disappeared into the bathroom, and Gethin heard the shower running.

"Come to lunch with me," he said through the door.

"I haven't had breakfast yet."

"Then come to breakfast with me."

Gethin listened to the water running. With a degree of embarrassment, he found himself tempted to replay the view of her standing half-naked before him. Wastelanders were paradoxically reviled and desired. Hollywood loved Outland-themed movies featuring pit fighters and feral women, grizzled tough-talking vigilantes with eyepatches and a dark past.

Celeste didn't have the eyepatch, but she seemed everything else the holos teased. Gethin thought about her body. From where had those other scars derived? What stories did they tell? Explanations suggested themselves like a barbaric grocery list: knife wound, bullet-hole, reset bone, burn scar, upon the canvas of a rippled eight-pack abdomen and size C breasts.

After a few minutes, he heard the water switch off. Celeste emerged wearing only a towel, hair combed straight back like a skullcap. "So how did it go with your old friend?"

"He hasn't confessed to interplanetary terrorism yet."

"A shame. Listen, I can't catch onto the fashion here. Some people wear trousers, while others…" She indicated Gethin's sable tunic. "Any suggestions for me?"

"Wear whatever feels natural."

"Is that what you're doing?"

"Well, I *am* Athenian. Aside from a few recent purchases, most of my wardrobe is scattered in moondust or stored in my mausoleum."

As he was talking, Celeste had been going through her bag of new clothes. Now she looked at him with interest. "Excuse me? A mausoleum?"

Gethin leaned against the wall, joints aching. "Arcology homes aren't terribly large. Once you have furniture, favored belongings, decorations, and tech, there just isn't space for a lifetime of collectibles. Most people lease mausoleum chambers."

"A safety-deposit box for nostalgia," she volunteered.

"I suppose."

He reflected suddenly on what would not be going into his mausoleum: the ten years' worth of redworld souvenirs and belongings. Real things tied to real memories: his walking staff worn to a nub from many jaunts around Mount Olympus; four anniversary champagne bottles finished off with Lori at romantic getaways; a canister of rocks collected from the awesome Valles Marineris and the plains of Cydonia and the lakes of Hellas; a terrycloth robe from Boccaccio's Thistle Inn; ceramics from Sakura's; personal letters written on smartpaper, bamboo paper, and rice paper. Gone!

He could order replacements, of course. Print them cheaply off an online catalog, rinse the tray dust from their surfaces. But they would never be the originals.

Like me.

Celeste undid her towel, letting it crumple to the floor. She slid into a new T-shirt and cargo pants. New black shoes.

"Will I fit in here?" she asked, arms spread.

"No."

"Good. Let's go."

★   ★   ★

Leda's was one of the arcology's most celebrated restaurants. On the 147th and 148th floors, it afforded a breathtaking view of the Apollonian Ring concourse, with quadrants of the restaurant set like floating Cycladic isles connected by grassy walking paths. Their approach to their table took them past winking satyrs, strutting centaurs, and coquettish dryads moving throughout the establishment. Celeste found herself watching the restaurant guests, though. Not one of them seemed interested in the myths in their midst.

They were seated in the Olympus hall by a wasp-waisted hostess. Food was arranged on buffet-table islands amid flowering bushes and real olive trees. On the ceiling, gods and goddesses gazed bemusedly from a backdrop of swirling clouds.

Celeste snatched up the wine bottle on their table and filled both their goblets. "If you work for the IPC, why are you alone?"

"I'm not alone."

"Where are the other investigators?"

Gethin swirled the wine, looking thoughtful. "IPC blueworld headquarters are in this very arcology. Right now, exactly two floors above us, they have analysts chewing over every piece of data that gets sent their way. I don't know many others are working this case, but I guess you're right: most work in teams."

"But you don't play well with others?"

He smiled slightly. Not a warm expression, but none too distant, either. "I'm what you call an asymmetrical investigator."

"Why?"

"Because history has shown that when you get groups of people together, even if they start off with many different voices, they quickly calcify into just a handful of camps. Usually two. It's the old us-versus-them mentality. A territorial quirk, I suppose. You can see it right now in the media. What are people saying about the tragedy? Who are they blaming?"

Celeste had spent most of the morning watching the newsfeed. "Most say that Prometheus Industries was conducting illegal energy experiments and it blew up in their face."

Gethin sipped the wine – a chilled retsina – and beckoned over a waiter bearing a tray of raw oysters. "And the other side is saying they were attacked by Stillness." He plucked some choice specimens and arranged them on his plate.

Celeste followed suit. "Okay…"

"Either side may be right. But few situations have just two sides. The asymmetrical angle is often better at conducting an inquiry untainted by groupthink. I was first on the scene to Kenneth Cavor's hospital bed. First to interview his coworkers. Now I've got the IPC keeping a watchful eye on Professor Peisistratos."

Celeste sucked the pale flesh from a half shell, looking at him curiously. "Why *you*?"

Gethin winked. "I'm very good at what I do."

A burst of commotion interrupted him. From an antechamber, a tawny horse with wings growing off its forelegs galloped into the room. It trotted indifferently past the gawking spectators, drawn to a dryad's fountain, and pretended to drink.

The sound of a little girl screaming sent Celeste to her feet. From across the room, a nightmare beast bounded out of an opposite chamber. Heart pounding, Celeste saw it had a mangy body, and a thick neck splitting to support three bestial heads: greasy reptile with flesh like glass, a fully maned lion, and a hell-eyed goat with stiletto teeth. Glistening wings flapped from its back, and a scarlet scorpion tail gave a menacing, mace-like whirl over guests who finally were paying attention.

The pegasus perked up from the fountain, neighed, and stomped one hoof warningly. The monster let loose a triple-voiced roar and lunged. The pegasus leapt into the air, wings flapping from its forelegs, as its would-be assailant took after it.

"Isn't Bellerophon supposed to be up there too?" Celeste whispered.

"Must be on bathroom break."

Many of the guests immediately glanced away, back to their meals or private virtuboards. Apparently, if they didn't have a monster right in front of their noses, their sense of wonder hastily evaporated.

Celeste felt a flush of irritation; even her wounds gave a convulsive itch where the nanites were toiling at cellular rubble. She swept up her goblet and clinked it against Gethin's in a collision that nearly shattered both. "To the dryads and nymphs and Proteus rising from the sea, or Triton breathing his wreathed horn!"

Gethin gave her a startled look. "Wordsworth."

"Yeah."

"Are Old Calendar poets popular in the Wastes?"

"We don't get holos out there. When we find books, we read whatever pages are still legible."

"I didn't realize books were…um…still widely read."

"They're not."

"Then why…"

"Because after a long day of ducking bullets and killing people, blowing trucks off the road, burying dead comrades, and sifting for edibles among the ruins, some of us like curling up with pure fucking fantasy. When you see babies broken open like eggs, or brains swelling like mushrooms from cracked skulls, you do something to keep yourself sane. When you're eight years old and hiding in a ventilation shaft, watching your mother carved up by a chainsaw, you need a place to recuperate. Even if it's just in the pages of ancient books from another goddamn age."

Gethin lowered his goblet.

Celeste pushed her dish of oysters away. "Like right now, I have a choice. I can dwell on the deaths of Jeff and Rajnar and Allie and Jamala. Scavengers have gotten to them by now. Did you know the eyes are eaten first? Birds rip them straight out. Next go the soft pieces of the neck. Then larger creatures come padding along…the dogs out there have gone completely feral, and those fuckers hunt in huge packs. Some glops will even make use of bones as tools. Maybe my friend Allie's skull is some land mollusk's drinking goblet. Maybe Jamala's bones are being smashed into bread. Do you know that old rhyme? 'Be he alive or be he dead, I'll grind his bones to make my bread.' Real monsters, Gethin, not this illusion shit!" She jabbed a fork at the sensoramics whirling above her, then let it clatter noisily to her plate.

Gethin lowered his eyes. "I'm sorry."

She glared. "Four nanite infusions. That's one for each of my comrades. What an age of fucking miracles this is, here in *civilization!*" Spit flew from her teeth as she said the word.

"Or is it sivilization, spelled with an S?"

"Twain. *The Adventures of Huckleberry Finn*. Do you think he would care for your world?"

Gethin slid his own plate away. "I don't know."

Celeste angrily gulped her wine, letting it burn her throat. As she set the goblet down, a renegade tear fell; she deftly caught it on her fingertip, blotting it on the tablecloth. It formed a circular wet blotch.

"I'm trying to find out who or what killed your friends," Gethin said softly. "The IPC has sent me after anomalies before. If what Disch said is correct, maybe this time it's for real."

"I'm not following you."

"Okay, listen. The IPC is sensitive to how fragile civilization is. We pulled ourselves out of radioactive rubble…after an unprecedented global collapse. If there's another Fall, maybe this time we don't recover. Maybe this time we die out, or revert to such barbarism that there is no healing. The IPC is concerned about threats that could do that."

"Okay…"

"Some threats are obvious. Nukes and antimatter, for instance."

"Right," Celeste said quickly.

Gethin hesitated, hearing something in her voice that suggested a thrumming tension, like standing next to power lines. "Right," he repeated. "But you don't often hear about other threats. Like the AIs. They're faster, smarter, more productive, and utterly foreign in goals and thought processes. Or the Ashoka…" He saw her blank expression. "They live out in space. Still human, depending on how generous your parameters are. Descended from the fledgling spacers and asteroid miners who were cut off from everything when the Final War transpired. Now they roam the solar system in rockships, keeping to themselves. Maybe they're all hopelessly insane. Or so insular that they have no interest in us. Thing is, we have no idea how advanced they are. Earth collapsed into a Dark Age, but the Ashoka were spared that, so they might have kept advancing.

"And you brought up glops. Who knows how many varieties exist on Earth, or how intelligent some breeds are? There's also the possibility of malevolent nanites. Or Ice-9 scenarios. Or…" He sighed. "The point is, we don't know, and the powers that be worry about such asymmetrical threats hitting us when and where we least expect it."

Celeste found herself warming to the conversation in spite of herself. "So you investigate every wild rumor?"

"Not every rumor."

"Ever find anything to justify the work?"

Gethin told her of the Ecuador anomaly.

It had been sixteen years ago, several miles outside Qito. The locals had reported unusual transgenics in the rainforest. *"We've been seeing 'em for years now,"* a farmer told him. *"Big, almost as large as a plowbot. Dark green color, usually. Bodies like massive termites. They're building cities underground! We see glowing lights from mountain caves!"*

And so Gethin had hiked into Ecuadorian volcano country. He found lots of stone mounds, and encountered small transgenic species attempting to carve their own niche in the jungle (but, ironically, most had the fatal habit of eating the indigenous and highly poisonous frogs). In the end, he found nothing to support the farmers' tales of hyper-intelligent termites building subterranean metropolises.

"Except," Gethin added, "I did discover an unknown species of bioluminescent moss that grew underground."

"Which you think was behind the rumors of termite city lights."

"Yep."

"And what did the locals say when you came back with your findings?"

"Nothing. I don't report to them."

"But you've a good idea what they would have said."

Gethin scooped up the remaining oyster on his plate. "Sure. They'd ask me if I crawled into every lava tube, or if I'd scoured every cave, climbed every tree, visited every island of the Galapagos. Then they'd smile and say, 'Well then, how can you be sure, señor?'"

"So why was the IPC interested in farmer stories?"

"Because if hyper-intelligent termites did exist, that's a potential threat."

"But…bugs, Gethin?"

"The unknown can be deadly. No one really knows what triggered the Final War, and the IPC doesn't deal in mysteries. Hell, that's likely the reason behind the colonization ban. They don't want humanity running smack into a nasty alien race. The farmers in Ecuador suggested there might be competition to human civilization, so my employers wanted to know for certain."

"Would they have exterminated them, if it was true?"

Gethin shrugged. "Don't know. We haven't burned the AIs off the map yet, have we?"

Celeste poured herself another glass of wine, her mind racing fluidly.

Maybe some big-ass anomaly will tear up these arcologies by the roots someday, or some extraterrestrial menace may descend from the stars in tripod death machines. She didn't have the patience to wait. Her hands trembled as she cupped her goblet and imbibed.

A cold thought flashed in her head…a thought which spoke with Jeff's voice: *What are you going to do, my love?*

Oh, Jeff! Would you look at me here? I've been kidnapped by goddamn arkies. I'm dining on oysters among immortals while a fucking pegasus soars over my head. I learned that the guy who killed you is not human. The StrikeDown missiles are still missing, and I haven't dared contact King D. since my abduction. How the hell are you?

She pictured his freckled smile, his beautiful eyes sparkling like river stones. *I'm dead, babe. You have to go to Europe without me.*

Jeff, I swear I'll help StrikeDown finish this for us. I'll do whatever I need to, I'll manipulate these arkies to my purposes. I've been remade and rebuilt. Got my sensorium working. And I know the Mantid *is not in Promethean possession. Fucking cunt Yamanaka lied to me, of course. Our ship sent me a message this morning. Two words: SAFE. WAITING.*

Do what you need to, my love. I'm there with you. And Jamala and Allie and Rajnar would tell you the same thing. Be glad we went down fightin'. I love you.

Sharp applause rang around her. Celeste realized the winged-horse-and-monster show had ended. She caught a glimpse of the chimera's scorpion tail vanishing into an overhead stable. Now, a trio of Sirens rose up from the same fountain the pegasus had drunk from, their hair like cherrywood, their topless bodies dripping as they strummed harps and sang in a language she didn't know.

"Gethin?" Celeste said, reaching across the table and clasping his hands.

He looked shocked by this sudden intimacy. Blushing, he said, "Yeah?"

"I can think of a better way to spend the afternoon than in this living wax museum. How about you?"

CHAPTER TWENTY-FOUR
Jonas Picks up the Trail

Jonas barely blinked as he sorted the newsfeeds, and his VR rig so completely enveloped his small head that he never heard his mother leave for the late shift. He had been in the rig all day, a hungry datahound sniffing for traces of his quarry, his wheelchair and home and country forgotten.

Base 59, Flight 3107, and the Pacific offshore rig that had sunk that morning, killing more than fifty people. The blueweb was screaming with conspiracy theories, accusations, online personalities circulating petitions for one cause or another. The latest fuel to the fire: an allegedly leaked Promethean memo, purporting to reveal the corporate powerhouse was embroiled in illicit energy experiments.

Jonas stayed away from the pundits and citizen-journalist cults with their rabid followers. He sifted the reputable agencies for salient data, then shut out the madhouse and logged straight into Arcadia.

Not to escape.

To dig deeper.

It was really the only modicum of privacy left in the world; a veritably Venetian masquerade crossing all boundaries, obfuscating all participants. Players could hail from any group, agency, political faction, or corporation. But Jonas had recently sniffed out a deeper truth. An entire cloak-and-dagger society existed in the blueweb under various personas, laundering meetings through fictional scenarios. A cold war boiled among digital shadows. Like ancient Brazilian martial artists who, forbidden to practice their craft, learned to disguise it as dance.

That Prometheus Industries, a three-hundred-year-old corporation and one of the architects of the New Enlightenment, could screw up so royally as to have two separate accidents – and on two different worlds – was preposterous. Jonas sensed other factors were involved.

If he stalked around as his famous avatar the Exile, he'd be beset by fans and enemies alike. Instead, he called up a Rolodex of other, carefully cultivated personalities. For half an hour, he became Jasper Manforte, one of the foot soldiers of an online conspiracy group. Stepping into one of their enclaves (rendered as an outlandishly complicated network of treehouses in freakishly tall trees) he mingled with the regulars, listening for their take on global events.

They didn't have a take on it. They had hundreds.

Netcreeps bellowing with absolute certainty that the Ashoka were behind it all, or that Prometheus had captured aliens and were experimenting with their alien tech (with disastrous results), or it was the Asteroid Federation, or the Frontierists.

Jonas dissolved away from the treehouse fanatics, and became a fake Vector Nanonics employee named Edwin Kim DeCosta.

As Edwin, he went to the Vector Nanonics Cave. It looked like a posh Tibetan restaurant set upon a snowy mountaintop, a Mobius strip bar enclosing the tables and booths. Vector security daemons resembling birds stood watch, but they allowed him to enter without hassle. His employee ID was real, after all; Jonas had hacked the corporate recruitment database to 'hire' himself as a VIP-sponsored intern…which could mean many, often lascivious things. It was the perfect cover. He mingled as a hybrid of low-totem pariah and privileged boy-toy with a backstage pass.

In fact, the closest he'd ever come to having his cover blown was from a fellow employee – a marketing analyst named Damaris. He'd run into her at a Vector Cave on the Bombay grid. She'd cozied up to him, much to his own discomfort, and propositioned him. Jonas figured the easy way out was to say he was happily married. That had been a mistake. His unavailability only seemed to embolden her pursuit, and her recent string of messages were embedded with graphic visuals. Jonas was terrified. Her unyielding fervor had gotten so constant that he rarely visited Vector any more, and had considered dissolving the DeCosta identity entirely.

Now Jonas strolled through the Tibetan Cave. The place was teeming with employees on break, and they were in a celebratory mood. The popular conversation was to revel in PI's misfortunes. A few were making bets on how soon the next catastrophe would occur. Jonas nodded, played along, listened.

Someone touched his elbow. Jonas froze, turned, fully expecting to see Damaris standing behind him.

"Exile?"

Jonas blinked; his smiling DeCosta face mirrored the action. An attractive young Indian girl wearing an aquamarine sari stood there, facing him. Her employee ID floated above her head: PRANILIKA ADALJA.

"I'm sorry?" Jonas said, his squeaky voice coming out as rich baritone.

The Indian woman held out her hand. Jonas hesitated.

An invitation to a private chat.

Exile. Whoever the hell this was, she knew who he was. Jonas felt his heart anxiously skip a beat.

Steeling himself for a hasty logout retreat, he extended his own hand until their palms were touching. Chat accepted, Jonas heard the woman's voice in his head, while her lips didn't move.

"Exile," she said. "I am Anju, your friend!"

Jonas felt his tension melt away, replaced by annoyance. "What are you doing here? How did you find me?"

Anju was an accomplished, but reckless, gamer. The online equivalent of a bank robber who, enjoying success, keeps upping the ante until arrest becomes inevitable. She didn't participate in the major online adventures, but rather made a fortune conducting sneak attacks when one group or another was down on their luck. A battlefield vulture, pecking at the dead or dying, flapping off before she could get caught.

Except that a month ago, she had gotten caught.

Posing as a high-level cleric, she found five marks – five wounded warriors returning from an ill-fated battle. Anju lured them to a private spot, and transformed her character into a goddamn manticore. Killing the warriors, she stole all their gold, weapons, scrolls…everything. From manticore to mouse, she scrambled away, intent on selling the items to online bidders.

It had been a grievous mistake. Her victims, as it turned out, had been high-level Judgment Fiends – a powerful brotherhood of online assassins. You didn't fuck with the Judgment Fiends.

Somehow, they discovered who she really was…and for the past four weeks, Anju had been a hunted woman. The Fiends were openly scouring Arcadia for her. They even started killing off her sideline characters…a feat not ordinarily possible. Apparently, the Fiends had gotten some real-world hackers to track her online footsteps. Anju's digital life was not long for this world.

She had repeatedly begged Jonas to intervene. However, he wasn't in the habit of flippantly doling out favors. He had no quarrel with the Judgment Fiends; they stayed out of each other's way.

"I'm not going to help you," Jonas said. "And how did you find me here?"

"I've known about this avatar of yours for a long while. I'm sorry, Exile. I—"

Jonas conjured his Exile persona. Visible only to Anju, the Kim DeCosta skin morphed into something horrific: a tall, spindly creature with a breathing apparatus and biomechanical survival suit. His eyes were bulbous black.

"How did you know I'd be here?" he demanded. "I don't like being stalked! Speak, or I'll kill you myself!"

Anju threw herself to her knees. "I put an alert on this Cave, to let me know the instant you showed up. I was losing hope that I'd ever track you down. You don't return my messages. You—"

"Your probems do not concern me. I have other matters requiring my attention."

The girl swallowed hard. "You mean details on the shuttle explosion?"

Jonas went silent.

"I know you've been asking people about it all morning. Requesting information."

His annoyance shifted back into anxiety. Just how long had she been tailing him around Arcadia? And the more frightening thought: did she know his meatspace identity? Did she realize he was just a dying child in Cappadocia?

"I have come into information," Anju said.

"What information?"

"I've been in hiding, you know. While sneaking about, I witnessed a secret conversation and recorded it."

"Let me see it."

Anju hesitated. "Mighty Exile, you understand the danger I'm in! The price for my information is your protection."

Jonas rolled his eyes, then coughed messily. It was a brutally sharp sound, and Anju surely heard it. His chest pained him as if glass jostled in his tender bronchial tubes.

"We will discuss terms after I have seen it," he said when he recovered.

"How do I know you'll honor your word?"

He seized her by the throat, his spidery fingers closing around her avatar's windpipe. No actual injury would be done to the girl herself, and he couldn't kill her in a Vector Cave where player-versus-player violence was disallowed. But Anju's eyes grew wide in terror.

"You have violated my privacy. Show me this recording, and if it has value, I shall consider helping you. If you're wasting my time..."

He released her throat.

Anju bowed. "Yesterday I was in the Biomech forest. I figured it was a good place to hide those hunting me. I changed into a raven and flew over the woods, looking for places of interest. And I saw a tent. I swept down to investigate."

"And?"

"Three people were having a conversation in the tent. I thought I might..." She trailed off.

"You thought you might attack them and steal their goods," he guessed.

"Yes, Exile. But their conversation was so unusual, I decided to listen and record their words."

A video file appeared in his VR rig. Jonas hit PLAY.

Three people crouched inside an animal-skin tent. They were dressed in simple rags. One was a young man with raven hair and many rings on his fingers. Another was a blond man, blocky, with the blank features of a stock design; few if any personal touches had been made to the boilerplate visage.

The third character was a woman, elven in appearance, elegant and beautiful, with silver hair. She was speaking as Anju's recording began.

But it was in a language Jonas had never heard. He brought up a translation option, which identified it as Latin.

Latin? Who the hell spoke Latin anymore?

"What does the piece do?" the elf asked her compatriots.

The blond man stared disinterestedly at a clay mug in his thick hands. It was the dark fellow who replied: "It can alter matter's charge. Perhaps allow construction of a Midas Hand."

The silver-haired lady looked startled. "They can do that?"

"It was only a matter of time."

"Then they can also—"

The dark man interrupted her. "The question now is how do we mobilize? How many of them are even left?"

The blond man growled low, like a jungle cat. "Four, maybe five. Perhaps fewer than that."

"But why would they expose themselves like this?" she asked. "Destroying that base and shuttle in such a public way? Surely they know we'll come for them."

The dark fellow stood swiftly, walked directly towards Anju's vantage point at the tent flaps. But he didn't seem to see her. He halted, pivoted in place. "There are two possibilities. One, they are setting a trap for us. Two, they are so near to completing their plans, which we can assume involves this negative matter device, that exposure is meaningless now."

The blond man hurled his mug to the ground. Gameworld physics were flawless; the mug broke into pieces, frothy fluid seeping into the grass. "Forget theories! Track them down and end them! For good this time!"

"They hardly expect you to be cautious, Sy'hoss'a," the elven woman said dismissively. "Perhaps that's their intention. Get you to come out of hiding. Get you to do something stupid. Doesn't take much."

The man growled again.

It was the strangest sound…primal and bestial and yet oddly electrical, like metallic wires sizzling as they came into contact. It made Jonas's eyes hurt.

In his VR rig, Jonas paused the video and hastily opened another screen so he could search for the words 'Midas Hand'. He also ran a search for variations on the name he had heard: Syhosa, Cyhosa, Sai-hosa, and the like. He was excited. Anju had not overstated her discovery.

Jonas was dimly aware that he was coughing again, that blood was dripping down his chin, his lungs shedding more pulpy, infected matter. The glowing screens of Arcadia began to wheel around him.

Quickly, he said, "I have seen enough, Anju. Transmit the entire video. I will agree to your terms."

Anju's elation was pure disbelief. "You…you will protect me from the Judgment Fiends? Really?"

"I will," he said, after muting his audio to get through another coughing fit. He was aware that in the real world, Maximilian was flashing a warning message, but Jonas couldn't read it. He couldn't even see straight.

"Thank you, Exile!" Anju was saying. "Thank you, thank you! I knew I had come to the right person. The Fiends have destroyed every one of my characters. Thank you so much for—"

"Transfer the entire file to me," he repeated, panicking as he fought to stay conscious.

"Of course, Exile. There's only another minute left to it, but I think you'll find it just as interesting—"

Jonas hacked up salty pulp. "*Now!*"

He tore the VR rig from his head and blindly groped for Maximilian. It was too late. The world seemed to spin away from him, and his head crashed into the corner of his desk. White lights exploded in his right eye like a supernova… darkening fast.

CHAPTER TWENTY-FIVE
Attack Patterns

The blue-green corridor leading back to Poseidon Suites smelled of fresh citrus – lemon touched with saffron – but Celeste felt nauseated with each breath. She steered her arky companion by the arm, the oysters shifting slimily in her stomach.

Gethin glanced sidelong at her as they walked. "Where are we going?"

She hoisted a grin onto her face. "Your room."

He raised an eyebrow. The wine had given a blush to his pale, stone-cut cheeks. "Why?"

Celeste gave an unbelieving look. "Judging from the way you fucking people dress, I wouldn't figure you for prudes. We wined and dined, and now I want to go to your room. Are you Greek or Victorian?"

"Neither, if you want to be precise about it. What I am is sensitive to loss and the need to mourn."

And who have you ever lost? she thought savagely. *Really, truly lost?* "I lost some coworkers of mine," she grunted.

"Still, if they were friends…"

"Better them than me."

The comment visibly stunned him, and he was quiet as they rode an escalator down past friezes of Greek titans and Peloponesian meadows. Some people riding the opposite way glanced at Celeste's raiment, at the scars on her arms, and then they looked away. Most appeared half-tranced by virtual fantasy, hands tickling the air, shuffling through private distractions.

Celeste supposed she had her own distractions too. As they stepped off the escalator and turned towards Triton wing, she found herself imagining Athens cracked open like a great Fabergé egg. A single antimatter missile could do it, launched from the *Mantid* or StrikeDown's other secret ships. Earth's lofty capitol would be transformed into a smoking crater like a new Yucatan smackdown.

Of course, as best she knew, Athens itself wasn't one of StrikeDown's targets. If your objective was forced negotiation, it was poor strategy to lop the head off your enemy. King D. wanted to chop the knees, not go for decapitation, and when the collective arky was bleeding at the stumps, he intended to shove a grocery list of demands under their snouts. The major Save centers were his targets…a carefully calibrated kick to the world's balls. Let the immortals get a whiff of the grave, a wake-up call for three centuries of segregation and cruelty, delivered by antimatter petition.

How many missiles has King D. stockpiled now? Twelve? Thirteen? And perhaps twice that in nukes.

The IPC could easily retaliate, sure. Hell, with their terrifying battleships patrolling Sol, they could turn the Outlands into one planetwide glass crater from orbit. But surely they didn't have the stomach for that. Arkies, shaken from their citadels, would demand negotiation. With cities lying in smoking ruin and the threat of further destruction, King D.'s demands would suddenly seem very, very reasonable to the peacekeepers in the sky.

Still steering Gethin, Celeste entered the final stretch of corridor leading to his room.

"What are the sexual mores of arkies, anyway?" she taunted.

"Anything goes," Gethin said thoughtfully.

"I'm sure it does. From what I've seen, you people probably download fantasy men and women to your optics, regardless of who you're actually screwing."

"I'm sure you're right."

Celeste shrugged. "Imagining someone else in bed is nothing new."

"Is that what this is about?"

"Do you care?"

"Not sure yet."

They were nearing the end of the corridor. The painting of the Garden of the Hesperides once again pixelated to insert her and Gethin into the mix; what had surprised her last night now only conjured derision. But suddenly she noticed two additional faces. Two men she didn't recognize. Large, blocky figures with glowing eyes.

"Don't turn around," Gethin whispered. "I just noticed them too. Closing in on our six."

Celeste had to fight the urge to turn. The spectral-eyed humanoids in the painting glared at her, as surely as the actual men must be glaring as they closed the distance.

Gethin palmed open his door and pulled her inside. He hastily twisted the deadbolt.

"My goddamn equipment hasn't arrived yet," he hissed. "Quick! Give me that chair!"

She obeyed, and made an instinctive grab for her pistol before remembering that all her weapons had been confiscated: they were, quite unhelpfully, sitting in some Prometheus Industries security locker in Babylon. Swell.

"Who are they?" she asked, handing him the chair.

He wedged it under the doorknob. "The same duo I noticed on Luna's Night Train. I'm calling Saylor to—"

The door was kicked open with such force that it shattered the chair, sending one wooden leg spinning madly around the floor to crack open a potted plant. Gethin cursed, staggered backwards.

Celeste sized up the men as they came. Both large, broad-chested specimens in the two-hundred-and-fifty-pound range. Flat, eerily clayish features and hooded eyes. Pit fighter bodies. Her first instinct was to aim for their throats and groins; a dragged-out scrap meant certain death. And it was death they were bringing too. Celeste was flooded with unaccountable certainty.

This is a planned assassination.

She had time to snatch two pens from the nightstand when, with no indication whatsoever that it was going to happen, both men disappeared into a vibrating blur.

★   ★   ★

Blurmods were military-grade augmentations restricted to corporate security, Republic peacekeepers, and IPC personnel. Outlanders desperately coveted them for their tactical advantage, and various black markets claimed to offer reverse-engineered knockoffs. At best, such imitations failed on activation; at worst, they killed the person using them. Accelerating a human being was tricky. The heart and brain couldn't keep up. Resonance frequency destroyed tissue, imploded organs, turned circulatory systems into gory ribbons.

To counter this, official blurmods required all sorts of fine-tuning systems implanted throughout the body. They spiked the nervous system with adrenal stims and neurosynths that, to a non-accelerated bystander, lasted five standard seconds. It was all the juice a blurmod cell could hold. Some blurmods could even be rigged for auto-triggering whenever a high-velocity shape – a bullet, or another accelerated individual – came within proximity.

Like Gethin's.

He was afforded a passing glimpse of the intruders before they blurred, and his own systems kicked in with a low-pitched whine. Suddenly there was a sensation of elastic bands wrapped around his universe, a rubbery resistance miring the world down to a crawl while he tacked against the pressure.

He looked to Celeste. She was a beautiful waxen doll, frozen in place, each of her hands closed around a pen.

The intruders barely registered her. Grinning, eyes shining, they fanned out to make the most of the small room.

Golems, he thought. But who the fuck sent them after me?

He was able to hop a half step backwards, towards the foyer counter and away from the locus of their center. The nearest assailant grabbed Gethin roughly, hauling him off his feet. Its mouth stretched impossibly wide. Double rows of serrated teeth glinted like broken glass.

Gethin realized the thing was going to bite for his throat. He headbutted the attack as it came, his dome smashing into the golem's nose. The force was enough to add slack to its grip, and he disabled the grappling hands, twisted his body inside their breadth, and flipped his assailant over him. Then he dropped to one knee and drilled a punch into its throat, collapsing its windpipe.

The low-pitched whine of his blurmod rose to a shrieking whistle.

The second golem tackled him. It was like getting impacted by a train.

Gethin's breath burst from his lungs and he hit the linoleum, slid a meter, and crashed into the kitchen counter's baseboard. From there, his attacker clubbed him with its fists, gorilla-like. Gethin was forced into a protective ball, squinting up at his attacker.

The face was blank. No anger, no murderous hate. It pounded him with the brute, detached efficiency of an assembly-line bot.

Gethin couldn't retreat. Already, he was scrunched against the baseboard. Each punch fell like a wooden bat on his arms, head, and legs.

He grabbed for the creature's head, but succeeded only in taking a blow to the face. He tried again. A blow caught him in the kidneys and he cried out. Once more he made a grab for the thing's head. This time he knitted his fingers behind the misshapen skull, and heaved down as he brought a knee into its face. Then he planted his foot against the construct's chest, shoving with all his might.

The creature toppled backwards, rolled with an odd grace, and was on its feet again. Gethin scrambled up to meet him.

The attacker with the crushed windpipe made a choking sound and groped for Gethin's leg. He sidestepped the clumsy attempt and edged closer to Celeste. She was moving now, as his blurmod timed out, his own speed reducing to match hers. With the slow-mo grace of being underwater, her right hand drew one pen back, reached the zenith of an arc, and began the gradual jab at an opponent who was no longer there: her eyes telling her brain there were still two intruders at the door.

The second golem lunged at Gethin again, swinging its heavy fists. Gethin tucked and rolled beneath the blows, rushing for the door. Predictably, the golem dashed after him, putting itself back in front of the Wastelander.

And the blurmod ended.

The world snapped back to normalcy.

And Celeste buried her pen into the golem's ear.

Black blood spurted from the injury. Gethin shoved the creature farther into the room. The other one, despite its ruined throat, was clambering to its feet, ready to re-engage.

Gethin tugged at Celeste. "Fall back! They've got blurmods!"

Celeste tossed her pens away, scooped up pieces of the shattered chair. Gethin wrenched open the door.

And as he did, a tornado seemed to fly into the room.

Gethin's blurmod kicked in once more.

The tornado coalesced into a large, formidable-looking man.

Jack Saylor.

The Promethean collided with both golems, tossing them about like rag dolls. Mr. Windpipe was hurled into the open bathroom, where he collapsed like a folded chair in the tub. The other golem, pen sticking from its ear, tried to bite his arm; Jack avoided the blow, and chopped his other hand on its neck, killing it.

Gethin rushed to Jack's side. They cornered the glowing-eyed monster in the tub.

"I've got it," Jack said.

"It's yours," Gethin breathed.

Jack slammed into the construct as it stood. The impact crashed them both through a glass shower door. Shards danced like magic crystals, spinning in dreamy cartwheels, all jagged edges and glitter clouds. Jack seemed to slap the creature around, neatly hitting the ears, neck, and ribs. Then the blurmod was screaming.

The floating glass tinkled onto the linoleum.

"Don't kill it!"

It was Keiko's bark. She came sprinting up behind them.

"Wasn't going to," Jack said, voice clean and neutral. He dragged the incapacitated foe into the foyer. Keiko reached for something in her beltline pouch.

The construct's eyes, dazed and faintly glowing, rolled white.

Gethin shouted, "No! He's suiciding! Goddamn it!"

Keiko scrambled forward. She pinned the golem in place with one knee against its chest, and rammed something like a medical cylinder into one of its eyes. Blood popped around the tube. The body twitched and kicked. She shoved the cylinder as far as she could.

The creature stopped kicking. Its hands fell aside.

Jack said, "Did you get enough?"

Keiko staggered to her feet. The cylinder was in her hands, dripping gore. Gethin recognized it as a magpie extractor.

She frowned. "Don't know. Looks like a good core sample. Maybe enough to trace the manufacturer."

Celeste tossed the chair legs aside and peered at the body. "He's dead?"

"He was never alive," Keiko muttered.

★   ★   ★

"A golem. Essentially a false consciousness planted into a homegrown body, given a set of directives, and set to self-destruct if it fails." Jack shook his head, enraged at the loss of opportunity. "The only chance we had was to knock him unconscious long enough to use the magpie. Maybe even get the time to do a flash-capture." He glanced to the mush in the cylinder. It was visibly bubbling, popping, disintegrating before their eyes.

Gethin looked dangerous, eyes large and rage-clouded. Celeste had seen the look before; a man clearly not used to this kind of battle, surprised that he had survived, and now galvanized by adrenaline thinning out in his blood, cresting the combat high.

But what did he have to lose? she wondered. *He's already died and come back once. Guess instinct runs deep.*

By comparison, Jack and Keiko looked as calm as monks. Keiko methodically withdrew a wicked-looking tool from her beltline and, without any fuss, plowed a retractable blade into the remaining golem's forehead. The blade slipped twice across the skull as she made short work of the skin, peeled it down over the nose, and broke into the skull. Chips of white bone came away like sawdust.

Using the other side of the blade, she produced a cone of light.

"Wetware circuits in a vat-grown substrate," she muttered, tilting the ruined head so Jack could see. She used the magpie again, took a sample with its spare tube. Celeste watched her rise tranquilly and rinse her hands in the kitchen sink.

"Worth a shot," Gethin muttered.

Jack stared hard at him. "Any idea who did this?"

"No."

"Where did you go earlier today?"

"The University to see Doros Peisistratos," Gethin confessed. "I had reason to suspect he might be involved with all this." He looked at the bodies. "I still do."

Jack gave him a bewildered look. "*Senator* Peisistratos?"

Gethin started to reply – intrigued by the awe in Saylor's voice – when Keiko cut him off. Blotting her hands dry on her clothes, she said, "You were the target of this, Gethin."

"Yes."

"How many people knew you were in Athens?"

Gethin sighed. "Doros did…but…"

"Yeah?"

"I recognize these two from Luna. They were on the Night Train with me. So I really doubt that Doros is behind this."

The hotel room looked ghastly. Two dead blodies venting oil-black blood, and debris strewn across the floor. Celeste squatted near the closest body. She stared into its blank, blood-spattered face.

"I still don't understand," she said. "If they succeeded in their mission, you'd just come back to life. So what's the point? How is this an attempted assassination?"

Gethin rubbed his chin. "Maybe to delay me. They followed me down from Luna. We'll have to check shuttleport logs. See what names they were using." He pointed to the magpie in Keiko's hand. "I'd like to see the magpie. In the spirit of sharing information."

Keiko gave a short, caustic laugh. "Don't trust us, Gethin?"

"Not entirely."

She handed him the device. Gethin pressed his fingertips against the cylinder's datareader, downloading the magpie's assessment of the neural composition. It would take a forensics team to get a good look at the sample on the microscopic level and attempt to sift for telltale residue, but he downloaded the preliminary data anyway.

"Prometheus doesn't make golems," Keiko said, watching him.

"Glad to hear it." He completed his scan and tossed the cylinder back to her.

"Prometheus has better things to do than assassinate you, Gethin. Now how about sharing with us. What did you and Peisistratos talk about?"

"I'll tell you in due time."

"Now, Gethin."

He saw her calm countenance blushing red with controlled anger. The eyes as slender as knife-blade flats. She had turned her body into a confrontational pose, squaring off to him, extraction blade still in her hands.

Gethin matched her posturing. "For the moment, I am classifying my conversation with Doros. The details of my inquiry are none of your damned business. However, you will continue assisting me as your superiors ordered you to."

<Gethin? Eight security personnel are converging on this apartment.>

"Good," he said aloud. "Arcology security is here."

CHAPTER TWENTY-SIX
Deathbots

IPC Colonel Leon Tanner was standing by the tall windows of the security office on Level 151 when they were led in. Tanner was a trim-looking man with Teutonic fair skin and elegantly sculpted features. He wore the smoky blue, gold-trimmed uniform of IPC admiralty. Although stationed in Athens, he was clean-shaven and wore his hair utilitarian short, an austere schoolmaster's presence in a land of hedonistic abandon.

The office seemed carved out of black glass. The tabletop crawled with the latest newsfeed headlines: the Actors' Guild was in uproar over rumor that *Cry of an Alien Midnight* producers had announced they would use a virtual copy of dead actor Salvor Bear to complete their film.

Tanner turned as his guests entered the room. "Mr. Bryce," he said stiffly. "What happened in Poseidon Suites?"

"We were assaulted by two constructs, sir."

"Just hours after you order a Hassan detail for Doros Peisistratos?"

Gethin grimaced. "It is pretty damning, but they're the same ones I noticed on Luna, not an hour after my resurrection."

Tanner regarded the Prometheans. They needed no introduction; their data was probably flashing red on Tanner's optics. He frowned at Celeste, however, who wasn't linked to any infosystem.

Speaking quickly, Gethin said, "This is Celeste Segarra from the Hudson Outlands. I reported to your office that she is a material witness."

Tanner's searing blue eyes were hard.

Right, Gethin thought. *The old enemy brought into paradise. A reminder of where we all came from.*

"Good afternoon, Colonel," Celeste said sweetly.

Tanner tapped his desk with one hand. It was an uncharacteristically anxious twitch from a man who, in Gethin's experience, was as stolid and cool as a block of ice. "I have a sweep team examining your assailants. Maybe there's enough to run a trace."

"I doubt that, sir," Keiko interjected.

Tanner looked startled at her edgewise interruption. He tilted his head. "Why do you doubt it?"

"Because they were top-line golems. Whoever went through the expense of creating them and setting them loose in Athens wouldn't be sloppy enough to leave their fingerprints over it." She swallowed. "Sir."

Celeste was amused by how subservient her compatriots were being. In the Outlands you showed respect to the powerful because they could cut your life off with one knife-flash or squeezed trigger. That shit didn't happen here.

She smiled thinly. But then, quite unexpectedly, she caught a whiff of danger too. Like the stench of overwarm electronics. The office was dim and quiet, like being submerged in murky water.

"Perhaps the behavior itself might yield a clue," Tanner suggested.

Keiko had already thought of that. "Hopefully."

"Colonel?" Gethin started. "Has there been any luck in tracing the other voice on that recorded call? The one between Peisistratos and someone from NoCal?"

Tanner continued drumming the desk. "I read your report, Bryce. We have sniffers tethered on all comlines to seek a vocal match. Either he hasn't used a phone since that conversation...or he was voice-cloaking from the start."

Gethin considered that. The voice he'd heard was edgy and savage, seemingly too genuine for digital fakery. Such raw ferocity had surely come from a fleshy throat; the sonics rooted in an excitable, dangerous spirit, someone capable of exploding like a supervolcanic eruption.

"Disguised or not, I believe I could recognize that voice if I heard it again."

"How?"

"The man seemed...uniquely dangerous."

Tanner grunted.

Except that it wasn't really a grunt. It was a low sound, nearly inaudible. Celeste, already on the hidden scent of danger, felt a difference in air or temperature or arrangement of molecules in the room. Again, she imagined they were all underwater, only now lava was spilling into it, gradually raising the temperature and releasing toxic compounds.

"So what's your theory, Bryce? Is this a Stillness plot?" Tanner asked.

"I doubt it, sir. This is too high-profile for them."

"Agreed. Peisistratos?"

"I doubt that too."

"Why?"

Gethin shrugged. "My judgment of his character. Of course there are groups he might support. The Frontierist radicals, for instance. Doros is not a fan of the ban."

Tanner had stopped drumming the table, but now he was gliding his fingertips over the surface. "You didn't mention them in your report."

No, I didn't, Gethin thought, trying not to stare at the rapid fingers. *Just like I won't mention that the IPC remains atop my list of probable suspects. Just like I've noticed that you aren't acting like yourself at all, sir.*

"I didn't mention them," Gethin answered carefully, "because there is no evidence to link their involvement. I simply bring them up to illustrate that some extremists have the technical reach to conduct this attack, and have procured sympathizers in our society. Stillness has never been able to do that."

"Is Peisistratos a Frontierist?"

"Not formally."

"How does he feel about Avalon?"

Gethin's confusion showed for a second before he regained control of his face. "The AIs? He never expressed any opinion of them one way or another."

Tanner rounded the desk. "Two minutes after the Base 59 explosion, a series of multi-spectrum communications were intercepted from the AI Lunar outpost of Camelot to Earth. To Avalon, specifically. Seven hours later, our satellites confirmed Avalon was abruptly shifting its collective effort into a new project."

Jack frowned. "How can you tell with them?"

"We keep a very close watch on the AIs," Tanner explained. "As I'm sure you can appreciate. We can penetrate right into their facilities and track changes in production. Seven hours after receiving the signal from Camelot, they shifted all manufacturing efforts into a mysterious effort."

Jack and Gethin regarded each other.

Keiko stepped forward. "Did you decipher the signal?"

"No. And not for lack of trying. Our analysts are losing sleep over the encryption. If it is encryption." Tanner wrinkled his nose unhappily. "But here we come to it: Avalon is keenly interested in preserving a technological edge over us, their nearest and most dangerous competitors. Prometheus Industries," he nodded to his guests, "has been working on the TNO project, which by its very nature requires research into experimental and exotic energies. We figure that your company developed something the AIs didn't have, and so they decided to conduct an acquisition."

Keiko's face went slack. She started to speak but checked herself.

Tanner continued. "You said there was only virtual data and a cathode rail at Base 59?"

"Yes."

"How easy would it be for Camelot to break in, download the data, and transmit it for planetside manufacturing?"

Keiko cleared her throat. "We were ready to perform field tests in the Belt."

"Avalon isn't waiting. It would appear that their entire race is working on it."

Keiko's face blushed with anger. "If true…"

"It is our working hypothesis."

"But it's a very good hypothesis."

Gethin stiffened at her eager tone. *Yes,* he thought, *it certainly seems reasonable. But it also feeds too easily into global fear.*

"How did you discover the Lunar signal?" he asked.

"You are not the only investigator working this, Bryce. I want you to examine the data from Luna and work in conjunction with other teams at our orbital facility. Naturally, I cannot order your Promethean friends to go with you, but as this does involve them, the IPC formally invites Yamanaka and Saylor to take part. We need as much input as possible. As for her," Tanner gazed penetratingly at Celeste, "I see no reason why an Outlander should continue to be part of this case."

Gethin was appalled. "You're pulling me off an independent investigation because you think *your* theory is correct? Pardon me, sir, but that is *not* how I operate. My skills are uniquely suited to asymmetrical inquiries—"

"Which is why we need you in orbit," Tanner countered hotly. "You have a knack for spotting patterns. We need you to pit your skills against Avalon's entire civilization. If we're wrong, you can return to your independent study. But right now time slips away from us."

Celeste felt a rush of terror like winter slush in her veins.

It all came back to her.

The humid evening, flies swarming in an orgy for her sweat. The adrenaline in the back of her throat.

Jeff's death.

The Stillness High Priest lunging at her, his expression of illimitable hatred, the flash of white.

Time slips away from us!

He had used those very words just seconds before she blew his damned head off. Celeste's panicked heart seemed to claw up into her throat, and she thought: *My God! It's the same man who murdered my beloved! He's here with us now!*

Tanner pressed a button on his desk. Two guards entered the room.

"There is an airship awaiting you," the IPC colonel said. "If you need a moment to pack your things, these guards will escort you." He was looking at Gethin, but as he spoke his gaze shifted to Celeste. She stared at those eyes.

The same eyes.

Wintry, pale, starlike irises in a four-pointed diamond shape around black pupils.

She could feel her blood draining away. Her fingers tapped in her pockets, drawing up a comlink tab to Gethin. Subvocally, she whispered, "Gethin. Are you sure this is Colonel Leon Tanner?"

Gethin heard the terror in her transmission.

As subtley as he could manage, he queried Ego.

<Colonel Leon Tanner matches his public profile,> the Familiar replied.

"Scan for wetware."

The response was instantaneous: <Colonel Leon Tanner has no detectable wetware.>

Absurd! Tanner was an IPC colonel; he needed a sensorium to conduct business and Cave conferences, to stay connected with the Fleet and his own staff!

"Mr. Bryce!"

Gethin looked at the colonel. "Of course, sir. I'll take the airship. But I want it on record that I object to this order. Just like I objected to the way you pulled me off the Ecuador inquiry."

Tanner's glower bored into him. "It is so noted, Bryce."

"Good. Then perhaps you'll grant me the favor of Celeste Segarra's expertise on advanced AI systems. I want her with me."

"What expertise?"

He told him about Celeste's ship. He hadn't seen it for himself, but had pried information from Keiko and Jack. It was advanced, unusual, and represented an unknown element in the topography of AI systems.

"Therefore Ms. Segarra," Gethin said, "is an important resource right now. She worked for years with an advanced mechanical intelligence. She may spot something familiar in the Lunar signal. Either way, she'll be a lot more helpful than that fool analyst you sent with me to Mars."

Tanner could barely hide his impatience. "Fine. If you feel she is useful in a professional capacity, then by all means take her. Move out."

★   ★   ★

Earth is mostly an ocean world.

Born from a fusion of necessity and hubris, Earth Republic had gazed at the rolling blue waters of their planet and, with sweet irony, began to build upon them. Here was the watery cauldron which life had crawled from, flopping and gasping, to escape the competition of the deeps. Five hundred million years later the descendants of those early pioneers were returning with newfound strength and sovereignty over Poseidon himself.

The Republic funded the creation of vast sampan villages. Like their namesakes, they were comprised of individual vessels, nodes, habitats, and pods, which linked together as a kind of mechanical Portuguese man o' war. In the event of typhoons they could break apart and submerge. The inhabitants sea-farmed, drew resources from the ocean, and soaked limitless energy through photovoltaic sails.

The sampan city of Effendi took its foundational cues from another maritime city: Venice. The ancient Italian province had originally been constructed in a marsh to escape barbarians; so too had the founders of Effendi taken to the ocean to escape the depredations of the Warlord Century, until the trilobed Republic ended the wars and brought Effendi into civilization's fold.

In the same hour that Colonel Leon Tanner was dismissing Bryce and his companions, Effendi floated seven hundred miles off the coast of Vladivostok, indifferent to global politics.

The sun was setting behind it. Several families ate dinner on the outer decks to appreciate the surreal crimsons and deep indigos blending heaven and sea. Some of the children were preparing a music recital of flutes, harps, and lyres.

There was no warning, screech of missile, or pulse of laser fire. As the recital was beginning, Effendi exploded with such force that it gouged a hole in the ocean a half mile down and scattered debris over a thousand miles. The energy signature was visible to IPC battleships in space.

CHAPTER TWENTY-SEVEN
The Airship

"Please select delivery method," the postal kiosk told him.

Gethin touched OVERNIGHT DELIVERY on the screen. He reviewed the order to Dion Bellamy, confirmed the man's last known address in the Bahamas, and pressed his fingertip against the payment pad.

"Please insert letter."

Gethin dropped the envelope he'd purchased from the kiosk into the mail-slot. Inside was a hard copy of everything Keiko's magpie had culled from the golems. Probably not very much. The IPC sweep team would comb the corpses down to the electron, but Keiko was right: if you didn't get your sample fast, you were wasting your time. Top-line golems were like flash-paper. When they died your window of opportunity closed in microseconds.

Under ordinary circumstances Gethin would have sent his hard copy to an IPC lab for trace analysis…but not now. He knew he needed someone as far outside IPC influence as possible. Someone he could trust. And he didn't want it sent over the web, where a tapeworm could intercept it.

"Thank you for using Republic Post," the kiosk intoned. "Have a terrific day."

Gethin returned to his compatriots. They stood by the elevator with their luggage like tenderfoot tourists, having returned to their rooms to hastily pack and check out. Gethin sighed, reminded yet again of what few belongings he had to his name.

"All set," he announced. He noted Celeste's pleading gaze and ignored it. Hopefully she would get the message: no more communications. Their hands brushed in the elevator and he interlaced his fingers with hers.

The floor numbers ticked off. The carriage ascended to the shuttleport with a placid hum.

Gethin reviewed what he knew of where Tanner was sending them. An orbital station locked in geosynchronous orbit over Avalon, the famous AI city. An observant eye on Earth's only known nonhuman metropolis. Access was harshly limited. No way in.

Or out.

Tanner was imprisoning them.

The elevator slowed and stopped.

"Air Terminal Five," the lift's honey-warm voice informed them.

They fanned out onto the arcology rooftop. The airship hovered directly above, its massive zeppelin shape pewter-gray against the overcast afternoon. Terminal Five was the zenith of the arcology, reserved for the largest aircraft. The wind raggedly assailed them. Gethin shivered.

"So what now?" Celeste asked neutrally.

Keiko thought the question was directed at her, and so she started talking about IPC battleships that could bombard Avalon from orbit. The Prometheus war wing would happily assist, sending Enforcers to scorch the metal cancer from lower altitude. Republic troops would then comb through the rubble and make sure every circuit was melted, while Luna would mobilize for the decimation of Camelot. The AIs would be a grim footnote in history.

Celeste interrupted her. "Gethin? What do we do?"

He stared at the airship. "We get onboard."

"But—"

"Come on," he said, taking her by the arm.

Keiko hesitated. "Is there a problem?"

Gethin shook his head. The guards herded them up the embarkation platform.

It was heavily air-conditioned inside the ship. Everything padded for optimal luxury: blue pashmina chairs and foldout desktops equipped with wetports and chargers. The cloud-diffused afternoon burned coldly through oval windows. The high ceiling was a bramble of nanosteel I-beams. A grand stairway connected all three floors: upper deck for crew cabin and dignitary seating; middle deck for general passengers; lower deck for cargo and luggage.

Gethin swallowed, agitated by his uncertainty. He could see no options. Mechanically, he queried Ego for the passenger manifest. It flashed instantly:

GETHIN BRYCE
JACK SAYLOR
CELESTE SEGARRA
KEIKO YAMANAKA

Not that the deserted middle floor left much doubt as to the company they would have. Gethin seated himself at a windowside table, puzzling over this fact. An *airship* for four passengers?

Why is Tanner imprisoning me? Have I somehow gotten too close to the truth? It sure as hell doesn't feel like it. Since death, I've been captured at a hospital, met with a university colleague, been propositioned by a Wastelander, and then nearly beaten to death by corporate-grade golems. That was a lot for a two-day-old human being...and I still don't know what the hell's going on.

To Ego, he muttered, "Identify surveillance fields around us."

<The surveillance systems on this ship are engaged.>

★They can be electronically jammed, Gethin,★ suggested Id.

"Yes, but that will tip them off."

He wasn't ready to deal with the awesome weight of implications happening here. Leon Tanner was not Leon Tanner. The man had been commandeered somehow. Replicated, imitated. A golem? No, the person he had been speaking with was too intelligent, too high-functioning.

And where was the real Tanner? Held hostage somewhere? Killed in a dampened room where his lifecode couldn't be detected and purchase signals could never escape?

The airship engines thrummed and the ship rose without fuss into the sky, leaving the skypad behind. Gethin leaned against the window. His beloved Athens sank like a luminescent dream into deeper layers of slumber.

Back to the darkness, he thought, chilled. The words of an ancient poem from Lord Byron floated into his consciousness:

> The bright sun was extinguish'd, and the stars
> Did wander darkling in the eternal space,
> Rayless, and pathless, and the icy earth
> Swung blind and blackening in the moonless air

"Gethin?"

It was Keiko, sitting across from him.

He blinked at her, but his words were directed elsewhere. "Do it."

Keiko frowned. "Do what?"

Jamming surveillance band.

Gethin leaned towards the Prometheans. "Okay, we don't have much time, so listen closely. I have reason to believe that Colonel Tanner is not Colonel Tanner. He has been replaced. Looks like the man, but sure as hell doesn't possess the man's memories."

Jack's eyes bulged. "*Replaced? By whom?*"

"The last time I met Tanner was eleven years ago. He was chock full of wetware. Sensorium, wetport, medcells. Some cutting-edge things too—"

"So?"

"So the Tanner I met today was a goddamn virgin. There wasn't so much as an earpiece on him."

Doros Peisistratos had no wetware, either.

Keiko looked unimpressed. "Stealth augs."

"I considered that. That's why I tested him as we left. Tanner never pulled me off the Ecuador inquiry. I finished the damn assignment, I reported my findings to him in person. And my Mars inquiry? Tanner never sent a partner with me to the Red Planet. I'm telling you, the man we just met was not the colonel."

Celeste sweated openly. "Gethin, that man—"

"Wait a minute," Keiko interjected, "Who else could he be? Are you screwing with us again?"

"The man in that office is a goddamn imposter!"

Something happened in Keiko's eyes. They developed a cold sheen like the patina of polished chrome, the kind of look from their Arcadium days, when they had worked together to carve up digital empires like ancient conquerors. He could see his words finding their mark.

Her hand strayed to the back of her ear.

"Don't do that," Gethin warned. "This is an IPC ship and they monitor everything. I'm jamming surveillance, but I can't cloak messages you might send to PI."

Gethin, my frequency jammers are being countered faster than I can adjust. You have three seconds.

"Just sit tight and play along," Gethin told his companions. He flicked Keiko's knee, gave her a meaningful look.

Two seconds.

One.

"Keiko," he said loudly, "Just what is your fucking problem? Sorry our marriage didn't work out, but if Tanner is right and Avalon is behind this, that's a bit more important than our personal baggage…unless you'd rather the machines take over during your protracted hissy fit?"

Keiko turned so red that Gethin worried she might actually deck him. "Same old Gethin Bryce. I *have* moved on! I got offworld. But you, even when you finally worked up the nerve to leave Mother Blue, nothing changed!"

"Part of my charm."

"Part of why you'll always be alone!"

They bantered, bringing up enough personal issues to make Jack and Celeste wriggle uncomfortably. The Outlander excused herself to use the bathroom.

"Wait," Keiko snapped. "Are we just letting this woman walk around alone? *She's got an AI ship.* Maybe she's working with them!"

"Celeste is fine," Gethin retorted, wondering if Keiko was still playacting or being serious now.

Keiko whirled. "Fine? Why, because she has a nice pair of tits? Another youngster to quicken you?"

Gethin's face flushed. "You're the one who brought her to civilization. You go watch her urinate."

"I brought her to Babylon, got what I needed, and was done with her. You insisted she come to Athens for reasons that are strangely unclear."

"Maybe I thought she had a nice pair of tits."

Celeste descended the stairs in a hurry, heart pounding. She reached the bottom of the stairs and suddenly keeled over, the emotional impact of reliving Jeff's death like a gut punch. She squeezed her eyes shut, sobbing once, hammering her fists into the floor.

"Can I help you, ma'am?"

She glanced up. A young IPC guard had rounded the corner and was watching her in concern.

"Sorry, but all passengers must remain upstairs."

Celeste dredged up the closest thing to a smile she could manage. "You prefer I piss all over the floor?"

The guard smirked, as if to say, *Well yes, I would prefer that.* He pointed to a door. "Bathroom is there."

"Thanks," she said, and went inside, locked the door. She studied the bathroom mirror. A scared girl looked back.

"*Mantid*?" she asked quietly.

Her optics gave a NO SIGNAL. They really were cut off here.

She didn't know where the *Mantid* was, but ships in King D.'s nascent revolution were highly protective of their owners. The last communication she'd had with it had been only two words.

HERE. WAITING.

Yet the *Mantid* knew she was in Athens. Invisible, it must surely be shadowing her. Was it outside the airship even now?

Her reflection offered no answers. Just grim commitment to a grimmer decision.

★　★　★

She emerged from the bathroom and nearly plowed into the guard, who had taken vigil directly on the other side of the door. The kid was a few inches shorter than Jack, but he didn't wear the height well; a toothpick man, gaunt and sunken in the way an arky should never be. Celeste had seen malnourished looks like that before in Outland folk all over the Americas.

Celeste smiled. "Trying to listen to the sound of my tinkle?"

The guard looked somewhat abashed. "No! I just to wanted to make sure—"

"That us Wastelanders know how to use the bathroom?"

"You...you're a Wastelander?"

"A frustrated Wastelander." She stared into his eyes and decided that he really was as young as he looked. Twenty years old if he was a day. "Those people upstairs? I'm in their custody, did you know that? They watch what I eat, drink...hell, I haven't been allowed to fuck since I got here, and I'm so frustrated I can barely think straight."

The guard looked conflicted. He stared to say something, stammered, then turned to make sure they were alone.

Stars, she thought. *How have men managed to achieve anything with their dicks acting as cosmic divining rods?*

The instant he looked away, Celeste shoved him so hard his feet left the ground. She dashed past him, rounded the corner, and flung open the cargo hold door.

She had no plan. The guard had merely commented that no one was allowed down here. That was excuse enough, knowing what she knew, to see why the cargo hold was forbidden. Why an immense airship was being used to cart four people to an orbital station.

As she stepped through the door, however, she froze in place.

Thirty additional people were huddled throughout the hold! They were a mixed crew, all armed with weaponry of crude, nasty variety. Fleschettes, multiguns, handguns...but Celeste only had eyes for the wet-looking, summer-green cloaks they wore.

Stillness cloaks.

Holy shit!

She heard the guard come rushing up behind her.

Celeste spun around and squatted as the man reached her. Her punch was aimed for his crotch, and it connected beautifully; he made a wheezing sound as he doubled over. Celeste caught his chin with an uppercut. Then she tore a pistol from his holster – a stunner as it happened.

The Stillness troopers in the hold scrambled to their feet. But there was a hesitation; Celeste realized they hadn't expected this turn of events. She could see it in their eyes: they were being secretly transported – to the orbital station or whatever the next stop was to be. They were supposed to stay secret; her sudden appearance confused them, gave enough time to save her life.

Celeste bolted for the stairs. Halfway up their length, she turned and fired the stunner at the first head that rounded the corner. The blast put the man down. She leapt up the rest of the way.

Her survival instincts cycled through the possibilities. *Thirty fanatical and armed soldiers who will gleefully die for their ideology. The IPC in collusion with them...*

...and we're in an airship at least thirty thousand feet up.

In the airship's passenger cabin, Gethin intercepted her.

"Stillness!" she cried. "Thirty Stillness troopers in the hold!" As she spoke, three IPC officers – or rather, three men dressed as IPC officers – appeared atop the grand stairs leading to the crew cabin, drawn by the clamor and shouts.

Gethin was looking right at them when they emerged. Their names should have appeared on his optics, but there was nothing.

Impossible.

All IPC officers were registered to the global infosystem. Standing in the clutches of panic, Gethin made the connection. These were Outlanders recruited by Tanner's look-alike. The famished look on their faces. The scrawny bodies. They'd been given uniforms. Weapons. Control of the airship.

Celeste pointed her stunner at the officers and squeezed the trigger. One of the men seized up, teeth locking, eyes white. As his compatriots dove to either side, he made a half spin and fell, rolling down the winding stairs like a bowling pin.

Keiko and Jack were up from their seats, sidearms out, moving in eerie synchronicity. They each flipped a table for cover. Keiko fired at the upper stairs, scattering the officers up there; Jack covered the descent to the lower hold.

A green-cloaked woman appeared from below decks and he killed her with a shot through the head.

Celeste retreated to Gethin's side, stunner in hand.

"Twenty-eight down below," she snapped. "Um...you don't have a weapon? That's just great."

"Isn't it, though?"

A multigun jerked over the rim of the lower level and sprayed an arc of needles into the room, forcing the Prometheans to tuck against their covers.

Gethin's blurmod kicked in.

At IPC Academy, blurmod training involved circumnavigating a gymnasium-sized room while automated turrets shot rubber rounds at you. Hurt like a bitch when they connected and left purple bull's-eye-shaped bruises. Cadets hated the course.

Hyperaccelerated, Gethin fell back on that training now. He scooped Celeste off her feet and moved away from the needle-sprayer.

From the grand stairs, there was movement. The two 'officers', matching his speed.

One of the officers leapt down the entire flight and landed well, pistol firing twice. Keiko took both shots in her chest. The bullets flattened against her uniform, the impact knocking her backwards. She hit the floor, rolled aside as a third shot tore a chunk out of the tiles where her head had just been. Stillness troopers surged from the lower floor like a green geyser.

Without weapons, about to be pinned down between crossfire, Gethin did the only thing that he could think of. He conjured the blueprints of the airship. Holding up one finger, he activated the fire suppression system. The room instantly filled with chalky mist, blanketing the oncoming Stillness troops with several hundred pounds of directed force. The troops were flattened or knocked aside in the extinguishing jets. One man had fallen face-first to the floor, the suppression system reading his presence as a hard-to-put-out chemical fire; he stoutly tried getting to his feet, slipping and weaving in the abrasive fog. Foam bubbled around his multigun, only meters away.

A multigun!

Gethin dove for it, grabbed it, opened fire on the prone troopers he saw, cutting them down as they floundered and stumbled in the miasma of sodium bicarbonate. Bullets and fleschette needles whistled past him. One came close enough to trigger his blurmod again. He snapped into hyperacceleration.

And noticed something strange in the air.

A black disc like a hockey puck was crawling overhead towards Keiko and Jack. The Prometheans were ringed by corpses, but their uniforms were also pockmarked by rounds they had taken themselves. Crouched together, firing together, their bodies seemingly frozen to Gethin's accelerated viewpoint. Blurmods recharging, bullets whispering through the haze around them, neither had noticed the black disc gliding towards them from above. The—

—grenade!

Thinking fast, Gethin leapt into the air, slapped the grenade out of its slow-motion arc. The wallop from his hand knocked it aside, but it detonated a moment later, the shell disintegrating into a flash of white that outpaced his own speed.

His blurmod died. Gethin was flung into the opposite wall.

<Wetware batteries depleted 70 percent,> Ego advised.

The airship seemed to have been consumed by a hurricane. Wind batted his ears. A pistol flew past his head towards the—

Open breach! The airship is breached!

The grenade blast had torn a gash in the airship. The vessel's hull grated and flapped like the wings of a mechanical bird. Everything not bolted down disappeared out into the visible sky.

Gethin barely had time to cling to a support column. His multigun spun away and was gone, followed by green-cloaked figures.

"Gethin!"

He managed to rotate his head in the tempest. Celeste was embracing a nearby column, gasping for breath.

"There's no way I'll survive this!" she screamed.

Gethin craned to look towards Jack and Keiko.

They were gone.

Two more soldiers flew past his head. They slammed into the ceiling, snapping limbs, bounced twice, and were blown out of the ship.

"You guys are immortal!" Celeste insisted. "I'm not!"

What happened next horrified him so much he almost let go of the column. Fighting to breathe, Celeste seemed to mutter something he couldn't hear in the furious wind. Then she released her grip. She sailed towards the rupture with an odd grace, tucked her head and arms close, and *let herself be sucked out into the open atmosphere.*

At thirty thousand feet.

CHAPTER TWENTY-EIGHT
Suicide

She was committing suicide to save her life.

The irony came on as giddy terror while she plummeted through the clouds, air bursting from her lungs in the thin sky. Her clothes flapped like a bat swarm at her ears.

Celeste twisted herself, seeing the airship dwindle to a pale point above her. Then it was gone, her world engulfed by pure whiteout, like a snowblind strike into someone's optics. She was engulfed by clouds. Crazily, she found herself thinking of the pegasus in Athens, effortlessly gliding around the restaurant.

The decision had been pure instinct. The life she was willing to trade for StrikeDown could not be lost on a hijacked airship. She could stay and die, or jump through the breach and…

She couldn't breathe. The air was so cold it burned her face. Free of the jamming frequencies, she tried again to contact her vessel. "I am here! I am here!"

In the absolute whiteness of cloud, she struggled against terminal velocity to open her virtuboard. The digital overlay appeared; the green font so light against the clouds she needed to squeeze her eyes shut to read it. Again, she said the words, watching them appear on her optics.

"I.

"Am.

"Here."

And from a lake sixteen miles east of Athens arcology, the *Mantid* raised an invisible rail-gun turret to the sky and fired.

★ ★ ★

The *Mantid* never slept.

Its intelligence circuits were sufficiently complex that, when its crew was away, it retreated into the gloaming of standby mode. There, systems powered down to a crawl, its consciousness floated in dream-shape abstractions not entirely unlike human REM, purging errors and anxieties that had accumulated in its higher processors. Even then, the *Mantid* maintained a hypnagogic awareness of its environment.

Its crew was dead.

Their absence upset an accustomed dynamic; they no longer fed their unique inputs into the *Mantid*'s considerations. Gone, deleted forever. Only Celeste Segarra proved recoverable, and the *Mantid* was pleased to have recovered her. There was a brief moment when it feared she had died in Babylon – when the Prometheans deactivated her sensorium and there was no way to reach her. During this uncertain epoch, the *Mantid* sent cautious surveillance feelers into Babylon and discovered Celeste alive, eating an apple, in a hospital food court.

But then she had been transported to Athens. The *Mantid* followed like a parent discreetly shadowing its child. Watching her transport land at Athens. Descending to the Mediterranean Sea.

To wait.

And now she was in the sky, falling, too far away for the *Mantid* itself to reach her.

Invisible on the lake, it tracked the pseudopod it had fired into the overcast sky.

★   ★   ★

Celeste plummeted towards Earth.

The clouds sheared away and she was gazing on wispy archipelagos of vapor, feebly strung together like pearls over a patchwork planet of muted green, brown, and black. So beautiful! She felt a sob welling in her throat.

I'm going euphoric, she thought, recognizing the sensation and its cause: glucose in her blood rising, blunting her terror into something more manageable. The frantic, impotent reflex of a sentient creature faced with oblivion. Denial at terminal velocity.

Keep it together, Celeste!

She rocketed downward through the airy isles like a bullet through cotton.

★   ★   ★

Gethin heard the airship ripping open around him and the metal squealing like a piteous creature. The violent pitch of descent tipped it into a nosedive. A maelstrom of wheeling bodies emptied into the sky as he clutched the column for all he was worth.

"Give me an audio readout of the ship's altimeter!" he shouted to Ego. He couldn't hear his own voice.

<Ten thousand feet.>

The airship dipped so suddenly that Gethin's legs were suddenly dangling above him. He amped his muscles to keep his grip.

<Nine thousand feet.>

He glanced around in the feeble hope of spotting his compatriots. Instead of finding them, he observed a woman hanging from the ceiling's I-beams, her face stretched into an awful inaudible scream. Her green cloak flapped around her. She might have been a superhero from old comics, hugging the beams as if to lift the entire craft against gravity.

<Eight thousand feet.>

<Seven thousand feet.>

<Five thousand feet.>

<Four thousand feet.>

★   ★   ★

Celeste fell.

She could breathe now; this consolation was just enough to suppress her giddiness and constrict her focus. She became aware of a small object hurtling up towards her, a black fleck visible against cropfields and roads.

The pseudopod came like a birdshot fired at a clay skeet. She dropped past it, watching her hope go wide as the pseudopod flew past, seemingly destined for space. But behind her, the device swiveled thrusters, shifted its straight trajectory into an arc, and swept around, descending towards the falling human.

Celeste saw the ground hurtling towards her.

[I am here, Celeste.]

The voice lanced into her thoughts. Celeste sobbed at the maternal tenderness in that synthesized harmonic. Alone without family or friends, without Jeff, she at least had her ship.

Peripherally she realized the pseudopod was now a few arm-lengths away, bridging the distance by inches. Screaming as it cut through the air to reach her.

Celeste grabbed for it, touched its hot and unexpectedly soft shapestone exterior. Her fingers snaked into handholds that deepened for her fingertips; within the molecular latticework, tiny commands flashing, directing reconfigurations, rendering handholds into a pliable substance not unlike rubber. Straps of this flexible metal-flesh snaked out and embraced her. The thrusters fired anew, exhausting themselves as they defied the grim gravity-well of Mother Blue.

Celeste glanced over her shoulder at the sky.

There, like a massive bomb from earlier, barbaric times, the airship was pitching through the sky. By the time Celeste's pseudopod had angled its descent into a gentle glide towards the treetops of an unknown woodland, the airship was plowing past her into those same woods, snapping canopy as it went.

The ship shrieked out of sight and exploded.

PART THREE
OUTLANDS

There should always be a wilderness.

Recognizing the delicate social contract between government and individual, there should always be a place for an individual to go if he or she decides they dislike the social contract or what's become of it.

The Outlands, the Wastes, the gloplands, we hear, are such a place. But the people who dwell there don't choose this exile; it is forced upon them by an accident of birth. They remain because they must, sharing that wilderness with the remnant fragments of Warlord gangs, victimized while we play in our ivory arcologies. They fight for scraps of food with beasts.

They deserve it, you say? Is it because their ancestors refused to cooperate with the early unification under Apollo, Enyalios, and the armies of Lady Wen Ying? Are sons and daughters to be punished for the sins of their shortsighted forbearers?

Is it the old religions that still dominate these communities, making us fear the insidious influence that destroyed civilization at least twice before? Haven't you wondered why these people cling to Bronze Age belief systems? Deprived of endless life, they will grasp at whatever crutch they can.

I have written these columns for fifty-nine years now, and have seen no change of attitude. The Wastes shall remain Wastes, you declare with your inaction, and to hell with the people living there! I have hosted programs, gone into the Outlands with people, brought them supplies. I have interviewed the ones who suffer there. Some of you have sent aid, when the newsfeeds stir you to action. But we are too far gone, as a society, to truly effect change. We dwell in our digital Xanadus and shall not be moved.

Earth can never shake off its past.

But I can.

Dear readers, I am leaving Earth for redworld shores. Mars! A world without war, without Wastes.

Farewell to Blue Hell! I embrace MarsAlone!

Gebhard Bleibtreu

CHAPTER TWENTY-NINE
Hanmura2 Goes to Club Nadsat

In his tearoom, Sakyo Hanmura2 broke meditation after a few minutes and, acting on an astonishingly atypical impulse, took a Lunarcab to New Shinjuku.

On Mars, he was accustomed to daily meditation in his corporate tatami room, where he could hear the dim gurgle of garden streams through rice-paper walls. There, too, he might thumb through the jade books of Basho or Miyamoto Musashi, or traverse the forested shadow of Mount Olympus. Hanmura had even written his death poem while contemplating the caramel Martian firmament that was, year by year, turning more violet, folding into bruised purple sunsets, and destined to imitate the heavens of Earth. Such loss! His death poem reflected that...the impermanence of worlds while he, Hanmura, was forever.

His company's Lunar facility accommodated his tastes well enough: a tatami-matted room with shoji walls and rich, buttery light radiating around rock gardens. The low gravity was a reminder that he was not on Mars, though. Even with magfiber footwear, he felt like a helium balloon every time he moved.

He was restless.

Anxious.

Needful of things he could not identify.

So he went to New Shinjuku. With only three bodyguards.

In the Lunarcab, he slid a skin-shell over his head and let the fiberoptic mesh conjure up a randomized Japanese face. They docked at the city's western gate and went straight to a club he'd often seen on the covers of glossy hedonistic magazines. Club Nadsat.

It was a structure four stories deep, each level boasting a different aesthetic theme of urban grittiness. Graffiti-sprayed walls, brick enclosures, Wastetown rubble, and a sunken abbey. Hanmura2 entered at ground level. The dance floor crawled with a mix of Japanese, Chinese, Thai, and Korean partygoers interspersed with dreadlocked Africans and gangly Caucasians.

The club's music was a thudding tribal heartbeat. Hanmura2 grabbed a table along the balcony, unsure of what to do with his strange impulsiveness. The club-goers roiled like green surf. It made him think of a cruise ship he had been on, back when he lived Earthside and frequented the Caribbean. He remembered a scuba expedition at night. The floodlights igniting the ocean. Like swimming in milky jade. For years afterwards, he'd made annual pilgrimages to Caricom just to experience that ocean again.

"Get me a *sake*," he told Hideo, newest of his bodyguards. The man was halfway to the bar when Hanmura2 called him back. "No, no. A beer. Whatever they have on tap."

He smiled behind his skin-shell mask. *Yes, let me not be Hanmura tonight. This body will be destroyed in a few weeks, memories and all. I will vaporize like some forgotten dream. So a dream I shall be then, and a good one at that.*

"Who drinks beer anymore?" a voice asked behind him.

Hanmura2 looked to see a round-faced woman smiling at him across the rim of her fluted champagne glass. She was Philippino, maybe Malay. Pretty. Imp-like eyes set above a dainty nose, with wide smiling lips. A dynamite fuck-me figure clad in a red, form-fitting cheongsam. Her hair was tied in a bun, set with red chopsticks.

And beside her was another girl, taller and paler. Real Japanese, by the look of those sculpted cheekbones and elegant limbs. Smaller breasted than her voluptuous friend, her hair in braids encircling her head, she wore a deep blue kimono.

"So? Beer?" the red-dressed woman teased. "Try a Godblood."

His true self would dismiss these frivolous tarts in favor of something more refined. His Olympus castle contained a geisha house, stabled with Renaissance women trained in no fewer than forty musical instruments, capable of reciting thousands of poems, able to sing in up to thirty languages, accomplished Arcadium counterparts and superb equestrians, who could storymod more tales than Scheherazade, and match his wit with lovely brazenness. What could these Lunar whores do to compare?

His true self would scoff, showing cold iron in his eyes and lips.

But this is a perishable me!

"Godblood?" he said. "That's a pheromod."

Both girls stared at him, unbelieving. They burst into laughter.

"Why, so it is!" the red-dressed girl exclaimed.

"Mocking me?" Hanmura2 asked, modulating his voice to inject playfulness into the words.

"Do I get spanked if the answer is yes?" She moaned sharply while thrusting out her head in a silly faux-orgasmic pose.

It was crude, obvious, overtly Western.

But dear gods! he thought helplessly. *I want her! I want them both!*

He regarded the nihonjin. "And you? Are you a spanker or spankee?"

"I'm Masami, and let me give you a clue what I like." She turned to her smaller friend, lovingly grasped the back of her hair, and with the other hand slapped her face. Hard. The girl's cheek matched the hue of her cheongsam for a moment. Masami drew the trollop closer, shoving her face against her neck where the girl began kissing, mewling submissively at her cleavage.

"Looks like three would be a crowd," Hanmura2 said, turning away.

"What do you think a girl has two tits for?" Masami challenged.

He stopped. Bodyguard Hideo was returning with his beer.

Hanmura2 looked at the girls. Looked back to Hideo.

"Send the beer back," he barked. "And get me a fucking Godblood."

Both girls giggled.

"Now you're talking!"

Hanmura2 straightened in his chair. "I talk all fucking day. Tonight, I'm not interested in conversation."

Masami's eyes were firestones. "Good, because that's not my game either."

Hanmura2 felt pinned by those eyes. Stars! Her gaze was pure predator, icy hot, the raw force of an instinctive dominatrix. He decided he had completely misjudged her age.

"Then let's play your game," he said, matching her steel. "And maybe you can bring your pet too."

"Oh, she comes wherever I want her to." Masami cruelly grasped the other girl's wrist and said to her, "Let's go, little girl! Let's follow the bad bad boy to a room."

He waited only to get the Godblood from Hideo. Then he eagerly tailed them to the next level down where bungalows honeycombed the walls. Masami looked at the drink in his hand.

"Try it," she ordered.

Hanmura2 brought the cobalt blue liquid to his lips. His sensorium deftly jacked the grayweb to look up what a Godblood was. The definition appeared in his eyes:

GODBLOOD. A synthetic pheromone and energy drink.

He swallowed a sip. His poison receptors weren't triggered. He swallowed more. It tasted the way a live wire might, if melted down to a drinkable fluid that diffused, not dispelled, its electrical properties. The tingling went swiftly to his loins.

Masami and her partner (whom she had introduced as Pet Momo) keyed into one of the bungalows. Hanmura2 had barely entered when they were already skinning out of their clothes. Momo's busty figure made him salivate. No way that was a natural body. She must have been grown from a patchwork genotype. Her nipples were swollen with excitement. Masami had the advantage in sleek legs. Hanmura2 fought to restrain himself, transfixed with animal hunger by two sets of rounded breasts.

He turned his back on them and undressed with cursory motions. Leaving his boxer shorts on, he folded his clothes and stacked them in the corner.

Then he glanced back to the girls.

They were gone.

In their place was a giant black scorpion.

Hanmura2 didn't waste any time standing in amazement. He tapped his left forearm twice to summon his guards.

The scorpion stretched its tail. The segmented appendage extended like a bristly, unsightly tree, the tip grossly swollen with venom.

Hanmura2 repressed the urge to run for the door or overturn the bungalow's futon to use as a shield. He was immortal. And this whole thing was probably some sick joke being played on him. Maybe by Gates or Bielawa. He wouldn't give anyone the satisfaction.

The scorpion's tail reached a zenith and began to bloat. At the same time, the lower portion of the creature was shriveling, retracting its pincers into its head, the body dwindling as if all its life juices were being pulled inexorably into its tail.

And the tail was becoming something else.

Hanmura2 gasped as the armored scorpion shapeshifted into a man.

In seconds, the arachnid was gone. The man was all that was left of it, and he floated lotus-style, like a grinning Buddha on an aerostat shelf. Hanmura2 gaped, knowing this was just an illusion but unable to look away.

He had never seen this man before. Vaguely Middle Eastern, bearing a swarthy pallor suggesting Arabian roots. Curly black hair crowned his oval head. His face was sculpted with a forbidding sharpness, and despite the hooked aquiline nose there was something in his elongated features that suggested reptilian origins. Black eyes peered beneath pitched eyebrows. A bristly chinbeard hung many inches beneath his mouth. He wore a very plain, pitch-black garment over his lank body.

He was smiling.

"I'm not impressed, Masami," Hanmura2 said. "Parlor tricks."

"And yet you currently exist on three worlds," the man said in a clear, crystal timbre. "Is that a parlor trick also?"

Hanmura2 walked straight at the apparition. "Allow me to show you a parlor trick." His hands clenched into iron fists.

An instant later, he was pitched against the far wall. The collision felt like it should have flattened him. He crashed to the floor, blinking stupidly, while his flesh crawled with pain as if he'd been splashed by hot water.

"I like that one!" the man said cheerfully, and he extended his legs to the floor. He strode over, peeled Hanmura2's skin-shell from his face as the CEO lay weakly. Then he lifted him up by his hair.

Hanmura2 glared weakly at his attacker. Every inch of his skin throbbed like a blistering sunburn.

"My name is Apophis and you are in violation of IPC law," the stranger said. "I am here to place you under arrest."

Hanmura2 stared dumbly.

"Will you come peacefully or not? Because −" the man's good-humored face became serpentine, "− I can be very unpleasant if I'm vexed. Dost thou vex me, you little insect?"

Hanmura2 didn't bother messaging his guards again. Whatever was happening here, his communications were being jammed. Hideo especially would have been here a half second after the command was given.

Apophis tossed him into a corner, like chucking a small suitcase.

Am I being hacked? Hanmura2 wondered. *Is this guy feeding false images to my optics?* Hanmura2 pressed behind his ear to deactivate his sensorium. The whirring in his head went silent.

The man was still there.

"I shall present you with a choice," Apophis said after a moment's pause. "I can haul your ass before the Redemption Board. They will be happy to make an example of the powerful Sakyo Hanmura. Edit you down to your core personality, I suspect. Not to mention the stocks in Hanmura Enterprises will plummet, horror of horrors!" The man chuckled, and he circled the bed. With each stride, his black tunic altered. The transformation was incredibly subtle. In four steps he was wearing a sable coat, pale trousers, and his chinbeard had reshaped into a Mongolian goatee.

"Your second choice," Apophis said, "is to rule within the new power structure of humanity. To be a satrap of the empire that is to come."

Hanmura2 waited. His heart thrilled with confusion and fear.

A skin-shell? That had to be it! But he had scanned both girls. They had no tech whatsoever.

"Is there some purpose to this?" Hanmura2 demanded.

"I represent Stillness," the man said, growing grave all of a sudden. Too grave, too grim, as if the mood change were done by the flick of a switch. Hanmura2 got the distinct impression that everything he was seeing was a carefully calibrated illusion; this maniac's emotions switched too rapidly.

Hanmura2 sneered. "Stillness. Earthly terrorist group. What of them?"

"They wanted me to pass along some very important information to you."

"I'm listening."

"The person responsible for destroying Base 59 and the shuttle was an experiment gone haywire. The Prometheans have rewritten the rules on what is possible, Hanmura-sama. If the IPC realized this…there would be war."

"So?"

Apophis's liquid eyes shimmered. "Whoever tips off the IPC to this illegal creation would slay the great Dragon."

Hanmura2 scowled. "I don't conduct business in this manner."

Apophis looked perplexed. "What manner? Negotiating with a scorpion man? Come *on!* It's the only way to do business, my friend!"

"If you have information, why not contact me in a more traditional way? Why this stupid lure?" *And how did he throw me so easily? Enhanced muscles? Cybernetic strength augs? That should have shown up in a scan. And my skin…why does it feel as if it's been burned?* "Answer me!"

Apophis's eyes watered. Tears ran down his face at a snap, his lips curling in anguish. *"Don't yell at me!"* he pleaded. "It hurts me when you yell! Those bad people at Base 59 made a bad thing and someone has to know. Punish those bad, crabby people! I thought…" He sobbed. "I thought you *cared!* Who else can I go to, if not you?"

Hanmura2 was agog. Was he serious?

Apophis sank down to the floor, grasping both knees and rocking back and forth. "They will just do it again! Make more bad things to hurt more people.

You can't let that happen!"

Hanmura2 looked to the door, calculating his chances of reaching it uninterrupted.

He looked back.

Apophis stood right in front of him. As if he'd teleported from the floor.

"Will you accept my proposal, or no?"

Hanmura2 panted. "No."

"Then it would be disadvantageous to allow you to live."

The corporate chieftain feinted for the door. Then he secretly popped the nanoblade from his arm. Turned to the side, it was virtually invisible.

Apophis was upon him. Hanmura2 let out a yell and dropped into a samurai's lunging stance, one leg splayed back while the other crouched like a spring. He shoved his blade into Apophis's heart.

The man looked stunned. Hanmura2 shoved it in another few inches, then pulled it out and ran for the door. He didn't bother retracting the blade; there was no telling what awaited him elsewhere in the club.

Suddenly he was seized from behind, spun around, and shoved against the ceiling. His body stuck there like glue.

Apophis held him there, grinning like a crocodile. But Hanmura2 knew rage when he saw it. The hate emanating from this creature was deep and powerful, far more than a child's demanding tantrum or a righteously enraged fanatic. Hanmura2 felt despised as if he was a parasite.

"May I see the arm that wounded me?" the man asked, brown eyes twinkling.

Hanmura2 didn't even have time to consider complying. As if an electric current were branching through his body and manipulating it like a sock puppet, his right arm extended. Hanmura2, pinned against the ceiling, couldn't budge.

"*Mittai desu, kudasai.*" The Japanese accent was perfect: *Watch this, please.*

And then Hanmura2 screamed.

It wasn't merely that his arm caught fire. The burn started deep in his flesh, setting every nerve ending alight with excruciating agony. A million swords sliced in his muscle. The skin cooked, shriveled, collapsed into red ash that danced like ants over the metal blade.

The stink reached Hanmura2's nose. He vomited at once, from pain and horror. The vomit splattered down from the ceiling. His head lolled, sweat spilling down his cheeks.

"Stay awake," Apophis purred.

The magical field holding him to the ceiling vanished. Hanmura2 plummeted to the floor and he flopped like a poisoned cockroach. The pain was too much to bear. He rammed his head into the wet floor.

His body's pain dampeners went to work, cutting off all sensation. But his arm! It had become a blackened twig, his nanoblade just visible against the ash and melted bone, like some hideous candle.

"Shall I continue?"

Hanmura2 shook his head. He could hear his ruined arm sizzling. Sleepiness overtook him. His mouth felt slurred and half-paralyzed. He knew it was the beginning of shock. His bodily defense, detecting this alarming shift in blood pressure, pumped him full of endorphins.

"Stay awake," Apophis said gently.

"What...do you...want of me?"

"I request that you inform the IPC of what I have told you. Prometheus Industries has created a terrible monster, and it destroyed the lab, the shuttle, and will certainly kill again. You must tell them about it. You must tell them where it is."

Hanmura2 shuddered, dangling in the man's grip. Voice slurring, he asked, "Where is it?"

Apophis stared at him as if he was unbearably thickheaded. "Why, right in front of you, Hanmura-sama."

CHAPTER THIRTY
Gloplands

Light.

Shadows moving around him, touching him. Pale afternoon and the sounds of a forest. Birds trilled in a dozen native cries. Gethin dimly recognized the steel-whistle chirp of a bluejay.

Something wet tugged clumsily at his tunic.

Gethin opened his eyes in time to see a pulpy, red-purple face inspecting him, tentacles prodding at his hair, face, and shirt. He stared dumbly, aware of sharp bristles of pain racking his body. His right leg was twisted and throbbing and his sensorium splashed a half dozen screens across his eyes.

But the immediate concern was the tentacled creature. Gethin swallowed, tasting an acrid ammoniac smell in the air. Suckers quizzically pulled at his shoulder strap and sash. A tentacle entwined his hair and yanked.

"Hey!" Gethin snapped.

The pulpy creature recoiled in panic, springing away and bumping into pieces of wreckage as it went. Gethin spied a dozen other mollusks scattering in every direction, propelling themselves on their eight legs in rapid, ungainly strides.

As soon as he sat up, he cried out from stabbing pain in his leg. His sudden movement summoned his medgrid overlay, congesting his vision with red crosses flashing around a diagram of his body.

He took a few seconds to appreciate what the medgrid was telling him. Nerve suppression was running high on his injured areas…but not high enough as far as he was concerned. There was trauma to his forehead; he touched the spot, found it sticky and swollen like a bulging insect hive growing out of his skull. His left wrist was broken and being flooded with synthetic glucocorticoids to arrest swelling. There were two pulled ligaments in his right leg, and his right foot was cracked at the fifth metatarsal.

A large, bearded piece of debris moved across from him. "Fucking glops," it said. "They probably shit all over us."

Gethin's breath caught in his throat. "Jack? You're alive?"

The Promethean nodded. "Keiko and I blurred to the pilot cabin. Then again at the moment of impact."

The security chief ambled over and helped him stand, but as soon as Gethin leaned on his broken foot, the pain blossomed. Jack caught and braced him.

"You okay?"

"Could have been worse. You look unscathed."

Jack held out his hands helplessly. "Not a damn scratch. Like I said, we blurred at the moment of impact. Took a hell of a tumble, but no injuries. Keiko was right behind me." The sector chief swallowed and glanced around anxiously. "I hope she's okay. We came down at four hundred miles per hour."

The airship looked like a marine creature that had somehow managed to beach itself in this deciduous inland and been picked at by scavengers. The ruptured shell exposed a whalebone frame. Fires crackled amid gushing smokestack plumes.

Gethin took a hobbling step. He wasn't concerned about his wrist; it was his right foot that would be the problem. Rescue craft were almost certainly on their way and Gethin had no intention of being here when they arrived. The only solution was to disappear into the woods. How far would he get on a broken foot? Again, he examined the medgrid overlay. If they could make a splint...and if he upped the painkillers...

From the smoking carcass, a shape emerged. It hacked violently and made a drunken stumble towards the pulverized forest. The ground sizzled from heat and the shape wavered, mirage-like.

Jack and Gethin looked at each other.

The stumbling shape tore through the mist in front of them. A Stillness soldier stood revealed, clutching her side as she weaved. She saw them. She froze.

Jack took a single step. That was the only incentive the woman needed; she whipped around and fled like a crippled spider for the woods. At the tree line, Keiko appeared and tackled her to the ground.

"Behind you!" Keiko yelled. "There's another one."

Jack noticed what he had originally thought was a piece of wreckage. Now he realized it was a Stillness soldier half-buried beneath his cloak. The man stirred as Jack rolled him onto his back.

"How is the one you have?" Keiko asked, shoving her quarry to her knees. Gethin recognized the soldier at Keiko's feet: she was the woman who had been clutching for dear life to the ceiling I-beams, howling for all she was worth.

Jack inspected the man he'd apprehended. "He's unarmed," he told his partner.

"I mean his physical condition."

"Aside from a few scrapes and bruises, he looks good."

"Fit enough to walk?"

Jack hoisted the man to his feet. "Yes."

"Good." Keiko drew her pistol, pressed it against the woman's head, and splattered her brains onto the ground. The muffled gunshot was like someone spitting; the impact of cranial matter on rocks was louder than the report itself. Keiko calmly holstered her pistol, making a visual scan of the steaming crash site and absently tucking her hair behind her small ears. "We only need one to interrogate."

"Two would have been better," Gethin said reproachfully. He limped forward a few paces to gaze at the bloody ropes of brain pulp coiled on the rocks. Jack was staring also, and Gethin caught a flicker of disapproval in the big man's face.

Some of the wreckage upended behind them. Keiko sprinted to the source and kicked over a section of floor. Two bloody soldiers stretched their hands feebly towards her. She shot them both in the head. This time she didn't bother holstering her weapon, but did a quick scour of the airship's exposed carcass for other survivors. She found one more, legs broken, and executed him where he had been dragging himself from the scene.

"It doesn't matter," Gethin called after her. "Witnesses or not, the IPC will dispatch airhounds. There's no way to evade that."

Jack hawked and spat onto the rocks. "Actually, there is." He tapped a yellow hexagon at his tool-belt.

Keiko marched back to them. Up close, she looked bad. A gory weal formed a crescent moon around her right eye. The wound bristled with glass fragments, giving her a frightful visage. A wide-eyed goddess of war.

She had holstered her pistol again and now bore three multigun rifles salvaged from the wreckage. The only remaining Stillness trooper stared at her, steeling for violence. Keiko gave one rifle to Jack, one to Gethin.

Jack checked the magazine. "We need to vacate this crash site ASAP."

"I know. Hold that bastard steady."

The soldier stiffened in Jack's viselike hands. Keiko extended her palm, moving it slowly over the man's face, head, neck, chest, limbs, and torso…anywhere a tracking device or other wetware could conceivably be stored.

The soldier grinned. "Healthy heart? Good blood pressure? You won't find any metal cancers in my sanctum."

Keiko persisted in her scan, however, until satisfied. "Maybe some metal cancers are woven into your clothing fibers, though? Strip him."

The soldier didn't protest as his cloak was torn off him. He even helped kick off his boots and stood proud, pale, and lean, thrusting his hips forward to show off his genitals. Jack produced a glasstic tie to tether the man's hands behind his back.

Their quarry was reduced to a naked white ape of strange proportions. His legs seemed too skinny. His arms were sinewy, and yet his midsection swelled with flab. There were faded stretch marks on his back.

The soldier laughed at their expressions. "You've never seen a real man, is that it?" He thrust out his genitals farther. His penis waggled in the air. Remarkably, it began to thicken.

Jack slapped one massive hand around the guy's neck and shoved him towards the forest. His bare feet were cut on the rocks and left dimples of blood which Gethin tried to avoid stepping into as he hobbled behind, using the rifle as a cane, muzzle pointed into the ground.

"Movement!"

Keiko snapped her pistol to the crash perimeter. Her augmented senses were running with manic efficiency, flooding her visual field with data-streams calibrated for motion. She zoomed in on two crouching shapes at the tree line.

Octopi.

Keiko relaxed. The glops studied her with cautious interest. One lifted itself up on a nest of tentacles and retreated a few feet behind a tree. From there, the shapeless head peeked at her. Its partner began gyrating its limbs in an odd rhythmic beat like a primitive drum circle. Not far away, three more mollusks followed suit, undulating tentacles in the same creepy coordination, which might have been a general broadcast of caution or an elaborate theological discussion on the arrival of four two-legged gods from a skyborne chariot.

Jack followed her line of sight. "Just glops. Forget them."

"Poisonous?"

"No."

A few steps into the tree line, she lowered her pistol an inch and looked beyond the transgenics to the deeper woods. "Our immediate priority is to disappear. Gethin, where are you hurt?"

"Looking for an excuse to splatter your ex-husband's brains?"

She stared from what seemed a grisly mask of blood and glass. He tried searching that face for signs of the woman he knew. Again, he wondered what her employers had done to train her. The chilling way she had executed those soldiers – no hesitation – played out in his mind. It made him wonder if such a reflexive talent for murder had always been festering inside her.

Keiko wasn't leveling the rifle at him, but a narrow few inches could create the threat. She hissed, "Right now you're aligned with an enemy power—"

"*Aligned?* Were you watching what happened up there? If there's a coup at the IPC, they didn't see fit to invite me. Their intent was obviously to sequester every investigator at the orbital station. Keep them distracted working on a false puzzle. At the same time, they were using the airship to transport these soldiers somewhere else."

"To where?"

"Don't know."

Jack shook his head. "Those soldiers were en route to the orbital station to contain us."

"I don't believe that," Gethin snapped, and he glanced at the smoking interior of the airship. "Why waste the personnel? An orbital station is an efficient prison all by itself. Once we were to be contained, imprisoned without realizing it, this ship was bound for other destinations. To transport those soldiers into civilization. What better method of smuggling than aboard an IPC vessel?"

"How can you be sure they were meant to be—"

"Because I'm brilliant, remember?" Gethin leaned awkwardly against his rifle. "We were never meant to discover the soldiers. Celeste stumbled on them by accident."

Keiko considered the deciduous woodland around them. "What happened to her?"

Gethin shook his head, not wanting to think of the way she had killed herself.

Jack detached the yellow hexagon from his beltline, wound his arm back and pitched an underhand toss into the air above the crash site. The device unfolded its petals and spun like a top, discharging invisible cargo. Countermeasures. Little anti-hounds which would swarm the area and create false leads for Hassans to track.

Jack said, "That should throw the hounds off our scent. But we need forest cover to hide from satellites. And the IPC can track our sensoriums. We need to power them down." He looked at Gethin. "You especially."

Gethin gave a quick, pained nod. He kept the nerve suppression active, but shut the main system; the soft thrumming spun down to silence. By contrast, the volume of the world amped up. A choir of birds, bugs, and frogs tickling his ears.

"If we head east we can reach Cappadocia," Jack continued, and he shoved his captured Stillness trooper ahead. "I think that's our best bet. Independent territory."

Gethin nodded, hobbling after them. "Fiercely independent. They politely tell us...the IPC, I mean...to go to hell."

"Hell is where you're going anyway," the soldier breathed.

Jack regarded him with all the empathy a man might show to the tick that's attached itself to his thigh. He started to speak, decided against it. Gethin thought: *Now here's the most cool-headed person among us. Gotta admire that.*

They pushed deeper into the forest, losing themselves beneath the deciduous canopy. Their march was brisk, and it was all Gethin could do to keep pace. His multigun cane made neat, circular marks in the soil and he grimaced. *Might as well leave our enemies a fucking map.*

★   ★   ★

The forest used to be a city. Fire hydrants appeared every so often like oversize mushrooms popping from the forest floor, their cast-iron toughness preserving their overall contours while the centuries had seen nature overtake the asphalt, concrete, and steel of whatever metropolis had been here. When the group finally halted after an hour's forced march, evening was pooling beneath trees and boulders and sheared-away walls of yesteryear.

Gethin panted, resisting the urge to check his medgrid overlay. It was separate from his sensorium, but there was little point in creating strange energy signatures out here. Along the route, he had pointed out a few good pieces of lumber to use for a splint, and Jack helpfully gathered the materials. With his beard, height, and the woodsy surroundings, Saylor looked like Paul Bunyan merrily at work.

The Stillness soldier was made to sit on a tree stump. The fellow didn't look anxious to escape, but the Prometheans never strayed far. If anything, he seemed amused by his situation. Every so often, Gethin caught him muttering prayers.

Jack crouched beside Gethin and set to work on a splint. He used his own shirt to tie the wood behind Gethin's leg, bending the bark as far as it allowed to support the foot. Then he stood, bare-chested and muscular. Less Paul Bunyan than Hercules now. Give the man a lion's-skin cloak and a club. Gethin noticed a curious tattoo emblazoned across Saylor's flat stomach. It resembled some kind of antiquated purple heraldry.

Ego would know it; Gethin made a mental note to ask his Familiar about it later. He tested the splint.

"Feels good," he said. The ground was worn away beneath him, and ceramic tiles showed through a tangle of weeds. Corroded copper piping jutted from a hillside.

This used to be someone's bathroom, he realized.

They were quiet for a moment, catching their breaths. Somewhere deep in the forest gloom, a creature howled. All heads jerked towards the sound.

Keiko cast a worrisome glance at the darkening sky. Where the clouds were visible, they looked like dull iron.

She wiped her neck. Went to the prisoner.

The man nodded agreeably. "Hi."

"I have some questions to ask you."

"Can I pray first before you kill me?"

Keiko reached into her tool-belt and removed the magpie claw. She gripped the handle with two hands, twisting one clockwise, and the cylinder lunged several inches, yawning its head open like a metallic piranha.

The soldier didn't even flinch. "If you think that thing intimidates me in the least, you never been to the Outlands. That's a toy."

Keiko smiled. "Think so?"

"Go ahead," he demanded. "Cut me, bleed me." His blue eyes closed, and he said in near-song: "You may violate the sanctum but not the soul, for I am bound for a better world." His eyes opened and glared. "You people are rotting meat, injected with preservatives and perfumes to dispel the stench. You spit in God's face! But He'll have you. The nova-fire of Judgment will find you, deformed and degenerated like the Grendels of Cain."

"Your—"

He persisted, smiling and defiant. "I'm the one forever fated, while demons get their death belated. I find—"

"You *are* forever fated!" Keiko insisted, and she held the magpie for him to see. "This is a Digital Capture sim-Cave. And it is an implement of Satan. This end pushes through your eye, guides itself like a hound-dog straight to your most recent grouping of memories...the ones fresh from consolidation in your hippocampus." She paused deliberately, seeing him process this information. "In other words, the magpie will rip out your recent memories. Not nearly as thorough as a DC. But frankly, I don't care about your childhood. I don't care what your musical tastes are, what your cognitive map looks like, what your emotional climate is. I want your recent memories, and this will get them."

"Then take them," he said, with noticeably less enthusiasm.

"It also takes your soul."

The soldier's lips formed an expression of hilarity, but before he could vocalize his amusement she continued.

"That's the secret your leaders are so angry about. We finally figured out a way to snatch the body's immortal soul from where it sits, in the hippocampus, and imprison it in these portable jails. Like Reverend Marlo Morris."

The name plainly registered on the soldier's face. His eyes flicked from the device to Keiko's cold expression. "You're crazy."

"Forty years ago, outside of Memphis. Morris was one of the masterminds behind the Stillness raid of a Prometheus transport. You're too young to have been alive for that, so I'll fill you in. They killed sixty of my people. Used heat-lances to knock our transport out of the sky. They cut into it, pulled out the survivors, and crucified them. Set up a live webcast. Nailed my workers to crosses and set them on fire."

The webcast had run for several hours. Women and men, still in their Promethean uniforms, being doused in kerosene and lit ablaze. The victims burned like torches until the screeching went silent and the agonized straining against their bonds ceased.

And then they sprang back alive, still crucified, only now charred and livid red.

Stillness burned them again. And again. The priest overseeing the ceremony dutifully informed a horrified public that the only people responsible for such torture were a society in which regenerative nanites and medpacks kept the meat alive, defying God and death with its blasphemy. Stillness was merely demonstrating how innately wicked eternal life was, and they illustrated this lesson over the course of eight hours of flame and piteous screams.

"On hour nine," Keiko said, "Prometheus retaliated."

"Killing children!" the soldier yelled in blossoming outrage. The spit flew from his teeth. "And whole families!"

"Some of them," Keiko admitted. "Others live forever, in sim-Caves like this." She shook the magpie. "Reverend Morris had presided over the torture of my coworkers, so Prometheus figured death was too much of a mercy. We snatched his soul. No eternal Paradise for him. Just endless suffering...on PI's all-time greatest hit list." She touched a button at her wrist.

It was difficult to tell where the hideous screams that followed were actually coming from. The magpie, or speakers embedded in Keiko's hand.

"*Pleeeeeease nooooo!*" the voice screamed. "*Dear God help me!!! Let me gooooo!*"

Another voice, childlike and soothing, cooed over the torture. "There is no escape, no escape ever. You belong to us forever."

"*God it hurts! Heeeeeeelp! Heeeeeelp me! Mercy! Mercy!*"

"Thirty years of this, thirty million more to go, thirty years of this, thirty million more to go…"

"*Noooooooo! Anything! I'll do anything! God have meeeeeeercy!*"

The ululations reached an inhuman crescendo, sounding more like a demented musical instrument than anything a human vocal chord could produce. Then it crashed into desperate wails and sobs.

"*I dennnooounce them! I…sttt…I denounce Stillness! Pleeeeeease! Letmeout! Ahhhhhhhh!!*"

"Thirty years of this, thirty million more to go, thirty years of this, thirty million more to go…"

Gethin saw the soldier blanch. The man looked searchingly at her face. "It's…a recording."

Keiko touched her wrist and the sound cut off. "Tell me what I want to know or you can join Morris in hell. Cooperate and I'll kill you quickly. Go straight to Heaven, tell your God what we devil-arkies are doing, why He gets fewer and fewer souls each year because we keep them imprisoned on Earth for all time."

"God will flood this world and release our brothers!" the soldier screamed.

Keiko shrugged. "Hold him steady."

Jack immobilized the man's head.

"No! Wait!"

The magpie claw came within a half inch of his face.

"Where were you headed?" Keiko demanded.

"Shimizu! We were going to Shimizu!"

"Why?"

"Following orders. Some upcoming assault!"

"What assault?"

The soldier's neck bulged with tendons and veins. "I don't know!"

"You fucking liar!" Keiko spat, and pushed the claw into his eye.

He squealed, kicking his legs out spastically. "No! I don't know! Fathers Tiamat and Apophis were going to tell us when we arrived! I swear! We knew nothing—"

Gethin leapt forward. "*Who* did you say? Fathers *who*?"

The soldier looked wildly at him. "Tiamat and Apophis!"

Gethin and Jack exchanged a meaningful look.

"Who are they?" Keiko asked.

"I've never met them! They…they are the leaders of the Crusade! They speak to us…and command us…for the Crusade!"

"What Crusade?"

"To bring Stillness to Earth!"

"You're already on Earth," Jack said with disgust.

"Stillness! Peace! Tranquility!"

Gethin seized the man's chin and yanked to meet his eyes. "How?"

The man inhaled a fierce lungful of air, and when he shrieked his red face pulsed with a spiderweb of veins. "I don't know!"

"Ask him if Fathers Tiamat or Apophis acquired some missiles recently."

The voice came from the woods behind them.

Keiko spun and planted one knee in the dirt, leveling her pistol like a gunslinger. The magpie claw dropped to the soil beside her, frightening a millipede into the damp sanctuary of a log.

Celeste Segarra emerged casually from behind the trees. A salvaged combat shotgun was slung around one shoulder, and she was wearing a Stillness robe turned inside out, so the stitching of the pockets was visible like crude surgical scars. Those pockets bulged with scavenged materials; Gethin noted the silver foil of prepackaged airship meals, although his attention was quickly drawn to the cobalt-blue pseudodopod she carried. It was about a meter long, and she had looped one arm through the back to grip it like the shield of a gladiatrix.

"How the hell did you survive that fall?" Keiko demanded.

"I'm feather-light."

The Promethean kept the woman in her gun-sights while she regarded the strange shield she carried. Gethin thought it looked heavier than it should be. His impression was one of condensed mass – it was clearly straining the Outlander's arm and shoulder despite her affectation of calm – and he had the impression that it could spread out this extra mass into a lengthier shape if need be.

Shapestone. Was that the secret of her legendary ship?

The look in Keiko's eyes told him she was coming to the same conclusion. "Where did you get that?" she asked.

Celeste leaned the pseudopod against a tree. The weight was obvious as it sank inches into the dirt. "From the *Mantid*," she replied.

Keiko instinctively checked the sky. "It's around here?"

"No. It's near Athens, lying low."

Keiko puzzled over this. "Are you saying that your ship fired off a rescue drone *from Athens* while you were falling? That it caught up with you at terminal velocity?"

"Expended every volt of power to do it. I was riding vapors to reach the crash site." The Outlander pointed. "Ask that asshole about the missiles."

Gethin couldn't help but smile. "Nice to see you, Segarra."

The soldier, as it turned out, didn't know about any antimatter-tipped missiles. But he had heard rumors that his Crusade was stockpiling weapons from around the world. What type of weapons, and for what ultimate purpose, he couldn't say.

And through it all, Celeste listened and thought of the fiasco at Quinn's compound.

We all underestimated Stillness, she thought. *They aren't scattered or leaderless. They're tightly knit and organized. What happened at Quinn's was no accident. It was one acquisition front out of many. They're doing the same as King D. Combing the Wastes for antebellum weaponry, stashing it away, building up for a massive strike.*

A cold wolf's paw of fear touched her heart. *If that was true, then there was another problem far closer to home for her. Two different groups fighting over the same Outland scraps meant that Stillness had likely learned about StrikeDown's own stash. Perhaps King D. was their next target.*

Fuck. The wackos would ruin everything.

Celeste cleared her throat with aplomb. "Soldier boy! Where can we find your glorious High Priests?"

"They find you," he said weakly. His pulse beat raggedly in his neck.

For another few minutes they interrogated him to learn what they could. Several 'teams' were being dispatched to the Shimizu pyramid, he said, for reasons unknown. He knew nothing about an IPC-Stillness arrangement, and didn't seem to have heard of Colonel Leon Tanner. But he did know the organizational structure of his faith, and the three High Priests that currently ran it: Mother Eris, Father Apophis, and Father Tiamat. This latter persona was the 'Great Master' who sat, spiderlike, at the center of the organization's web. He preached about pure life, a life without tech, machines, and 'noise'. Once the world walls tumbled, all mankind would return to this state of anarcho-primitive utopia.

Stillness. The return to a simpler life. The death of machines, industry, and arky tech. The end of immortality and of humanity's desire for the stars.

"He knows nothing else," Gethin said thickly, turning away.

Keiko lifted the claw.

The soldier had calmed considerably since Celeste's arrival. Better to die and plead forgiveness in the afterlife than suffer eternally in a digital inferno. Seeing the magpie again, however, his ashen face shivered.

"I told you everything!"

Keiko shoved the device into his eye. This time it was no bluff; the guiding probe drilled straight through the organ, spraying juices down the screaming man's face. It took three minutes to cull the memory dendrites, while Jack kept their wailing victim steady with one hand and clamped the other over the man's mouth. When the claw retracted, he snapped the soldier's neck.

He dropped the body into a small gulch. Then he looked back into Keiko's satisfied eyes.

★   ★   ★

They marched another thirty minutes in silence. When they halted again, this time sandwiched between boulders and the gnarled flanks of serpentine trees, evening was in full gloom.

Keiko wiped her forehead and met Celeste's gaze. "So your ship can throw you a lifeline from Athens? Have it pick us up."

"Not a chance in hell."

"Why not?"

"Because satellites must be scouring the area for us, and I won't risk exposing my ship to the goddamn IPC. You people pulled me into this whether you meant to or not. And I intend to live…with all my cards intact."

"Kill your sensorium," Keiko warned. "Power it down so they can't track you."

"Already done. You think I need schooling on how to stay off the grid?"

The woods were incredibly dense. The saws and bulldozers of civilization hadn't run through here in at least four centuries. Only Gethin had seen environments like this up close and personal, in the tropical Ecuadorian mountains, in the deeply shadowed woods of northern Russia. It was disconcerting how easily nature reclaimed the bones of mankind's ingenuity, and as Gethin considered the devastation of the Final War, he calculated (as he had done many times) that a few more megadeaths in those fragile days might have rendered the entirety of Earth into a timberland like this. Cockroaches crawling through buried pipes. Colonies of algae and bacteria forming furry carpets over unused papers and plastics.

He checked his splint, tied and retied the bands. "Keiko, that was one hell of a bluff back there. The soul-in-the-hippocampus bit. Incredible." He grinned coldly. "It *was* a bluff, right?"

His ex-wife was carefully plucking slivers of glass from her face. "It's an effective bluff," she quipped. "We've been running that routine for twenty-five years, and the results you saw are textbook. Success-rate eighty-seven percent of the time."

"So it was just a recording? You pay a voice actor?"

Keiko raised an eyebrow. "Grown squeamish with age?"

"Digital prisons are against IPC policy."

"Squeamish."

"Maybe I'll drop a line to the Republic and have them petition for full disclosure. If Prometheus is using digital prisons—"

"We're not," she said flatly.

"—they'll have your top brass frozen for a thousand years."

Keiko flicked a glass shard off her fingertip, looking unconcerned. "What I said about the attack on our transport was true. We sent Hassans and CAMO agents to investigate. Reverend Marlo Morris was just another Wasteland prophet; every few years, someone like him pops up. Our agents recorded his sermons. When we wiped out the villages, it was decided we needed a new method of interrogation. Strictly bluff stuff."

"A magpie *does* snag memories," Celeste said carefully.

"Not with any real efficiency," Gethin explained, but his heart was pounding. He felt the tickle of possible futures unfurl like a ribbon in the wind, twisting like a bifurcating trunk into new pathways…each eventually connecting to the three flavors of *The Divine Comedy*.

Celeste gave a crisp, bitter laugh. "Oh, the cleverness of me." She spat on the ground just a half inch from Keiko's boot. "Your crash site must be crawling with reporters and agents. Tanner will quickly realize we're not among the dead. He'll come after us."

Jack shrugged. "Cappadocia is two days east. What other choice do we have?"

"Two days in the gloplands? You ever try to survive out here before?"

"I'm not worried about mollusks," Jack said sullenly.

"Ever see a dire dog pack? They typically run three hundred strong. A flash flood of oversized wolves. Goddamn turret couldn't mow them down in time."

Gethin paled slightly. He *had* seen dire dog packs. "This region is dotted with Wastetowns," he said. "Let's find one."

Celeste folded her arms and gave them a sneering, up-and-down appraisal. "You guys waltz into a Wastetown dressed the way you are, you'll end up on a chopshop's table. Keiko's tool-belt alone is worth murder. Hide it, sister. In a bag or up your snatch."

As if on cue, the howling they'd been hearing at various intervals came again, nearer, more numerous and from different directions.

They're triangulating our location, Gethin thought. *Sniffing us out and communicating to the pack.*

"Maybe it's just wolves," Jack whispered.

Celeste took an anxious breath. "If natural wolves survive out here, they've become runts of dire packs." She ran her fingers through her sweaty hair. "Take off your uniforms. Tie them around your waists. Anything that has a PI logo has to be hidden or discarded. You too, Gethin. Throw some dirt on you. Good."

They obeyed her instructions in silence. A light rain began to fall. The forest glittered like black glass, and Jack, already half-naked, now gave the appearance of a Paleolithic Goliath.

When they were done, Celeste surveyed them. "It will have to do. Those Promethean pants still have logos on them."

"It's nanomesh," Jack explained. "Untearable."

Celeste scooped up fistfuls of mud and splattered it over their legs. She touched her fingertips to Jack's belly tattoo. Anger rose briefly to her eyes, and she was about to give an acidic editorial on how shameless arkies were to steal the heraldry of Outland clans, like nineteenth-century American frontier soldiers pillaging woven beads and feathered headdresses and deerskin tunics without a care to the cultural significance they represented. But the temptation passed, her blood cooled, and she resumed her work.

Finally, she stood back to admire her handiwork. They were a dirtied, grim-looking crew. She wondered how they would fare against her original squad, tech-toys aside, in a pit fight. Jamala might be able to take Keiko. She had seen Gethin fight and he was resourceful but inexperienced; without blurmods, he wouldn't last long. Jack was a different story. She'd seen Outlanders of his stature. A good, hulking genotype, instinctively inspiring respect.

The thought flashed crazily in her head and it spoke in Jeff's tone: *Here's your new squad, Celeste!*

Her eyes flicked to the rifles they carried. Each was pointed at someone in the group. A cold-blooded diagram of mistrust: the Prometheans were wary of Gethin. Gethin was edgy towards his ex-wife. And all were unsettled by Celeste.

Some fucking squad, she thought.

Sourly, she asked, "What happened in that office, Gethin? We both know that wasn't your colonel, but I know something else: he was the same guy who nearly killed me in the Hudson Wastes."

Gethin looked shaken. "That's not possible."

"Listen to me," she began, and told the others about Tanner's choice of words. About his eyes.

Jack shrugged. "Coincidence. We're thousands of miles away."

"It's the same man." She hesitated, caught Gethin's wondering eyes, and said, "Or not a man, remember? Something that can shapeshift. Become whatever it wants."

"The man who exploded in the Hudson is dead," Jack insisted. "Pardon me, Celeste, but he's fried now. We all saw the video."

"It was him," she maintained. "I feel it."

Keiko laughed bitterly. "Are psychic powers cropping up in the Wastes?"

"Is basic attention to detail disappearing among arkies?" She looked at Gethin. "Tell them what your colleague found."

He did. He related Disch's analysis. The phasing of matter. The insistence that Segarra's assailant had been inhuman.

Keiko gave a skeptical grunt. "Not human? What the hell does that mean? What do you think he was?"

Gethin cleared his throat, the rain collecting around his face. "An anomaly."

CHAPTER THIRTY-ONE
"They Made Me."

The moon is made of green cheese.
   The moon is made of green cheese.
   Why green? Hanmura2 wondered as he let his people wipe his perspiring brow while the grafter isolated nerve strands and closed down their avenues of pain. The clinic in his corporate suite on Luna was drafty with filtered air, gloomy, reminiscent of old noir flatfilms about gangster hideouts. The walls were painted crimson. Circular lights riddled the ceiling like bullet holes and the windows were digital renders of a faux Kyoto landscape with a daimyo fortress rising above groves of chinaberry trees.
   But all Hanmura2 could think about was that silly myth, over and over:
   The moon is made of green cheese.
   His right arm was completely encased by the grafter. The machine hummed, fit snugly around his mutilated limb to weave newly printed muscle fiber to bone. There was no sensation; they'd reactivate his nerve endings soon enough. But the memory of agony made him delirious. His nostrils felt caulked with the stink of charred flesh.
   Hanmura2's attendants ringed him like glum, stricken slaves. They were sworn to obedience to protect him, to die for him, and yet this grievous thing had happened on their watch. Someone would pay. The group was almost gibbering with panic. After all, they had all signed Hanmura corporate release forms, and therefore getting fired meant a memory wipe. That meant years for some people. Decades. An entire life swallowed by a whiteout nova.
   Thus far, he hadn't fired anyone. Bodyguard Hideo begged to be allowed to die, but Hanmura2 refused.
   How can I blame him? he asked himself. *It was my idea to go to Club Nadsat. To tail those women to the room.*
   Hanmura2 sipped water. Choked on it. Swallowed.
   "Show me the clip," he said at last.
   Hideo ruefully fired up the holodisplay. Club Nadsat appeared. People were screaming and running for exits. The music and colored lights were gone. Bodies were strewn on stairs and draped over railings.
   In the center of the main dance floor was a freakishly tall version of the man named Apophis. He hung magically over the room, drifting around as if

wheeled by invisible wires, and was booming, *"They made me! They made me! It won't stop in my head! They won't let me stop! I kill for them! I kill for them!"*

He was wearing pale brown vestments with the PI logo on one sleeve. His right arm was encased in a grotesque biomechanical sheath, stone blue in color. Veinlike rigging and tendons fused into mechanical joints and servos.

Hanmura2 leaned interestedly at this.

Using this freakish cybernetic arm, Apophis was flailing madly at the shrieking club patrons. Wherever he pointed, people burst into flame. One couple was cowering behind a table; Apophis hovered above them, howling, and aimed his prosthesis in their direction. The couple erupted in fire; the girl ran like a living torch across the room, thrashing and shrieking. The boy dashed in the opposite direction. Like two moths streaking apart from each other after a brush with a campfire.

And Apophis kept howling. *"They made me! They made me!"*

Stars! Hanmura2 thought. He found himself enthralled with the expression of gut-wrenching desperation and agony on Apophis's face. It looked so genuine; some out-of-control Frankensteinian thing consigned to murderous impulses. A man strugglingly helplessly against a programmed violence instilled by his creators.

But it was all an incredible deception. Even that augmented arm casing. Hanmura2 knew from his own experience that Apophis needed no enhancements to wield his phenomenal power. The Promethean garb, the cybernetic arm…

It was just cinema.

But why?

And what the hell was he?

The footage ended. Hanmura2's attendants let out a collective gasp. Slowly, all eyes went to their corporate master…this man who had survived an encounter with the devil.

"Hideo? Send my message to IPC command."

His bodyguard scurried off. Hanmura2 narrowed his eyes at the others.

"You are each sworn to utter secrecy. This creature is an abomination of Prometheus Industries. Let the IPC handle it. We stand to profit. Each of you will be rewarded for your silence."

They all knew what that meant. The rewards he could bestow were far greater than anything they might get from leaking this info to datahounds.

But they were clearly troubled. If Prometheus could create a devil-thing like this, how soon before other companies followed? It reeked of superstitions, witchcraft, devilry, Dark Age horror.

Hanmura2 settled back into his chair. The medprogram tirelessly worked its spinnerets.

Apophis won't trouble me again, he thought. *He wants to use me as a pawn in his unknowable game? Fine.* Nonetheless, he felt a measure of comfort knowing that his security forces were on high alert. His Lunar compound was sealed tight.

He closed his eyes.

He tried to see the end of this game.

Apophis was surely not a PI creation. He was a father of lies, shuffling appearances and treachery like Mahjong tiles. And besides, if revenge was really his intent, why not attack Prometheus direct?

Because he *wanted* the IPC involved.

He wanted war.

Hanmura2 shuddered. *All I need to do is position myself and company to benefit from that war. Grease the right palms, make the right deals. Prometheus Industries is going down. Hanmura Enterprises will be ascendant.*

Unless…

What if Apophis was playing the same game with Gates and Bielawa? Maybe he had tracked them down too. Appeared like a giant scorpion and offered them the same strange deal. *Rule within the new power structure of humanity. Be a satrap of the empire that is to come.*

What new empire?

Hanmura2 felt his breathing constrict. He could still hear that wretched howling in his skull. The attack on Club Nadsat was *the* story on the newsfeeds. Apophis wanted that. He was mugging for the camera. Playing his part to the hilt. Showing the corporate logo on his sleeve. It was as if Apophis was truly a devil in disguise, a *hengeyokai* trickster, and Hanmura2 struggled to remember if such tricksters had weaknesses according to bygone legends. Bow to a kappa, that sort of thing.

Hanmura2 heard a sudden rattling. He realized his arms were shaking; his arm in the grafter unit trembled against the sheath.

Please! he asked the gods of his ancestors. *Please let this creature have a weakness. Or at least an enemy who is stronger than him.*

CHAPTER THIRTY-TWO
Anomalies

The rain had taken on a steady, icicle-thin quality. They marched through the drizzle, Gethin talking as Celeste supported his right side, seeking refuge from the wet and cold. The crash site lay several miles behind them to the west. When they stumbled on a large drainpipe jutting from a mountainside, Keiko insisted they hole up for a few hours to regain their strength. She shone a flashlight inside to make certain it was unoccupied; the pipe ran on for twenty meters before it was pinched by collapse.

Keiko erected a hasty blockade at the drainage pipe's entrance with an armful of twigs and branches, corking them inside. Water ran beneath them from an unremembered sewer system within the hillside.

Gethin lay with his splinted leg flat. "The IPC has recognized the need to research outside established parameters. To investigate mysteries from an asymmetrical angle."

Keiko reduced her flashlight's beam to a dull glow. Her ex-husband's features gathered shadows – for an instant, she was reminded of their life together in a fourth-tier Athenian wing, wedged among the arcology's HVAC systems. Eating hasty lunches together before donning the VR rigs and vanishing into Arcadium fictions…like drug addicts, scarfing down just enough sustenance to keep alive through the next binge. The drainage pipe reminded her of that damp, cramped life together, and her flashlight's glow could be the HUD display of a loading screen.

"What mysteries?" she asked, shooing the unwanted memories away. "What kinds of mysteries are really left in the world, Gethin?"

He related what he'd shared with Celeste. AIs. Glops. Ashoka.

Celeste said unhappily, "The thing that attacked me was no Ashoka."

But Gethin looked unfazed. "You can't justify that declaration, Segarra. Maybe they can make surreptitious planetside visits, walking among us now. Or maybe we're in an actual first-contact extraterrestrial situation." He saw the others roll their eyes. "Hear me out. And forget all the holos you've seen, with their conceit that extraterrestrial organisms would descend to Earth in dazzling saucer-shaped UFOs. A real extraterrestrial might be a seven-thousand-foot-long pyramid that pushes itself along a sluglike mucous foot."

Keiko gave an impatient sigh, but Jack, stretching out his legs in the tunnel, was warming to the discussion. "Okay..."

"Or an aerostat jellyfish that can turn invisible at will," Gethin added. Both Prometheans looked at him, stricken by his reference to the Base 59 footage.

Celeste thought about the way the High Priest had managed to hold himself together despite the weaponfire pulping him. She remembered those search-beam eyes.

"Ashoka or aliens," Jack muttered.

"Or artificial intelligence," continued Gethin. "Personally, I'm discounting it because Tanner – I mean Tanner's doppelganger – used it as his preferred scapegoat, one that played right into Keiko's favored boogeyman. I submit it only to underscore how quickly threats to human dominance can arise in our brave new era. It took more than a hundred and thirty thousand generations for humanity to evolve from tree dwellers to emailers. How many generations of machine intelligence has Avalon undergone?"

Jack said, "Everyone predicted conflict with the machines. They were wrong. They keep away from us."

"Biding their time," Keiko quipped.

For a moment a babbling argument erupted, Keiko and Jack sparring in what was clearly the latest round of an enduring match. Then Gethin laughed coldly, and they stopped, words hanging from their lips, to gape at him.

He looked genuinely amused, his laughter pure and real. "What is it about our species that we insist on perceiving everything in goddamn binary code? Black or white. On switch, off switch. Humans versus machines."

Keiko drew herself into a *seiza* squat, better suited to the drainpipe's constraints. "Are you saying there isn't a potential conflict between us?"

He smiled wryly. "Between you and me, Keiko?" When she blushed at this, he changed subject. "Again, even in this discussion we're falling into binary. Aliens or AIs? There are other possibilities. We have yet to conduct a comprehensive investigation into transgenic ecologies on Earth. Before the Fall, we know that genetic tinkering had become available to numerous civilian, academic, and extremist groups. Think of those mollusks we ran into earlier. Almost nothing is known about them, and yet they clearly demonstrated inquisitiveness and intelligence."

"Glops can't outcompete us," Keiko snapped.

"No? One hundred thousand years ago evolution produced several distinct groups of would-be champions. Most were megafauna. The cave lions, sabertooths, bears, a species of wingless terror bird in the open prairie. A few were a varied handful of hominid species. At a glance, you'd be hard-pressed to pick a winner from that motley ensemble, and you sure as hell wouldn't bet on the hominids. They were small, vulnerable, lacking claws, armor, or poison sacs. They were unimpressive. Yet those primate runts would soon drive out all competition. This is an important point, and it should rein in our impulse to dismiss glops as irrelevant curiosities."

"You think humans could be crowded out by competition?" Keiko sneered. "With our weapons and technology? Not a chance."

"Yet you pathologically worry about AIs."

"Because AIs are different than glops!"

He smiled broadly. "How do you know? How can you be certain that a transgenic species in the Wastes doesn't possess the biological equivalent of quantum computers in their heads? There are strange breeds out here, propagating. While we were blowing ourselves up, maybe some superslug built a rocket ship and colonized Pluto. Maybe that explains the IPC ban."

"That's insane."

"Is it? Why? In a way it's ironic. There were several sentient species around when humanity first started. We killed them off. Now, our sorcery has engineered new intelligences. Who knows what they're capable of? That's why investigators like me check every credible report we get."

"Like termites in Ecuador?" Celeste chimed in.

Thunder sounded outside their barrier. The small stream trickling under them swelled, and Keiko checked to make sure the water could escape through the blockade she'd fashioned.

"Don't want to drown in our hideout," she muttered, managing an awkward expression that might have been a smile.

Celeste sighed. "All this speculation gets us nowhere. What was impersonating Tanner? What are we dealing with?"

All eyes were on Gethin. He looked from one person to the next.

"How the hell am I supposed to know?"

Keiko groaned.

But Jack looked thoughtful. "Let's table the discussion. Get two hours' rest and we'll resume our march."

A hideous chorus of lupine howls pierced the rain. The glop world's trumpets of war.

Yes, Gethin thought with a chill. *Pleasant dreams.*

CHAPTER THIRTY-THREE
Haventown

The steady deluge created a mesmerizing sonic pattern on the pipe. It sounded like the march of armies, and Gethin hugged himself sleepily. When he came to, Celeste was peering in at him from outside the drainage pipe. Night was in full bloom, blacker than pitch. In the backsplash of flashlight lowbeams, he regarded Celeste's rain-plastered hair, her eyes bright beneath the tangle.

She looked beautiful. The Prometheans waited behind her, armed and ready to break camp.

"How long did I sleep?" he asked.

"A few hours." She helped him out of the pipe. He climbed into the rain, and carefully shifted his weight to his good foot.

Without a word, Celeste pressed a syringe of some kind to his broken foot. He felt nothing; nerve suppression made his foot feel like wood.

"Nanite infusion?" he asked, astonished. "Where did you get that?"

"From the wreck. You geniuses didn't bother salvaging anything other than rifles and some food. By the time I got there you were already gone, so I nabbed some packaged arky meals and two medkits. This shit is priceless out here."

Gethin regarded his broken foot. "Thank you."

She gave a cold smile. He had the greenest eyes she'd ever seen. Like a serpent. She remembered thinking that arkies were no longer human, and Gethin's saurian gaze underscored that impression. "We're even. You saved my life with that S-jack in Babylon."

"That was my pleasure to—"

"Shut up and move your ass."

Within minutes they were marching again, following a line of fire hydrants and concrete foundations overgrown with furry moss. Jack aided Gethin as his foot slowly healed under the nanite infusion, while Celeste trekked far ahead, tirelessly scouting.

"There's a town about eight miles due east," she told them when they caught up to her. "I saw it on my descent from the airship."

"Why didn't you go straight there, then?" Keiko demanded.

It was Jack who answered, and he sounded irritated. "A stranger floating down from the sky into your town? They would have shot her like a clay pigeon, Keiko. She's probably as much a foreigner to these parts as we are."

"I'm just saying—"

"Enough."

Incredibly, Keiko shut up. Gethin was awed. *What does it take to rile Jack Saylor? Poor night of sleep? Or is he one of those guys who comes to a slow boil, cool under fire until things reached critical mass? Either way, when you riled a giant, you stayed out of its way.*

Then Gethin glimpsed Celeste as she was crawling uphill, flattening herself at the crest to peer into the next valley. Her legs coiled, her ass thrust out, she put her chin into the dirt. Jack's breathing changed and color flushed into his cheeks.

Ah! Gethin thought amusedly. *Maybe the call of the wild is dividing loyalties among the Prometheans. Merciless Aphrodite.*

The next valley led to a forgotten highway. Asphalt showed through the forest, and knobby streetlamps – shorn of their ancient height – dotted the Turkish wilderness. The next few miles were flat and steady along the old freeway pass. Gethin had seen antebellum videos of highway traffic in the days before the compact nature of arcologies forever changed the philosophy of city construction. This old highway must have afforded a quaint view of the wilderness, back when it scuttled with personal vehicles.

Where the highway terminated, the road dipped steeply into another valley. A high-walled town lay nestled in that deciduous enclave.

"That it?" Jack asked.

Celeste nodded. A distinct line of defense bunkers ringed the town wall like minarets, familiar from her descent as she'd clung ferociously to the *Mantid's* pseudopod. She'd only had a quick glimpse of the town from altitude before the rescue drone dipped below the canopy, running low on battery juice. She hadn't liked the look of those minarets then, and she didn't like them now. They exuded hostility.

She ordered the arkies to withdraw into foliage. From concealment, she studied the gates and barricade. There was no telling who governed the town. They might be insular maniacs, itching to shoot any foreigner on sight. But few Wastetowns were so self-sufficient that they could afford outright xenophobia anymore.

Then again, it might be the case that only approved traders and caravans, bearing specific standards, were allowed to approach Turkish towns. The Brasstown megaplex in Hartford observed such rules; a stranger in the dark, creeping up to their front door, was fair game for someone's target practice.

Celeste sighed, a nervous ache in her chest. One thing was certain: they could not stay out here in the woods tonight. Too cold, wet, and far too many howls. She remembered once, in the ash-bowl Wastes of Minnesota, she and Jeff had been camping when they heard a discordant symphony of beastly ululations. Jeff looked at her with large eyes. "Dogtown," he said. In other words, no place for humans.

She pointed to Jack and Keiko. "Your mud wore off. You look like two Prometheans caught in the rain. Yamanaka, give me your flashlight."

While they re-dirtied their clothing, Celeste continued. "We can't let anyone think we're arkies. Only humanitarian groups are tolerated by Outlanders and that's because they arrive as virgins. Most arkies are stuffed with wetware. Outlanders want that shit."

Keiko cocked her head. "Then why not pretend we're humanitarians?"

"Sorry, none of you can pull that off. But we *could* fake being a squad... though that would mean acting like a tightly knit group of soldiers who respect and trust each other."

"Ouch," Gethin breathed.

"Just follow my lead. Look people in the eye, but don't challenge them to a fight. There's a pecking order. Outlanders know it. Be alert, not anxious. Don't wear your emotions on your face. Turn to stone, *comprende?*"

She had their attention. As long as they kept quiet, let her do the talking, they might just pull this off.

She broke cover, striding to the town gate with a boldness she didn't feel.

The highway switched to gravel closer to town. Celeste activated a flashlight in her left hand and moved it in a sweeping arc, back and forth twice.

From the gate came an answering flash.

Good, she thought in relief. At least some customs were universal. She was worried enough about what to say when she got there. English was the lingua franca, but there were a million dialects and no Rosetta Stone for Outland slang.

At the gate, Celeste held up her right hand, palms out. "Cabin and food for the night! Tradestuff will pay!"

A man's face appeared above her. A surprisingly handsome, youthful gatekeeper. She was accustomed to leathery-faced town guardians, jaded and world-weary. This kid looked like a band front man.

"How many in your party?" he asked. In English.

"Four."

He studied her face. Celeste felt good about it; let him see the grime, the lean features, the scars. She kept her expression neutral.

"What tradestuff, lady?"

"Packaged arky meals. Tech-stuff. Medkits."

"Where did you get it?"

"We..." Celeste hesitated a fraction of a second at this break in Outland protocol. "There's an airship crash forty miles west of here. Practically came down on our heads. We stripped what we could. You must have felt the explosion here."

The kid considered this. "Call your party out."

Celeste signaled with the flashlight. The town's spotlights snapped on, cut through the rain, and located the arkies in golden lances as they appeared over the ridge. The arkies halted at the gate, looking grim and dangerous.

"Weapons," the kid prompted.

Celeste saw her comrades hesitate. "Weapons!" she barked. "Now!"

Gethin forked over his rifle. He was let through the gate while Jack and Keiko followed his lead. The guards inspected each person with a handheld scanner. Celeste guessed it searched for microtech trackers, killbots, and explosives. She'd heard of a town in the Wichita Wastes that once bought a dozen crates of grenade-rockets only to discover too late the casings were crammed full of waspbots. The grisly lessons of Troy repeated.

"You too, sister," the guard said. "You chief?"

Celeste noticed he had warmed considerably to her. She softened her features as she passed her multigun to him. "Yes."

"Name's Howd." He handed her a hard plastic red ticket with a chipped "67" in white paint. "Hold onto that to get your weapons back. Welcome to Haventown."

★   ★   ★

Haventown was akin to places she'd seen in America: an Outland community with plastic tarps stretched over the jagged remains of concrete buildings. It was as if an unthinkably large spider had cocooned the forlorn relics of man. Seen from the inside, the barricade was built from similar detritus: smashed cars, piled tires, and stunted pylons. Armed guards lounged in lawn chairs, cigarettes burning tiny holes in the night.

Within the barricade, the town sprawled as a collection of corrugated shanties, plywood commonhouses, and residential burrows like ancient baseball dugouts, all awash in the Halloween glow of barrel fires and kerosene lamps. Rain tinkled into gutters and trenches.

Celeste's heart ached in unexpected nostalgia. She was suddenly a pre-teen again in the dinner lines, content to lose herself in the obscurity of ragged crowds who put aside their troubles for a turn at the fifth-rate replovats and cooking pits. She remembered the thudding radio beats during those gatherings…festive music only possible from mortal beings. What did arkies know of real music? What could they? Jeff liked to say that art would never survive among immortals, and from what she'd heard in Athens and Babylon – with their stale, precise recordings and pompous harp strummers, her love had been right on the money.

For her companions, the Wastetown was a vivid realization of images glimpsed from afar. Classroom virtual tours treaded the gutter-strewn paths of the Outlands; you saw the suffering of the damned, sick, diseased, and dying. You watched traders brave dangerous roads to mountaintop bazaars. You yawned at farmers toiling in the dirt. You glimpsed a screaming child searching for its mother. Sometimes it moved you. Sometimes it didn't. Either way, the classroom bell would ring and the virtual tour would end.

Celeste located the local food pit. A noisy replovat chugged away, strips of vat-grown meat dripping from the spigot. People took sidelong notice of the newcomers. They saw what she wanted them to see: a trader or hunter with her posse, just passing through. If anyone toyed with the idea of picking a fight, they were quickly discouraged by a look at her hardened face and the dried blood she wore with disinterest.

The people were primarily Turkish in breed, mixed with the darker-skinned stock of India. What shocked her was the sight of a Zulu on the woven bridge above the pit. He was carting away a malfunctioning replovat, but he glanced her way, locked gazes across the distance, and gave a friendly nod. She nodded back. Refined bone structure from prime nourishment. His left collar sported a faded, sideways Y.

It was a historical irony that for all the African wars over diamonds, oil, gold, and ivory during the antebellum, it was Africa which had dissolved tribal lines to form a single state…while Europe, America, and Asia collapsed into cannibalistic in-fighting. When Apollo the Great began his unstoppable conquests, the Zulus readily joined forces, essentially handing an entire continent to his cause, becoming the first pillar of what would become Earth Republic. Since then, the Zulu had become emissaries of peace and stability, the classic embodiment of order over chaos.

"Don't look so nervous," Celeste whispered to her crew as they gathered around an umbrella-shielded table. "What the fuck are you scared of, anyway? If these people rape and kill you, you'll just wake up in a squeaky clean regen center."

Jack and Gethin exchanged looks. "Maybe not," Jack said. "The IPC controls all Save clinics."

Celeste considered this.

So we're finally even. Sort of.

After a few minutes, the Zulu approached them.

"You came from the crash, eh?" he asked.

"Me look like airship rider?" she said, mirroring his accent.

"You no local girl."

"No. *Loco* girl."

He threw back his head and laughed. "No doubt, sister!"

"You got network here?"

The Zulu's eyes shimmered at this. "Sure. But come straight. You from Paradise?" It was what Africa's sprawling cities were collectively known as.

"No, but me longtime friends with Zulu," Celeste said, speaking in half truths. She had interacted with his people from time to time, when they descended to the Outlands bearing humanitarian aid. Decent folk, as arkies went.

Her attempt at diversion failed. The Zulu gave her a meaningful look. "You tell me where you from?"

"Odessa," she lied. Odessa was King D.'s birthtown, where he first established his rep by unifying the street gangs of the Ukraine. "You trader-man 'round here?"

He nodded, gazed past her shoulder to her companions. She used the moment to look around for a ship – the scintillating African ships that brought aid to the despondent. But there was nothing in sight. Most likely, a Paradise vessel would swing by in a few days to bear him away.

"We salvage from airship crash. Medbot program. Arky prepmeals. You buy?"

The Zulu inspected the items she dug from her coat. "These good. What you want?"

"Meals for squad, two days' worth. Place to stay one night."

"Just one?"

"We make for Cappadocia tomorrow."

The Zulu smiled and yelled an order to the replovat counter. *Sweet*, Celeste thought. *One arky meal buys two or three plates of replovat crap. A fair enough exchange rate.*

A fresh-faced pit worker carried a tray to Celeste's table; she caught the aroma and guessed it was grown from cattle stock.

"Got these too." Celeste showed him the medkits. The Zulu inspected them, quickly found the nanite infusion clips, and wrinkled his nose. Nanite infusions were illegal in the Outlands. Could regrow bone, tissue, vessels, organs, and limbs...but deadlier applications were possible in the hands of skilled reverse-engineering labs. Turn a plaque cleaner into a brain chewer.

"Bring these to Doc Tiptree," the Zulu said, and he gave an ironic smirk. "Just follow the gravel path to town center."

"Good."

"Cappadocia strange choice, woman," he added. "They no deal with outsiders. But you take the old highway when you go. It be neutral ground for all. Just wait for daylight and you be safe."

She caught the troubled undertone in his voice. "Glops at night?"

"A real problem 'round here. We lose more to them than to spats, you best believe that."

"Dire dogs?"

His smile slipped. "Me, I don't advocate the killin' of Earth's beautiful beasts. But these woods hold nothing beautiful. Nothing true-beast."

She thanked him, feeling a twinge of guilt at the realization that if she did discover he had a ship around here, she might have to kill him for it; the *Mantid* was running dark again, and she knew her only chance to escape back to King D. was out here, where the arkies were at a disadvantage. "Hey," she said, "You got commonhouse for travelers?"

"Passed it on your way in."

She thanked him again and turned away.

"Hold on," he said. "My name is Siyanda. You looking for work? Less risk here than scavenging."

"Like what?"

He indicated the entirety of Haventown with a sweep of his arm. "All this will be a state in six years. Outland Charter, you know? We got schools in operation now."

Celeste felt a thrum of vicious rage, and had to fight to keep the smile on her face. "You going Republic?"

"We have need of new teachers."

She laughed caustically. "Do I look like a teacher to you?"

"We all learners and teachers, sister."

★ ★ ★

Some arkies got bitten by the Wastes. Like children in love with dinosaurs, bugs, or birds, there were people who obsessed with the colored history of the Century from the Final War's nuclear holocaust to Enyalios's blood-drenched conquest of the Americas and subsequent global unification. Lots of pirates, dynastic struggles, conquerors, biowars, sordid affairs, and civil strife wove a tapestry of events that fascinated some people.

Jack was one of them.

"Warlord Eyeblaze made his famous wedding attack around here, somewhere on the outskirts of old Istanbul," he was saying, speaking between spoonfuls of soup. "After thirteen years of fighting with neighboring clans he finally agreed to a truce. His enemies wanted a mass marriage to unite the tribes, so an entire city square was prepared for the wedding. But Eyeblaze learned it was a ruse. His enemies wanted to lure him under a banner of truce, and then assassinate him and his entire staff."

Keiko stirred her soup listlessly, not really interested. However, listening to him was better than thinking about this peasant meal of old replovat protein structures and a meat program almost certainly grown from local fauna. She needed the calories for tomorrow's march. Gethin had already scarfed his meal down and was leaning back in his chair, observing the town with a calm, thoughtful gaze.

"So what happened?" Keiko asked.

Jack tapped the table with his fingers. "Eyeblaze performed one of the most stunning feints in history. The day of the wedding, his enemies arrived with their military entourages. They saw Eyeblaze at the head tent, laughing and drinking, seemingly ignorant of what they had planned. But it wasn't Eyeblaze at all. He'd rigged a hologram of himself. The *real* Eyeblaze was miles away, looking down on his own wedding ceremony with binoculars. At a prearranged moment, his staff snuck into a bunker. Then Eyeblaze gassed the entire party with cyanide. Killed everyone." Jack snapped his fingers. "Just like that. The next day, he mounted up and *walked* into their respective kingdoms."

Gethin groaned. "And a few years later, his own brother poisoned him, ripped out his colorful eyes, and hung them, optic nerves and all, from the palace until his wife killed *him*, chopped him up…"

"My point," Jack insisted, "is that if Eyeblaze had lived, he might have united Europe two generations before Apollo was even born."

Gethin shrugged and finished off the last of his water. "Maybe. Who cares?"

Jack gave him a quizzical glance. "I figured *you* would find that period interesting. Aren't you a history professor?"

"Doesn't mean I like every era."

"Sure, but—"

"Want to know a disadvantage of immortality? You're never quite so far from the ugly past. What is it, just a half dozen generations since Eyeblaze?" He broke off his editorial as Celeste returned to relate her conversation with Siyanda.

"And there's a doctor in town," she added. "Last chance to get fixed up before the march to Cappadocia."

Gethin stood, eager for whatever medical ministrations this town could provide. Then he hesitated, remembering the tattoo on Saylor's stomach. "Eyeblaze," he said, "created a special order of bodyguards to protect him."

"The *colossi*," Jack said.

"Right, the *colossi*. As I recall, anyone under six foot five need not have applied. Eyeblaze himself was a large fellow and he wanted his escorts to match." Gethin gave a small, genuine smile. "The Saylors have done well for themselves since those grim days, haven't they?"

Jack actually blushed. It took Celeste a moment to appreciate the comment, and when the reality sunk in, she gently punched the security chief's arm. "*You* are descended from the *colossi*? That's why you sport that purple tattoo on your belly?"

"Out of the past," he quipped.

Gethin said, "Just remind your son and daughter of that, Jack. Tell them how the Saylor clan ascended and…" He grinned. "Your daughter is going to Venus, right?"

Jack looked stunned. "Yeah. I mean, we don't know yet, she has to apply, but she wants to go." He frowned. "You looked up my family file?"

"I like to know things." Gethin smiled in a way that bordered on pleasant. "Up to the stars indeed," he added, and the big man smiled appreciatively.

★   ★   ★

Doctor Tiptree looked more like a frazzled, exhausted butcher than a health care professional. He had a trollish body, squat and powerful, with broad shoulders and huge hands. A swirl of black, wiry hair sprouted from a cancerously mottled scalp. His gourd-shaped face was scarred by what might have been a bear's claw but, more likely, had been a long-nailed human patient. His chubby fingers trembled as he examined his new patients.

The clinic was a rusted shed that had once been a gas station. Corrugated steel sheets welded over the windows, the interior holding six beds; Keiko eyed the filthy mattresses with open distaste.

"One medkit." Celeste let him examine it. The other one she decided to keep for herself. Aside from Gethin's broken foot, the group's injuries could be treated in more traditional ways. No point in wasting arky magic on what amounted to bruises, gashes, and splinters.

Tiptree carefully extracted the glass from Keiko's face. He frowned when he saw Gethin's forehead gash, and sewed it up with black thread. He prodded Gethin's cracked wrist and wrapped it.

Celeste watched the proceedings in silence. As the doctor finished dressing their wounds, she said, "The medkit will buy us a room too. Siyanda gave his word."

Tiptree locked the medkit in a metal cabinet and nodded solemnly. "I'll radio ahead and tell 'em."

Most Wastetowns had commonhouses. This one was a fugitive's dream. Down from the main square in a sunken patch of earth, overhung by a half circle of maples. The innkeeper was a matronly creature listening to a radio via headset when they entered, and she handed them a brass key without a word.

The room was on the fourth floor. Two bunk beds crammed into square accommodations like an old college dormitory. It had a cloying stench and the nose-tickling aroma of mold. There were black streaks on the walls that made Gethin think of striated fossil shales.

He took the lower bunk, nestling himself into a shadowy corner. Celeste lay above him, her bed pressed against the room's single window. His foot throbbed with warmth, the nanites industriously toiling on his bone and tendons. Like a tiny construction crew, working in calcium instead of concrete.

Lying awake in the darkness, Celeste reflected on their situation. If there wasn't a way to contact the *Mantid* – and she figured it was lying low because the IPC was scouring the entire region – then Cappadocia really was the only reasonable option. The Turkish metropolis was an autonomous state. Among the Folk, she'd lie low. Wait. The IPC wanted her companions, not her. When the heat cooled, she could call the *Mantid* for evac.

She contemplated the peeling plaster ceiling. And then what?

Celeste rolled onto her side. Beyond the streaked window, Haventown was a dark, rainy blur. Barrel fires twinkled in the night.

War was brewing.

The arky factions seemed ready to go at it, gladiator-style. StrikeDown could sit back and wait. Hide in the cracks of the world like rodents in the age of dinosaurs, unseen and forgotten, while the mighty toppled. Then they could more easily storm the fortresses, haul out vitals, erase the borders.

And then what?

Celeste realized her heart was pounding like a lead drum.

King D. seemed to think that he could bring the Repbublic and IPC to the negotiating table. She believed in his cause. But what if they were all wrong? What if open war meant total global collapse, as Gethin Bryce had described in Athens? Then Outlanders would literally move underground, and what remained of the IPC would duke it out with every other scavenger in the solar system. Belters and Prometheans and Frontieriests, brightworlds and deepworlds. Such was life. Hiding from sabertooths, or from conquering legions, or from nuclear fallout. Each time the human race burrowed deeper like moles. Deeper, deeper, clawing their way blind, like maggots squirming to the still-warm center of a corpse. Some fifty million years from now, when human civilization wasn't even a rusted stain, the next dominant species might discover five-fingered, albino, eyeless parasites gnawing at their garden roots.

An anguished howl pierced the night beyond Haventown.

Celeste shivered.

Maybe it had already begun.

CHAPTER THIRTY-FOUR
Apophis and the IPC

Dark drop.

Twenty-eight men and women fell through inky blackness, landed easily on the powdery Lunar surface, and scampered into position around the Williams Sports Dome. Their obsidian-colored transport drifted high above them, poised on the periphery of Luna's gravitational web, running cold and unseen.

IPC Mission Commander Michelle Hyde crouched by a loading crate, fixing the dome in her binocular sights. It was the largest stadium on Luna, enclosed in a concrete shell fifty meters north-west of her position. It sat on the remote borders of Luna City. Hyde was thankful for that. Most traffic arrived here by subway, but the dome wasn't a regularly scheduled stop on the main lines, and the route had already been shut down by local police. Air traffic was also being diverted.

Hyde's optics crowded with data overlays. In her left eye, she saw her attack squad represented by twenty-eight green dots. The other overlays were a veritable Rolodex of the dome's blueprints, list of personnel, fire escapes, and garage. She also kept several radio frequencies open on her codex. The comlinks from inside the building were silent.

Maybe the terrorist was gone?

Hyde was eighty-one-years old, tall and auburn, built like a Valkyrie. Earthborn but now a proud Lunar, she privately held out hope for the overturn of the colonization ban. She had, after all, always entertained fantasies of working on a frontier colony like some sci-fi holostar. Maybe be the first to discover intelligent extraterrestrial life.

The voice of First Scout Mikhail Popova sounded in her ear: "Readings are clear. No sniff of explosives."

Hyde nodded, tense and excited. Luna had been a frenzy of activity these past few days. The IPC was working closely with Lunar authorities, who demonstrated a level of cooperation only fear could engender.

Because it wasn't just the shuttle or base explosions any more. An hour ago, Club Nadsat was attacked. The culprit was caught on camera: a Caucasian male of unregistered identity. He had killed everyone in the place using an unknown Promethean weapon. Then he'd hijacked a moon buggy and driven to the Sports Dome. The dome's seating capacity was forty thousand; mercifully, no games were scheduled today.

But there *were* employees there. Some two dozen maintenance workers and security guards. The security station was hit first; a guard managed to squeeze off one panicked emergency call before the dome went entirely silent.

Hyde had the Nadsat footage stored in her sensorium. She had studied the terrifying footage during the flight here. The IPC's best and brightest were analyzing it, but presently no one could give her anything better to go on other than a generic "Be careful, Michelle." They would all be watching through her eyes as she conducted this mission. So, too, would IPC Lt. Donna McCallister.

I'm a television station today, Hyde thought grimly.

"Alpha Team, move up."

Six soldiers rocketed up the dome on controlled bursts of pressurized air. They landed with precision on the building's hull, a few meters above the row of glasstic windows. Each took a window, covering as much of the interior as they could. Then they shifted into CAMO.

"I've got eyes on," an Alpha Team sniper said a few seconds later. "Main floor lobby, sitting down near the ticket booths. He's still armed."

Alpha Team worked quickly, placing sealed sniper mounts over the windows to maintain dome pressure when the nanoblades set to work on the glasstic. You couldn't just shoot through glasstic.

Hyde was tempted to give a kill order when the window was breached. She wanted a clean mission, over and done. A bright jewel on her corporate résumé. But McCallister had comlinked her on the transport, made it clear that IPC brass wanted the man taken alive.

Priority One: Non-lethal takedown.

Priority Two: Recovery of subject's armaments.

Hyde skipped in the low gravity to the dome doorway. There she hesitated, her tech specialist overriding the door locks.

How had the terrorist gained entry to the dome in the first place? You couldn't just drive up in a moon buggy and waltz past security.

"Alpha Team," she said, "let's see him."

A signal crackled in her head. She linked to a sniper's optics. There! The terrorist was slouched against a ticket booth, legs splayed out. The blue metal weapon still encased the subject's right arm, showing bright red through the creases and joints. Analyst chatter had been a confused mess about its capabilities. It appeared to fire a plasma-based discharge, though there were no visible storage tanks. It could also immolate people from a distance of at least three and a half meters, if the Club Nadsat footage was any indication. And then there was that eerie business of floating around the club like a goddamn phantom. The analysts didn't know what to say. Magnetism? Nanowires? Was the terrorist himself an aerostat construct?

No visible powerpack or ammo clips. The unknown weapon looked grafted to his flesh.

"Let's see the rest."

Feeds flowed in from the other snipers. Gradually the interior of the dome assembled itself to her optics. The Sports Dome lobby was a grisly sight. Human carcasses strewn about, still wearing orange maintenance coveralls. One poor woman draped over the ceiling pipes. Topical damage on the walls, but hull integrity was not compromised.

"What do we make of the weapon?" she asked.

"No heat. Looks powered down."

The dome doors popped open, making Hyde jump. She motioned to her forward team and they rushed in through the gap, fanning out in the lobby interior.

"What about the subject?" she whispered, imagining she could feel the weight of so many people watching through her sensorium. This mission was being watched in real time by the universe's elite. Leon Tanner, Donna McCallister…and almost certainly IPC President Song in his situation room.

Alpha Team's report came in. "No wetware, commander."

Hyde frowned. No wetware?

She went through the airlock and switched to infravision. The darkened interior snapped into green focus. She stepped carefully around the bodies. She stopped at the corner, sightjacking with the Alpha Team sniper above her for a visual on the target.

"My name is Commander Michelle Hyde," she called out. "I am a negotiator for the IPC. Can we talk?"

The target spoke in a soft, dejected tone. "Are you here to kill me?"

"No," she said, instantly running the voice against the Nadsat recording. Positive ID. "I'm here to talk with you. But you have caused a great deal of suffering and death. I am prepared to use deadly force against you if necessary. *If necessary.* Do you understand? We can either have a conversation, or you can die."

"I would very much like to talk," the man said brokenly. "I'm a bad thing. You must understand that I can't help myself."

"May I approach?"

"You may."

"Would you consider removing your weapon?"

"It's part of me. I can't take it off, as much as I want to."

That certainly seemed to be true. Whoever had done this to him must have surgically melded the weapon to his limb. Ridiculous! Why do that? Hyde's mouth felt dry. She licked her lips.

She turned the corner, seeing him with her own eyes for the first time. He was dressed in loose-fitting brown slacks and a matching long-sleeve shirt. It gave the impression of being a monastic garment. The man himself was lank and unspectacular. His eyes were dazed. He was sprawled out as if he'd been shot. His hair was plastered to his forehead.

"What is your name?"

"You can call me Apophis."

An instant list of possible etymologies sprang to her optics:

No citizen in the IPC database of registered voting planetary bodies goes by the name of Apophis.

There are 121 avatars named Apophis in Arcadia.

Apophis is the name of a fictional laboratory in Sloan Goodman's *Reynard Pond* series.

Apophis is the name of a defunct Persian Jazz band from last century.

Apophis is a comet discovered in the Old Calendar, long since harvested by the Ashoka.

39 references to Apophis occur in films and television.

In Egyptian mythology, Apophis is the God of Chaos.

"Apophis," she repeated.

"Michelle Hyde," he said with a wink.

She held his gaze, while peripherally studying the damage to the room and the dead bodies. No burned corpses this time. No energy burns. Unlike the club, the damage here looked strictly mechanical; blood spatters, necks twisted at odd angles, toppled chairs. It was as if the perp had run out of ammo, and been forced to bludgeon his victims to death. Maybe that's why the weapon was cool. Even the woman's body hanging from the ceiling pipes…a strong enough assailant might easily fling a person up there in the low-G.

But why do it at all?

In the club's video, he had insisted he couldn't help himself. It was conceivable. There were lots of ways to induce behavior.

But it was also possible he was purely psychotic.

In fact, this was one of the few points the analysts were in agreement on. Nothing in his behavior suggested a man struggling against programmed instincts. The analysts likened it to watching an obsessive-compulsive trying to resist the ritual of handwashing. OCD sufferers were angry, even furious, as they indulged the hated compulsion. They scrubbed their hands raw and *hated* doing it, though they *couldn't* stop. You could see the anguish in their eyes.

Not with Apophis. He clearly enjoyed his destructive appetites, regardless of what he said.

"You wanted to talk," she prompted.

Apophis nodded. "Quite right. I'm sure you want to know who blew up Base 59."

Hyde's heart skipped a beat, seeing the moment of revelation – with her name attached to it – about to unfold.

"I would."

"Prometheus Industries made a nasty little plaything. They built it, groomed it, and it blew up in their faces."

"What did they make?"

"Me."

She took another couple steps into the room. There was another ticket booth, and she hesitated beside it, maintaining eye contact with the target. "You destroyed Base 59? How?"

"'How?' Wouldn't the better question be why?"

"Agreed. Why?"

"An empire's ambitions are nothing without the power of its soldiers. Was it Caesar alone who conquered Gaul? Or was it the Roman legions, whipped into seamless military perfection, clad in the best armor, and protected by the best shields?"

Hyde nodded, but her senses were attuning to his right arm. If he jerked that weapon up, she decided, she would simply blur away from him.

She said, "I agree, but that doesn't answer my question. *Why* did you destroy the base?"

"Destroying is what I am good at, madam. It's how they made me. I am an experimental prototype shock trooper. Prometheus Industries plans to annex one world at a time. They can do it too, if they develop others like me. A technological edge without rival."

Hyde steadied her breathing. She tried to imagine what the people back at HQ were going to make of all this.

"Was it revenge? Is that why you attacked the base?"

"'Cursed, cursed creator!'" He looked forlornly at the ceiling. "'Why did I live?'"

Hyde was considering what to say next when a signal flashed from command. Donna McCallister.

"By all means and at all costs," McCallister said through her audio, "take him alive, Michelle."

Hyde saw the wisdom in this. *She* could be regenerated, while this Apophis was invaluable.

Then she glanced at the bodies around her. Her heart gave a long, agonized pang of fear.

"*Where* did Prometheus Industries make you?" she asked, aware of her audience listening in.

"'In a secret lab,'" he said miserably. "'It is a scene terrifically desolate. In a thousand spots the traces of the winter avalanche may be perceived.'"

"Tell me about the lab."

"'Conceive an enormous cylindrical space, a quarter of a mile across, perhaps, very dimly lit at first and then brighter, with big platforms twisting down its sides in a spiral.'"

"Were you the only one? Or did Prometheus create others?"

"I'm the prototype," Apophis said. "Others will follow. 'Millions of flaming swords, drawn from the thighs of mighty Cherubim!'"

From her helmet, a voice crackled. McCallister again.

"Watch yourself, Michelle. He's quoting from various books. Frankenstein. H.G. Wells. Wait a minute…John Milton was that last one."

Keeping the man in her targeting reticle, Hyde asked subvocally, "What the hell for?"

"No idea. Just keep him talking, and *take him alive.*"

Apophis was suddenly coughing, choking violently. "Oh! Goodness! Help me!"

Hyde held her ground. Her troops spread evenly behind her. "What is it?"

Apophis peered at her between bouts of hacking. "It's so *hot* in here!"

The falsity in his voice was mocking. Hyde glanced at her suit's thermostat. The temperature in the room was 30 below. But he was right. The heat in the room had increased by four degrees since the start of their conversation.

Apophis put his head in his hands. Slowly he split the fingers, like a child playing peek-a-boo. "*Memento mori, plaga! Mors omnibus instat!*"

"Michelle!" came McAllister's voice. "He just said he's going to kill all—"

Hyde fired at his knee. The projectile hit the kneecap solidly, shattering cartilage and lodging there, releasing an incapacitating neurotoxin. She was concentrating on her next shot when he vanished.

"He's blurred!" she cried, but then realized this couldn't be. Her own blurmods should have sprung into auto-activation in response to a hyperaccelerated body. They hadn't.

She looked to the vending machines, then up at the ceiling.

If her mods didn't trigger, then he *couldn't* be moving at hyperaccelerated speeds. So the bastard must still be there, disguised by CAMO mesh or implanted chromatophores like a fucking chameleon.

A half dozen voices were piping through her suit.

"Where did—"

"—nothing on sensors—"

"Bullshit! Radiation is spiking. Something is here—"

"Michelle! *Behind you!*"

She spun around in time to see Apophis standing there. Somehow he had increased in height, his body stretched long like a funhouse reflection. A bullet whined from an Alpha Team sniper and her optics illustrated its vector as it hit Apophis in the shoulder: a neurotoxin that could put down an elephant. Then she was pitched violently away as if smacked by an invisible hand. Hyde hit the wall hard, rattling her teeth. Her team sprayed the room in barely controlled bursts, but the target was gone again.

The bastard is toying with us, Hyde thought angrily.

That wasn't the half of it. She'd seen him get hit by the neurotoxin round… but that didn't seem to be working. He should have dropped like a lead balloon. Maybe the perp possessed an advanced nanite immune system operating on picosecond reflexes, countering the toxin before it could work. Hyde had heard rumors of corporate research labs cranking out experimental wetware implants. She struggled to keep her thoughts together.

"I've got nothing!"

"Did he blur?"

"Exits are sealed with nanomesh! He can't go—"

"Michelle! Your suit temperature's spiking! Get out of there!"

Her biosuit turned oven-hot. The heat crawled over every inch of her body, between her toes, on the backs of her knees. Spikes of pain swelled in her limbs. Hyde staggered back, stricken. The ugly sensation of being probed filled her. Scorching unseen fingertips kneaded her joints, making a very obvious ascent from her toes up to her neck…then her scalp and face…

There was a soft popping sound from her eyes. One after another, her capillaries were bursting.

Get out of here!

She retreated for the lobby, knowing that Apophis was touching her, he was *inside her suit and feeling her body!*

Inside her suit, her hair burst into flames.

Michelle ran straight into the wall, shrieking terribly. She clawed at her helmet. Smoke erupted from the seams of her biosuit. She found the release locks, tore the helmet from her head, and slapped at her roasting scalp.

Her squad fired into the lobby. One of her squadmates was abruptly flung by an invisible force into the ceiling. His back struck the overhead pipes and jackknifed around them. Another man burst into flames and flopped around like a fish.

Michelle had dropped her rifle, but she groped for it now. Her wetware augs were clamping down on her pain, clipping nerves. The lobby was a haze of gunpowder and smoke. It cleared just enough for her to see a chamber of horrors. Men flailing in agony, flames gushing from their mouths.

One fiery body was slamming its head repeatedly into the vending machine. It jerked away as if by an invisible hook, smashed into the nearest wall, and stuck there, affixed, while the head – couldn't tell if it was a man or woman – was peeling away in great sizzling strips of meat inside its helmet.

I won't remember any of this, she thought. *When they regen me these things won't even be a memory.*

Then she saw *it*.

In the center of the room a source of heat manifested. It was a shapeless, ever-changing blot of power, tentacled and holding position like a jellyfish floating in the ocean void.

The video feed cut after that. Alpha Team couldn't see anything in the smoke and fire, but they heard their commander screaming shrilly. It took ten minutes for Michelle Hyde's purchase signal to be received at Wyndham Save. They never found out exactly how Apophis had killed her except that her bones were found in one room, while her jellied flesh was plastered like a glob of mucus affixed to the ceiling of another.

And hours later in her new body, she didn't want to know.

CHAPTER THIRTY-FIVE
Reflections

The next morning Gethin awoke and climbed carefully out of bed. The air had a damp, invasive quality. He glimpsed Keiko in the adjacent washroom, where she was examining her face in a smeared body-length mirror. There was no sign of the sector chief or the Wastelander.

Keiko noticed him in the mirror.

"Your face will heal in time for corporate elections," he said.

She turned and leaned casually against the doorway, thumbs hooked into her pockets. He knew that pose. She was feeling confident, in control. Nothing to prove right now. Her Noh mask discarded in the face of certain victory. Impressive, actually, considering all they'd been through so far.

"How do you know I'm running for office?" she asked evenly.

"Are you?"

"I'm planning on pursuing a Promethean governor post in '30 or '35."

Gethin nodded and massaged his foot. It was sore, but he couldn't locate the loose bone any longer. The nanites had been busy during the night. His next urination might expel their used-up carcasses. "What post?"

Keiko's eyes narrowed a millimeter. "Looking to be my campaign manager, Gethin?"

"Just curious, is all." He deactivated his nerve suppression and stood, testing out his foot. The pain came on like a hammer at first. He let its full intensity course through him, gritted his teeth, and realized he could cope with it.

Gethin hobbled towards the washroom. Keiko stood aside and watched while he stripped off his shirt and rinsed his upper body. Dried sweat and grime swirled in the sink basin.

He patted himself dry while the shirt soaked in the sink. "Where are the others?"

"Jack is using the local hub to contact HQ. The IPC has almost certainly taken over airspace for fifty miles, so an extraction is unlikely. But I want Prometheus to know where we're heading."

"And Celeste?"

"No idea." Keiko hesitated. "You think Doros is one of these *things*, don't you?"

Gethin sighed and paced once through the room to test his balance.

"I know he is." When he saw her eyes flicker, he added, "No, I never suspected anything while working with the guy. It makes a creepy kind of sense now, though. Doros is probably one of the things that replaced Tanner."

"Maybe he *is* what replaced Tanner."

"No."

"The attack on you in Athens?"

"Unrelated," Gethin insisted. "At least as far as Doros goes. And I'm starting to suspect what the purpose of the attack was. And maybe even who's responsible."

"Oh?"

"Think of the timing. Those golems tailed me from Luna. They could have attacked me on Luna, or Babylon, but they waited until I was in Athens. If I'd been killed, the IPC would blame Prometheus. Prometheus would counter that the IPC was framing them. Someone out there wants the two greatest powers in the known universe at each other's throats."

Keiko thoughtfully tapped her fingers on her pants. "Not the AIs, huh?"

He returned to the sink and wrung dirty water from his shirt. "They're merely a convenient scapegoat. You have to admit, you were ready to gulp that bait."

"So if it isn't them…"

"Let's run through what we know. A new order of intelligence exists, capable of shifting between matter and energy. It can assume any shape it wants. It attacked your Lunar base, I'm guessing to obtain the exotic-matter cathode designs your company pioneered. As it left, it collided with my shuttle."

Keiko's lips compressed into a thin line. "The image on the recording…"

"Was our first look at one of these things." He snapped his shirt around the shower curtain rod and stood across from her, bare-chested, emerald gaze lively and alert. "It went to Earth, we all saw that."

"And then it – or another one of these things – attacked Segarra."

"The attack on her was purely incidental. Its real purpose was to ensure that Stillness acquired antimatter missiles."

The connections, coming on the heels of each other, almost physically staggered her. Keiko absently clenched and unclenched her feet in her boots. "And then it impersonated Colonel Tanner in order to sneak Stillness troopers onto an IPC airship bound for Shimizu." She tried to pace in the small bathroom, driven by a curious cocktail of fear and awe. "What about the attack on our Pacific base? And the Lunar editorial?"

"Editorial?"

She told him about the damning newspaper article.

"Ah." Gethin reflected for a moment. "I doubt that's related to these creatures. But it's almost certainly related to the people who sent those golems after me."

"A Promethean competitor," she said softly.

"Precisely."

"Who do you think?"

"Can't be that long a list. TowerTech is the obvious choice." He grinned. "You and I always *did* have a habit of making enemies."

She laughed. "Especially of each other."

"Someone's gotta keep us on our toes."

"Because shapeshifting energy creatures aren't enough." She hesitated, wrestled with a confession, decided. "We were too similar to ever work out in the long run. Competitive, ambitious, arrogant, adversarial."

"That might just be the sweetest thing you've ever said to me."

Keiko's smile slipped. "It comes with a barb."

"Of course."

"A mutual barb. When we were conquistadors of Arcadia, it overtook our lives. Instant gratification, affirmation, fake friends and social media circuses... but none of it was real. Meaning no disrespect, but I think I realized it before you did. I remember logging out of Arcadia one night, and looking at you in the other rig, and..." She struggled to put it into words.

Gethin took a breath. "A drooling online addict, right?"

"More than that. I started feeling like we had both been captured in some web, preventing us from ever truly taking flight and doing something that mattered." Keiko rubbed her chin thoughtfully. "So when our marriage ended, I willfully unplugged. I applied for the corporate life, and I've never felt better."

"You look good, Keiko. I mean it."

She gave him a sly look. "So do you, even if you had to go to fucking Mars to kick your habit. Speaking of which, I have to ask, who was the girl who got Gethin Bryce to settle down on the redworld?"

"Her name was Lori." He glanced to his reflection in the smeared mirror. "The details are unimportant."

"You loved her," Keiko observed with a gasp. "Gethin Bryce actually fell in love with someone."

"No one's perfect."

"Not even the great *bodhisattva* of Faustus?"

"Don't," he said, giving a mock glare, "start with that."

She handed him the damp shirt from the curtain rod. "Come on. Let's meet up with Jack and get the hell out of here."

★   ★   ★

Outside, the rain had diffused into a soupy vapor, making Haventown seem a haunted waystation in the damp mists of Limbo. Pale sunlight suggested it was morning. Perhaps eight or nine a.m.

Gethin saw a small huddle of men outside the commonhouse. Keiko noticed them too, and she shot him a worried look.

"Let's not chance it," he advised.

They turned off the path and melted into the fog. Somewhere from the main road, three women began singing a Turkish melody about underworld spirits and the brevity of life.

"We make for the center of town," Keiko whispered.

Together, they rounded a shed. Gethin felt a stab of pain in his foot and he stumbled. His nails dug into the corrugated steel, flaking rust, while behind him came the sounds of sudden pursuit.

Keiko snatched his hand, pulling him under the awning of a tool shop. An old woman looked up from her workbench as they crouched by a bin of nails, and four seconds later a group of youths jogged past.

Gethin watched them go. "Nine people," he said morosely. "At least two of them have clubs. Think they're recruiting for baseball?"

"We've got another few seconds before they realize their mistake."

They fled the shop, cutting across the street, and made for the main road and sound of singing. The congested shops thinned and there was a low building, with about a dozen residents milling about on the porch. The food pits weren't far, but Gethin heard their pursuers again, and he knew they'd never make it.

Keiko's tranquil face lost some vitality. She made a rapid survey of their surroundings and considered the narrow alleys.

"Blur," Gethin told her. "It's the only choice. Risk powering on your sensorium or get clubbed over the head and dragged off to a chopshop."

She gave him a worried look. "What about you?"

"Depleted batteries. But I'll manage. Go."

Her finger went to her ear, but she hesitated. The youths saw them and dropped out of their collective jog, grinning cruelly, spreading out to meet them.

"Good morning," Gethin tried.

"No," she said, withdrawing her hand from her ear. "I'm not abandoning you."

Gethin didn't look away from the kids but he hissed. "*Yes.* Get Saylor."

"No."

He couldn't identify a clear leader among the kids in the leering, scrawny bunch. He did see deadly urgency in their eyes, the violent intent. How many visitors to Haventown had come to *this* fate?

Then a shotgun blast sounded over their heads.

From behind the kids, Celeste's lean figure materialized in the grimy morning air. She closed the distance to them, and when a new group of slightly older males ran up behind her, she barely acknowledged them with a look. Her shotgun leveled at the younger crew.

"Drop the weapons!" she shouted.

The crew hesitated.

"You speak English?" she demanded, in a tone that taunted them to truth. A few heads nodded. "Good, then you understood my command. Drop the weapons, now."

No response. The two groups of men, young and old, silently conferred with each other.

The shotgun blasted.

Celeste didn't waste it on another warning shot. This time, she discharged at the group of youths dead center. At twenty feet, the impact blew one of the boys off his feet, and he was dead before his body hit the mud.

"You murdering bitch!" an outraged cry rose up behind her.

"Self-defense!" she roared back. "My squad visits Haventown and you *assault us* like dickless cowards? Why are *we* your enemy? All of us here share the same common threat to our lives! The arkies! *They're* the ones who prosper while we die like ants in the dust!"

The mist darkened with more bodies, the town's inhabitants drawn to the gunshots and voices.

"*This is why you fail!*" Celeste's voice yanked their gazes up from the corpse. "Killing each other in the shadows, while the arky world laughs at us. I've been to the arky world, I've heard what they say. We're *rats*! Outland rats who cannibalize one another. We're better off dead, they say. We're sick and diseased, in body and spirit."

Someone muttered.

She glared in that direction. "What was that?"

"I said fuck them," a kid said sullenly.

"Exactly! Fuck *them*, not each other! 'Steal the scepter and the crown!'"

The man blinked in surprise. "StrikeDown."

"StrikeDown!" she echoed. "StrikeDown!"

She fist-pumped in timing to the rhythm, latching onto each pair of eyes in turn. The youths joined her chant warily. The older men added their voices. Gethin shivered as the chorus grew. Even the morning singers, a trio of frightfully emaciated women, began chanting the refrains of the revolution song making its way among the world's pariahs.

"StrikeDown!"

Gethin looked to Celeste, saw the lusty glitter in her eyes as she shouted with unstoppable conviction above the crowd.

"StrikeDown!"

CHAPTER THIRTY-SIX
Urgent Action

Jonas's eye was itchy after surgery. Impact with the computer monitor had detached his retina, the doctor told him. It was an easy fix, but now he had to wear an eye patch for a few days and he hated it. It was so uncomfortable. The doctor offered him a packet of mild painkillers to help, but Jonas declined, since painkillers made him drowsy and he would rather suffer than have his concentration blunted by meds. Especially now, with all that was going on in the world.

Maximilian had called the doctor when he blacked out. Jonas remembered nothing of the ordeal that followed; his mother said the emergency ward had drained his lungs the best they could and fixed his eye. He awoke to his mother weeping and stroking his hand. He asked if they could go home.

The doctor wanted to talk to him, but Jonas wasn't interested. Time was more precious now than ever. He knew he was doomed...why pretend otherwise? By the ghastly pallor on his mother's face, Jonas guessed what the doctor was going to tell him anyway.

Home. He just wanted to be home.

And they let him go. Bahara signed the discharge papers.

"You look like a pirate now," she told him, carrying a box of pink foam into his bedroom. Wonderingly, he watched her use the stuff to injury-proof his room, blunting the sharp edges of his monitor and desk. When she was done, it looked like his workstation had been dipped in raspberry cotton candy. "Good?"

Jonas nodded weakly. Sitting in Maximilian's wheelchair form, he reached for the VR rig.

"Wait!" His mother's eyes were bloodshot. "Jonas, do you have to do this right now?"

"Of course."

Her forehead creased with anguish. She hesitated, clearly on the cusp of confession. Finally she bowed her head in resignation. "Do you mind if I do my needlepoint while you play your games?"

He told her he didn't mind. She fetched her colored threads and canvas graph and sat on his bed while he set the rig over his head.

His first order of business was to confirm that Anju's transmission had gone through. Good! The recording was saved in his files. Now was the tricky business of making good on his word: he needed to start a war with the Judgment Fiends. It was going to be disastrous, a shrieking melee, a cataclysm of digital gore and death that would snowball through Arcadia. It would be the gameworld equivalent of another Final War. The very thought made him weary.

But before he could log into Arcadia, he noticed the newsfeed headlines. An Athenian airship had crashed into the Turkish Wastes. The mainstream news wasn't reporting any details yet, but Cappadocia surveillance had scooped them. The airship belonged to the IPC. Spybots confirmed that there were at least a dozen bodies strewn among the wreckage, that many of them had died from *gunshots*, and that most were dressed in Stillness regalia.

Ah!

Jonas was so intrigued that he almost didn't bother with the other headlines. Then he saw the pictures from Luna, and his jaw dropped.

Club Nadsat. Williams Sports Dome.

Jonas lifted the rig and peeked at his mother. She smiled up at him from her needlework.

"Is that a new game?"

"Yes, Mother." He returned to the feeds. Luna was under martial law. Not just Tanabata City, but the *entire moon*. A terrorist named Apophis had murdered dozens of people, and managed to repel an IPC elite anti-terrorism squad. Details were so sketchy it gave Jonas a chill. President Song was urging everyone to be calm, but he had already mobilized two battleships to Luna. The dome was under nanomesh quarantine; it was believed Apophis was still inside.

And everywhere, the headlines.

APOPHIS: ESCAPED MONSTER FROM PROMETHEUS INDUSTRIES BIOWEAPONS DIVISION

Jonas breathed hard. His lungs felt sore; the bronchial passages recently scraped of diseased tissue gave the sensation of being overly congested. In a few days, they would be again. Jonas smiled grimly behind his breathing mask.

It took real effort to return to the airship crash story. Jonas knew it must figure into the puzzle somehow. Besides, it had practically crashed in his backyard. The world rarely came to Cappadocia.

Jonas cracked his knuckles and began digging.

Cappadocia security systems used quantum encryption, but even the best systems were prey to human error. In this case, Jonas had the unwitting help of his mother. Two years ago, she had dated a security guard named Erkan, a likeable enough fellow who came by for dinner one evening still wearing his security badge on his jacket. While Bahara and Erkan sat watching old holos in the living room, Jonas quietly lifted the badge, scanned it, and used it to hack the camera grid in the local station. Cameras were quite helpful when they were poised above someone's desk...and keyboard...

Now Jonas tapped his list of pilfered passwords and began nosing around the security database until he struck pay dirt. The Cappadoccian government was taking a keen interest in the airship crash. They had authorized spybots to both comb the wreckage and perch nearby when IPC investigators and cleanup crew arrived. Everything the outsiders had said was recorded and delivered to Cappadoccian security. Jonas spent the next forty minutes listening to streams of audio.

From the cleanup crew's conversations, he gleaned that two Prometheus Industries investigators had been aboard the doomed ship: a Keiko Yamanaka and Jack Saylor. Mention was also made of a 'Wasteland girl', and an IPC investigator named Gethin Bryce...

The name almost stopped Jonas's heart.

Gethin Bryce? And Keiko Yamanaka?

From the age of five he had known all about Arcadia's former stars. Prodigies from Greece who had built an online empire! Jonas had studied Bryce's strategies in particular, feeling closer to this man than to any other male figure in his life. Fact was, Jonas sometimes fantasized he was playing under Bryce's tutelage, and that he might glance over and see his green-eyed hero nearby, nodding in satisfaction.

But of course, that was impossible. Bryce and Yamanaka's greatest moments had been long before Jonas was born. He knew the man had relocated to Mars. Any fantasies Jonas had of meeting him were preposterous.

Was it conceivable that Bryce was back on Earth? *And working for the IPC?*

Maximilian's alarm lights flashed. Jonas took slow, stabilizing breaths through his mask to steady his excited heart.

Bahara darted forward. "Jonas!"

"I'm all right, Mother."

"Maybe you should stay off the web right now? Jonas?"

"Give me one more hour," he pleaded, worried suddenly by the tone in her voice. Bahara could be heavy-handed. It wouldn't take much right now for her to shut down his rig by force and wheel him into the other room. One more alarm from Maximilian was all it would take. "I promise I'll stop in one hour."

"Five minutes, Jonas." The fear was coming out as anger. "You'll stop in five minutes. I'll make some lunch and we can sit together on the couch and watch a movie."

"Mother—"

"*You have to give me some time, Jonas!* We don't know how much—"

"You're right," he said. She stopped, glassy-eyed, her sob caught in her throat. "Give me my five minutes, and we will have lunch together."

Five minutes. He sighed, turned back to the computer.

Jonas promptly conducted a search for all news containing the name 'Gethin Bryce' for the last few years. The only thing that popped up was the Flight 3107 explosion. Bryce had been killed *while returning from Mars!* Perhaps *that's* when the IPC recruited him for this investigation. Now, the poor man was involved in *another* accident.

The cleanup crews, by their conversations, were clearly tasked with finding Bryce's body. But they'd been unable to. Bryce, Yamanaka, Saylor, and the unknown Wastelander were not among the dead. Therefore they must have survived the crash, but for some reason, hadn't waited around for first responders.

With mounting excitement, Jonas conjured a GPS map of the region. The airship crash was seventy miles outside the Apollonian Ring's borders. Deadly gloplands. Why on Earth would Bryce disappear into some of the most perilous forest of Europe? He surely must know what the region contained.

Jonas studied the Cappadoccian security footage. Stillness bodies.

How did it all fit together?

He steepled his fingers, thinking.

The Stillness terrorists must have hijacked the airship; their presence almost certainly accounted for the crash. Bryce and Yamanaka probably expected more enemies to show up, so they figured their best prospect was to melt into the woods. Either they didn't know how monstrous the local fauna was – and it wasn't Bryce's style to be uninformed – or they estimated it to be safer than sitting still for rescue.

Jonas pored over his map of the gloplands. Scattered towns studded the region, connected by a thin spiderweb of trade routes but otherwise remote and alone and autonomous, hiding from the brutal wilds as much as counting on it to dissuade hostile neighbors. Cappadocia monitored its Outland neighbors; Jonas, therefore, knew all about them. By his ninth birthday, he'd even hatched a silly plan of building a database on every local Wastetown which supported Stillness, with the intent of selling it to the Republic in exchange for the cure to his condition.

No one reputable had taken his offer.

Now his fingers flew nimbly, opening up a half dozen lines. Bryce's best bet was to make for Cappadocia. And he had to cross the deadliest terrain in Europe to do it.

Jonas decided it was time to drop an anonymous tip to Derinkuyu security.

"Five minutes is up, Jonas," Bahara said behind him. "Let's have lunch together now."

CHAPTER THIRTY-SEVEN
Consequences and Complications

Chief Enforcer Howd was a model of controlled fury.

He looked less like a boy-band leader now, and more like a no-nonsense military lieutenant, trim and ascetic. His attractive features hardened into a scowl, eyes blazing in their sockets, as he paced up and down the line of townspeople with his rifle slung at his back, arms straight at his sides. That rigid posture underscored intense rage. His jaw muscles visibly bunched between stinging, vitriolic bouts of condemnation.

It looked like the entire town was gathered at the square. The pack that had pursued Gethin and Keiko had been corralled into a line. Young and old men alike, looking sullen. One bearded fellow off to the side cradled broken fingers. Several gaunt teenagers in the back looked absolutely terrified. The corpse of the local boy was sprawled before them.

"You've put the entire town at risk!" Howd said again. He whirled on the bearded guy with broken fingers. "Twenty-five hundred people. Fathers and mothers! Families! Step out here *now* and admit what you did!"

Without hesitation, the bearded man shuffled forward. Celeste saw resignation in his eyes.

"I tried assaulting her," he said, motioning with his head to Celeste. "I wasn't going to shoot her. I just…I…"

"Wanted some fresh pussy?" Howd's voice was merciless. "Wanted to *rape* a visitor to Haventown? Explain to everyone what you desired so much, that you put everyone at risk. We are only *six years* away from charter incorporation! Tell *everyone* why you jeopardized that!"

The bearded man gave a hollow look to Celeste. Thirty minutes earlier, he had come at her from an alley as she was talking to the locals. King D. was the subject of discussion; an easy, accessible subject that broke the ice wherever she went. Celeste had headed out early in the morning, intent on gathering intel, intent on being careful since Haventown was part of a loose network of towns up for incorporation, and therefore Republic spies might be nosing around, seeking any excuse to delay or deny the charter.

Celeste realized now that the teenagers had started talking to her to distract her, to give their accomplice time to make his move. But when conversation turned to StrikeDown, the façade melted. She told them she had met King D.

personally. Their eyes widened. Their conspiracy dissolved. By the time their accomplice came for her, they had changed their minds about abducting her. They tried calling him off as he popped out of the fog like a lecherous jack-in-the-box, but it was too late, and Celeste put him down easily and stole the shotgun from his quiver.

And there he was now, singled out in front of the entire town. She caught his empty eyes.

"I wanted her," the bearded man said.

Howd looked disgusted. "You were willing to sacrifice us because she gave you a hard-on?"

"Yes."

Celeste read the lie in her attacker's voice. Likely, rape was only going to be a prelude to what they really had planned for her. Chopshop. Knock her out, strap her down, slit her throat, and start excavating her carcass for goodies. Sensorium, Familiars, whatever mods they could find. Her late Uncle Tony employed a fat butcher who went by the name of Nicky Christ. Could ransack a body of tech and still have time to scrub his hands for dinner in seven minutes flat.

Howd made another pace in front of the townspeople. Siyanda was there, but the Zulu barely paid mind to the teenage ruffians.

"Turn him out," Howd bellowed. "And alert the grid. If in twenty-four hours he's still local, he will be shot on sight."

The townsfolk were deathly still.

Howd pointed to the others. "The rest of you. Dig a grave for your companion. Then…" He hesitated fractionally. "You are mandated to roadwork for the next thirty days."

The road in question was the gravel path stretching west. Essentially, a crude welcome mat to arky society for the day when they would formally arrive to welcome Haventown into civilization.

"Dismissed!"

The gathering disintegrated in grim quietude. Howd marched to Celeste, Siyanda in tow.

"Do I get roadwork too?" she snapped. "Or a grave?"

"You get out of my town."

"Why? Because your dogs attacked us?"

"You did the right thing," Howd said. "But you have to leave anyway."

"Reason, please?" Gethin asked.

"You know *damn well* why," the kid growled.

Celeste folded her arms. "Enlighten me."

"That'd be a waste of breath. You were leaving today anyway, right? March to those gates —" he pointed, "— and don't ever set foot in my town again."

Jack still didn't get it; the outrage showed in his red complexion. "I don't understand what the hell we did to deserve—"

Standing nearby, Siyanda said to Howd, "Her accent is pure Hudson, chief. The same with her fellows."

"So?" bellowed Saylor.

Howd's hazel stare burned. "You came here from the Hudson to spread StrikeDown propaganda? With the sky about to crash down around us?"

Celeste spat. "*That* crap? I spouted off the only thing I thought would work to prevent a fucking lynch mob. They had marked us for arkies. I grabbed at the best defense I could muster."

"Sounds reasonable. But I don't believe you."

"Like I fucking ca—"

The enforcer's eyes turned to icy hate. "*Out* now. You'll get your weapons once you're through the gate." He marched away with the forcefulness of a drill sergeant.

The Zulu watched her, shaking his head sadly.

"What the fuck do *you* want?" she asked, ashamed by the judgment of his stare.

"The only enemy is chaos, sister. You been away from your comlink? World's going to chaos, again. It's the only real enemy in the universe. Chaos is all that StrikeDown will bring."

"I don't belong to StrikeDown."

"Of course."

"It was a clever deception."

"Not half as clever as you imagine, sister."

★　★　★

At the town gates, Celeste traded in the ticket for their weapons, half expecting to be denied. The Haventowners were good as their word, though; soon, they were out in the wilderness again with everything they had arrived with. Aside from birdcalls and rain dripping off branches, the forest was a portrait of solitude. It might have existed there for a hundred million years. She could easily imagine a long-necked sauropod lumbering forward, munching wet leaves, reptilian skin glistening from the dewy air.

The highway lay ahead, crisscrossed by weeds and tufts of grass.

Celeste felt a whirlwind of rage, undirected and amorphous, the StrikeDown mantra still thudding in her head like tribal drums. A steady burn of adrenaline had her energized, ready to fuck or fight. You got that when riding a combat high sometimes, and Celeste figured that the last few days constituted one drawn-out battle. She hadn't even dealt with Jeff's death yet.

Dangerous. With emotions riding high, it was easy to make a mistake.

"We need to run," she said, without turning to the arkies trailing her. "The longer we stay out here, the poorer our chances."

Keiko shoved Celeste from behind as they reached the road. "StrikeDown, is that right?"

The push nudged Celeste forward a step; she braced on her left leg, leaned, and fired a sidekick into Keiko's gut. The strike was fluid and perfect. Keiko doubled over, staggered back, drew up her multigun, and froze.

The double barrels of the Outlander's shotgun were aimed between her eyes.

"No DC," Celeste reminded her, and she winked. "Blurmod powered down. For the first time since we met, we're even. You want to scrap, Yamanaka? Just say the word."

Keiko held the Outlander's stare but said nothing.

"We could kill each other right now," Celeste continued, flushed and panting, "or return to a world that's about to incinerate. There's a battle in heaven right now, or haven't you heard? The pillars are gonna fall and I can't *fucking wait*."

Gethin raised an eyebrow. "You were speaking to the Haventowners? What do they know? What did they say?"

Whatever attraction Jack might have been developing for Celeste didn't sway his loyalties; he jerked his rifle towards Celeste. "Gun down. Now."

She did, somehow making her compliance seem tremendously defiant. Cards out, masks shorn away, Celeste only wanted to be back in her ship, en route to King D.'s Odessa fortress, where they could sip from an excavated case of Dom Perignon while the missiles launched and the Republic burned like a goddamned Viking funeral pyre.

Gethin's gaze was a bright green knife. He glared as Keiko's fingers tightened around the trigger. "Don't even think about it, Keiko."

Celeste gave a sharp hiss. It was pure Wastelander whisper, a ventriloquist trick that threw her voice without an ounce of tech behind it.

In the mist ahead of them, a row of mounted horsespiders emerged in efficient, ruthless unison.

Keiko and Jack instantly crouched and took aim at the interlopers. Then Keiko saw a bead of ruby light crawling on her hand. It drew itself up her forearm, kissed her eye, and stopped on her forehead.

"Guns down," Celeste snapped. "We're caught."

"By who?" Keiko demanded.

The horsespider line approached. They were massive animals, biogengineered from Clydesdale stock centuries ago as speedy six-legged warhorses. Their riders were small atop such muscular steeds; black-haired men and women with caramel-dark skin and copper-colored uniforms. No green-and-silver livery of Prometheus. No smoky blue-and-gold of the IPC. And no patchwork marauder rags.

"Throw your weapons down," a mustachioed rider told them. "You will not be harmed if you cooperate."

Keiko tossed aside her rifle. "I'm Internal Affairs Officer Yamanaka of—"

"Prometheus Industries, yes, we know. And Babylon Security Chief Jack Saylor, and IPC agent Gethin Bryce are with you. From the airship crash, yes?" The man touched his ear, reporting to his superiors. He didn't look at them again as he wheeled his mount around. "We are taking you into the custody of—"

Gethin nodded. "Cappadocia."

The security forces had brought spare mounts with them; the airship survivors were made to saddle up, safety restraints across their thighs and midsections. Horsespiders had been used as armored warhorses in the Century, but their greatest strength was speed. A healthy specimen could outpace a cheetah. The extra set of legs looked ungainly, protruding wide from their flanks. But the addition made a difference. When the security chief gave the word, the herd broke into a breakneck gallop.

An hour later, the clouds were sleeting, tinkling against their clothes like shards of glass, and continued until they reached the borders of mysterious Cappadocia.

CHAPTER THIRTY-EIGHT
The Folk

"Prometheus will send an extraction team for us," Keiko was saying between sips of hot Turkish coffee. "We'll be off your hands as soon as I can get a message to them."

Two dark security officers sat at the desk across from her in the spacious security office of Derinkuyu. Icy rain pelted the windows. Other than the mint-green glow of holopanels, the room was sunk in rich, comforting shadows.

Both officers, a man and woman, were mocha-skinned and of roughly the same build. The woman boasted a crescent-shaped scar down her face. It was almost too perfectly stylized; Gethin wondered if it was cosmetic, or some form of dermally advertised rank, given the way her peer deferred to her.

"Send a message?" the scarred woman said. "Yes, well, the premier's office will have to authorize that."

Keiko blinked. "I need the premier's permission to make a phone call?" She didn't sound angry; it could have been tact, or the comfort she was drawing from being out of Haventown. Gethin, Jack, and Celeste sat on a couch of black leather behind her, watching the exchange.

The scarred officer hesitated. "Ordinarily, no. During your time in the Wastes, a lot has happened. I have been authorized to grant the four of you sanctuary in Derinkuyu until it passes."

"Until what passes?" she asked.

The officer tapped her desk display; the green holo reversed so the new arrivals could read it where they sat. A series of time-stamped headlines, all less than an hour old, burned against the black. Keiko felt her stomach push into her throat.

THIRTY-TWO KILLED BY PROMETHEAN ATTACKER
Click for more

MONSTER ON THE MOON?
Click for more

PROMETHEUS UNHINGED
Click for more

IPC TROOPS SEIZE CONTROL OF PROMETHEUS
TERRITORIES IN EUROPE
Click for more

IPCS ALEXANDER, NOBUNAGA THREATEN PI
GRAYWORLD FACILITIES
Click for more

"Cappadocia maintains steadfast neutrality in matters of this kind," the woman explained. "What hasn't hit the news yet is this: the IPC has commandeered the airship crash site. A Promethean Enforcer arrived a short time later and attempted to land, I presume to conduct their own inquiry, or extract their missing employees, or both. Whatever the case, their presence wasn't welcomed. There was a firefight."

"*What?*" Jack cried, leaping to his feet.

The woman fingered her scar, looking apprehensive. "The IPC vessels shot first. Strafed the Enforcer, took out a wing rotor. The vessel fired back. People were killed on both sides."

Keiko felt the muscles in her body turning to lead. "And?"

"The Enforcer tried to withdraw, but was shot down. We don't believe there were any survivors."

Silence thickened in the room like a cancerous weed. The officer killed the holopanel. "I can grant you temporary sanctuary until your request is processed. But you see now why communications must be handled carefully."

And so ends the *Pax Apollonia*, Gethin thought uneasily.

They took a tram down into the underground city.

★　　★　　★

Gethin knew the mountaintop metropolis was just for show; the real Cappadocia bustled in the ancient clay caves below. He had often hoped the IPC would send him to investigate it, just for the otherworldly joy of exploring its forbidden passages. The community of the so-called 'Folk' dwelt in a hive of carved mazes of volcanic ejecta. Wooden doors punctuated the tortuous, forlorn length of halls. Algae-lanterns glowed like constellations in the murk.

It was a place that conjured both the oldest and most modern modalities of human habitation. Was true change even possible? Gethin wondered, feeling a bout of weighty fatalism. How much of history is part of an ever-revolving wheel, turning and creaking? *Here we are again in the caves. And once again there are hostile tribes and gods and monsters…dragons prowling the wilderness and archangels splitting the heavens asunder.*

"No satellite can penetrate these caves," Keiko said, drawing up beside him. "And see the picosurvs everywhere?" She indicated the dark green boxes set between the wall and ceiling of each archway they passed through.

"Yes."

"These people survived the Warlord Century here."

He nodded, pretending to scratch his neck while he wondered whether or not to fire up his sensorium. In the Outlands, the energy signature would have been detected instantly. Here he should be safe...as long as he stayed off the web, kept his uplinks dark, and maintained a low profile. There were certain advantages in letting the IPC think he was dead.

He pressed the dermal button.

<There are fifty-one levels to this structure,> Ego advised at once, unfurling in his head. <They sprawl for three miles and connect to other underground districts. Indeterminate data available. Census lists a population of 25,121.>

Gethin glanced sidelong at Celeste. She appeared strangely comforted by the corridors and doorways; people watched them without lechery or menace as they passed. One silver-haired lady was sweeping her porch step, spotted them, and stared without expression.

Impressive security, Gethin. Id's voice was almost conversational. *Picosystems appear to be a match for all known intrusion techniques.*

Gethin breathed the menthol-like quality of the air. "We may need it," he muttered, thinking of the thus-far-unreported firefight between the universe's two grand powers. Holy fuck. What had been the sequence of events? The IPC would have claimed jurisdictional rights. Prometheus should have known that, but Gethin could hardly blame them for wanting to pull their own people out of the area and, even likelier, wanting to see up close what the devil was going on. It wouldn't be just curiosity, either; they would have justified the invasion of temporary IPC airspace under probable cause, considering the Stillness bodies visibly strewn about the wreckage.

Or had the imposter of Colonel Tanner given the order to fire? More kindling for the blaze?

As if reading his thoughts, Keiko said, "Gethin? We have to decide what to do now."

"What do you mean?"

"War has begun."

He shook his head. "One incident."

"You don't believe that. The IPC is bringing their battleships into orbit. How do you think *my* superiors will respond?"

They were coming to the end of the corridor, where a commercial zone materialized in hazy dens of indigo lights. A café was first on the left and locals sat, craning their necks to view overhead viewscreens of ticker-tape headlines and live footage.

Gethin stepped into the café and said, "Your superiors will bring out their own fleet. But you'll lose in the end, Keiko. You have to believe me."

"You don't know our abilities."

"I know causalities. You'll make a good show and kill a lot of people, but the IPC will eventually destroy you. I'm not rooting for teams here. I'm telling you it won't work."

"Jack and I need to know where *you* stand in this."

"Depends."

The old glare burned in her eyes. "On *what?*"

"Neither one of you has told me what you discovered about Kenneth Cavor."

Her righteous wrath died instantly. She averted her eyes and exchanged an anxious glance with Jack.

Gethin grunted in satisfaction. "If he was innocent you would have brandished that fact by now. He *isn't* innocent. Your people were supposed to look into it. What did you find?"

Keiko stiffened, breathed deep, and said, "Cavor was a Stillness agent."

Jack's eyes bulged. "You...why the *hell* didn't you tell me?"

"Fincher ordered me to silence, even from you," she professed. "Besides, it only came to light a couple days ago. Fincher called me in Athens to say they had dug through Cavor's personal records and discovered he had been falsifying his whereabouts on numerous occasions. Fincher then let a hard query team go at him. They conducted a full scan, synapse by synapse. Turns out that Cavor is a terrorist sympathizer. More than that, he's an active agent. He was reporting every stage of Base 59's research into exotic matter to a Stillness High Priest named Father Apophis."

Celeste rounded on her. "Apophis is the name of the creature on the moon right now!"

Keiko swallowed. "I don't know what that thing is, I swear it." She looked stricken. "Gethin, you said yourself we're dealing with a new order of intelligence here. They want war between us!"

Jack paced through the café, looking exasperated. "You could have told me, Keiko."

"I was ordered not to tell anyone!" she pleaded. "Jack! I had no choice."

"It doesn't matter," Gethin said. "Our enemies have wormed their way into *both* the IPC and PI, playing on our fears and biases."

The conversation was attracting the attention of the café crowd. Discreetly, the group slipped out of earshot. The market was relatively deserted at this late hour. Fiberoptic cables were secured against the walls and ceiling like biomechanical ivy. Above, a trellis hung, on which pale plants glowed to provide dim, shadowless light. A newsbox stood at the corner of an intersection, displaying a new breaking report: two IPC satellites had been shot down by Promethean land-based lasers.

They were passing the newsbox when a small voice snaked out from its speakers.

"Mr. Bryce? Miss Yamanaka?"

They both whirled around, staring in surprise at the newsbox.

The voice piped up once more: "Gethin Bryce and Keiko Yamanaka?"

Gethin noticed that the holo was suddenly displaying their faces. "Who is this?" he demanded.

"I think I can prevent the war," the voice said softly. It was harmonically distorted, although Gethin thought it sounded very young and weak. "Would you both please come to room G7128? I have much to tell you."

CHAPTER THIRTY-NINE
The Exile

<This room is registered to one Bahara Polat, 41 years old and employed by the Derinkuyu Education Board as a Learning and Development administrator. She has one son, Jonas Polat, 11 years old.>

Jack and Celeste elected to stay behind in the marketplace, for their own reasons and for the fact that neither had been included in the mysterious invite. Room G7128 was on the seventh floor, residential district, accessible by lift and Ego's helpful map overlay.

Gethin knocked, and the wooden residential door swung wide. A pleasant-faced woman stood revealed, wearing an apron, her hands splattered with flour.

Gethin felt his prepared introduction dry up. "Um. My name is Gethin Bryce. I received a message—"

"Oh yes!" the woman said. "Jonas gets so few friends who arrive in person. My name is Bahara." She stared with brief concern at them, noting their battered apparel and wounds, clearly wondering what kind of ruffians her son had granted an audience to. "This really…is a treat. Please come in."

Bahara drew aside. In the doorway of the next room, a wheelchair rolled into view. It held a small boy. A black breathing mask was strapped over his face. The boy was emaciated and pale, no muscles of any worth were visible through his T-shirt. He wore a silken eye patch.

The boy seemed to smile. The breathing patch made it impossible to tell, though his blue eyes crinkled merrily. "Gethin Bryce and Keiko Yamanaka in my mother's house!"

Gethin approached the boy. "You have me at a disadvantage."

"Impossible."

They beheld each other in silence. Gethin stared past the boy into an adjacent bedroom with VR rigs and computer support equipment.

Gethin no longer participated in the addictions of Arcadia, having weaned himself off following the end of his marriage to Keiko. During his tenure as a university professor, he had occasionally indulged in online raids, battles, and explorations with what remained of his gamer clan, using new avatars that didn't link with his famous days. Mostly, though, he stayed out of the events himself.

Nonetheless, he kept current on the new stars of Arcadia. Therefore, the

Turkish boy in front of him looked mighty familiar: the breathing mask, the retro design to his wheelchair.

Gethin said, "The Exile?"

Jonas gave a short, delighted chuckle. It sounded like a crackle of static through his breathing apparatus.

Keiko came to Gethin's side. "Who?"

"You mean to tell me you've never picked up an Arcadium newsletter in the last couple years?"

She was going to retort that she had been too busy in the real world, making real achievements and progress to the future. One look at Jonas stayed her tongue.

"I'm sorry," she said. "I...haven't really followed the games since our glory days."

The boy brightened. "No apologies necessary." His voice was squeaky, like a chinchilla given the power of speech. "Mother? Today we are hosting two of Arcadia's brightest stars. Gethin Bryce and Keiko Yamanaka."

The last threads of concern faded from Bahara's face. She shook their hands, apologizing for not having recognized them (neither Gethin nor Keiko mentioned that avatars were used instead of real photos, so recognition was impossible) and then insisted they stay for dinner.

"May I get you something to drink?" she offered. "We have excellent sodas here."

"No, thank you."

"I'll leave you to talk, then." She departed, and something about the movement inspired sorrow and hope in Gethin's heart.

He stepped fully into the boy's bedroom. To his bewilderment, the walls were papered by hard-copy photos – not of fictional online worlds – but of the far shores. He recognized the plateaus of Osiris, the tidally locked world of Epona, the richly forested vistas of Midsummer Dreams, and the stormy skies of Tempest. Worlds that were many light-years away.

"Ah," Gethin said, peering close to one frame of gray forest that appeared to have coalesced from enormous cobwebs. "Osiris, right? Latest images?"

Jonas swiveled in his wheelchair to track Gethin. "A magnification of the forests, yes, hugging the Jormungand shoreline. A single ocean wraps around the planet like a blue belt. An exotic ecosystem. The probe has detected large shapes moving beneath the sea."

"Probably not the best choice for colonization," Keiko said.

"Must we colonize everywhere we go?" the boy inquired.

Gethin turned away from the photos. "You wanted to see us. You said you can stop the war. How?"

Jonas swallowed. "May I ask you to sit? The story is long..." His breathing mask shifted awkwardly around his sudden smile. "But I think you will enjoy it!"

★   ★   ★

"Someone wanted us to think the AIs were responsible for the Lunar incident," Gethin explained. "Probably because of the airship crash and all the inconvenient press it's getting, they seem to have abandoned that lie, and are now openly pushing for war between our respective powers."

Bahara had brought them a plate of *sigara borek*, hot and crispy from the oven, with dipping sauces and lentil soup, and now she sat on the corner of Jonas's bed to listen. The visitors were hungry; their rapid march from Haventown had been made on an empty stomach.

"I agree," Jonas replied. He so desperately wanted to detach his breathing mask, but since his last collapse the doctors said that could be fatal. Even his food was being fed intravenously.

"What do you know?" Keiko prompted.

Jonas made no movement or reaction. He looked like an alien Buddha, Keiko thought uncomfortably. There was something dreadfully fascinating in the look of that gaunt face merging into black plastic, the tube hanging down and curling into the guts of Maximilian.

Suddenly Jonas extended a skeletal arm to his virtuboard, activating his VR rig's projector function. A viewscreen splashed onto the bedroom wall.

"I possess a formidable network of contacts in Arcadia," the boy explained. "And I have known for some time that corporations make use of its Caves. This is not wise of them. Fearing nothing in the real world, they naturally deem themselves infallible in virtual. I have associates who look for the ripples they make. I know who was responsible for the attack on the Promethean offshore rig."

Keiko straightened at this.

"It was rehearsed in Arcadia before the actual event. In a game called *Tengu Castle*. Most people do not realize this, but *Tengu Castle* is entirely run by Hanmura Enterprises. They are the ones who attacked your ocean base."

Something happened in Keiko's eyes. Like plates of black glass sliding across each other, a cold flame glinting and reflecting in each facet.

"And yet they are a minor player," Jonas continued. "A vulture pecking from the sidelines. Hanmura Enterprises is not your true concern."

"I'm listening," she said.

Gethin said, "Our true concern is a creature called Apophis, and the Stillness troops it commands."

The boy cleared his throat, a wet, slimy sound. "An associate of mine recorded a most peculiar conversation in a remote landscape of Arcadia. Three beings discussing something secretly." Jonas weakly touched Gethin's arm and his eyes crinkled. "I believe you will find this recording most—"

Bahara leapt to her feet. "Jonas! Wait!"

Her little boy gave a startled jump.

"You need to think this through," she pleaded, and she whirled on Gethin and Keiko. "What will you give us for this information? My boy found something that can benefit you? Why should you get it for free?"

Gethin pushed aside the plate of food and folded his arms. "What's wrong with your son?"

Bahara trembled as she spoke in a hurried rush, as if to delay would miss this single, shining opportunity. "A weaponized nano-replicating cystic fibrosis. He contracted it while just a *baby*, do you understand?"

"Why does he still have it?"

"You're an arky," she said flatly. "We are not as fortunate as you. There is no cure."

"There is."

She compressed her lips into a hard line.

Gethin spoke decisively. "I'll have the two of you transported to an Athenian hospital."

"I have petitioned Athens and *every* enclave for years!" she said angrily. "What power do you have, that my letters lacked?"

"You're not civilized," he said plainly. "Keiko and I are. We can do it."

"Then you had best do it *soon*," Bahara said bitterly. "Because he won't survive his next collapse." Her eyes went to her son, to his fogged breathing mask, to how frail he looked in his robotic wheelchair. "The doctors told me straight. His life is over in weeks. Maybe less."

"Your boy is remarkable by any standards. We will have him brought to Athens and treated there, you have my word." He touched Jonas's pale hand. "Show me what you found in Arcadia, Jonas."

Bahara began to protest. She caught herself, and at long last sank back onto the edge of the bed, rubbing her hands as if kneading dough.

The bedroom wall sprang to life with projected images and audio.

"What does the piece do?"

"It can alter matter's charge. Perhaps allow construction of a Midas Hand."

"They can do that?"

"It was only a matter of time."

"Then they can also—"

"The question now is how do we mobilize? How many of them are even left?"

"Four, maybe five. Perhaps less than that."

"But why would they expose themselves like this? Destroying that base and shuttle in such a public way? Surely they know we'll come for them!"

"There are two possibilities. One: they are setting a trap for us. Two: They are so close to completing their plans, which we can assume involves this negative matter device, that exposure is meaningless now."

"Forget theories! Track them down and end them! For good this time!"

"They hardly expect you to be cautious, Sy'hoss'a. Perhaps that's their intention. Get you to come out of hiding. Get you to do something stupid. Doesn't take much."

When the recording ended, Gethin slowly drew back.

"Thank you, Jonas," he whispered.

"It is intriguing, yes?" Jonas said, watching his guests.

It answers everything, Gethin thought. *Now, what can we do about it?*

CHAPTER FORTY
Blackmarket

Celeste prowled the drafty underdark.

The corridors were porous and sepulchral, like Wasteland tunnels she had encountered but with a clean, after-the-rainstorm aroma which made her feel young and savage. She pictured herself as a primitive hunter, bow at her back with a deerskin quiver, stalking prey along a night-shrouded trail.

Derinkuyu was remarkably advanced for a colony of burrowers. There was an aug shop not far away, and she went there, aware that Jack Saylor was tailing her. She didn't know what Keiko and Gethin were up to, but it had to be serious if stakeout duty was being assigned to a seven-foot-tall Samson.

She lost him a minute later, ducking through the warrens of the main plaza, hiding behind a clothing rack until he went hurrying past, and backtracking to a web café she had noticed earlier. It was modeled on the Paleolithic caves of Lascoux. The walls were porous stone, splashed with ochre handprints and charcoal reindeer, bison, and stick-figure hunters. The tables were slabs of stone. The chairs resembled tree stumps. Veins of bioluminescent algae burned in the walls.

The shopkeeper was a copper-skinned Turk, burly and cherubic. "Hello!" he roared. "Please tell me I can assist you!"

"I need to use a terminal."

"You have your choice." He indicated the lack of people with a sweep of his hand. "Business is slow tonight."

"I also need a blurmod."

His face petrified in an expression of bemused interest. "May I see your Republic ID?"

"It was eaten by dire dogs," she said with a smile. "But they spared my wallet."

The shopkeeper chuckled. "I'm afraid a blurmod is military-grade tech. We commoners aren't allowed to peddle such things."

Celeste glanced around the café. "You might consider turning the lights up."

"It's night. Doesn't the sun still go down topside?"

"So you dim the lights to pretend?"

"Gotta respect the circadian rhythms. Listen, I'm sorry about the blurmods, but there are plenty of other things here that might interest you."

Celeste peered over his shoulder and inspected an entire wall of devices for sale in shiny plastic covers. There were wetware armbands, sensorium upgrades, eyepads, mnesis cubes, sleep-deps.

So much glitz and glimmer. Like a shopping mall for the gods.

These were the things King D. wanted, so he could hand them out like Santa Claus on Solstice to the world's unfortunates. The strict distinctions of capitalism and socialism were absurd, he often said, when civilization had attained post-scarcity divine power.

A scarce post-scarcity, she thought. *Let them eat mortality!*

The shopkeeper laughed suddenly. Celeste looked at him, having forgotten he existed.

"You spaced out on me, my dear," he said. "May I get you some coffee? Or maybe a soda. We have wonderful flavors here."

She ordered a coffee just to give the guy something to do. Then she took a table and clicked onto the web, found a StrikeDown ghost site, logged in and went to the forum. There, she posted a message for StrikeDown's people to decipher: *Star Lady here. In Cappadocia. Squad all dead, killed by greentribe. Believe they are behind Lunar attacker. Will attempt to reach Alpha rendezvous point ASAP.*

The shopkeeper brought her the coffee. "Where are you from?"

"Odessa," she said. "I like your decorating tastes."

"The Planning and Zoning board encourages every café to use culturally themed designs," he eagerly explained. "They encourage the celebration of Derinkuyu's colorful history. Many different peoples have called these caves home, all the way back to early man. The shops and stores around you celebrate this historical diversity. I do like mine."

"Did you choose it yourself?"

"I bid on it. Planning and Zoning gave us a pool of designs to select from."

"Planning and Zoning sound like a bunch of fascists."

He threw his head back and laughed. "We are very proud of history here. I was only too happy to celebrate a chapter."

Celeste nodded absently and stirred her coffee. It smelled obscenely strong.

"So is there anything else you'd like?" he inquired with a curious tilt of his head. "Perhaps a hot egg bagel?"

"No, thank you."

"An artichoke-and-chicken sandwich?"

Celeste shook her head.

The man smiled warmly, his eyes twinkling. "How about a blurmod?"

★　★　★

Jack adored Derinkuyu.

The Stygian city fed into his greatest fantasy of being on another world – the dark blasted-out tunnel work of colonists. It was the company line to *say* you wanted to go to the stars. He knew Prometheus was destined to take over the galaxy someday, and there would be thousands of worlds as destination points for the seedship diaspora which was sure to follow. Prometheus thirsted for frontierist souls.

And Jack really wanted it. He knew it would be a while, even without the colonization ban. He was still young, and his short résumé had plenty of competition from otherPtometheans who could boast interplanetary postings from all over the solar system. An entire generation of PI veterans, centuries old, had purposefully served on every outpost, planet, moon, spaceship and space station just to sculpt a perfect résumé for the day that the far shores were made available. Even Keiko's experience paled next to theirs; Jack was probably dead last in the roll call.

Derinkuyu made it easy to pretend he was already in that distant future. He didn't even care that Celeste had lost him. Let her have her freedom. He fancied he was patrolling a colony, and the few Derinkuyans he saw at this late hour unwittingly aided the fantasy. From what he could see, they were an industrious lot, what he imagined frontier folk would be. Optimistic, social, helpful, friendly, cognizant of how much everyone depended on one another, bound together like an offworld colony would be against the collective threat of nature. For wasn't that the ultimate enemy anyway? Nature was constantly the archnemesis throughout humanity's short career.

Jack nodded pleasantly to people as he entered the main shopping plaza. It looked like a peculiar fusion between an eleventh-century Islamic city and classical Parisian streets, with the arabesque doorways of the former and the patio cafés of the latter. The architecture was also painted in biolume so that it glowed like black-lit neon.

On holopanels high above, images from Luna were playing. Apophis killing and screaming, destroying everything around him while professing his innocence. The PI logo on his uniform.

Jack's good mood faltered.

What the hell is he?

The holopanel froze on the entity's twisted face. Panelists began discussing the IPC shutdown of Promethean properties. Jack contemplated that crimson visage.

Maybe nature wasn't the only enemy, he mused.

From the holopanel, the monster seemed to be staring straight into his soul.

★　　★　　★

In the café backroom, Celeste sat perfectly still while the man took her measurements with a handheld scanner. He was impeccably professional, like a carpenter wielding a stud finder, even when he pressed it between her breasts to determine the depth of her sternum. His eyes remained fixed to the tiny screen on which her data composite was being configured. Then he wheeled over a medcart, complete with an array of tubes, drives, and industrial syringes. Celeste felt her skin crawl.

The Turk, whose name was Onat, chuckled. "You're thinking I raided a mechanic's dumpster, glued everything together, and didn't bother washing the needles?"

"Remarkable deduction."

Onat pointed to the gunmetal storage cylinder. "Nano seed-clusters." He pointed to the nearby drive. "Programs and etchers. I'll give you the full spread, and throw in a blood rerouter." He touched the syringe and grinned. "Needle. It hurts."

Celeste considered, reconsidered, and re-reconsidered. Finally, she skinned out of her shirt and said, "My body has some defenses. If any of those seeds tries for my sensorium, I'll know it instantly. Then I'll be fighting mad, *señor.*"

He shrugged. "*I* offered you a blurmod."

"And I changed my mind, now that I've seen the extent of your operation's secret menu. Something better than a blurmod. More practical for…um …me."

Onat lifted the syringe in one hand, scanner in the other, and set about finding the best entry points."When I am done, you'll be nearly as nifty as your arky pals."

Celeste looked at him. "My scars do give me away, don't they?"

"I could remove them for a bit extra."

"Why? I worked hard to earn them."

"They become you. Now exhale completely."

Celeste obliged. The syringe made a snapping sound like a crossbow and she felt the first seed-cluster driven hard into her body. Onat circled her, an artist contemplating the next step in his project.

"So what's the deal with you people, anyway?" she asked after the third cluster. "Why not join the Republic? You could pass the Outland Charter in your sleep, from what I can see."

"Selling autonomy is too high a price. Exhale please."

She obeyed. A cluster snapped into her stomach wall and she gritted her teeth from the pain, managing to say, "You just have to submit to global hegemony."

He flashed a smile. "We don't like the word 'submit'. We are very proud."

"Pride goeth."

"Ah!" He had been pleasant and friendly, but now his eyes lit up in real interest, as if he had been performing an automated task until this moment. "Pride goeth before a Fall. But *we* never did fall. We shut ourselves up here, lying low, munching in the shadows. And when arcologies grew from the ash, we were still here. These caves are more than my home…they are my heritage."

Celeste hopped off the chair and paced around the room, rolling her shoulders and testing the sore patches in her body. "My paycard really afforded me all this?"

"No," he said with a cautious smile. "Your credit line was tagged for Babylon and Athens only."

Celeste froze. The thought possessed her that this blackmarket peddler had injected a suicide seed into her, to blackmail her into returning with regularity to make future payments. Her heart galloped for a fight.

"I depleted your paycard," he said quickly, holding up his hands. "Channeled it through a dummy shop registered to Athens. But you don't owe me the remainder of the cost. I simply ask that you give me good word-of-mouth when you return to the Wastes. I can arrange for outside customers to come here."

She halted. "You have a business card I can hand out?"

"You, my dear, are the business card."

CHAPTER FORTY-ONE
The Price for Arcadium

In the Bolat residence, Jonas detached his breathing mask. His mouth had the wrinkled texture of shriveled fingertips. He sipped water, watching his guests in quiet, studious fascination.

"Would you rule the universe if you could, Mr. Bryce?" he asked suddenly. "The Faustians believe you were born to help them do just that. Arcadia was a training ground for a mind like yours, they say. The future must be unification."

Gethin tiredly rubbed the gash on his forehead. "The age of the Warlords is past, Jonas."

"Is it?"

"I'm just an investigator with the IPC now. I have no dreams of conquest."

The boy looked at Keiko. "And you? Do you share this sentiment?"

Keiko gave a curt nod. "I was planning on running for governor of a far shore, should the ban ever be lifted. That's an administrative post, not exactly known for despotic powers."

Jonas fumbled to reattach his breathing mask. Keiko helped affix it. His shoulders were damp.

"I received a message from an associate of yours, Gethin. A man named Dion Bellamy. He received the sample of the golems you sent him, and made some discoveries about them. He wishes to meet you in Arcadia to share the results."

Keiko looked at her ex-husband. "You sent the samples I obtained to *Dion?*"

He raised an eyebrow. "I wasn't in the mood to trust the IPC." He went to the VR rig to log into the web.

The boy stayed him with a small hand. "I am unable to login to Arcadia from here. My body is too frail for a wetport or sensorium, but there are uplinks at the net café."

"I don't need to wetlink merely to speak with Dion…"

Jonas shifted uncomfortably in his wheelchair. "Perhaps not, but I am regrettably forced to insist that you do. Forgive me. The information I provided you comes at a price, as does interface with your friend from Caricom. You see, I need your assistance with something." Jonas smiled weakly, as if embarrassed by the request he was going to make. It was the expression of someone squirming to get an autograph and nervous to ask.

★   ★   ★

Jonas's computer room was not sufficient for what needed to be done. Gethin was amazed, actually, that the boy had achieved so much with so little. Arcadia was meant to be experienced through a sensorium. You *tasted* the ozone of laser fire, you *felt* the crackle of sonic grenades or the rumble of your Ashoka asteroid tank as its treads crushed enemy resistance. And while you never experienced actual pain, an injury in virtual meant a decidedly unpleasant vibration.

The eleven-year-old Turkish boy was too sickly to have an implanted sensorium. When he played Arcadium hubs, it was on flatscreen monitors. The depth of experience was lost on him...and yet, he had excelled.

Gethin and Keiko went to the district's net café on the same residential level as the Polat household. It was nearly deserted at the late hour. Two young girls were jacked into an overseas concert in one dim corner, while Keiko and Gethin quietly seated themselves at the wetports of another.

Gethin felt his heart pound at the *thump!* of the hub loading. The crimson pinwheel of Arcadia flowered into his optics. He was suddenly standing at the arrival port: a massive steel ring suspended in blackness. Galaxies swirled above, behind, and below like gold hurricanes rotating spiral arms. Each galaxy represented Arcadium hubs. Gethin narrowed his eyes at the pinkish-purple shape of the *Faustus* hub far below...an unpleasant island to be avoided during this brief voyage.

On the reflective steel of the ring, he regarded his appearance. He was his old avatar again: black hair, silver eyes, skin the color of quartz. He was dressed in a form-fitting black tunic which worried Gethin in its resemblance to the Wyndham Save Center's post-resurrection complimentary robes. He hadn't accessed his avatar in many years. Must have been the last outfit he was wearing when he retired.

The steel ring looked empty. Of course, there must be hundreds or thousands of other players here, unviewable to each other. You were only allowed to see members of your team at the loading hub. A smart arrangement really, since it was neutral territory and anonymity kept it that way.

Keiko appeared beside him in a flash. She was also wearing her old avatar, which looked exactly like her, aside from the silver retro-futuristic bodysuit cladding her body like shrink-wrap. In her heyday, it had been in vogue. Now it served to make her look like a charmingly outdated pop star sexpot.

Jonas was last to arrive. Stars! Gethin thought, awed by the little boy's virtual appearance up close. The Exile was a preternaturally tall, spindly, shiny black exoskeleton.

"Are you both prepared?" the Exile asked. "I fear there is little time for a refresher course." His voice was deeper here, authoritative and serene. Who would ever imagine it belonged to a prepubescent invalid?

Keiko gave a soft laugh. "When we arrive, just point out who you want us to kill. I'm ready."

The insectile form strode to a glowing circle in the floor of the ring. "There is a gathering of Judgment Fiends in a fleshfactory on Dilok, Zone 6882. I've set coordinates. Your friend Dion shall meet us there."

Gethin tingled, the old excitement like bubbles in his stomach. "Let's go."

They stepped onto the circle and instantly materialized in a world of organic walls, muscular piping, and skeletal rib-vaults. It was like being in a gigantic heart. Valves branched off in every direction. The air was oven-hot and fans twirled uselessly in the high flesh-colored ceiling. It smelled like an old meat locker.

Keiko wrinkled her nose unhappily. "Now I remember why I *stopped* playing."

Jonas nodded towards the balconies – cartilage overhangs whose points of attachment appeared infected and swollen.

In the past, Gethin would have studied everything about Dilok and its strange fetish for wetwork constructions. He would have spoken to all locals, collecting data to feed into his tactical analyses. Only then would he craft a strategy.

He had neither time nor desire for that now. He, like Keiko, was realizing why he no longer came here. Arcadia was illusion. What the Martians would call noisy flash. There was enough drama occurring in the real universe to make this unnecessary.

"You can tell the Judgment Fiends by their uniforms," Jonas said, indicating the many balconies. "Notice the women and men clad in those spiked maroon armors? Foolish if you ask me. *Your* group never wore matching uniforms and yet you acted with uniformity. People could never pick your squad out in a crowd. That made all of you dangerous."

As Gethin was peering at the cartildge balconies, a pair of Judgment Fiends pulled out cheesy-looking laser pistols and shot someone they had been conversing with. The body blew apart messily. The corpse's companions backed away, hands up in submission. All heads turned to the action. One of the Fiends was squaring off to the retreating players, daring them to fight. In this fictional city of Dilok, the Fiends were open and unafraid, like 'made men' of ancient mafia families.

Gethin grinned. "The more things change, eh? I count sixteen Fiends in this room."

Keiko glared. "Always hated people like that."

"Yeah. But not people like *that*." Gethin pointed.

A smiling black man in forest-green fatigues was approaching them. Forty years ago, he had worn yellow armor with a winged helmet, but he apparently was more up-to-date on Arcadium fashions than his old teammates.

"Dion!" Gethin smiled.

Dion Bellamy wore his real-world face. A resident of Caicom, he must have been patching in from the Bahamas, at his wetport in Nassau.

"Bryce and Yamanaka?" Dion threw back his head and guffawed. His laughter was so rich and contagious that they were all chuckling in an instant. "Holy stars!"

Gethin noticed three more Judgment Fiends coming into the fleshfactory, walking with a purpose. Something was going on. The place was going to clear out soon.

"You got my delivery?" Gethin asked Dion in the few moments they had.

"Did indeed." Dion's grin dropped. "Had several of my sources run that golem sample against everything we had."

Keiko sighed. "But you found nothing."

Dion raised an eyebrow. "*Au contraire*. Found everything."

"Who made the golems?"

"Xibalba."

"So?" Keiko scoffed. "Dion, that doesn't tell me—"

"Vector Nanonics placed the order."

She stopped. Conversations wafted in the humid air. The fans spun noisily in their swollen slots.

Even Gethin raised an eyebrow. "You know this, or you're guessing?"

Dion hugged himself. "Me, guess? I took your sample to *my* people. Golems were off the rack, nothing special. But I thought, 'I can't be disappointing my friend Gethin!' So we did some datamining, found that the nanorod imprinting matched profiles in Xibalban subcontractor labs loaned out to Vector Nanonics."

Keiko narrowed her eyes. "First Hanmura Enterprises. And now Vector?"

Jonas's Exile avatar was suddenly in their midst. "Seems that your corporate rivals have agreed to a disconcerting marriage."

"And there's at least one more in the mix," Keiko added. "TowerTech. They've been orchestrating a media circus to time with our misfortunes."

"You'll never prove that one," Gethin muttered.

Keiko's eyes shimmered. "Don't need to convince a jury."

Dion was giving the Exile an appreciative, up-and-down appraisal. "Nice skin! So, we going to war with these local punks or what?"

The Exile turned expectantly to Gethin. "What do you suggest?"

"Spread out," Gethin advised. "Four against nineteen, not the best odds. And there might be more outside."

"I have the outside covered," Jonas retorted. "A friend of mine, who can turn into a manticore."

Dion laughed anew. "Miss these days!"

They diffused into the crowd. The Exile was attracting attention; people knew who he was and were wondering why he was here.

Jonas addressed his admirers. "I am about to go to war. It will become legend, talked about for years to come. Are there any volunteers to assist me?"

Several of the Judgment Fiends were noticing the sudden hoopla.

"Mr. Bryce?" Jonas said in his audio.

"Yes, Jonas?"

"Thank you for this, my friend."

The Exile withdrew fanciful pistols from his holsters, turned towards the Judgment Fiends on the balconies, and opened fire.

★　　★　　★

Gethin disconnected from the wetport, sweaty and gasping. He glanced to Keiko. Her eyes were closed, perspiration dotting her forehead, and her pulse visible in her neck. When she opened her eyes, she looked at him for a long time before she spoke.

"*That's* why we played," she managed. "And that's why we can never go back to that world."

"Agreed on both counts."

The two girls were gone and the café was empty. The clock showed that four hours had passed. The battle of the fleshfactory seemed to still be exploding around them. Gethin's fingers twitched with the pulling of virtual triggers, his eyes playing the afterimages of the fleshfactory lighting up in the wondrous violence of battle. His face was fever-flushed. The Judgment Fiends had been cut down, and were being cut down, by Jonas's webwide call to arms.

Gethin touched his ear. "Jonas? You okay?"

There was silence on the other end of the comlink.

"Jonas?"

The audio crackled. "I don't know how to thank you," the boy replied in his high-pitched, natural voice again.

"I do," Keiko said gently. "You had a lead on that Pacific offshore assault. Follow it and keep me posted until we send an extraction unit to bring you to Athens."

"Done." A pause. "Derinkuyu security is about to summon the both of you. It appears that your request for an evac has been granted, and Prometheus has agreed to send a transport." He sighed unhappily. "It's too bad, actually."

"Why?"

"I was hoping you both could stay for dinner. My mother makes the best *okonomiyaki*."

CHAPTER FORTY-TWO
The Headlines

PROMETHEAN, IPC FORCES CLASH IN
MEMPHIS, AKIHABARA
Click for more

DID PI MURDER SALVOR BEAR?
Click for more

TWO IPC SATELLITES SHOT DOWN BY PROMETHEUS
INDUSTRIES, CLAIMS SELF-DEFENSE
Click for more

IPCS SHAKA, BATU, AUGUSTUS DEPLOYED TO
EARTH ORBIT
Click for more

CHAPTER FORTY-THREE

Rescue

At 5:09 a.m. they reunited in the Derinkuyu security office, were offered coffee, and then escorted to the topside tram. The storm had not abated, and the sound of rain on the tramcar was mesmerizingly rhythmic. At the station they were met by the scarred woman coming off her shift, and she agreed to drive them to the western gates not far from where they had entered.

"In and out," she told them. "Your transport has been granted access to Cappadoccian airspace just long enough for your evac. Can't guarantee that the instant you *leave* our space, the IPC won't shoot you down, however."

"Expect another transport, from the IPC, to evac one of your citizens," Gethin said, riding in the front passenger seat of her jeep. It was a six-wheel model, maneuverable, resilient, and the officer obviously enjoyed driving it down the narrow channel winding around the mountain's base.

She looked at him in surprise. "What transport? What citizen?"

"Jonas Polat is a Derinkuyu citizen essential to my investigation. I need to bring him to Athens for medical treatment."

The woman was quiet for a while. Accessing Jonas's file, presumably.

The jeep passed through one small gate and stopped before another. The fence slid open, and she pulled over to let them disembark into the rain.

In the relative security of a large oak they waited. At 5:47 a.m., a small blue PI transport parted the rain and glided into the clearing. Its bay doors slid apart. Half a dozen armed troopers waited within.

Keiko waved to them.

One of the officers waved back. "Officer Yamanaka, Chief Saylor. Let's get you both out of here."

"They come with us," Keiko said, pointing to Celeste and Gethin.

She thought the officer was extending a friendly hand to them, but instead he leveled his rifle at Gethin.

"We're authorized to take the two of *you*," the officer told Keiko. "No others. Sure as hell not the IPC agent."

"The IPC is *hunting* him," Jack explained. "He's proven invaluable in—"

"No. These orders come from the top. They stay."

Jack hesitated. "Then we stay."

The transport's wing rotors whined sharply, flinging rainwater.

"Jack?" the officer said. "Get onboard or we drop that IPC spy where he stands. War has begun."

Gethin spat. "The four of us have learned that your war is—"

"Another word," the officer snarled, anger twitching a vein on his forehead, "and we send you back to your superiors through a purchase signal."

"No!" Keiko shouted, placing herself in the line of fire. "He has invaluable information! Don't kill him!"

Gethin's heart pounded ferociously. He touched Keiko's shoulder.

"It's okay," he said.

"Get onboard," the officer repeated. "That is an order from HQ. Now!"

Keiko looked at Gethin sadly. "*Gomen nasai.*"

"Not your fault. You better go."

The Prometheans climbed aboard the ship. The pilot wasted no time; the transport tilted away from Gethin and ascended at a diagonal angle, vanishing into the storm.

"That might have been for the best," Celeste said, watching it disappear. "Not my kind of company."

"And I am?"

Celeste smirked. "I don't know what to make of you, Gethin."

"Ironic. I know exactly what to make of you."

"A StrikeDown rat, right?"

He shrugged. "Doesn't really matter now. The two biggest powers in the known universe are going to destroy each other for the wrong reasons."

Celeste wiped the merciless rain from her face. "Why precisely should I care?"

"The thing that killed your friends? It's still at large."

"So?"

"Don't you want revenge?"

"We have no idea what it is," Celeste snapped.

The rain ran off Gethin's chin like a liquid beard. "Actually, I do."

"Really?"

"Yes."

Celeste stalked around him in a circle. Her hair was plastered to her face and neck. "Yesterday we were spinning our heads, trying to figure out who was responsible. Now you've got it all figured?"

"I'm something, aren't I? If you want details, we need to get out of here first."

As soon as he finished speaking, a remarkable thing happened. The rain was no longer falling on them. Gethin could still hear it, but he realized it was magically sparing the two of them, as if an invisible umbrella had appeared over their heads.

Gethin looked up.

The *Mantid* materialized.

PART FOUR
SHIMIZU

History seduces us into wondering how the future might have turned out if pivotal events had gone differently. Such a fragile thread of chance and choice determines our lives. Some used to believe that every moment could shoot off into wildly different futures. Oatmeal or bran for breakfast? Shower at night, or in the morning? While these microhistorical moments can occasionally have far-reaching effects (choking to death on the oatmeal when you wouldn't have with bran, slipping during your groggy morning shower and breaking your neck on the linoleum floor) we can now be confident that these microhistorical events typically disappear into the 'white noise' of our lives without much consequence. Computer models have demonstrated this beyond doubt.

When a microhistorical flowers into the macrohistorical, it is a different matter entirely. The remarkable events of 322 remain a matter of endless interpretation, debate, and mystery, though the little we do know terrifies – not seduces – our fragile sense of security. Perhaps there are indeed alternate universes where those events turned out differently…and the Earth is even now a lifeless rock in space, spinning with dull repetition. Or that it fell under the sway of a frightful despot.

Instead, we are left with the way history did turn out. The human race so hopelessly fragmented that they can barely be called human any longer.

And we know that it is all the fault of Gethin Bryce and his conniving conspiracy operating in the shadows.

– Points of Impact, Human Liberation Front, December 17, 561

CHAPTER FORTY-FOUR
Lord of Chaos

It was an unusual place to hold a meeting.

King D. kept repeating that in his head, trying to come to grips with the bizarre course of events over the last few days that had twisted, turned, and now led to this eccentric location for an Outland parley. As the newest messiah of StrikeDown, King D. was accustomed to clandestine huddles. He appreciated – even relished – the fact that he was embroiled in the deadliest conspiracy of recent centuries. He figured an unexpected location was, well, to be expected.

King D. was tall, thickset, and massive like a fleshy tank, with muscular, tattooed arms. He wore a trim moustache, and with his wide, flat cheekbones and small eyes, he exuded a vaguely Mongolian visage. His wide frame lent the impression of being inert, plodding; most people were therefore surprised by the speed at which he moved, as if he were a Godblood junkie itching for action.

"The point," King D. bellowed to the crowd below him, "is not to dwell on our ideological divisions, but to find middle ground for compromise. We *both* have a common enemy. Only through collaboration can we bring the Republic to its knees. Unless you *prefer* being their slaves?"

At these words, the audience murmured. Father Chadwick, local shepherd of this Stillness flock, scowled. The first hint of real emotion washed pink into his pasty face. The man was shaped like a top, wider in the middle than the terminating points of his head and feet. He wore a full Abrahamic beard, and he licked his lips anxiously in that weedy mass.

Some two hundred Stillness troopers, a dozen priests, and King D.'s own elite bodyguards gathered in the granite passages beneath the Sinkiang Mountains of China. No satellite could spy on them here. No Hassan would ever seek them this far underground.

And that was part of the strangeness. They were nearly *two kilometers down*. King D. doubted the upper world even suspected this network of caves existed; certainly no references existed anywhere on the blueweb. When he had hailed the local Stillness cairn demanding a top-level conference, he expected to be summoned to a clever hideout. But this?

Incredible.

And there were other oddities.

For starters, although Stillness had clearly been using the place for many years (by the look of the open dormitories, replovats, generators, and the rusting, industrial-sized inclinator that could move fifty people at a time to higher levels of the hollowed-out mountain) it seemed that some structures – namely the colossal pillars and support beams – had existed here for an impossibly long time. King D.'s eyes kept straying, seduced by the suggestion of antiquity…far older than the earliest whispers of Chinese civilization dared imply.

Secondly, there was a damnably strange machine down here.

In the bowels of the mountain, beneath the airy cavern bustling with green-cloaked troops, a mad contraption had been assembled. A chimera of many mechanical fathers, it bristled with magnetic ventricles and an angular peak of quill-like spindles that jabbed straight up a narrow mountain shaft. Power cables snaked into it from four fusion generators. A cathode rail unlike anything King D. had ever seen formed the centerpiece of the monstrosity. And most disturbingly of all, *six antimatter missiles* were set into the sanctum that housed the infernal machine; they ringed it and connected to it via a forest of cables.

Six missiles!

My missiles, he thought bitterly.

Father Chadwick headed the local cairn, and he seemed an amiable enough fellow. But negotiations were making little headway; King D. was already weighing the logistics of stealing the missiles back. He had been granted safe passage, and even been allowed to bring a contingent of armed bodyguards. Unlike Stillness, his guards were jacked with enough pilfered technologies to represent a serious threat, despite being heavily outnumbered; Stillness's visible strength was triple his own.

It was the eccentric contraption that worried King D. more. He didn't know what the hell it did, except that six goddamn antimatter missiles were part of its design, and he didn't want to mess with something he didn't understand.

So he turned back to the priest. "There is a tremendous lot that we share in terms of goals," he said, "the least of which is the overthrow of the Republic and IPC."

"Yes," Chadwick replied, voice echoing musically in the cavern. "But the advantage of the current situation is obvious. Arky devilwork is in the hands of arky devils. It's therefore contained, while most of the Wastes are spared such metal cancers. We may suffer in our transitory world of the flesh, but eternal paradise awaits us."

"Promises of eternal life," King D. bellowed in his rich baritone, "don't erase the fact that you spend part of your lives on Earth. We must help those who suffer here."

"Yes," Chadwick agreed. "If StrikeDown and Stillness were to unite, we could do much to improve the Outlands. But here we come to an irreconcilable juncture: you wish to crack open the arky shells and let their poisons unfurl into the rest of the world. This is not acceptable to us."

Murmurs of approval from the crowd.

King D. maintained his composure and decided to change tactics. "Can I speak plain?"

"Of course."

"Is it more acceptable to you the way the Republic slaughters your people by the thousands? Is death more acceptable than a unified front against tyranny?"

"At least in death, our souls remain pure."

King D. smiled. "Ah! Then *end your life now*. Kill yourself and rocket into the hereafter. *Do it!*" He turned his gaze outward to the crowd of young parishioners, men and women in their late teens and early twenties, a few elder heads in the crowd like aging dandelions. "Why don't you *all* kill yourselves and rush to God? I'll tell you why: you are not cowards! You wish to fight those who oppress us. *My* people are committed to that fight, and we are your allies. This is why I propose a compromise. Neither of us will get everything we want. Not StrikeDown, and not Stillness."

He strode away from Chadwick, gazing directly into the crowd. The priest was an old, complacent, weak-willed fanatic. The *masses* needed to be addressed…and it was what King D. excelled at.

"If we work together," the StrikeDown leader said, turning up his crystal baritone, "we will *bring down* the arky devils! We will seize their world by its balls! Slap a fiery delivery stamp on their Save Centers, and ship them all by antimatter express to Hell! Threaten them with permadeath! Why should they continue running things? Make them answer to *us* for a change!"

Murmurs of agreement rippled among the crowd.

"The arkies have kept us divided for centuries, squabbling over garbage like dire dogs. How about we make them suffer for a change? Break open their cities. Rescue their children from sinful illusion. With our two organizations in charge!" D. beckoned to Chadwick to join him at the ridge. The priest stood awkwardly, uncertain. "Call it a rescue, call it revenge. But they *will* hear us. They will hear StrikeDown, they will hear Stillness, and people can decide for themselves what they want. The arkies don't give them choice. *We will!*"

The approving voices multiplied.

"Who wants to kill the infidels? The IPC just declared war on Prometheus Industries. It's gonna be a bloodbath!"

Outright cheers from the crowd.

"But in time, they will wind down and talk peace. *That's the time to strike!* Capturing their Save Centers is essential, I'm sure you agree. After all, how can you save souls when they keep coming back in new bodily shells?"

He was delighted with the ease with which he had possessed the crowd. He caught Father Chadwick's glance. The priest gave the briefest nod, conceding defeat.

For the next several minutes, King D. whipped the cavern into dizzying heights of frenzy, filling their minds with dancing wheels of fiery images.

Maybe, just maybe, we won't have to steal the missiles back after all, he hoped. *We can fight over ideological divisions in the aftermath. If I can just convince them to let me use the missiles smartly, as opposed to whatever harebrained plots they are hatching...*

A voice sounded in his sensorium. Holly Gibbs, his chief intelligence advisor, spoke urgently from his gathering of bodyguards: "Someone's coming, D."

He noticed two men entering the cavern from a passageway. High Priests, judging by their golden robes.

"High Priest Tiamat," Gibbs informed him, running her recognition software. "And High Priest Apophis."

Interesting, King D. thought.

Born in the ashes of the Final War, the Stillness movement had long been a Balkanized, unpleasant stew of provincial kingdoms, loosely tethered by a mantra of purity to contrast with the fallout from a fallen age. Eventually, self-professed prophets began appearing. Three prophets who welded the believing masses into a unified cause. Three prophets who could somehow travel the world unseen and uncaught, across the decades.

They called themselves Tiamat, Eris, and Apophis.

King D. had never thought much of the stories before. He himself was a committed atheist, seeing the usefulness of evangelistic rhetoric as a means to ammunition and strategic objectives. Nothing built an army better than the double-sided promise of eternal goodies for one's own tribe, and eternal punishment for everyone else.

Now he watched with interest as two of these famous prophets passed by barely a hundred meters from where he stood. Tiamat was the more imposing figure, with spiked blond hair and luminous, wintry eyes.

The lankier figure was Apophis, trailing Tiamat in a stooped, subservient manner.

"High Priests Tiamat and Apophis!" King D. shouted. "It is my honor to meet you both!"

Tiamat didn't so much as glance in his direction; the man was bound for the bowels of the mountain. To D's surprise, it was Apophis who halted momentarily, smiled, and nodded...in simple acknowledgement, or approval, who knew? But it was a start.

★   ★   ★

In the Midas Hand chamber, Tiamat leaned over the machine controls with an expression of repugnance. There was a bone-chilling draft in the alcove, breathing in from high above where the mountain's natural hollow had been expanded by nanorod-enforced diamond drills over the course of decades. Like the flue of a blacksmith's cliffside forge, where the high-altitude breeze was sucked down to cool a smelted array of swords, axe blades, and sickles.

Tiamat no longer resembled Colonel Leon Tanner, or any other registered human being. He had melted into a blank slate of a man, facial features as crude and simplistic as something a child would shape from clay.

"Need I inquire the status of this thing?" Tiamat asked softly.

Apophis bowed. "I am integrating the last piece. In another day or two, we can run a field test."

Tiamat ran his hand over the controls. "Another day or two?"

"We have waited a billion years. What is forty-eight little hours?"

Tiamat craned his neck to peer at the steeplelike extensions.

"I asked the technicians about this cathode rail I obtained for you," he said thickly. "They couldn't explain how it fits into this. Perhaps you can, Apophis? You said Prometheus had succeeded where your efforts failed." He jabbed a finger at the phallic rail. "What is so special about this...that you couldn't invent it yourself?"

Apophis grinned like a jackal. "I'm the cleverest creature you've ever encountered, but *they* have billions of minds at their disposal. And they're inventive little fuckers. Always were."

"Run the test now."

"The opening shots of war have begun. We've worked hard to stir the nest. Why not let them fly about, stinging each other? It will be more effective to deliver the fatal blow when they're distracted."

Tiamat's clay features sharpened into a doppleganger of Colonel Leon Tanner once more.

"If this machine works," he snapped, "what does it matter if they're fighting or not?"

Apophis licked his lips. "Because when I trigger this, *they'll see where it comes from.*"

"What of it? It will be too late by then."

"And if it doesn't work to the extent we wish? The humans will unite in the face of common threat. They could strike from orbit, destroy the machine. We will lose...again."

He could see his words were having an effect. Tiamat growled low, backed off. He gave another disgusted glance to the machine, to this mechanism of steel, nanomaterials, glasstic, cables, and concrete bedding.

"The IPC tracked a mysterious explosion in the Pacific," Tiamat said gently, arctic eyes glinting suspiciously. "A sampan village was destroyed by unknown means, and the blast radius is...curious." He regarded Apophis.

Apophis hid his stab of fear behind his false face. "Oh?"

Tiamat didn't say anything for a long while. Apophis soon realized his friend was done speaking, having voiced his suspicions and content to let them drift, floating between accusation, inquiry, and conversational camaraderie.

"I don't know anything about that," Apophis said at last. "But I do have news you may enjoy, my friend. Lady Wen Ying is dead. Eris destroyed her in Shimizu...and will impersonate her, waiting for the others to arrive."

Tiamat gave no indication he had even heard. He bowed his head before the machine. He was no longer breathing – none of them needed to breathe like the pestilent inhabitants of Earth. His face quivered in painful, needful contortions. In a small voice, he whispered, "We have lost so many from our side. They would have wanted to be here…for this moment of victory and peace. Their loss must be marked."

Apophis extended an invisible tendril to his friend, filaments streaming out from his human manifestation to offer an electrical touch of comfort. He was reminded of the astonishing limitations of *Homo Sapiens*, with their simplistic extremities, sensory organs crammed into a head, and the way skin separated them from the environment.

"We must sing the litany of the lost," Tiamat maintained, and the color of his body faded until he was translucent as milky glass. The Tanner manifestation bled at the edges and began to dissipate.

"We will," Apophis said tenderly. "Purity will return."

"When the dust settles—"

"Understand that this time, there will be *only* dust, and it will *never* settle. You understand what this machine will do?"

"Yes."

"And what of us?"

Tiamat had reverted entirely to his base form; a swirling phosphorescent plasma. The colors washed in indigos and twilight dusks. "When stillness has arrived, we will join it. Do *you* understand?"

"Of course, my friend. Of course."

CHAPTER FORTY-FIVE
Aboard the Mantid

Celeste Segarra nearly collapsed in her relief, the emotion moistening her eyes. Being back aboard her ship in its cramped compartments was like returning from cold years into a warm and cherished home…far more secure than anywhere else she'd ever known.

The central bay was just four meters long; stuffy when Jeff, Rajnar, Allie, and Jamala shared it for mission transports. Celeste glimpsed the dried blood flaking on the floor and medtable. It took her a moment to realize she was seeing her own residue from the airfield rescue at the Hudson.

She saw, too, the chair where Jeff liked to sit. Where he had been sitting in the moments before their final, fateful mission.

Twenty-four soldiers? he had asked. *Really? Quinn will expect this…*

It wasn't Quinn we had to worry about, Jeff. It was a nonhuman Egyptian God unleashed upon the Earth.

Gethin gave the place a methodical viewing, noting the weld points, equipment locker, and five resin lockers arranged side by side like tombs in a mausoleum: ALLIE, PRANILIKA, JEFFREY, RAJNAR, CELESTE.

<This ship matches no existing models,> Ego told him.

No doubt, he thought. He remembered Keiko's preliminary report on the ship's unique properties. Where had a Wastelander obtained it?

The most obvious hypothesis – that it was a refurbished Warlord transport – was clearly wrong. The *Mantid* had rescued its owner, assessed the extent of her wounds, and made the decision to bring her to Babylon arcology. That in itself wasn't so unusual; there were drone-ambulances which could do the same.

But Celeste's protector had also negotiated for medical treatment, deceived PI security, and then exercised both the skill and sense of self-preservation to vanish off their radar. It had managed to jettison the tracking device Keiko installed, was able to stay hidden from surveillance sweeps, had rescued her a *second* time through an astonishingly daring pseudopod maneuver. Had any Warlord state possessed artificial intelligence of this sort during the Century, it would have dominated all conflicts faster than even Apollo the Great. Like a twenty-first-century aircraft carrier sent back to the Napoleonic Wars.

Gethin tabled these speculations. "I need to access my email. That'll trigger a few IPC bells."

Celeste shrugged. "Route your access through the system here."

"That won't stop a trace."

"Um. Yes, it will."

He heard the certainty in her voice. "Indeed?"

Celeste went to her locker, drew it open, and started poking about inside. "The *Mantid* can route a laser transmission through concealing channels."

"A lot of people can do that."

"Not like this ship."

"Through whom does it route the signals?"

Celeste shrugged and continued her digging.

Gethin decided to try something. He sent his Familiars to tap into the ship's logic circuits.

<The *Mantid* is protecting itself with a rotating quantum encryption membrane,> Ego reported.

Not well enough, Id cut in. *Last several communications were calibrated for unknown receiving stations along the Carpathians.*

"Line of sight to Avalon," Gethin muttered knowingly. Before he could continue, a new, unfamiliar voice spilled into his head with the sensation of chilled fog.

[Any further attempts to access my systems without permission will be construed as an attack. I do not wish that.]

Gethin's eyes grew wide and he chanced a nervous laugh. "Neither do I." He noticed Celeste peering over her shoulder at him. She had not been privy to the conversation, but by the look on her face she had a good idea of the content.

"She means business," Celeste advised.

"Sorry. I'm just checking my email, *Mantid*. No need to be rude."

[I wasn't being rude. Any further attempt to hack my systems will be met with lethal force. Not rudeness, Gethin Bryce. Honesty.]

He pressed the access pad behind his ear. His inbox unfolded.

Two new messages had arrived, joining the unread message from Lori, which continued sitting like an unopened Solstice gift.

The senders' names were there for perusal:

KEIKO YAMANAKA (Unread)
LT. DONNA MCCALLISTER (Unread)
LORI GOSSAMER AMBERMOON (Unread)

"Anything?" Celeste asked.

"Ex-wife, ex-employer, ex-wife," he said. He noted the timestamps. Keiko's had come in just minutes ago. McCallister had sent hers around the time he was leaving Haventown and running into Cappadocia's scouts.

He was afraid to hope that McCallister was emailing to let him know that spies in her organization had been ferreted out, Tanner's imposter dispelled, and the war machine's engines downshifted to a rumbling idle.

"Wait." Celeste stood and pointed at him. "You said you had figured out what was happening."

Gethin gave her his attention. His email screen formed a semi-translucent overlay across her face. "Researchers don't deal in absolutes," he said.

"Your working theory, then?"

"You know that professor friend of mine in Athens?"

Celeste nodded.

Gethin leaned against the wall. He gave a reluctant sigh, and the shadows of the bay formed a map of inky pools and plateaus across his countenance.

"Yeah. He's actually Apollo the Great."

She blinked a few times, like a sleeper uncertainly sloughing off last night's dream. "As in, the Warlord Apollo?" she asked.

"The only."

"Gethin, Apollo lived and died three hundred and fifty years ago. Before immortality and DCs. All the Warlords did." Her mind raced to weigh the possibility. "But not before cryonics, right? Are you suggesting that Apollo had himself frozen at the time of death to await a secret resurrection?"

"No." He minimized his email tab with a short, conductor-like sweep of his hand. "Celeste, we both grew up hearing stories of Apollo's divine power. Calling down fire from the sky. Sprouting wings and battling angels of darkness. Turning night into day by his radiance. We live in a highly rational age now, so we realize these tales are just mythologized attributes of his military successes. It fits the model of earlier religiosity: burning bushes, angels bearing black stones, water turning into wine. It's the 'awe factor' of our species, and it isn't limited to gods. Secular hero-worship is alive and well. Look at the outcry over Salvor Bear's death." He panted, wiped sweat from his lip. "But what if this time it isn't mythology? What if Apollo really had the powers ascribed to him?"

Celeste frowned. "Am I hearing you right, Gethin? *You're* converting to the old faiths?"

He shook his head vigorously. "It's not faith. Apollo is still alive and he calls himself Doros Peisistratos. His longevity is almost inconsequential compared to the other things he can do. Convert the matter of his own body into energy. Imitate anything or anyone he desires."

"So if Apollo is still alive...then why not Enyalios?"

He nodded. She shuddered.

"And others," Gethin said, a clammy hand touching his heart. "I think we have been tossed into the midst of war between two different, roughly equal factions. I think they have been fighting since well before the Final War. And I think I've never been more scared in my life."

★   ★   ★

The ship landed beneath a rocky, gourd-like overhang south of Cappadocia to conserve fuel while they discussed their next move. The bay viewscreen displayed a local map in blobs of green and blue vector lines.

Celeste cracked out a beaker of brandy from her locker. She poured two deep glasses, handed Gethin one, and gulped half of hers before he had taken a sip. It burned like corrosive acid in her throat, spread warmly into the pit of her stomach, tingled along her limbs.

If there was one thing she could count on, it was the *Mantid*'s storehouse of liquor. Like the hold of a pirate vessel, enough loot was aboard that her entire squad could remain sated for weeks, eating canned soups, dried meats, dehydrated easy-prep meals, and washing it all down with stolen spirits.

She swirled the remaining brandy. "If there *is* a war going on, Apollo and Enyalios are presumably on the same side. They both signed the non-aggression pacts, along with Lady Wen Ying."

Gethin swished his brandy in the glass. "True enough. But I don't have to remind you of their differing methods. Apollo was an enlightened philosopher king, a uniter, the founder of a new civilization. Enyalios was a butcher. Eighty million people killed by his predations."

Celeste felt her breathing coming hard and fast. "Those estimates are considered low." She threw back the rest of her drink and was surprised by a warm, lustful tingle in her body. Warlord Enyalios. Mass murderer or not, he was the first man she had ever loved from afar. The deliverer of brutal justice for a brutal people.

Gethin drained his glass in one long, steady trickle. He placed it on the counterspace. "We both need to undergo a DC as soon as possible. This knowledge can't die if we do."

Celeste was stunned. "Why me?"

"Why not?"

"I thought you needed to be a citizen to have a sentient pattern registered with a Save center."

Gethin laughed. "I'm betting it won't be a challenge to get you registered."

"And if I die?"

"Then you come back, like Ishtar from the underworld."

"The goddess of love and war?"

"Aren't you both?"

"Check your fucking messages," she snapped, and stepped into the narrow shower cubicle, stripped, and disappeared beneath spraying water and steam.

He opened the email from Donna McCallister.

The IPC lieutenant's face was a solemn rectangle, long and worn in a way befitting the dignified visages from antebellum currency, back before the advent of the IPC tradenote. More than two centuries old; to flip through her photographic record was to witness willful fluctuations between youth and matronly maturity, like the frames of an antique film projector looping the illustration of the human life cycle. She appeared young at the start of her career during the Saturnian Miners' Revolt of 117. The photos of her began to show a swiftly aging matriarch by the time of the infamous Stillness attacks of the 200s. Then, in time for the unveiling of the IPC's newest battleship fleet, she was young again. Donna McCallister. Summer to autumn to winter to spring.

Currently, she was in her matriarch season.

"Mr. Bryce?" she said to the recorder. "I must assume you survived the crash and are alive, in the Wastes, and deliberately evading our search teams." She sighed deeply, giving an appreciative nod. "We found the bodies of Stillness troopers amid the wreckage, and last night discovered the charred remains of Colonel Leon Tanner in a maintenance tunnel beneath Old Athens. We don't know all the details yet, so please bear with me. The man you spoke with was not Tanner. He was an imposter. We...don't really understand how this happened."

"Tell me something I don't know," Gethin muttered.

McCallister continued. "When we discovered Tanner's remains, we downloaded his last Save and brought him back. He has no idea who was responsible for his abduction and murder. His imposter has vanished...as if into thin air."

I'll bet he did, Gethin thought. *Or perhaps through a ventilation shaft like in Tycho Hospital to finish off Kenneth Cavor. Transforming his physical mass to energy and then worming into the vents, scorching them as he goes.*

The silver-haired woman looked weary and exhausted. "Bryce, the airship recorder was disabled by the hijackers, but we have a pretty good idea of what happened. I'm guessing you think the IPC is in collusion with terrorists. This is *not* the case. We need you back, to help us shed light on the situation. Contact me as soon as you can."

Gethin got McCallister on the line and started talking before she could cut in. "We know about the imposters," he told her. "In fact, I have reason to believe there are two factions of these shapechangers involved in all this."

McCallister looked pained. "Who are they, Bryce?"

"Doros Peisistratos is one. I need to find him right away."

He expected McCallister to continue drilling him, and was mildly surprised when she said, "Just a moment. He left Athens for Japan aboard REP Flight 54021. His passport was scanned at the Shimizu pyramid yesterday at 6 p.m. Wait. I can't get a lock on him."

"Because he has no wetware," Gethin explained. "So far that's the only way I know to detect these...imposters. They possess no internal technologies. No detectable tech of any kind."

"Stealth augs," McCallister suggested. "I'm contacting our security forces at the pyramid right now to—"

"No!" Gethin insisted. "Do nothing of the sort. Doros trusts me, and if he feels threatened he'll disappear. Literally."

"Then we'll put the pyramid on lockdown."

"That won't work either," he said irritably, unwilling to get drawn into a deep discussion on this. Celeste emerged from the shower and treaded past the screen. McCallister stared at the naked apparition but offered no comment.

"Let *me* talk to him," Gethin persisted. "When I get to Shimizu, I'll keep an open channel to you, but it's *my* show, got it?"

"Fine. Where are you right now?"

"You'll understand why I won't answer that query."

The old woman regarded him solemnly. "What would you like us to do?"

"Your Shimizu office is compromised. The airship was transporting terrorists to the most advanced arcology on Earth, and that can't be done without insiders. Issue a standing order to all Shimizu officers. Tell them local IPC personnel are to immediately confine themselves to their homes and offices until further notice. Then run a priority scan on every citizen. Tag all those who lack wetware, or possess signs of recent wetware implantation, and send me the list when I arrive. Should be a short list for Japan."

"You don't want a security detail? Gethin, if you're right and more terrorists are there, what do you expect to do?"

"I'm going to reach out to the one group that couldn't possibly be associated with Stillness," he said, and disconnected the call.

Then he contacted the Faustians.

CHAPTER FORTY-SIX
Out of the Past...

Gethin ended the call with the Faustians and realized he was sweating. He poured himself a second brandy and drained it in a painful, inexorable swig, concentrating on the parching sensation in his stomach and knowing the pleasant numbness of intoxication would follow. The *Mantid*'s stealth thrusters thrummed, the vessel en route to the other side of the world.

Celeste leaned across from him, dressed in a fresh pair of cargo pants and pale red T-shirt, her thumbs hooked into her beltline. "That sounded serious. Did you just sign with the Devil?"

He looked at her sharply. "No, that's *your* modus operandi. During one of my earliest anomaly assignments, I was asked to investigate reports of miracles among Abraham's Flock. Ever hear of them? A bastardization of Old Calendar faiths. I hung out in their villages, watched their sermons of judgment and damnation." Gethin sat up, his sinewy arms as taut as tree limbs. "And they did perform miracles too…with stolen arcology medpacks. But the fanaticism, the thirst for hellfire and destruction…well, it wasn't really so different from your StrikeDown pals, huh?"

"I'm not with StrikeDown."

"I'm smarter than anyone you've ever met, Celeste. I had you pegged when we had dinner in Athens."

Celeste said nothing.

"This ship is an illegal AI," he continued, "subcontracted by your StrikeDown associates. Now, that could be lots of people. However, you made a point of telling Howd that you were from Odessa. I thought that was interesting. You know who else is from Odessa? Konrad Dal. Known to the Outlands as King D. A savvy political genius in the mold of Warlords. He commissioned an entire fleet of *Mantid*s, right? All carting their squads around, waiting for the acquisition of enough weapons to make StrikeDown dreams a reality. Weapons like those two missiles your doomed posse grabbed in the Hudson. Once things reach a critical mass, Dal pushes the buttons and gives Earth another dark age."

The blood rushed to her cheeks. "We do what we can to survive."

"The cry of the fanatic. At least we arkies are trying to improve the world, step by step."

"We'll see," she hissed, mask off, talking straight to her enemy.

"And you know what else?" Gethin said in afterthought. "This clever ship might pull off a few hit-fade strikes, but IPC battleships will eventually scorch Avalon and every ship it made from the face of the universe and—"

Celeste hurled her glass at his head. It missed him by several inches…enough that he realized she hadn't actually been trying to hit him. Then she crossed the distance to him, seized his tunic, and kissed him.

There was nothing sweet or soft about it. Gethin grunted, feeling her hands at his throat. She tore his tunic open, grasped the back of his head, forced him to look into her eyes.

He saw rage there.

And anguish.

And fear.

"Celeste, I—"

"Shut up."

She tore the rest of his tunic away. His bruises and lacerations formed an attractive pattern of scarring on his arcology hardbody. Celeste yanked his sash through its belt loops and threw it noisily to the floor. Then she peeled out of her top, gripped him by the back of his hair again, and pulled him towards her.

Gethin instinctively took one nipple into his mouth, feeling it harden against the ministrations of his tongue. He was shivering, the past days of madness washing away in an emotional monsoon. He sucked one breast, then the other, while she pulled her cargo pants down over her sharply accentuated hip bones, letting them crumple at her feet. Celeste dragged her adversary to the floor after them. The steel was cold against her knees.

"Celeste—"

She pressed two fingers against his lips. They were slick with her wetness. Gethin's protests evaporated as she lowered herself onto his mouth. She reached around and gripped his hardened member, beginning a maddening stroke that made Gethin groan helplessly as he pressed his mouth and tongue to her. Celeste began to grind in a steady, deliberate circle against him, hips rolling.

Gethin let himself be used. The floor vibrated behind his head, the brandy swam in his veins, and he thought of their hypersonic flight above thousands of feet of Earthly landmass. Celeste's moans increased in pitch, and her first orgasm shocked him with its intensity. Her muscles were still contracting when she dismounted his face, flipped around towards his feet, and took him into her mouth. The suction pulled at every nerve ending in his body. When she finally mounted him, he was twisting in desperation for release.

It was a four-hour flight to the Shimizu pyramid. Their coupling seemed a delicious agony, a contest of willpower that ended in the first orgasm of his new body. Celeste's hair was plastered to her face and neck. She curled against Gethin's chest, her face wet with tears, never meeting his eyes or letting their fingers interlace. Neither had spoken more than simple words, urgent and bestial.

Gethin listened to her breathing. A half hour before their descent to Japan, they joined one last time. She lay on her stomach, feeling the seams in the metal plates. Gethin straddled the backs of her thighs and penetrated her slowly, teasing at the threshold, pressing deeper with each thrust, withdrawing completely before returning, over and over until he was buried to the hilt. When he came again, it felt like his insides were twisting into knots.

He placed his hands on her supple shoulders. There was an old knife scar just above the scapula.

At last, Celeste stood. "Get dressed," she ordered, tying her hair into a ponytail.

Gethin complied, regarded her quietly. "What was that about?" he asked.

She closed her eyes and felt the change in pressure as they began the descent to Japan.

"Life," she said.

CHAPTER FORTY-SEVEN
Ten Thousand Thunders

For all its tricks, the *Mantid* could not possibly approach Shimizu without triggering a dozen surveillance tools designed to look for heat signatures, real-time optical distortions, wind modulations, ladar net, and the feedback from sonic air buoys. The pyramid's AI net knew the positions of every bird and fish in a ten-mile radius, and Gethin feared that he and Celeste had already picked up an unseen automated escort. Without McCallister's support, they would be blasted to shrapnel over the Sea of Japan.

At 7,000 feet tall, the Shimizu pyramid was the highest manmade structure on Earth (though not the largest – both the Apollonian Ring and Transatlantic Railway bested it in terms of mass and scale.) It floated on the water, chrome in the late afternoon sun, and the ocean could have been a mercury desert undulating around it…a surreal reinterpretation of the age of pharoahs, as a race of machines might have envisioned it.

Gethin had been to the pyramid twice in his youth. The people of Shimizu were like those of the rest of Japan; bright, eager technosorcerers who seemed to exist in a state of perennial optimism. And why not? Technology had been their timeless savior and had merged with the mystic's promise of magic.

The *Mantid* maintained invisibility as it splashed down and cruised through one of the pyramid's hangars. Thanks to McCallister, the docks were deserted of security personnel.

Celeste handed Gethin a fully loaded multigun with a bejeweled undercarriage of EMP cannisters. She also gave him a knobby, navy blue glove that felt far heavier than it looked.

"Ever used a shieldfist?" she asked, seeing his expression.

"I'm not a soldier."

As she helped stretch it across his left hand and a portion of his arm, she explained its use. "The trigger is the rubber ball in your palm," she said. "The harder you squeeze it, the larger the shield. This was slotted to my friend Rajnar…meaning that it won't recognize you as its new owner. Make sure you keep it out in front of you when you deploy it, or you'll decapitate yourself."

Gethin breathed out slow and hard. "Good safety tip."

There were no CAMO suits remaining aboard. Even her own suit, painted with phosphire back during the Hudson attack, had been fried during the blast that almost killed her, and the *Mantid* had been forced to slice it off her during medical treatment anyway.

There *were* layers of shapestone armor, however, and she helped Gethin fit loosely into Silent Rajnar's slacks and shirts.

"Just follow my lead and do what I tell you."

He took her hand, squeezed it, his gaze bright. "Good luck to us."

To her surprise, she squeezed his hand in return. "Yeah."

They disembarked the invisible ship. If anyone *was* watching, it was as if a pair of interdimensional mercenaries were popping out of empty air.

Celeste strode briskly alongside him, scanning the hangar for activity. They passed a series of abandoned security booths. A lone cleaning bot patrolled the lobby carpet, swallowing skeins of dust.

Gethin felt his breath coming hard and fast. When a message from McCallister arrived to his optics, he nearly jumped out of his skin.

"We've done all you asked," she insisted through his comlink. "Shimizu security has verified that Peisistratos is having dinner, alone, in a Sakura restaurant. He's renting a room in CW-0782. There's more: I've confirmed that a large number of unregistered pures are in Shibata Ward. Sending you their biosignals now."

"Let me guess," he said. "Is that around the corner from CW-0782?"

"Yes."

"*Domo*," he said, receiving her emailed list and handing it off to his Familiars. "And standby."

They proceeded to the inclinator, hit the call button. Celeste adjusted the strap of her rifle. "You said you had friends here? Those people you contacted...?"

"They're not friends, but they'll aid us against the Stillness troopers here."

"Who are they?"

"A bunch of very dangerous lunatics."

"Figures."

Gethin felt the gentle ping of Id and Ego latching onto the local security grid, sifting each dataflow, worming into every electronic niche, evading countermeasure software, settling into various cubbyholes to provide logistical and technical support.

The inclinator descended and the doors slid aside. Gethin and Celeste hurried aboard, feeling small and exposed on its airy platform. The lift began its implacable ascent to one of the many smaller pyramids comprising Shimizu's inner structure. There were no personal vehicles anywhere in the pyramid beyond security jeeps, maintenance buggies, and ambulances; the local populace moved by lift, escalator, people-mover, shuttle, and tram.

Ego spoke in his head: <There are 61 unregistered people in CW prefecture.>

"Sixty-one Stillness troopers." He shook his head. "Fuck me."

The inclinator opened onto a courtyard of rock gardens and shops. Bright daylight filtered through high windows, suffusing the chamber with an overexposed quality, like a photo with the contrast dialed up too far. A crowd of roughly fifty people milled in the open stores, or drank at the café, or studied train schedules, or mingled like teenagers around benches and gardens, or stared with open contempt at the technical display of advertisements that turned the air into an aquarium of holos.

Id hijacked the security cameras and Gethin's optics splashed with overlays. Most of the crowd, it seemed, was packing heat; Id drew silhouettes over distinct bulges in their neo-Victorian coats, or the suspiciously cumbersome loads in carry-on satchels. Beneath their coats, thin nanomesh armor betrayed itself with the muddy rainbow of oil-slick reflectivity.

Gethin felt his resolve weaken. "About half of these people match McCallister's list. Looks like every single one of them is armed and deadly. Tanner's imposter must have cordoned off this entire wing from security so they could roam free."

Celeste considered that. "And your friend Doros?"

"He's not with them," he insisted. "He may or may not know they're shadowing him. I think they're here to try killing him."

"If this fucking professor really is Apollo the Great—"

Gethin held up his hand to silence her, pointing to one of the holos. A dragonfly the size of a condor flew high into the air, glided towards them, and broke apart into a blizzard of moths. The moths, however, were each a different color; they swarmed into the pattern of a pixie-like, androgynous face...bald and with violet eyes.

He waited for the visage to speak, but when the discomforting silence persisted, he hazarded a greeting. "We still have an agreement, right?"

The face made no expression. "And we will hold you to it, Mr. Bryce. Your last meeting with us was most unpleasant."

"Water Basilisk could use lessons in tact."

The face scowled. What Gethin had taken for a genderless quality went deeper, suggesting an amalgamated entity grown from numerous individuals, stirred into a melting pot until their distinctions boiled away, then poured into a human-shaped mold. Even the violet gaze was comprised of a multitude of other eyes. Gethin imagined he could see the future bottled up in this *gestalt* thing: a gout of humanity ejaculated into the cosmos...all the bad seeds and darker appetites, the sadism, tyranny, and fundamentalism set free upon the universe after centuries of careful IPC dictatorship.

Gethin twisted his grimace into a grin. "If you don't help me now, I won't be around to lead this revolution of yours and—"

"Count to ten," the face intoned, "and then walk to the escalators."

Gethin scanned the busy concourse. He spotted the escalators two hundred meters away.

The moths burst into their individual components and were gone. The air, however, was thickening with something other than holography; sensoramics, like the pegasus and chimera in Athens, only much smaller: butterflies, wasps, hummingbirds. First a few dozen, then dozens of dozens.

With security standing down, the Faustians were hacking every sensoramic in the pyramid.

"Eight seconds," Celeste reported in a flat tone. She was making finely tuned notations of enemy positions. Potential targets leaned against overhead terraces, shop entrances, park benches, and amid the pedestrian traffic.

"Five seconds." Gethin felt himself turning to lead. *What do the Faustians have in mind?* The hacked sensoramics were useless; they would explode harmlessly off an armored soldier.

One second.

He grasped Celeste's wrist and began crossing the courtyard. Instantly, eyes fell on them. A disproportionate number of Caucasians made up the crowd, and they were taking a keen interest in the armed couple strolling past them.

Then the crowd began to cough.

The vents of Shimizu housed fleets of microscopic devices like miniature submarines, programmed to cruise the currents of air viscosity. Not dissimilar to the highly specialized castes of an ant colony, they formed an unseen freeway of nanite cleaners tasked with removing rust, algae, and fungus off struts; nanite warriors to hunt viruses of either organic or mechanical origins; nanite engineers to comb the length of pylons and cables for stress damage; nanite recyclers and processors. There was no arcology on Earth as hive-like, and no people so willing to submerge into the veritable gravity-well of networked intelligence, as the pyramid dwellers of the Rising Sun.

Locals rarely reflected on this invisible, behind-the-scenes traffic. Even if you inhaled a cleaner or sentinel, you might sneeze or piss or belch it out without ever realizing. A single nanite was undetectable.

However, a *cloud* of nanites surging into your airways, acting under the same puppetmaster…that made for a somewhat different prospect.

Like a thunderclap, the loosely disguised Stillness troopers began hacking, clutching their throats, staggering into rock gardens, running about like people chased by bees. One woman dashed from an ice cream parlor, her eyes gouged out and thick jets of bright blood flowing down her cheeks. She raced sightlessly for Celeste and Gethin, crossed their path, and tried to hurl herself to a lower level. Instead, she succeeded only in colliding with the rail. She tumbled backwards and screamed, slapping the floor with her hands.

"*Make it stop! Make it stop!*"

Celeste unholstered her sidearm and blasted the woman's brains onto the tiles. She and Gethin broke into a dash for the escalators. A stampede of men appeared, hollering and shrieking and rushing *down*.

She stepped aside to let them pass…but they didn't pass. They died on the escalators en masse, as nanites burst them from the inside out.

The upper ward was deserted. Sort of. At the end of the corridor was a dead teenager, shotgun in mouth, still clutching the trigger he had pulled moments before. Blood and tissue dripped in a gory nimbus behind him.

Gethin felt sweat again on his upper lip. He went to the door marked CW-0782.

"Override." The word half stuck in his throat.

The door popped open. They went in.

★   ★   ★

They didn't have long to wait. Within ten minutes of the massacre, Ego reported that Gethin's old professor had departed the restaurant by way of the smoking lounge and was proceeding by lift to the CW wing. Heading back to his rented room, presumably. He wouldn't see the horror of the concourse massacre. Just as well.

Or does he somehow know what just happened?

Gethin led Celeste up more escalators, trying to outpace the lift. They reached Doros's hotel room door before the professor did, and Gethin overrode its lock, drew Celeste inside, shut the door.

Only a few minutes later, the door swung inward. Professor Peisistratos, former senator, former paleontologist, former friend, entered the murky suite.

Gethin and Celeste emerged from their shadowed corners, rifles trained on their target. The bearded professor saw them and halted.

"Doros," Gethin began, "kindly take my advice and make no sudden moves."

The professor nodded. Celeste went to the door and drew the dead bolt.

"This is not entirely unexpected, my friend," Doros said. "You remain my friend, no?"

"That depends on your answers."

"Then ask your questions."

Celeste circled the man, keeping him in her rifle sights. "We know you're Apollo the Great," she pronounced.

Doros made no reply.

Gethin exhaled with some force. "Warlord Apollo from four *hundred* years ago. History said you died before immortality was available. I don't know if you *can* die, but you don't need technology to pull your tricks." He tried to see something of the legendary warrior in this fat, bearded, cherubic figure. "The conqueror became a senator, then a teacher full of sage advice and honeyed lies."

"Men lie about their age," the professor said with a shrug. He chanced a smile, resembling an overweight, impish Zeus. "And sometimes their nature too."

"Sophistry won't save you. The IPC believes you're involved with Stillness."

"Do you?"

"No." Gethin lowered the rifle. "Apollo the Great allying with anarchists? Doesn't fit."

"'Anarchists'," Doros quipped unpleasantly, "is woefully inadequate to describe Stillness. Anarchy still implies life."

Gethin gazed at that familiar bearded visage. He remembered the evenings of dinners, drinks, walks, and fiery classroom discussions. He knew every kindly wrinkle in that antiquarian visage.

How do I reconcile this jovial Kris Kringle with the Warlord Apollo, conqueror of nations, founder of one third of the Republic?

"You didn't establish the Republic by yourself," said Gethin. "There are at least two others like you. Enyalios and Lady Wen Ying."

Doros nodded.

"The three of you worked together to end the wars and pull civilization back together. It was part of your grand plan."

"Yes."

"But you have enemies. Like this Apophis."

Hideous thoughts pierced Gethin, and he was afraid to ask his next question, desperate to ask it, though it was Celeste who beat him to it: "Can they be killed?"

"There were once thousands of us. Yes, we can be killed."

Gethin interjected, "What the hell are you? What do you want from any of us?"

The old man took a breath, made up his mind. "Long ago I made something. I'm proud of what I made. I don't want to see it destroyed."

"What did you make?"

"Life." His eyes twinkled in the room's blue-shadowed gloom.

★　　★　　★

Doros's beard was vanishing. It neither pixelated away like a diminishing holo, nor dramatically retreated into his face like reverse footage of follicle growth. Rather, the bushy hair surrounding his mouth lost its distinct outline, like a mist burned away by the rosy-fingered dawn. The professor's face was suddenly as smooth as new leather. He had simply *willed* the hair away.

He was growing too. Taller by inches, as if cybernetic joint extensions were raising the level of his head. His portly torso altered, thinning in places, swelling in others, muscles sprouting along his arms and chest. His hair thickened and flowed over his shoulders. It occurred to Gethin that this manner of shapeshifting was as easy for him as metamorphosing a slouch into an upright posture. His friend's molecules reshaped themselves in swift, nimble metamorphoses.

Celeste gaped. Doros's face was altering, the bones sliding into new configurations. And then she realized.

Warlord Apollo was gazing at her.

The entire transformation had taken mere *seconds*.

<Doros Peisistratos has no detectable wetware,> Ego said, and then added somewhat dejectedly, <I do not understand how this is possible.>

Apollo held out his hands, palms up. "Let me assure you that despite our differences, Gethin, we share a great many things in common. We are both children of *this* world. We oppose those trying to ruin it. In the beginning..."

He gave a start at his choice of words, then he laughed freely. "Yes, that is the *proper* way to explain this, no?"

Celeste swallowed hard. "What the fuck is he, Gethin? Tell me what's going on!"

The air seemed to grow heavier and darker. Apollo was changing again… but this time, into a decidedly non-humanoid form. He collapsed into a mist that billowed around them like tendrils of dry ice. The room's aquamarine carpet wavered into ocean swells; Celeste instinctively tried recoiling from the threat of falling. Gethin grasped her hand, arresting her retreat.

<I do not understand what's happening,> Ego said, falling back to its factory default response.

"I do," Gethin breathed.

Apollo had melted away, yet his voice tickled their ears as if he was standing right beside them. "I need to *show* you the truth. This is my body, memory, and history. This was the Earth when I was born."

The vapors had spread into a radius of several meters. At some hidden command they ignited into mad colors and geometries. Orange-red landmasses blazed and steamed, managing to achieve both translucence and opacity, like stained glass. Gethin gained abrupt new insight into the abilities of this new – or very old – order of life.

They are truly *amorphous beings*, he thought. *They condense their energies into matter when they wish. They project onto that condensate whatever they desire, the non-mechanical equivalent of a holobox drawing a digitized image through the calibrated tangle of laser light.* Apollo was no more a corporal entity than a mythical ghost. He could disperse himself and *become* anything he wanted. Any person. Multiple persons. A quivering mass of tentacles or a burning bush or a living screen.

"Uplink and record," Gethin mumbled on his subvoc channel, and connections were established with Keiko Yamanaka and Donna McCallister.

It was suddenly raining in the Shimizu apartment.

A thick downpour slashed diagonally into the molten landscape below the floor. Apollo's outline manifested amid the deluge, little more than a phantom saturated in the primordial dusk. Geysers of steam erupted, converting the rain into superheated gas. The black sky was split by vermillion lighting.

"Nothing could live in such a place," Gethin muttered.

Apollo's voice snaked into his ear. "Nothing could live *on* such a place, perhaps. But I was born above it."

The view ascended to the sky. Colossal cloudtops rotated in hypercane eddies. They looked like monsters stabbing at each other with electrical lashes. Like sped-up footage of Jupiter on a particularly nasty day, the entire firmament choked by a twisting, churning maelstrom.

"We were born in these clouds," Apollo explained. His voice felt very near, though when Gethin glanced sidelong he only saw Celeste beside him. Gold light played across her face. Two search-beam eyes appeared near her, alighting on her angular jaw, slender throat, catching her eyes in a crystalline glint, and vanished.

"I and the others were the birth of consciousness on Planet Earth. How can I articulate the experience? I became aware. Anticipating Descartes, eh? I gradually discerned my existence, and that of the neighboring globes of plasma around me. The storm was our mother. She birthed the ten thousand thunders that were *us*."

The clouds enkindled. A jellyfish-like shape of a thousand vibrating colors emerged. In time another followed, and then a third, a fourth, a fifth, moving like a shoal of fish drawing together for protection. It reminded Gethin of an aquarium he had seen in the London stalks, where a cylindrical tank displayed jellyfish. Apollo's celestial skycreatures moved like that, exhibited the same organic sense of life...

Then he realized *what* he was seeing.

It was the energy shape that had destroyed Shuttle 3107. The patterned light banking sharply towards Earth. It was the brief, frozen image that had murdered Celeste's squadmates.

Standing abreast of him, Celeste lowered her weapon. "They look like sea creatures," she whispered.

Once, when she was fourteen, she was involved in a lethal knife fight with a neighborhood boy. They had circled each other by a marshy lake of drainage pipes. When her opponent rushed her, Celeste buried her knife in his trachea. The boy staggered backwards, squawking like a duck on the blade, fell into the marsh. She pinned him, crying, until the water turned warm and he had stopped moving. And when it was over, she noticed that the water had life in it: bioluminescent jellies cautiously approaching the corpse, changing color from white to red.

"What are you?" she asked helplessly.

"There was no one to ask," Apollo explained. The voice enfolded her and she whirled one way, then another, trying to see through the illusion. "We existed. Pure consciousness. We fed off electricity in the atmosphere. We learned we could increase in size, or shrink and dissipate. We consumed the energy of the new world like young caterpillars. Self-organizing helical structures as your own species has long noted in dust storms and plasma clouds." The clouds in the vision broke and a hundred of the skycreatures were whirling around an immense, mushroom-shaped cumulonimbus.

Gethin heard Keiko gasp in his head. He had almost forgotten his channel was opened to her.

Apollo materialized, humanoid again, on the far side of the room. He gazed fondly at his illusionary creation. "It must have been millions of years that we existed in this childlike state amid a cooling Earth. The rain began to linger on the planet's surface, sizzling, forming the first boiling rivers, emptying into oceanic basins. As the planet cooled, the atmosphere changed...and our 'birthrate' tapered off. It came to pass that no young ones were forming from

Mother Storm. No new generations. We were the first, and last, of our species."

Gethin noticed Apollo had become Doros again. But thinner, sleeker, an exceptional hybrid of the Doros and Apollo templates.

A vast onyx sea flowered open below, miles beneath the phantom floor. Some of the skycreatures floated as fireflies, draped their tentacles into the boiling surface and appeared to skate along, creating ripples as they glided.

"We had great debates in those days," Apollo continued. "The world was changing. Cooling. Becoming solid. We discussed the implications of this. We speculated on how far it would go, wondered if the same process of creation had occurred on other worlds…the worlds we could see above the cloud towers."

"You went into space," Gethin said without thinking, and then recalled the shuttle footage again. *Yes, they can go into space. They swim up from the Earth's surface to the moon, perhaps even beyond. Gravity doesn't hold them.*

"We never strayed far," Apollo said, and gave his impish grin. "Space is terrifying, Gethin. There are no maps there. To enter its domain is to be cast adrift on a wine-dark eternity, a gulf of endless emptiness and cold stars. Earth is the blue mother in a nightmare of isolation. She is the Middle Kingdom, the jade heart, the home turf, and the cosmic womb. Beyond her waits the terror of constellations and worlds." His grin deepened into a grandfatherly affection. "*You* are the only species to connect the stars in constellations and imagine friendly, far-distant shores."

McCallister muttered something in Gethin's head. He silenced her with a sweep of his hand.

Apollo continued. "Fearful of the Void, some of us plunged into the ocean to investigate. We descended into the murk, stroking the softly glowing sea bottom, charting the terrain of valleys and marine mountains, the cones of volcanic activity, the shapes of permanence. How different this was! Permanence! The heavens were a pot of endless protean formation by contrast. And then, after uncounted eons, we realized that the ocean had become infested with tiny shapes."

"The first organisms," Celeste whispered.

Apollo's eyes revived into search-beam incandescence. "*We* had created them. Without realizing it, of course. The touch of our plasma bodies in that mineral stew must have sparked the bonding of self-replicating protein structures. Accidental and beautiful. Word spread, others followed our precedent. For many of us, it brought renewed excitement to a wearied world."

"But not all felt that way," Gethin guessed.

"There were those among us who considered the formation of life—"

"The Permian Extinction…"

Apollo faded away, expressing a kind of grim anguish in the act. "Some of us considered life to be an infection, that those responsible had contaminated the world's purity. They said we had ruined the natural state of things. That we had brought chaos into the *stillness of the universe.*"

Celeste felt cold needles hatch all over her body.

"It was a suggestion at first," said Apollo's voice. "Then a belief that sired conviction that sired dreadful action. The oceans were teeming with life by then. Tendril-weeds, petalled flowers growing on lilypads, fish staring with unblinking glassy eyes. Our debates turned angry. Once again the heavens shook with thunder, and our society divided into three groups."

Gethin jerked his gaze away from the coalescing patterns of sea creatures. "Three?"

The images fell away like a curtain and the room returned, shadow-drenched and dull. Apollo was a lonely figure again, dressed in drab monastic garments, arms folded across his chest, head shaven in a cross between devout Zen Buddhist and Trappist ascetic. "One group," Apollo explained, "considered life a natural development, just another branch of the cosmic tree which had produced us. The universe was constantly changing and life was but a symptom of that change. Another group opposed this. A third group took no sides in the debate at all, instead proclaiming that we had lost sight of a grander quest to fly out from the wombworld and investigate the stars. They reasoned that we were not alone, that atmospheric conditions of other planets must have repeated this miracle. They wished to seek them out."

Apollo approached Gethin and took his hands. In three steps Apollo was dressed as an early twentieth-century tycoon, pencil-thin moustache and neatly side-combed hair. "The third group – call them the Farseekers – made a reasonable suggestion. They would travel to the nearby worlds of the solar system and seek other intelligences if they existed; an attempt at finding an outside mediator. The Farseekers departed for Mars and Venus and Jupiter…worlds we knew not by name but by luminosity and position in the dappled night sky."

"They never returned, did they?" Celeste guessed.

"No," Apollo said. "And neither did we wait for them. Some of the purists had begun exterminating life in the seas, and others tried to stop them."

"How?"

Two patterned globes of energy blinked into the room suddenly, darting across the foyer through the living room. They stabbed at each other with pulses of crimson light. Each impact blew off jellylike tatters where they struck. The quarreling lights fled into the far wall and vanished.

"I don't think any of us realized we could kill each other. Our earliest battles were simply attempts at cowing one another, dominating so one set of beliefs could prevail in the world. But when we realized murder was possible – the concept so new, understand – the war became terrible and savage. Enough wounds can shatter us so we are unable to reconstitute. The helical scaffolding whirls apart. We can soak incredible damage, but there is a threshold that, once crossed, disperses us."

Apollo moved to the liquor cabinet and retrieved a flagon. He poured a drink. Gethin approached and before he could say anything, Apollo handed the drink to him.

"My side won that first war," he said. "There were terrible losses, but by the end we were the last ones standing, so to speak. Life was free to develop undisturbed. It moved to land and we wandered among it. We mimicked them. We tried our hand at terrestrial society. We lived as reptiles and insects and plants. Experience was our religion. We killed, mated, dined, died...only to shed our mortal coils and return to heaven."

Gethin gave the glass of liquor an absent consideration. He handed it to Celeste. She placed it, untouched, on the nearest counter.

"Then the dinosaurs were killed off," Apollo said with a sigh.

"Your enemies again?" Celeste asked.

"An asteroid. A chance billiard ball from space. We were so involved with our earthly experiences that we had ceased paying attention to space. Life had gotten interesting. A civilization had sprouted among the Troodons." He laughed at Gethin's expression. "Yes, I *saw* it and *lived* among them. Their culture lasted a million years before death came from above..."

"But they left no cities..."

"They left *many* cities," Apollo admonished. "But *different* from what you would build. Natural materials. Stone, wood, iron...they really never progressed beyond their Iron Age. But the comparison isn't fair. They created technologies no human culture would. They recorded their stories in pottery played by sunbeams. They had musical instruments of crystal and water. Oh! Their music! Haunting melodies of terrible majesty sung to rituals of fire.

"Their extermination devastated me. I wandered the deathly world of ash, taking small solace in the rodents that emerged from burrows to feast on the dead beasts. And in that grisly twilight, our enemies returned. This time, they coordinated their vengeance not against terrestrial life, but against *us*. It was a hateful, relentless battle. Eventually, we seemed to have won again, yet a Pyrrhic victory it was, reducing us to a meager handful. Three! Our enemies were likewise reduced, dead or licking their wounds deep in the Earth."

Apollo bowed his head, quiet for such a stretch of time that Gethin thought he had fallen asleep. In that silence, Keiko's voice came into his head:

"Ask him how they can be destroyed, Gethin. We have to know how to *kill them!*"

Jack's voice countered, "Let him finish telling our history, for gods' sake!"

Apollo looked up. "Even I didn't appreciate the small, dwarfish ape-things in the African trees. Who knew *they* would become masters of the world? The world had sprung back from reptilian holocaust to a time of fur, tusks, and mammalian claws. And so here we stand."

The visions faded. The room returned in drab, blue gloom.

Gethin was breathless.

"Your enemies have returned," Celeste prompted. "At least two of them are back."

Apollo smiled. "But I have friends, as well. Come with me to the gardens. I have someone I'd like you to meet."

CHAPTER FORTY-EIGHT
Peacemaker and Warbringer

King D. set a playdisk of popular music in the Sinkiang underdark while he excused himself to use the lavatory. The troops cheered and danced to the tunes, slapping each other on the backs, forming circles to clap in delight. Nor could Father Chadwick complain; this was not bland arky music, but the pounding, vivacious rhythms of mortality. The soldiers were mostly young too, and they grinned in lustful delight to the stirring bass echoing off cavern walls.

Near the inclinator, two bathrooms had been cut into the rock wall. The stalls were dirty, and the toilet tissue was like sandpaper, but King D. didn't care. A newsfeed piped into the caves with an incredible report: The *IPCS Nobunaga,* crippled into a deteriorating orbit by Promethean Furies, had just exploded over Canada.

And so ends the Pax Apollonia!

How to exploit this? King D. contemplated his reflection in the streaked and dirty mirror while he washed his hands.

There were sixty regen centers on Earth. StrikeDown, for its part, possessed nine low-yield antimatter missiles and six tactical nukes, already loaded onto its invisible shapestone fleet positioned carefully throughout the world. Their captains had the attack schedule. Six nukes for major Save centers. The resulting megadeaths would be routed to the nearest backups.

It was then King D. would use his antimatter stash. By then, the arkies should be gibbering with panic, eager to meet his simple demands: the end of the apartheid. No more Wastes, but a free and open world to all.

King D. realized that he had been scrubbing his hands raw. He twisted the faucet, blotted his hands on his pants, and left the bathroom.

His sensorium flashed with an incoming call.

"Celeste," he muttered. "I'm sorry, but I'm not at the rendezvous yet. Something came up and I have an intense negotiation going on now."

"Can you spare a minute?" she asked quietly.

"Go ahead."

"Did you recover the missiles?"

"Funny you should ask. I'm meeting with the High Priests of Stillness right now. We're all waiting to see how this IPC thing plays out."

Her voice was edgy. "Can StrikeDown work without them?"

"The missiles? Sure. It'll work better than ever," he said, still weighing his options. "War is good for us. They'll be so busy looking at each other that our attack will come like a knockout uppercut."

"That's why I'm calling. Peace is being brokered. If I read this right, the IPC and Prometheus are about to turn their collective focus on the Wastes and go after Stillness for good."

King D. chewed over this.

Celeste was still talking. "Did you hear me? If you're hanging with Stillness, you better get out *now*."

"I need to speak with Father Apophis first."

Silence descended on Celeste's end. "Apophis? That thing on the moon?"

He laughed. "Just a coincidence, I'm sure."

"No, you're not," she snapped. "Something important has happened, D. I don't have time to explain it. I don't know how much of it I believe. But you can't be with Stillness when shit goes down. I...*oh my God!*"

"Celeste?"

The call ended.

"Celeste!"

CHAPTER FORTY-NINE
Midas Hand

The Sea Gardens of Shimizu were a tropical delight of bright flowers and green bramble. It was the usual port to receive diplomats and VIPs when they arrived at the pyramid. The floral wonderland of bamboo forests drank from desalinated streams. Lilypads drifted on a mirror-perfect pond.

The moment Gethin stepped into the gardens, however, he was stricken with tension.

As if to confirm this, McCallister's voice sounded in his ear: "Cameras have gone dead! Gethin? Do you hear me? The cameras in the gardens have blacked out!"

He nervously cleared his throat. Apollo strode ahead with steely confidence.

When they rounded the circuitous rock garden, Gethin spied a lone figure waiting for them. She stood by a patch of chinaberries, displaying herself as a woman of surreal height and shape. Gethin gauged her at eight feet tall…but her body was stretched out like a warped reflection. Her arms were like ropes. Her hips were narrow to the point of absurdity. Small-chested, with a neck like a swan, her head elongated and oval. Gethin had only witnessed such freakish appearances on ancient Cycladic statues.

As if this appearance wasn't unsettling enough, the mystery woman had elected to display skin the color of real bronze. Under the garden lights, that unearthly carapace glinted in a burnished sheen, and the face she wore set Gethin's heart thrilling with panic. Her features might be called elegant, even lovely, but for their nightmarish distortion of length.

She looks like a humanoid praying mantis, he thought. His stomach contracted in a nervous spasm. If not for Apollo's fearless approach to this *thing*, Gethin knew he would be running for the nearest exit.

Apollo, for his part, seemed bemused by it all.

"May I present Lady Wen Ying," he said, grinning. "My co-founder of Earth Republic."

Gethin felt the color drain from his face.

Here was the second component of the trilobed world government. The aftereffects of the Final War had been especially brutal in Asia; with China's central government nuked, the sprawling region collapsed into bloody despotisms not seen since the Warring States period. The Dragon Kingdom bled from hundreds of wounds hatched within and without, while the surrounding nations of Thailand, Vietnam, Japan, India, and Korea found themselves embroiled in a tidal surge of vicious border disputes and resource wars.

And then Lady Wen Ying arrived.

It was during the same decades as Apollo the Great's campaigns in Europe and Africa. Historians shrugged at the coincidental timing; Gethin now saw that Apollo's faction had deliberately coordinated it under the guise of political hegemony. Lady Wen Ying was believed to have arrived from the north and, like northern hordes of another age, delivered a single Mandate of Heaven. Like her counterpart in Europe, strange powers were ascribed to her, assassins repeatedly failed to kill her, traps proved unable to contain her. The Mandate was hers.

Gethin gaped at this figure of legend. Unlike Apollo, there were never definitive images of the elusive Lady Wen Ying. Depending on the source, Wen Ying was a stocky milk-white *yakuza* ruler; a tall green-clad Chinese empress; a brown-skinned CEO in a sleek business suit; a scarred Mongolian horsespider rider; or a simple peasant clad like a rice-field worker.

She had *never* appeared as this freakish apparition.

Lady Wen Ying tilted her insectile head at their approach. "Friends of Doros in an hour of need?"

Apollo grinned. "Tiamat's allies are operating publicly. So shall we."

"Why now?" Gethin asked. "If you've beaten these things in the past, why would they reveal themselves so openly? Why not lurk in the shadows and try assassinating you?"

His old friend looked thoughtful. "The creatures known as Apophis and Tiamat have infiltrated Stillness. Likely, they founded the movement in the Warlord Century. They're clever and resourceful, and their plans unfold over millennia. And they have been unwittingly aided by your species' own inventiveness."

"The cathode rail on Luna," Gethin guessed.

The two entities shared a look. They seemed to be passing messages with their eyes. And maybe they were; Gethin considered the millions of years their breed must have communicated without voice, flashing messages across the stormy skies of primordial Earth.

"We don't precisely know," Apollo conceded at last. "But let us consider what we *do* know: our enemies despise life and seek its total, final extermination. Their manual efforts have failed them. But you—"

"We believe," Lady Wen Ying interrupted smoothly, "that our enemies have endeavored to apply the best technologies from your civilization to their purposes. In the past they attempted genocide through painstakingly localized attacks, showering life in lethal energies. Burning it away inch by inch. Far too ineffective."

Apollo gave a very human sigh. "Humans have changed the battlefield. Nuclear weapons, bioweapons, antimatter, plagues…Tiamat views intelligent life as the worst affront, you see, but his plans now depend on you."

"How many of these twisted creatures are left?" demanded Celeste.

"Three of them. Three of us." He was suddenly Doros again. His beard flowered out of his chin, his stature shrank. "We are the last."

Celeste prompted, "Stillness is collecting antimatter. That would cause a hell of a lot of destruction, but it wouldn't exterminate life."

Apollo moved to the bamboo trees and stared absently at their rigid stalks. "There are ways...in theory..."

Gethin watched his face. "You and your allies had a meeting in Arcadia. You mentioned your enemies might be constructing a Midas Hand." He spun around to Celeste with real panic in his eyes. "That's why they wanted the antimatter missiles *and* the cathode rail."

She didn't follow him, but his burst of fear was contagious. "What is a Midas Hand?" she asked helplessly.

It was Apollo who answered. "Some of us theorized long ago that it might be possible, knowing what we did about the nature of matter and energy. But there was never a technological means to..."

Gethin picked up from his friend. "A Midas Hand is a hypothetical device which acts as a switch. It can 'flip' matter into antimatter and vice versa. Just think of it: turn one half of a planet into antimatter and disintegrate everything. Absolutely...everything."

Something strange and cruel happened in Celeste's eyes, but Gethin barely noticed. He found himself reflecting, most unexpectedly, of his childhood in the stalks of London's arcology. Of waking up early with the spectral light of a rainy morning at his bedroom window, the horizon engulfed in milky fog, the metallic canopy of Upper City blotting out the firmament. Dad and Mom in the kitchen sharing coffee, enjoying the precious minutes they had together before work. It came to him as a crashing wall of anguish, the acute realization of how much would be lost and how fragile the world was.

And the shuttle explosion! Great stars! *The missing ingredient to apocalypse must have passed through my body on that shuttle!*

Apollo looked weary. "Gethin, there is so much more to tell, but now..."

Lady Wen Ying touched his shoulder. She was grinning, and the air was suddenly uncomfortably hot and pregnant with danger.

Something happened in Apollo's eyes. The moment of contact from his lady friend triggered an awful realization.

"Eris!" he cried.

Gethin wasn't certain what happened next. Dimly he realized he was flying outwards from where he had been standing. His eyes stung with whiteness, there was a vibration that implied sound, and then he crashed through bramble. His skin felt like it had been scrubbed off his body with a grater.

He blinked, felt his face with slow, groping fingers.

Whiteness. Searing and painful.

He was blind.

In his ears, voices were speaking in short, panicky tones. He couldn't make out the language being used; the pain in his skin soaked all his attention. But he realized there was a horrifying storm raging around him, bursts of hot air and thunder.

"Gethin!" Keiko screamed through his sensorium. "What's happening? *What's happening?*"

He tried to stand. His feet tripped over a heavy, immovable object. Then Celeste's rough hands were on him, dragging him backwards, and her strained voice came to his ear. "Gethin! Can you hear me?"

Strange shapes began to materialize in his vision. Fuzzy, indistinct, gyrating shadows behind a murky veil. He heard rapid-fire explosions and sonic booms.

"Celeste?" he asked. "My eyes…"

His vision began to focus. Red lights flashed in his sensorium, advising him of first-degree burns to sixty percent of his body. He discerned the Outlander, her scarlet hair, and the gardens over her shoulder. Depth perception returned and with it he saw Apollo, like a crushed bug beneath the pincers of a giant praying mantis.

The entity that had passed itself off as the great Lady Wen Ying had increased in size and transformation, and she hung over her victim with the triumphant glee of an alpha predator. In the explosion's aftermath, she had sprouted a half dozen pincers, lancing Apollo's torso and limbs like pins through a butterfly. He was trying to dissolve away into mist, but somehow she held him steady…her pincers glowing. Apollo shivered in place, attempting to vanish; each time, he was yanked back into solid form.

And his body! It was burning away beneath her terrible pincers. Fading to translucence…

His attacker leered. She drew near as Apollo strained against her. Here was a grotesque mockery of the female mantis, in the orgiastic moment of copulation, a half second before decapitating her mate.

Eris, Gethin thought. *That was the name of the last of the High Priests of the Outlands, the ones who had unified Stillness into a persistent threat.*

Only she, like Tiamat and Apophis, was much more than that.

Apollo attempted again to dissolve in her grip. The phalanx of pincers flashed, keeping him in place. He continued to fade.

She's devouring him, he thought, numb with panic. *She's gorging on his soul.*

McCallister was screaming in Gethin's ear, but he couldn't bring himself to look away from the awful scene. Eris sprouted new pincers to aid in her hideous evisceration.

"You killed her?" Apollo was saying, dissolving into vapor. "You killed Lady Wen Ying?"

"As I will consume you too," the creature hissed above him. "Vulnerant omnes, ultima necat, no?"

Apollo glared weakly. He was a glass ghost, curls blushed with gold, marble muscles taut where she impaled him.

And he was whispering something. Like a dying man needfully offering prayers to any god that would listen.

Gethin amped up his hearing. The crackling energies of the two entities swelled into a buzzing, discordant cacophony.

And through it, he caught what Apollo was saying.

"*Sy'hoss'a!*"

It seemed that a meteor flashed through the room. It struck Eris headlong, ripping her off her victim. One moment Eris was there, and the next she was gone and the eastern wall of the gardens was a gaping hole leading out to sea.

There, on the marine horizon, two plasma clouds were spinning in hideous embrace. One was clearly still Eris – Gethin amped his optics and made out her mantis-like shape. But a caged mantis she was, since a larger cloud of charged particles had surrounded her with imprisoning tentacles. Her attacker enfolded her, the tentacles burning into her 'body', and Eris shrieked. Forked red lightning crackled between them.

For an instant, Eris broke free of her assailant and dove for the ocean. The larger cloud snapped out tentacles and caught her before she could submerge, halting her escape so abruptly that the seawater dimpled as if hit with a jet of high-pressure air.

"Gethin!" Celeste cried behind him.

He tore his gaze from the sea battle and gazed onto a protean haze. Freed from his attacker, Apollo the Great was trying to reconstitute into a tangible structure again. The haze compressed into a vaguely humanoid silhouette – flesh appearing, a hint of a face – only to whirl apart. Clever geometries of willpower reverting to formlessness.

"*No!*" Gethin cried, driven by instinct to help this defiance against oblivion. He rushed into the mist; the charged air caused the hair on his arms to stand up. He smelled the clean odor of ozone.

Out at sea, Eris gave a screech unlike anything Gethin had ever heard. She – *it* – attempted another piteous dive to the sanctuary of the ocean. Once more, its opponent caught it, yanked it back into a firestorm of plasma. Flaming debris tattered and sloughed off Eris's body like party streamers, sizzling, collapsing, into the Pacific.

"*Gethin.*"

The voice hummed by his ears, felt more than heard.

"*You must find where Apophis and Tiamat are hiding. If they have indeed created a Midas Hand…*"

"I don't know where they are!" Gethin said helplessly, running the possibilities in his head. He unmuted McCallister and told her to conduct an aggressive search of all known Stillness hideouts.

Celeste stepped into the mist, breathing hard. She took a breath and said, "Tiamat? Apophis? I know where they *both* are."

The ancient entity made another attempt at human form. Again, it whirled apart, only this time managed to create an aetherial countenance in the mist.

Outside, Eris gave one final ululation for mercy. Gethin didn't want to look, hating it absolutely in that instant. But Celeste tugged and pointed. Eris burst like a fiery piñata. Only a single entity hovered over the sea.

"You realize who that has to be, right?" Celeste said. "Maybe we should get the hell out of—"

The entity hovered over the rolling waves. It had grown luminous, and very much like images of jellyfish, its tendrils draping loosely.

Then it vanished.

And reappeared in the chamber with them.

Gethin and Celeste were knocked aside as the jellyfish-thing materialized around Apollo. It grew new limbs to offer a loving embrace...as if trying to manually keep Apollo from total dissolution.

Gethin pulled himself back to his feet. "Will he die?" he asked. "Please tell us if there's something we can do! Please..."

He trailed off, as the jellyfish transformed, midair, into a festering wall of malefic eyes, burning with lunatic fury.

And then it was upon him.

CHAPTER FIFTY
Dealing with the Devil

King D. didn't worry about being assaulted in the caves. He rarely worried about being assaulted at all; the streets of Odessa were a tough place, and he had climbed its pecking order through brutal acts of survival. He figured he could clobber a dozen Stillness purity-freaks without tapping more than an ampule of the tech marketplace distributed throughout his body.

He wasn't worried, therefore, when a shadowy shape intercepted him as he returned from the lavatories.

His bodyguards were a different story. They darted in, shieldfists snapping open to create a glassy barricade around him. As the shields linked, King D. stared through them to the shape.

Father Apophis himself.

"Stand down!" King D. barked to his retinue. The shields retracted. He bowed in apology. "Father Apophis? I am deeply embarrassed by this. My guards are jumpy in the best of times. Please forgive me."

The High Priest smiled pleasantly. "You are forgiven, honored visitor."

"Wait for me at the junction," D. told his guards. They moved off, six men and one woman, like scolded, shaken children.

He abruptly understood their shame and confusion. They must have swept this corridor for intruders. Their optics were so finely tuned that they could zero in on a single gnat...

So where the fuck had the High Priest come from? A secret passage?

"Your Grace," King D. began. "I am honored by your presence."

"And I'm honored by yours! We honor each other!"

This was the nearest King D. had ever been to the upper brass of these maniacs. He knew what his field operatives knew: the fundamentalists claimed leadership by an unusual triumvirate: Father Apophis, Father Tiamat, and Mother Eris. In all probability, the three were merely the public face of the movement, while an underground cabal made the strategic decisions.

Apophis's proximity was such that the StrikeDown prince could see pores in the man's nose. "You read my proposal?" D. inquired.

"I did."

"I urge you to consider it in the face of our common enemies."

Apophis wore green vestments that he had personalized with curious markings and snakelike glyphs. "Tiamat has no intention of returning your missiles," the priest said flatly.

"I see," King D. said.

"Do you, indeed?"

"Yes," the StrikeDown leader replied, abandoning the pretense of diplomacy. "I see plainly that Stillness is in the hands of a true fanatic, and unless you are prepared to defy your master, we have little else to say to one another."

Apophis smacked his lips. "You can't possibly believe that a cache of well-aimed missiles will bring the InterPlanetary Council to its knees. They have built their very foundation on the status quo: solidarity against the common enemy of the Outlands. You won't change that with your meager resources. Better men than you have tried."

"You underestimate the power of fear," King D. replied with conviction.

"Ha!" Apophis staggered back, genuinely amused. "Fear is my specialty! And yes, it is a most powerful tool indeed. But *you* hardly have the means to exploit it, sir."

"We disagree," King D. replied, noting the odd grace with which Apophis had moved. The fucker was certainly a lanky specimen of man, but he possessed an unsettlingly feral agility. A martial artist could move like that. Fluid, almost like a cloud.

"Then let us return to where we agree," Apophis said evenly, and there was something obscenely flattering in his voice. "The overthrow of the system. Earth Republic cut off at the knees."

King D. kept his voice neutral. "I'm listening."

"That *is* what you desire, yes?"

"You know it is."

"What if resources were no longer a consideration?"

"How so?"

Apophis stroked his lengthy chinbeard. "Suppose, for only a minute, that your strategy did not depend on missiles. Pretend with me. Let us imagine that there existed a wellspring of limitless energy, granting you the freedom to focus on strategy itself. No supply lines to be cut. No mills to be pillaged. A wellspring of power for you to tap, unendingly?"

D. felt his impatience mounting. "Sophistry. Why waste our time this way, Your Grace? There *are* no limitless wellsprings."

"Allow me to rephrase. If I were to offer you an energy source vast enough to accomplish your objectives, what precisely would that be worth to you?"

"I'd have the resources I need if Father Tiamat would cooperate!" King D. let his anger show at last. "This is how rebellions fail...through in-fighting and ego-driven games." He regained control, looking past the priest. His bodyguard Lalania was visibly tuning in to the argument. "I fear we have nothing more to say to one another."

King D. stalked away, cursing what had to be done now. There was no alternative. The missiles were on site and a group of fanatics stood in his way.

He would send his bodyguards to kill them all. It would be messy. Costly. Yet he could not afford to let these weapons *sit in a cave*...not with war breaking out.

D. was halfway to his guards when Apophis was in front of him again.

"*King* D," the High Priest sang, looking more amused than ever.

The StrikeDown leader froze. *What the hell?*

"You *must* permit me to finish," Apophis chastised. "I do not idly approach people with the offer I'm about to make."

Lalania was already coming down the hallway, ready for business. D. stopped her with an outstretched hand.

"Then tell me more," he managed, stricken by this unsettling display of teleportation. For a superstitious moment, he wondered if this holy man was somehow the same terrorist on Luna. He had joked about it on the way over, he and his bodyguards. But beyond sharing the same name – a sheer coincidence, certainly – the terrorist and this lanky priest looked nothing alike.

But thinking it, he suddenly realized that there *was* a vague resemblance. Both sported a Middle Eastern swarthiness, and the same oil-black hair. Still, the Williams Sports Dome was two hundred and thirty-nine thousand miles away. It couldn't be the same man.

Could it?

Apophis steered him by the arm, down the corridor and into a branching passageway. King D.'s audio crackled with Lalania's worried voice, but he muted her.

He went into an alcove.

And froze in place, his heart flipping around in astonishment.

The missiles! They were here!

★　　★　　★

The room transformed as they stood there.

A contraption unlike anything King D. had ever seen remained the nexus of the rocky alcove, sporting its eccentric array of metallic quills. But the missiles! Six antimatter missiles were set into the chamber's pillars, which, King D. noted, were not for engineered architectural support but rather as...what? Power generators for the weird-ass machine? Cables snaked into it like umbilical cords.

As Father Apophis stood beside him, however, the reliquary changed. The scuffed granite walls blushed into sandstone. Fresh paint materialized on the rock face, slithered into hieroglyphic friezes of cats, falcons, decorative papyrus trees, and herons. The air flooded with rich, honeyed light hailing from a source King D. couldn't discern.

Only the machine was unchanged. A static fixture. As constant as a fabled time machine.

Indeed, for the first few seconds of this metamorphosis King D. wondered if it *was* a time machine. What else could the goddamn thing be? How could this room transform itself so radically, and without any indication of sensoramics, holos, or vidveils? Father Apophis couldn't be hacking his optics; he had powered them down. Then he realized that even if it *was* a time machine, that wouldn't explain the Egyptian motif; if they were shuttling backwards several thousand years in China, they would still be in *China,* not in this openly Egyptian locale.

Without warning, someone else was standing in the chamber with them.

"Father Tiamat," King D. said, bowing, struggling to contain his awe and confusion.

High Priest Tiamat didn't so much as glance in his direction. He was as blocky as Apophis was lean; in fact, the man gave the impression of deformity in a manner that wasn't immediately apparent. King D. squirmed uneasily.

Tiamat fixed an impatient wintry stare on Apophis. "We do not need your distractions right now."

Apophis shrugged and, still walking, transformed. His Stillness robe flowered into a new design – or rather, a very very old one. He was abruptly clad in a golden cloak, his face painted like some demented clown. A cobra-topped crown adorned his head.

"Promethean forces have attacked an IPC military outpost," he said. "With the *Nobunaga* burning up, now is the time for our test."

"I know that," Tiamat snapped, and King D. realized the man had neither eyebrows nor ears. But hadn't he had both a moment ago? And why...

The High Priest disintegrated into a nebulous mass of colors that, oddly, resembled some kind of massive ribbonfish or centipede. Maybe a jellyfish.

"My God," King D. whispered.

Apophis seated himself before a control panel at the front of the contraption. "I was thinking of the IPC base in Madrid. What do you think, King D.? There's a Save center there. Good enough for a test? Yes?"

Tiamat's voice came from every direction at once. "Proceed."

Apophis bowed his head. He threw a switch.

A hundred red beams erupted from the machine's quills and pierced the Tiamat-thing as if with pencil-thin, flaming spears. His mercurial jellyfish body jerked and twisted in the trap.

There were no nerve endings in the children of storm. They had never known pain, not even when they assumed physical forms. Masters of pattern, they rarely saw any need to grow a functioning nervous system, or bother filling their ersatz veins with blood, or stuffing their bodies with fleshy specialized organs.

The only pain the children of storm knew, in fact, was the psychological terror of oblivion. It afflicted even those who advocated the return of lifelessness. The horror of losing oneself.

Penetrated by the beams, Tiamat shrieked and caught fire.

"Apophis!" Tiamat's flashing, vaporous form cried. "*What's happening?*"

The titan attempted to flee the bars of red light. They held him fast. He batted against the sandstone walls, screeching in betrayal, transforming into a six-headed reptilian creature, growing leathery wings, vomiting caustic flame at Apophis through the web of light. But the fire never left the containment field. The colorless flames ricocheted off the luminous cross sections and blew back into Tiamat himself.

He began to break into fiery, sizzling streamers.

"I have finally accepted that I differ with you," Apophis announced, wondering if Tiamat's consciousness was anything more than a soup of thrashing electrons now, flying apart in the phantom impulses of willpower, surrendering to implacable, superheated chaos. "Your philosophy no longer suits me. Embrace the light of nirvana. Ashes to ashes, dust to dust, plasma to plasma. I bid you farewell, my beloved friend!"

His friend cried in a thousand voices.

King D. staggered backwards, sick.

"*Apophis!*" Tiamat cried, and then the voice cut out as his ever-changing body burst apart, raining fiery scraps that vanished as if they had never been.

For his part, Apophis gazed at the disintegrating fireball. He didn't smile or show any expression except for the glint in his eyes. The effect was precisely as he had expected…and yet strangely beautiful as well.

Beautiful. So very beautiful…as was everything in life.

Apophis disengaged the device. The beams cut out. The only evidence of Father Tiamat's existence was garlands of swiftly dissipating smoke.

King D. realized his mouth was dry.

Apophis grinned wickedly at him. "Where were we? Ah yes! You desire equality among the peoples of Earth. I shall satisfy that wish. Listen *closely*."

CHAPTER FIFTY-ONE
Warlord Enyalios

In the ruined Shimizu Gardens, Gethin expected to die. There was just enough time to realize that death would come at the hands of the most ruthless mass murderer in the history of history…the man who was not a man after all… the unifier of two continents…the tyrant who had conquered the Americas by butchering the Americas themselves.

The wall of furious eyes rushed him.

And then, without warning, Gethin felt arms draw protectively around him.

"Do not harm them, my friend."

The cloud of eyes sprouted razor claws and many mouths. The air was oven-hot; Gethin's nanonics were functioning, and he was alarmed to realize that his own body temperature was spiking. 103 degrees! 104!

"Sy'hoss'a, these are allies. They are not to be killed. Please."

105 degrees. 106. Gethin heard the popping of capillaries in his eyes.

And then, just as easily, the heat diminished. The nightmare thing floating in front of him changed into a nebulous cloud, its killing mood, perhaps, passing away for now.

Great stars! Gethin rubbed his injured eyes. His fingertips came away wet with blood.

Celeste glistened in sweat; by the luminous creature floating in the air, she glittered as if powdered in diamond dust. "We're not here to harm you. We couldn't even if we wanted to," she said.

"Is Eris dead?" Gethin said stupidly. He knew the answer. He couldn't think of anything else to say.

Warlord Enyalios assumed human form then, the cloud distilling into arms and legs and head and chest. *Yes, it really is Enyalios.* Gethin and Celeste gazed in unabashed shock at this figure of history returned to life.

Enyalios, for his part, paced with the cagey energy of a sabertooth in a throwback zoo. The Shimizu Gardens were rubble, melted plastic, and scorched leaves. The sea breeze blew in through the gaping hole in the windows, smelling of salt and rotting kelp.

"She is purged," the mad Warlord hissed.

Apollo appeared faintly. "They have a Midas Hand, Sy'hoss'a. Celeste knows where they are. She can lead us there, yes?"

Celeste couldn't find her voice. She managed a stiff nod.

Enyalios whirled towards her, looking savage and dangerous, eager for violence. "*Where are they?*"

"The High Priests are in a mountain retreat in China."

Enyalios looked to his friend. "You can't go, Hy'ala." He lapsed into a rapid staccato tongue that matched nothing Ego had on record. Apollo replied in the same forgotten language. It was clear they were talking about Apollo's health; he was, quite literally, barely holding himself together.

In the end, Apollo made some parting shot and Enyalios stormed away, solemn and angry but grudgingly compliant.

"You're sending us with him, aren't you?" Gethin asked Apollo. "Jesus Christ, Doros…I mean…whatever your name really is."

"It was never Jesus Christ," Apollo said, and suddenly he was the ghost of Doros Peisistratos standing there, looking corpulent and impish.

Gethin swallowed. "Is there anything we can do to help you recover? *Can* you recover?"

The professor-shape ignored the question. "Enyalios will go with you to China. He has agreed to defer to your judgment and command. You must understand how difficult that is for him." The ancient being smiled weakly. "Oh, and he agreed not to kill you."

Celeste gave a nod. "That was nice of him."

"It was necessary. Sy'hoss'a has never cared much for the human race. To him, you are still rats crawling in the sewers of long-forgotten troodon cities." Apollo drew a painful sigh and his color shifted like sunlight through a spectrum, apple-red to evening-blue, and then to nothing at all.

Gethin and Celeste shared a look.

"I guess we're going, then," she said, and turned to Enyalios.

But Enyalios was gone.

CHAPTER FIFTY-TWO
Hanmura3's Last Call

Aboard his airship high in the Swiss sky, Sakyo Hanmura3 imagined himself as an orchestra conductor as he manipulated a 360-degree wraparound of holopanels. They were like overlapping sheets of tinted glass, marked for a dozen recipients and in various stages of composition. Hanmura3 fervently rotated to each, dispatching commands and listening to reports from his advisory boards on three worlds. His actions would decide the future of his company. There was no way around it: Hanmura Enterprises could not afford to stay neutral in the burgeoning conflict.

And that window of opportunity was already zipping shut. A Promethean bitch named Keiko Yamanaka was skillfully positioning herself as peace broker, and the cunt had seen fit to fire a very public salvo at *his* company. Claiming that Hanmura Enterprises was behind the attack on the PI offshore rig.

How the hell did she know?

He pushed aside the question. There was a far more pressing matter. An issue of longer term consideration.

His other self on Luna, Hanmura2, had already warned him about a creature calling itself Apophis. Hanmura2's email dripped with fear and irrationality, referencing ancient Japanese gods and evil trickster spirits. Great stars! Hanmura3 figured his other self was fraying.

After all, there were no gods or trickster *hengeyokai*. This Apophis was just a brilliantly calibrated psychological strike from either Bielawa and/or Gates, and Hanmura3 grudgingly admitted that the trick had been most effective. His other self was a wreck; private messages disorganized, repeating the refrain of universal cooperation against the 'real enemy'.

I must have gone batshit insane, he thought, struggling to contain the fear that if his Lunar counterpart was now psychotic, then he himself was potentially psychotic, given the right jab.

Hanmura3 gave a long, musical sigh. The important thing now was to publicly discredit this Keiko Yamanaka. He needed to harness the public's emotional reactionism, remind them that a *Promethean lab* had been destroyed, a *Promethean memo* warned of dangerous experiments, a *Promethean monster* admitted its origins. Why listen to a *Promethean cunt*? The truth didn't matter. Victory was the only goal that—

One of his screens flashed an incoming message. Hanmura3 touched it open. A black silhouette appeared.

"Hanmura-sama?" the silhouette asked.

The great man glared. "Who is this? How did you get this—"

"Am I speaking to the Sakyo Hanmura on Mars, or the one on Luna, or perhaps the one on Earth?"

The CEO felt his blood turn to cold slush. Before he could muster a reply, his mysterious caller gave a sickeningly wet cough lasting several seconds. It might have been a sound-byte…a crude joke hinting at death and ruin.

"Who," Hanmura3 sputtered, "the hell is this?"

"Information is of more relevance than names," the voice said. It was a deep, resonating voice, richly timbered and articulate. "There are few secrets in Arcadia, Hanmura-sama. The one from *Tengu Castle* is out. I know that Hanmura Enterprises rehearsed the attack on a Promethean offshore rig. The IPC Senate will be receiving the full record of that rehearsal, along with the confession of one Taku Miyamoto. I have already contacted him. He made a confession tape at my urging."

The corporate leader felt his body petrifying. "I—"

"Deny nothing," the voice snapped, and before it could continue there was another series of horrible, lung-shredding coughs. "My…my name is unimportant. No one shall remember me. But they will always remember that Sakyo Hanmura violated IPC law so he could manipulate world events to his own greed and glory."

Hanmura3 struggled to control his face. Beyond the airship windows, the Swiss mountains seemed painted on the sky.

"You have shamed the honor of your ancestors," the voice accused, and Hanmura3 actually gasped, so powerful was this condemnation. "Hanmura Enterprises shall wear the mark of your wickedness for a thousand years. Unless you choose to rectify the situation."

The CEO rubbed his mouth in a nervous habit. "How?" he asked softly.

There was another eruption of wet coughs, worse than before. It was a hideous sound, a terrible reminder of mankind's frailty. That *had* to be the lesson here.

Hanmura3 considered his options. "Perhaps we can make some arrangement?"

He let the suggestion hover, waiting for a reply. No reply came. The line remained active. The CEO tried several more times and was answered only with merciless silence.

In the end, he had to disconnect the call himself.

And quite suddenly, he realized what he needed to do.

CHAPTER FIFTY-THREE
Siege

The *Mantid* hung like an invisible dragonfly over the Sinkiang Mountains. They were a rounded collection of verdant peaks, their crests peeking through wreaths of fog so that they appeared like the Floating Isles themselves. The central peak towered over its brethren as a jade tooth curling towards heaven, and Gethin thought: *This is as good a place to die as any.*

"D. said there's a tunnel access near the base," Celeste was saying. "And a tram that's used to ferry supplies and personnel. Below the fog line, I'm guessing." Onscreen, the mountain flashed past as the *Mantid* circled outward.

Gethin buckled the last strap of the CAMO suit; he had stripped it from a carcass in the hallway outside Doros's quarters. The suit stank of blood and didn't fit right. He also worried that the horrific nanite chewers were still on it, possessed by the last Faustian command to pulverize the wearer.

He watched Celeste squeeze into her own pilfered suit. Stars, he felt exhausted. His eyes were bloodshot and they ached. His chest ached too. He wondered if there had been electrical damage to his augmentations.

There had been no sign of Enyalios during the voyage. Leaving Shimizu, he realized he was expecting the demon to appear on the ship with them, but it never happened.

"This mountain range is a black blot in global records," he said, distracting himself from a thousand concerns. "The Republic declared them a zone of protection. They're a void, a hole in the maps." He paused. "Perfect place for Stillness to set up shop, huh? Right under APAC's nose?"

"D. said they have some kind of communications center. The heart of the mountain is hollowed out."

Gethin looked at her sharply. "What?"

Celeste gave a shrug that betrayed her own tiredness. "That's what he told me."

He mulled that over. How long did it take to carve out a mountain? And why? Was it for sanctuary, so their wicked gods could retreat to a subterranean Xanadu to plot their next move in a billion-year war? Or did they utilize it as a spacious recovery room, licking their wounds by geothermal balefires?

Acting on a hunch, Gethin ordered Ego to search the etymology of this high peak of Sinkiang. It had been named in the earliest days of the Old Calendar, perhaps a millennium before the birth of Confucius, Ego replied. Back in the Xia Dynasty. The name meant: *Mountain of Dragons.*

He regarded the Outlander. Her mask was peeled up so he could view the lovely oval of her face. "I don't suppose your inside man noted the kind of security waiting for us?"

"Lots of troops and cameras," she said. "But Stillness is able to keep a low profile because they're low tech. When you want a hideout, you don't pump it full of ultrasonics."

"You would know."

She winked at him. "Better than you think."

[Celeste, I have located something of interest,] said the *Mantid* on the standard comlink. There was a trace of excitement in its delivery.

"Show me."

The screen splintered into fly-eye quadrants. The fog peeled away under thermal imaging.

The thermal view flushed into blue, umber, and orange. Gradually, a large tunnel became evident. It was well-hidden, overhung by vegetation and crowded with trees too well-placed to have grown there naturally. The image sharpened. A shape appeared, resembling an oversized insect. But it could only be...

"A ship," said Gethin. "That's another one of your invisible StrikeDown vessels, isn't it?"

Celeste grunted, "King D.'s transport. The *Cobra.* Running dark."

The *Mantid* zoomed view on the cave. Men were stationed at the mouth, costumed in beetle-black armor.

"Stillness Seraphs," Gethin said, heart sinking. "Terrific."

Celeste contemplated the images. The falling water obscured the finer details but she was able to count thirteen Seraphs. Thirteen! And there was something else of note at the waterfall tunnel ledge: the black steel underframes of tortoise microshields. The shields themselves were invisible, comprised of micromolecular binding that could be tailored to whatever height, depth, or shape you desired. Impenetrable. The Seraphs must have sealed off the entire passageway.

Gethin touched the screen. "Can you give us audio?"

The *Mantid* dialed down the roar of the waterfall. The Seraphs were discussing the physical attributes of someone named 'Lalania'. Apparently, her hindquarters were really something to see.

"Cut that," Celeste ordered, and she rubbed her temples, trying to think. "Microshields will stop a railgun. There's no way past them."

"Enough heat will melt the microfilaments," he suggested.

"Do we have that kind of time?"

"Do we have another choice?"

Celeste licked her lips. "Your pal Apollo insisted that we be subtle about getting in there and taking out that maniac before—"

Onscreen, the Seraphs burst like wet balloons.

It had happened so quickly that Gethin felt his mind go blank. He wondered if he was having a stroke; the excitement and stresses of post-regeneration life finally unhinging his brain.

But after several seconds, the bodies were still there at the edge of the waterfall. Blood had squirted out so forcefully it had painted the tunnel ceiling where it hadn't flung out from the cave in long red gouts against the microshielding.

Then the microshielding itself came down as someone deactivated the controls.

A man formed out of nothing and stood at the cave entrance, gazing straight at the *Mantid*. The viewscreen zoomed in on his glower.

"Subtlety," Gethin whispered. "Thy name is Enyalios."

★　　★　　★

They hopped from the *Mantid* and landed on the viscera-soaked cave entrance. The waterfall washed some of the remains away. Enyalios strode into the tunnel, halted at the tramline.

"Enyalios!" Celeste called after him. "Can you analyze security detection systems?"

The Warlord frowned. He fixed her with his hazel gaze – for the first time he really seemed to *see* her as more than an obstacle or annoyance. "No," he replied, and his tenor said he understood her point.

"Let us go first then," she said. "Bryce and I will perform stealthy takedowns. We don't want alarms going off, not if they have a doomsday weapon, right?"

"True."

Celeste and Gethin vanished under CAMO activation. A dozen Stillness guards, mid-rank, were congregated at the tram station; foldout tables opened for an in-progress poker match. The tram tracks ran east to west. The stash of tradenotes in play made Gethin's jaw drop; the terrorists were in the middle of a big bet. Crazily, he was tempted to stall to see the outcome.

For her part, Celeste moved throughout the chamber, taking note of two security cameras. She pinged Gethin; he let Id hack them with false looping images of the poker game, forever on the verge of the bet's outcome.

"Stand back," she messaged. "I'm calling Enyalios."

"Wait," Gethin said.

"What's wrong?"

He considered the troopers. The poker game was a study of spring and winter. There were young soldiers and old veterans crowding the table, chummy and tense at the fate of the cards. The youths were in stiff-looking new cloaks of the same sheen and odor of rubber (though it was not rubber but woven layers of nanomesh sandwiching impact-gel). The elders wore cloaks several shades darker. A few smoked cigarettes, their aged-leather hands affectionately rubbing shoulders like grandfathers and grandsons at a family reunion.

"What are we waiting for?" Celeste demanded in outrage.

Gethin sighed. "Never mind. I just—"

The poker players exploded, strangled by the invisible monstrosity that had rushed into the tram station like a mad poltergeist; Gethin actually felt the wind of its arrival.

Enyalios reformed by the security door. "I have other ways into the base," he said, jerking his head towards the vents above their heads.

Gethin choked on the stench of carnage – the ammonia of vomit, odor of bowels loosened at the attack, the suffocating copper-stench of blood. He drew a hand to his mouth and asked the Warlord, "It was you in Tycho Hospital, wasn't it? You interrogated Kenneth Cavor and then charred him to pieces when you were done."

"Yes."

And then the creature was gone. The grate of the vent melted, dripping into black puddles.

★   ★   ★

They rode the tram into the heart of the mountain. Gethin sent Ego to latch onto the local security grid, and sightjacked the real-time datafeed directly to Celeste's sensorium.

<There are 1,647 people in this facility,> Ego reported. <Thirty-one of them are registered in the local database as guests of the terrorist group StrikeDown. This structure has fifteen levels.>

The lower tram station was unguarded, and Gethin and Celeste climbed aboard the transport. Its run was brief, and they exited unseen into the mountain's chalky interior. Music resonated in the airy space.

Celeste tugged him to a sloping corridor. He glimpsed a white banner on the wall, scrawled with red: PURITY FOR ALL.

"Remember," said Celeste, "there are antimatter missiles down here. We plant the grenades, grab King D., and get the fuck out."

"I'll remember," he promised.

Pressing onward, they arrived at a hewn stairway leading into a lower sanctum. Celeste halted so abruptly that Gethin crashed into her.

"You okay?" he sputtered.

"Shh! Look! What in the holy hell is that?"

He looked.

The Midas Hand machine was *there*.

Gethin sucked in his breath, committing it all to his digital memory. Perhaps reacting to his stricken gasp, or anticipating his query, his Ego Familiar began describing what it could discern of the eccentric device. He silenced the speculations. There would be time for analysis later.

But still…

A Midas Hand? Was it really possible?

"That's King D.," Celeste whispered.

But Gethin had already noticed the StrikeDown prince. He looked past the thug…to the *other* being in the chamber.

★   ★   ★

"Are my terms acceptable, King D.?" demanded Apophis.

The StrikeDown leader hesitated. When he spoke his teeth chattered as if in a Siberian chill. "They are acceptable," he whispered.

Apophis laughed richly and uproariously. "Glad to hear it! Long ago they called me Pharaoh. They cried my name in glory and fear when I swept over the plains of Sumer and Mongolia. Together, we will melt the Republic for the bricks of a new empire. *All shall be equal* beneath my throne. Equal subjects to the supreme power of my divinity."

Apophis changed his form. Suddenly he was a multi-armed blue-skinned goddess with human skulls displayed around his neck.

The abomination began a stomping dance. "But first, the wakeup call! Apophis versus the Republic. Signal your ships, my friend. Tell them to strike all Save centers now. When the IPC responds, I shall light the heavens with flame." He clapped his four hands together and took a bow.

Effortlessly, he shapeshifted again. A Roman despot this time, in Tyrian purple cloak, a wreath of gold oak leaves encircling his head.

King D. licked his dry lips and touched his ear. "All Save centers?" he asked of the shapechanging creature.

Apophis's patrician face tilted. A third eye blistered and opened on his forehead. "Getting cold feet?"

"No!" King D. said quickly. He licked his lips again and realized his tongue was even drier than before, like a wad of sandpaper. "I want this. I've wanted this all my life."

"Then strike the world down!"

King D. conjured his command screen. His fleet of criminal ships appeared in a tight grid throughout the world. They had their orders. All he needed to do was kick off the unholy bonfire.

He stiffened as someone touched his back.

A voice whispered into his ear. "This isn't the way we want it," the voice said.

His eyes widened. "Celeste?"

"We're here to rescue you."

Apophis floated up into the air, as if lifted by invisible wires. "Have you given the order?" he demanded.

King D. turned away from Celeste's phantom presence. "Yes."

"Good. I expect honesty from my apostles. Do you understand?"

"I do."

"Do you swear allegiance to the new order?"

"Yes."

"Then tell me," Apophis growled, "who else has joined us in this room?"

The floating creature held his arms. At once, the room's illusory projections began fluctuating, cycling through dozens of environments too quickly for Gethin and Celeste's CAMO processors to match. There were eccentric green cities like termite mounds; shorelines crowded with tentacled pink flora, Martian valleys, crystalline geodes…

In that explosion of color, two humanoid outlines appeared.

"Unmask yourselves!" Apophis cried.

He didn't wait for compliance. Celeste and Gethin were blown back against opposite walls. Their suit circuits crackled and fizzled.

"Celeste," Gethin panted, tearing off his dead facemask. "Run!"

She stripped her mask but remained, feet planted like tree roots. Apophis descended from his floating posture, landing between them.

"Well, well," the creature said, grinning. "Is this your doing, King D.? Do I face a Judas on the eve of our new age?"

"It's *my* doing," Gethin snarled, sweating furiously as he held the creature's gaze. "And Horus shall banish the Devouring Serpent, and chase him back to the Halls of Judgment, where the Eater of Souls shall feast on his ichor and the world will know only gold and lapis and the throb of life!"

Apophis's grin fell slightly.

Gethin's heart palpitated wildly as he began to circle the entity. "Apophis, right? Refreshing to think I can sneak up on a five-billion-year-old god." He shivered, hoisted a smile he didn't feel, and added, "Are you the same Apophis who started the Final War in the nuclear silo, beating that American woman to death? The Apophis of ancient Egypt, devourer of the sun?"

The creature's eyes shone like silver coins.

"Mother Eris is dead!"

A pained expression filled Apophis's face. "I will sacrifice a million lives to her memory." He bowed and began muttering. With sudden dread, Gethin noticed that the beast was standing suspiciously close to where he had quietly placed one of Celeste's bombs, in CAMO mesh, against an antimatter missile's carapace.

"Who are you?" Apophis demanded.

Gethin swallowed the lump in his throat. "I was hoping for a chance to—"

The bomb materialized from invisibility.

Apophis made a lassoing motion with his hand and pretended to harness the explosive. It leapt off the missile as if shot from a cannon. Sailing into the air, it whirled about, flew past their heads, up the stairs and into the room above. There was an explosion and wild screams from the Stillness crowd. Apophis hopped about like a joyous goblin.

Gethin withdrew his multigun from its sheath and pulped Apophis with a storm of fleschettes. The needles mulched the creature's head, spattering tissue and brain in a wet supernova against the sandstone walls. The torso bifurcated as if by an invisible zipper. King D. and Celeste ducked the mess, but Gethin noticed the StrikeDown leader was not trying to escape. Didn't the man know what he was dealing with here?

What deal did he make?

Apophis's body collapsed. A fountain of blood emptied from its headless trunk like champagne from a bottle; it formed a strange, scorpion pattern on the ground that, slowly, was rising as an actual scorpion of massive proportions.

Gethin screamed at the StrikeDown duo. *"Get out of here!"*

Celeste tugged again at King D. The StrikeDown leader hesitated, staring not so much at the arachnid but at the machine and the promise that it held. Celeste saw him make up his mind.

"We don't want it this way," she told him.

The great man looked pained as he said, "Agreed." Then he followed her out of the chamber.

And burst into flames.

The fire shot out from King D.'s flesh, peeling the skin and tissue away from his bones. The man screamed and flailed, forcing Celeste to duck his fiery arms.

"*No!*" she shrieked.

King D. missed the doorway and slammed into the wall, bounced off, flopped on the floor, burning and sizzling. Celeste tried to throw herself upon his body. The flames shot up in terrific splendor, blasting her back. King D.'s howls died.

She recoiled from her leader, gaping in horror at what remained of him: a glowing skeleton, white-hot, steaming in a bed of ash.

"*Goddamn you!*" she screamed. "*Apophis!*" She stalked around the chamber, face wet with tears. "Fight me!" She hurled her multigun aside. "Fight *me!*"

An invisible force snapped her head back. She toppled, rolled over once, scrambled back to her feet, eyes wild.

"*Fight me!*"

The next blow sent her headlong against the rock wall. A ribbonlike trail of blood streaked from one nostril to her ear. Gethin darted to her side, impotently scanning for a target.

Celeste laughed hideously. "Beautiful dreamer! Wake unto me! Starlight and dew drops are waiting for thee!"

Her body twirled into the air like an ice-skater.

Gethin fired below her, hoping to score a hit that would, however temporarily, release her from the demon's grip.

Then she was hurled against the far wall. There was a snap like a wooden broomstick breaking over someone's knee. Celeste crumpled.

Apophis appeared again in human form, crouching over her. Gethin put his rifle against the creature's head when, as if by magnetism, the weapon tore free from his grip. Two fingers came out of their sockets; Gethin was suddenly cradling a disfigured stump.

Celeste glowered weakly at her assailant.

"Sounds of the rude world heard in the day" she managed.

Apophis cradled her face. "Lulled by the moonlight ..."

"Have all passed..."

"Away," Gethin said, and blurred.

His uninjured hand formed into a fist and came down like a hammer on Apophis's skull. The bone collapsed with the sound of a smashed grapefruit. There was no blood in the damp cranial cavity, no pulpy mass of brain tissue. The monster fell like a stringless marionette.

And vanished.

Gethin dropped out of his blur, not wanting such a sensitive system running for any length of time near an entity that could easily char the circuits of his body. He scooped Celeste into his arms.

He saw at once that the impact with the wall had killed her. She just didn't realize it yet. Her head hung limply from a neck twisted in a peculiar direction.

"Behind," Celeste muttered wetly, "you."

A powerful viselike pincer crudely seized his neck. With Celeste still cradled in his arms, Gethin was yanked into the air, his feet cartwheeling over his head. He was abruptly fixed in place, upside down, a fly ensnared by a spiderweb's translucent tethers. He clutched Celeste to avoid dropping her.

Apophis glided below. The ancient god had shed his Roman form and was once more dressed in sumptuous Egyptian linens, serpent-crowned and terrible.

"Was it Doros Peisistratos who talked?" the monster asked, halting and running long fingernails through Gethin's black hair. "Did he let you in on our secret, *plaga*?"

"Maybe it was Enyalios," Gethin challenged. He could feel the pressure pound at his temples. "You gonna take him on? I just watched him rip Eris apart over the Sea of Japan."

Apophis hissed with mere inches separating them. "He's here, isn't he?" Not waiting for a response, the creature snapped his head back and issued a squealing howl.

Gethin never learned what had delayed Enyalios. He didn't bother asking Ego if the mad Warlord had taken it upon himself to butcher every living thing in the mountain on another of his psychotic rageaholic frenzies. But when Apophis issued that shrill alarm, the war god streaked into the control room like a meteor once again, eager to battle his nemesis in their final confrontation.

A switch on the machine flipped as if of its own accord. A phalanx of red lights shot from the mechanical quills, piercing Enyalios in mid-flight.

The war god didn't look like the jellyfish shape that had devoured Eris. He looked, instead, like an inaminate chunk of meaty, volcanic eruption, marbled and ugly, crisscrossed with flaming eyes and claws. He boiled in place, pin-cushioned by merciless rays of energy.

"*Ha!*" Apophis yelped, giving an oddly majestic twirl. "Look what I have reeled in! Sy'hoss'a!" His eyes radiated, though he kept a respectful distance from the festering wad of white-hot matter. "My, my, my. Ragnarok arrives at last!"

Gethin strained against his immobilizing levitation.

Celeste breathed shallowly in his grip. Blood slimed her face, dripped into Apophis' greedy mouth that was shifting into the scaly maw of a crocodile. His eyes turned opulent jade.

The monster extended his hand, and Celeste was jerked sideways out of Gethin's grip. She collapsed in a broken, ghastly heap.

"It's hot in here, don't you think?" Apophis taunted, showing scimitar teeth.

Gethin held the monster's stare. "It's about to get hotter."

He waited to burst into flame, or be hurled against the rocks. Waited to be squeezed until he popped. But then a remarkable thing happened. Celeste was moving! She had been paralyzed, neck broken…but now her head lifted, and she was pulling herself to her feet. Her neck popped back into place, healing as if she had arky-grade nanites flooding her system.

Even Apophis seemed surprised by the resurrection. Before he could react, Celeste dashed to the Midas Hand machine.

And threw the switch.

The red beams transfixing Enyalios flickered and disappeared.

Apophis's crocodilian visage filled with terror. Gethin, forgotten now, dropped out of the air, struck the ground, scrambled to his feet.

And Enyalios collided with Apophis in the air above his head. The control room was bathed in blinding luminosity. The gods wrestled, while he scrambled to Celeste, seized her hand, pulled her towards the corridor.

"We have to stop them!" she insisted. "Kill them both, now!"

The two creatures were as intermingled as a pair of storm cells combining into a typhoon. Gethin pulled his sidearm. He aimed at the nearest of the antimatter missiles.

"Nice knowing you, Bryce," Celeste whispered.

"And you," he said, and squeezed the trigger.

Gethin blurred as he did, scooping Celeste into his arms one final time to bear her in a hyperaccelerated dash from the chamber of death and—

CHAPTER FIFTY-FOUR
Oblivion

For the second time that week, Gethin awoke to blinding pain. A strangled cry escaped him as he tried to sit up, his entire body twisting in agony. He swatted away the medgrid loading screen when it flared in his optics. The trauma had rebooted his entire sensorium.

His world was pitch-black. For a moment he wondered if his eyes had been scorched out. Then he felt the closeness of the air and heard the spilling of sand between the mountain's rubble. It wasn't blindness he had to worry about. It was being buried alive.

His clothes, too, were wet, heavy, and reeked of blood. Gethin felt the knobby flesh of his mutilated hand. He ground his teeth from the pain. Crazily, he found himself focusing on how thirsty he was. His tongue moved thickly between chapped lips. He felt sand in his teeth.

"Gethin?"

Celeste's voice was paper-thin in the blackness.

"Yeah."

Gethin found her hand and squeezed it with his remaining fingers.

"How are you?" she asked.

"Dying, probably." He wondered what the medgrid did when its subject was mortally wounded. Were the crosses replaced by reaper scythes?

Celeste coughed weakly. "Yeah. Me too."

"You upgraded yourself in Cappadocia, didn't you?"

"Not enough, apparently."

The matter-of-fact coldness in her voice caused his heart to spasm. "Celeste? Tell me where you're hurt."

"What does it matter? We're buried beneath a fucking mountain and the whole world is going to war."

A surge of defiance rose in him. "It *does* matter. Can you move your legs?"

"They're both broken."

"You sure?"

"*Yes I'm sure!*"

He released her hand as his sensorium finished its reboot. His medgrid flashed automatically, and while there were no reaper scythes, there might as well have been. Wine-dark lettering appeared against the blackness:

VITAL SIGNS CRITICAL. USER DEATH IMMINENT.

He heard a soft, perilously weak cackle in the pitch dark. It took him several seconds to realize it was him.

Fighting delirium, he switched his optics to infravision. The cave-in appeared in soft blue blobs of shape. The ceiling was inches away, sandwiching them into a narrow shaft.

"Ego, can you detect any com signals?"

<No. I am sorry Gethin.>

Sorry? he mused. *That's interesting.* He had used his Familiars for years and never heard remorse from them. Maybe this was a factory default that sprang out when the host was about to exit the stage of life.

Gethin reached for Celeste's hand again. She was a blue phantom beside him, an angel of shadow and cobalt hues. "Be right back," he promised.

Celeste's face was marked by splashes of black blood. "No hurry." She imagined their bodies being found many eons from now and displayed in some museum. MAN AND WOMAN. Someone might write a damned sonnet in speculation on what these corpses were doing so far beneath the ground.

Gethin grunted, sweaty and constricted in his pain, as he crept towards the far end of the cave-in. It was difficult to see. He thought he could discern a faint pinpoint of light at the end of the tunnel.

I'm going to wake up on Luna again. No memory of any of this.

It was a paralyzing thought. For him, Celeste Segarra would never have existed. Later, Donna McCallister would likely say he had worked with a female Outlander. He would wonder what she had been like.

And Jack? A name only on a report he would not remember having wittten.

Keiko? No reconciliation or renewed history.

And Lori?

Gethin curled into a fetal crouch, throbbing with his injuries. He called forth his email inbox and selected Lori's message.

He expected to see Lori's pretty face, slender figure, the chestnut-brown hair hanging loosely over her shoulders. He thought he would see her desk terminal, the beige walls, Cody prowling on the carpet.

Instead, when the email opened he was surprised to see a bed of grass, and a long-stemmed Martian rose freshly planted in the soil.

"I plant this flower in memory of Gethin Bryce," came Lori's voice. She was not in frame. "Gethin was my husband of ten years. We loved each other very much. He was from Earth. He was my partner and confidant."

Lori took a breath. Gethin remembered that sound. He remembered how her shoulders would lift.

"Gethin Bryce was killed during a shuttle accident from Mars to Luna. Some people may think he can come back from the dead with Earthly tricks and replications, but my husband no longer exists. This flower is offered in his memory, and I have planted an oak tree in the Elysian Fields of Olympus so that I may see it in years to come…and remember his life and death."

"Farewell to *you*, Lori," he whispered in the darkness. He hit delete. The email dissolved.

And then, it seemed, so did he.

★   ★   ★

Except that he didn't. The wave of dizziness passed.

"Celeste!" he cried in a ragged whisper.

Silence filled his ears. He took a fierce breath of the diminishing air and was about to scream her name when he heard shuffling in the blackness.

"Not dead yet," she managed.

Gethin crawled, galvanized by pure, hateful defiance like some damaged crab scraping across the rock-studded sea bottom.

Where was Enyalios?

"Sy'hoss'a!" he managed. "Sy'hoss'a!" Even to his own ears, his voice sounded like the grating of gravel.

"Already tried that," Celeste whispered. "While you were out. Practically said a fucking rosary. The missiles ruptured. Enyalios, Apophis…they had to have been killed."

"*We're* still alive."

"You blurred us to relative safety. Those two weren't going anywhere. Locked in hate to the finish."

Gethin stared at the ground. He noticed the iron tracks of the tramline. He looked to the impossibly distant speck of dim light and realized that they must be in one of the tram tunnels.

"Hold onto me," he said, shoveling her into both arms.

"Can't even see you, Bryce."

"I can see *you*."

Holding her was the toughest part. Gethin felt her hot tears against his neck as he hobbled, his broken bones cutting into muscle like glass.

"Don't…want…to…die," Celeste muttered.

"I won't let you."

The light ahead grew wider.

It might have been minutes or hours or years before he finally reached the end of the tunnel, and he saw that a landslide had collapsed the mouth into a dead end. Any hope that the *Mantid* was waiting for them with medical miracles and a glass of brandy evaporated.

He closed his eyes and could hear the sound of the waterfall through the tiny fissures of rubble.

"Id," he said, voice slurring. "Send an emergency IPC broadcast."

★Already did Gethin. You don't have to tell me everything.★

He slumped against the wall, holding Celeste. Her pulse thudded delicately in her neck and, acting on impulse, Gethin kissed that small spot of life. Then he passed out.

Celeste Segarra died in his arms a few minutes later.

CHAPTER FIFTY-FIVE
Triple Suicide

It was Sakyo Hanmura1, in his corporate palace on Mars, who made the decision in the hours to come.

While the citizens of Sol were gaping at the mushroom cloud that had flung Sinkiang Mountains into rubble that reached the periphery of space, and the *IPCS Nobunaga* was little more than fireworks over the Pacific Ocean, and a massacre was being reported in the Shimizu pyramid, there were riots on Mars.

Newsfeeds were too busy to pay attention when the CEO of Hanmura Enterprises broadcast a special announcement. In fact, only two stations chose to run it at all.

The real-time communication began simply enough. The famous man appeared onscreen in a white kimono, surrounded by the cherry blossoms of his garden. There were pagodas and babbling streams. Hanmura1 was no stranger to public broadcasts – he was a well-known face and common panelist at economic summits. He always thought that was important; his competitors were hidden hydras, while he humanized his corporation. He usually wore his trademark black suit of eelskin.

Not this time.

"I have betrayed you," he announced. "I have violated the IPC Multiple Extant Sentience Law. During a time of chaos, fear, and war, I have exploited these tragedies for my own personal gain. And I cannot live with this shame."

Exactly how he had arranged it, no one could later be certain. The screen split into a tri-panel. At precisely the same minute, two other Sakyo Hanmuras emerged, similarly dressed in white kimonos and kneeling before a mat. Three *tanto* blades went into three hands.

"As is my right," Hanmura continued, "I formally request the deletion of my DC file from all Save centers, everywhere, to atone for these crimes. I pray that in time, the worlds may forgive the actions of a flawed human being."

Three Hanmuras undid the front of their kimonos, and in eerily perfect unison, spoke the same death poem. Three Hamuras drove three *tanto* blades into three stomachs. Three assistants finished them off with flawless decapitations.

Video of the triple suicide became the most downloaded clip in the history of mankind, until Harris Alexander Pope's victory during the Partisan War, twenty-six years later.

CHAPTER FIFTY-SIX
Reborn in the House of the Living

Thirty-nine hours after the mysterious explosion at Sinkiang, Gethin Bryce found himself in a jade-green room staring at his hands.

A sweep of horror rushed through him and he bolted upright, the bedside monitor beeping wildly, as he struggled to recall recent events. Dimly, he remembered clutching Celeste in the underdark. Beyond that? His memories ended like a map with a chunk ripped away.

He glanced around. No black robe hanging from the wall.

It was *not* a regen center.

"Please lie down," the bedside's monitor intoned in a crystalline female voice. Chinese calligraphy was engraved along its framing. XIANYANG MEDICAL CENTER.

But Gethin was too riled for easy compliance. He activated his sensorium, immediately checking his messages.

Thirteen messages appeared from Donna McCallister. He skimmed them quickly, gaining a cursory idea of events following the explosion. The Sinkiang mountains had been transformed into a smoking caldera. The landslide had buried surrounding villages, and China's regen centers were working round the clock to accommodate the flood of purchase signals.

War between Prometheus and the IPC was over.

He was scrolling through further messages when the door to his room opened, and Keiko Yamanaka and Jack Saylor stepped to his bedside.

"Celeste!" he cried. "Where is she?" He was dragging himself out of the hospital bed when a third shape hobbled at the doorway.

"*You!*" Gethin roared in a sob of relief and heartache. "How the hell did you survive?"

Celeste Segarra approached his bedside with both legs in support braces. She was purple with bruises and recent surgeries, though the tiny twitch at her lips could pass for a smirk. "My purchase in Cappadocia was worth every penny, apparently. How did *you* survive, Bryce?"

"I'm stubborn."

"And pulverized," Keiko told him, nodding solemnly. "Broken ribs, internal bleeding. They had to regrow your hand. It would have been easier just to regenerate you."

He grimaced. "No, thanks. Though I'm guessing my insurance premiums will go up now."

Keiko shook her head. "Are you kidding me? The world doesn't have all the details yet, but they know our names. Gethin Bryce won't have to worry about insurance premiums. President Song mentioned you by name as one of the architects of peace." Keiko's lips were a thin line. "Seems he's angling to have the four of us endorse his re-election campaign."

"That's because he doesn't see what's around the corner."

"And you do?"

"Yes."

They waited for him to say more, but after several seconds it was evident he had neither the strength nor desire to elaborate.

He reached for Celeste. She took a precarious step to the very edge of his bed, evaded his questing hand, leaned down to his face, and kissed his lips. They beheld each other, drinking in the other's poignant gaze.

Are we still enemies? she asked with her eyes.

He offered his tenderest smile. *Let's try not to be.*

Jack said, "There are some APAC officials outside, wanting to talk to us. I think we're going to be here a long time."

"Apophis?" Gethin asked. "Enyalios?"

"No sign of them." Keiko took a breath. "I don't think anyone actually believes the story Apollo told you. I don't think *I* do. I mean, they could have been AIs programmed to act as primordial intelligences. Anyway, there's a lot of gossip out there. Charges of conspiracy. You know how people are."

I do, he thought.

Gethin lay back in bed. He could already hear the clamor of an approaching crowd. Keiko and Jack rushed to the door and yelled for hospital security.

Alone for the moment, Celeste touched his face. "What did we do, Gethin?"

"Don't know yet," he said, and before he could elaborate a new email sprang to his eye. He read it where he sat, while the noise from the crowd – reporters and police, mostly – coalesced into a riot.

"Lynch mob?" Celeste asked, looking concernedly towards the door.

Gethin didn't reply.

"You okay?"

"For the moment." He looked her up and down. "You look like shit, Segarra. The next time you upgrade yourself, make sure I'm with you to get the best deal, okay? Now go rest. We're going to be here for a while."

She kissed his cheek and joined the others by the door. People were yelling, angry voices competing to outdo one another. Someone screamed. The crack of a pistol sounded from the hospital lobby. Over the intercom, a voice boomed in Mandarin.

Gethin closed his eyes. In his private darkness, he read the mysterious email once more:

TO: Gethin Bryce
FROM: Unknown sender
DATE/TIME: 07/28/322, 1132 ET
SUBJECT: None
MESSAGE: *Your turn now, my friend. We had the world long enough. No gods, no masters, no lords, no monsters. It's up to you to decide what to do with that.*

Gethin ignored the chaos from the corridor.
It was weeks before he came to his decision.
It was years before he could do anything about it.

FLAME TREE PRESS
FICTION WITHOUT FRONTIERS
Award-Winning Authors & Original Voices

Flame Tree Press is the trade fiction imprint of Flame Tree Publishing, focusing on excellent writing in horror and the supernatural, crime and mystery, science fiction and fantasy. Our aim is to explore beyond the boundaries of the everyday, with tales from both award-winning authors and original voices.

•

Other titles available include:

Thirteen Days by Sunset Beach by Ramsey Campbell
Think Yourself Lucky by Ramsey Campbell
The House by the Cemetery by John Everson
The Toy Thief by D.W. Gillespie
The Siren and the Specter by Jonathan Janz
The Sorrows by Jonathan Janz
Kosmos by Adrian Laing
The Sky Woman by J.D. Moyer
Creature by Hunter Shea
The Bad Neighbor by David Tallerman
Night Shift by Robin Triggs
The Mouth of the Dark by Tim Waggoner

•

Join our mailing list for free short stories, new release details, news about our authors and special promotions:

flametreepress.com